For ge... ...et
by str... ...m
owner... ...er-
ful, noble, and refuse to relinquish their birthright. But
three cunning, beautiful lasses are about to band together
to bring order and goodwill to their beloved homeland.
Yet when the campaign moves from the battlefield to the
bed chamber neither laird nor lass will be able to resist the
passions unleashed...

PRAISE FOR
SUE-ELLEN WELFONDER

"Few writers can bring history to life like Sue-Ellen Welfonder! For anyone who loves historical fiction, the books
in the Highland Warrior trilogy are a true treasure."
—Heather Graham, *New York Times*
bestselling author

"[Welfonder] continues to weave magical tales of redemption, love, and loyalty in glorious, perilous mid-fourteenth-
century Scotland."
—*Booklist*

"With each book Welfonder reinforces her well-deserved
reputation as one of the finest writers of Scot romances."
—*RT Book Reviews*

TEMPTATION OF A HIGHLAND SCOUNDREL

"4½ stars! Welfonder's second installment in the Highland Warriors trilogy is even better than the first! This finely crafted, highly emotional romance is populated by heroes whose lives are defined by the concept of honor and strong-willed heroines who don't accept surrender as a possibility."

—RT Book Reviews

"Kendrew is quite the hero! Readers will love his rough ways, as much as they will love Isobel's fire and spirit... an enchanting mix of romance, history, and the smallest bit of paranormal."

—RomRevToday.com

"This series fulfills all of my Scottish historical romance requirements...fierce men with feisty women, magic everywhere, and the amazing landscape of Scotland. Ms. Welfonder is able to place the reader in Scotland with such accuracy you feel the mist upon your face and see the men in kilts standing on the hillside embracing the women they love."

—TheReadingReviewer.com

"Sizzling...This story was magical...I look forward to reading the next book in the series."

—SeducedByABook.com

SINS OF A HIGHLAND DEVIL

"4½ stars! Top Pick! The first installment in Welfonder's Highland Warriors trilogy continues a long tradition of well-written, highly emotional romances. This marvelous novel is rich in love and legend, populated by characters steeped in honor, to make for a sensual and emotional read."
—RT Book Reviews

"Sue-Ellen Welfonder has truly brought legends and love to life...I cannot wait for the next two."
—FreshFiction.com

"A richly enjoyable story. Welfonder is a master storyteller."
—ARomanceReview.com

"One of the finest books I've read in a long time. The characters are so rich and vibrant, and Sue-Ellen Welfonder writes the most realistic descriptions of Highland battles. I was transported to the Glen and could almost smell the forest and the peat fires in the castles...I'm looking forward to the next story in the series!"
—OnceUponARomance.net

A HIGHLANDER'S TEMPTATION

"[Welfonder] continues to weave magical tales of redemption, love, and loyalty in glorious, perilous mid-fourteenth-century Scotland."
—Booklist

"4 Stars! A fascinating, intriguing story that will definitely stand the test of time."
—RT Book Reviews

MASTER OF THE HIGHLANDS

DEVIL IN A KILT

SEDUCTION OF A HIGHLAND WARRIOR

SUE-ELLEN WELFONDER

FOREVER

NEW YORK   BOSTON

Copyright © 2013 by Sue-Ellen Welfonder
An excerpt from *Sins of a Highland Devil* copyright © 2011 by Sue-Ellen Welfonder

Forever
Hachette Book Group
237 Park Avenue
New York, NY 10017

www.HachetteBookGroup.com

Forever is an imprint of Grand Central Publishing.
The Forever name and logo are trademarks of Hachette Book Group, Inc.

The Hachette Speakers Bureau provides a wide range of authors for speaking events. To find out more, go to www.hachettespeakersbureau .com or call (866) 376-6591.

The publisher is not responsible for websites (or their content) that are not owned by the publisher.

Printed in the United States of America

OPM

First Edition: January 2013
10 9 8 7 6 5 4 3 2 1

With love and much affection to Aurora Mata, dear friend, loyal reader, and all-around special and generous soul. Above all, Aurora is a Scotophile extraordinaire.

Cuban-born, now a proud American, her heart is all Scottish.

Aurora also walks the walk: She's stood atop the heathery hills, knows the heady scent of peat, she's journeyed on the Loch Lomond mail boat, experienced true magic on the Isle of Mull, and she's charmed the staff at my own Duncan MacKenzie's castle, Eilean Donan near Skye. Stateside, she's a well-kent face at Highland Games.

Aurora, I love you bundles. I'm sure you were a Highland chieftain's lady in a past life. And I'm wishing you many more Scottish adventures in this one.

Alba gu brath!

(Scotland forever)

Acknowledgments

My books are always inspired by my lifelong love affair with Scotland, home of my heart and land of my ancestors. It's also no secret that I believe in Highland magic. I experience it whenever I visit Scotland. And even when I can't be there, I look for tartan whimsy in my day-to-day world. I often find it when I'm writing and slip into the "zone." The story then springs to life, each touch of my fingers to the keys taking me back to the breathtaking Scottish land- and seascapes that fire my imagination.

For me, setting always comes first. A place has to captivate me, its atmosphere stirring my blood and making my heart pound. Only then, when I feel the heartbeat of the land, do I also pick up the pulse of the lives once lived there. The characters then stride out of the mist, telling me their tales.

That's how my stories are born.

My Highland Warriors trilogy was inspired by a place

of spectacular beauty, an area known for its rugged and remote splendor even today. The Glen of Many Legends may live only in my imagination, but its real-life counterpart is a corner of the Western Highlands known in Gaelic as *Garbh-chriochan*, the Rough Bounds. This area was home to men and women every bit as bold, proud, and devoted to their beloved land as Alasdair and Marjory in *Seduction of a Highland Warrior.*

But it wasn't just my passion for wild places that sparked this trilogy.

I was also inspired by my admiration for women. The original multitaskers, women are simply wonderful. Courageous, daring, full of love and caring, and I truly believe the world would be a better place if women ruled. So I love writing proud and strong heroines who band together to right wrongs, protect kith and kin, and, of course, win their hero's heart.

The heroines in my books are a reflection of the many strong women who have crossed my life's path, inspiring and influencing me, always earning my respect and esteem.

They are too many to name and I don't want to slight anyone by omission, so I will just say thank you!

Most especially, I want to thank my agent, Roberta Brown, and my editor, Michele Bidelspach. A true angel on earth (even if she denies it), Roberta is also my dearest friend. Michele and I also have a long history. She helped me wrap my debut title, *Devil in a Kilt*, when I was orphaned by my first editor. Recently orphaned anew, Michele once again took me under her wing. She's phenomenal and I'm blessed to work with her.

As always, all my love and thanks to my very handsome

husband, Manfred, who guards my turret as fiercely as a Highland Warrior. And my little Jack Russell, Em, the keeper of my heart. He's sat on my chair through the deadlines of every book I've written. I hope he knows how much I love him.

SEDUCTION OF A HIGHLAND WARRIOR

The Honor of Clan Donald

❦

In the beginning of days, before Highland warriors walked heather-clad hills and gazed in awe across moors chased by cloud shadows, old gods ruled the dark and misty realm that would one day be known as Scotland. Glens were silent then, empty but for the whistle of the wind and the curl of waves on sparkling sea-lochs.

Yet if a man looked and listened with his heart rather than his eyes and ears, he might catch a glimpse of wonders beyond telling.

For Manannan Mac Lir, mighty god of sea and wind, loved these rugged Scottish shores. Those who haven't forgotten legend will swear that stormy days saw Manannan plying Highland waters in his magical galley *Wave Sweeper.* Or that on nights when the full moon shone bright, he favored riding the edge of the sea on his enchanted horse Embarr of the Flowing Mane. All tales claimed that wherever he was, Manannan never lost sight of Scotland's cliff-fretted coast. One stretch of shoreline was said to hold his especial attention, a place of such splendor even his jaded heart swelled to behold its wild and haunting beauty.

That place was the Glen of Many Legends.

Storytellers agree that when the day came that Manannan observed a proud and noble MacDonald warrior stride into this fair land of heather, rock, and silvery seas, he was most pleased.

Those were distant times, but even then the men of Clan Donald were gaining a reputation as men of fierce loyalty and unbending honor.

They were the best of all Highlanders.

Even the gods stood in awe of them.

So Manannan's pleasure grew when this MacDonald warrior, an early chieftain known as Drangar the Strong, chose this blessed spot to build a fine isle-girt fortress. Here, Drangar the Strong would guard the coast with his trustworthy and fearless garrison. And—the tale spinners again agreed—the great god of sea and wind surely believed Clan Donald would blossom and thrive, gifting the Glen of Many Legends with generations of braw Highland warriors and beautiful, spirited women.

The world was good.

Until the ill-fated day when Drangar took a moonlit walk along the night-silvered shore of his sea-loch and happened across a lovely Selkie maid who no red-blooded man could've resisted.

Her dark hair gleamed like moonlight on water and her eyes shone like the stars. Her lips were seductively curved and ripe for kissing. And her shapely form beckoned, all smooth, creamy skin and tempting shadows.

MacDonalds, it must now be said, are as well-lusted as their hearts are loyal and true.

Drangar fell hard, succumbing to the seal woman's charms there and then.

But such passions flare hotly only for a beat, at least for the woman-of-the-sea who soon suffers unbearable longings to return to her watery home.

Nor is any Highlander unaware of the tragedies that so often befall these enchanting creatures and the mortal men who lose their hearts to them. Such tales abound along Scotland's coasts and throughout the Western Isles, with every clan bard able to sing of the heartbreak and danger, the ills that can break good men.

Or, perhaps worst of all, the tears of children born to such unions.

Drangar could not allow such sorrow to visit his people.

Nor did he wish to see his seductress in anguish.

So he did as all good MacDonalds would do and followed his honor.

Rather than carry her into his castle and have his way with her, he took her shining sealskin from the rock where she'd discarded it and, returning the skin to her, he'd stood by as she vanished into the sea.

Then—the bards pause here for effect—before the waves settled, Manannan himself rose from the spume-crested depths and made Drangar a great gift of thanks for his farsightedness and his honor.

The gift was an ironbound treasure chest heavy with priceless amber.

These were enchanted gemstones that, according to legend, would bring Clan Donald fortune and blessings, aiding them always in times of trouble.

But life in the Highlands was never easy.

And even magical stones can't always allay feuds, strife, and the perfidy of men.

Years passed and then centuries. Times were good and then also bad. Bards embroidered Manannan's fame and nearly forgot the role of the seal woman in explaining Clan Donald's chest of ambers. Soon other tales were added until no man knew what was real or storied.

Then the day came when even Drangar slipped into the murk of legend.

Worst fates followed and the MacDonalds' once-mighty fortress was torn from their grasp.

But the clan never lost their honor.

Centuries later they even regained their home.

Now a new Clan Donald chieftain rules there. Alasdair MacDonald is his name and he's a lord of warriors. A man worth a hundred in battle, well-loved by his friends and respected by his foes. Drangar's heart would've burst with pride if he could have known him.

To Alasdair, honor is everything.

Yet he lives in troublesome times. And although his beloved glen is quiet, the truce that keeps it so is fragile. Two other clans now share the Glen of Many Legends, and while one can be called an ally, the other remains hostile. Many would credit Alasdair's repute and authority that disaster hasn't yet struck.

Those less generous would say the strength of his sword arm is responsible.

Whatever one believes, he is not a man to cross. Unfortunately, ill winds are blowing ever closer to the fair glen once so loved by Manannan and Drangar.

Alasdair's passion for the glen is equally great.

But soon his love for a woman will challenge him to abandon everything he holds dear.

When he does, he will lose more than his honor.

His actions will unleash a calamity worse than the Glen of Many Legends has ever seen.

And every man, woman, and child there will be marked for doom.

Chapter One

❦

LUGHNASADH HARVEST FAIR AT
CASTLE HAVEN

The Highlands
Late Summer 1398

If she'd had any doubt that the day was a disaster, Lady Marjory Mackintosh knew it by the time she landed at the fair's crowded row of cloth stalls.

Most years she loved Lughnasadh.

A lively gathering to give thanks for the season's first harvest and to mark the end of summer, the ancient festival offered one of the few markets that ever visited the Glen of Many Legends.

All three glen clans attended, glad for the entertainments and an opportunity to replenish supplies now that the sun was on its descent into winter darkness. Folk from neighboring lands also took advantage. Everywhere, visitors jostled to examine wares not readily available in the glen. Others flocked to the cook stalls and refreshment booths, while some chose to watch the jugglers, musicians, and dancers who paraded past rows of brightly painted wooden stalls.

Bards spun tales for eager listeners. And young girls wearing flower garlands threw crumbled oatcakes to the birds so that the glen's smallest creatures could take part in the celebration.

Somewhere a woman laughed, her voice light and full of merriment.

Marjory felt a spurt of envy.

She would've enjoyed a reason to delight in the day's excitements. Unfortunately, she couldn't feel anything beyond a nagging frustration, disappointment clouding her pleasure.

Alasdair MacDonald wasn't anywhere to be seen.

Not that she'd truly expected to encounter the dashing Clan Donald chieftain. He'd been away from the glen nearly a year, after all. And whatever his business, he hadn't bothered to send a single word offering felicitations or even inquiring of her health.

He'd undoubtedly forgotten her.

And wasn't she a fool to let that bother her.

To wish for even a moment that the feelings she'd once imagined he held for her were true. Sadly, she'd misread him. She needed to forget the heat in his eyes and the flash of his smile. The way his body brushed hers in a passing moment. And how his scent took over her senses and left her weak in the knees.

The time had passed when his mere proximity would infuse her with delicious warmth, making her skin tingle and stirring potent desire deep inside her.

She knew better now.

His feelings for her, if they'd ever existed, had clearly turned as cool as the shadows on the hills in the hour of gloaming.

So she set a deliberately intent look on her face and

began perusing the artfully displayed silk ribbons offered by the nearest cloth vendor. It wouldn't do to let anyone who suspected her attraction to Alasdair think she might be suffering under his absence.

Her face heated, her pulse quickening in annoyance at how eagerly she'd scanned the crowds upon arriving at the fair. Slipping away from her brother and his wife, she'd worked her way through the stalls and past countless traders' carts, so hopeful to catch a glimpse of the tall, strapping man she ached to see. Now at the cloth stalls, placed at the farthest end of the fair, she had to admit defeat.

And for more than not spying Alasdair in the bustle, although the other soul she'd hoped to find certainly held no place in her heart.

A Norseman not adverse to fattening his purse, he was the latest in a long line of self-seeking men who accepted coin and jewels in return for helping her thwart her brother Kendrew's attempts to see her wed.

She had her own plans.

At least, she had until Alasdair vanished from the glen, never to be seen again.

Even so, she cast another glance down the row of cloth stalls. Regrettably, she saw little but the noisy throng and drifting smoke from the cook fires. She certainly didn't spot the one-eyed Norseman with a gold ring in his ear whom she desperately needed to see. More important, she also failed to see the warrior chieftain whose mere glance sent hot shivers racing through her blood.

Marjory frowned.

Alasdair wasn't worth the thoughts she wasted on him.

No doubt he wasn't at the harvest fair because he was occupied with a maid he deemed more pleasing than her.

Indeed, she was quite certain that was so. Alasdair was known to be a well-lusted man.

He wouldn't lack for female companionship, wherever he held himself.

Sure of it, she fought against the resentment that slammed into her. Her head began to ache.

"Sweet lass, you brighten the day more than if a ray of sunlight fell to earth."

Marjory froze, her breath catching at the deep, rich voice she hadn't heard in so long. *Alasdair.* His big, masculine shadow fell across her, melding with her own in an intimate joining. His scent swirled around her, a heady blend of man, peat smoke, and the sea, as familiar as if she'd breathed him in yesterday. But she hadn't. And that truth burned in her chest, a tight coil of injured possessiveness she had no right to feel.

Still...

She bit her lip, aware of the fair's atmosphere shifting, the air almost igniting around her.

The fine sapphire ribbon she'd been admiring slipped from her fingers to curl on the grass. Before her, the cloth stall dimmed, as did the colorful wares piled on its display board. Everything around her ceased to exist, the fairgoers smudging to a blur as her heart leaped, her body and her emotions responding to him in ways she knew she should squelch at once.

Unfortunately, she couldn't.

He stood right behind her.

So near that her skin prickled, tingling as if he'd touched her. Pleasure swept her, a sweet, warm tide. But his presence reminded her of the other reason she'd made certain not to miss the harvest fair. The peril she faced with each new day: forced nuptials with a Viking lord of high rank who'd expect an amenable wife.

A pity she didn't feel at all willing.

Marjory bristled, straightened her back.

Her brother meant well in trying to find her a titled and wealthy Viking husband, a man who would bring status to their clan and forge a bond to the Mackintoshes' ancient ties to the northern lands. Even so, she had no wish for such a match. Nor could she bear the thought of leaving her home, the Glen of Many Legends.

She didn't want to marry a Norseman.

She wanted...

"Alasdair." She turned to face him, anger chasing her elation. "I didn't think to see you here. You've been away many months now."

"So I have, aye." He stepped closer, giving her a slow, deliciously wicked smile. "Can it be you missed me?"

"Surely not." Marjory flushed when he cocked a disbelieving brow. "I've had much to do of late." She spoke true, just not adding that many of her thoughts had been of him. "You cannot believe the glen stilled in your absence, pining for you. There is aye work and—"

"I spoke of you, lass, no' the glen." His gaze locked with hers and she could feel the heat of him, the power of his strong, hard body. His rich, auburn hair gleamed in the sun. A bit longer than she remembered, the ends brushed his shoulders, while new, harsh lines in his face hinted he'd been long at sea. He also seemed larger and more roughened than she remembered.

She flipped back her braid, not liking how his rugged appearance made her pulse quicken. "I am not your concern, Alasdair MacDonald."

He let his gaze roam over her, as if seeing her for the first time. "Aye, well. You are a Mackintosh and your brother and I are no' friends, that is true."

"You never forget that, do you?" Marjory's chest tightened, his words a knife jab to her heart.

"There is much I dinnae forget." He gripped her chin, slid his thumb over her lips. "I'm also thinking I was gone too long, much as I needed to make the journey to Inverness. A good seaman watches o'er the building of a new galley, howe'er skilled the shipyard. Now I'm returned." He stroked the corner of her mouth, his touch leaving her breathless.

Shivery, almost giddy with happiness, and more than a little annoyed.

She wasn't a child's toy to be cast aside and ignored, retrieved at a whim.

She was Marjory Mackintosh of Nought and a proud and strong woman.

So she stepped back, away from the madness of his caress. The unsettling things his attentions did to her insides, making it so hard to think.

She did lift her chin. "Will you be staying?"

"Aye, that I will." His voice deepened and he appeared even more different. Not just larger than she remembered but a bit dangerous. His eyes darkening, he leaned in, so near that his breath mingled with hers. "Seeing the splendors of these hills, I regret I was away."

"Indeed." Marjory held his gaze, challengingly.

"So I said." He flashed another smile and then bent to retrieve the fallen silk ribbon. "You dropped this." Giving her the ribbon, he closed her fingers around its length and then raised her hand to his lips. "Have you ne'er learned no' to let something of such beauty slip from your grasp?"

"This past year, I have learned things I would never have believed." She didn't say her greatest lesson was that he cared so little for her. That truth surely blazed in her eyes. "Were you aware how many wayfarers pass through this glen? Traveling men who gladly carry messages if asked?"

"Such men also journey north, my lady. They sail Hebridean waters, where I spent time after leaving Inverness with my new galley. If the wind changes in Glasgow, it's known in Aberdeen by nightfall." He stepped back, narrowing his gaze. "Tongues wag even faster in our beloved Highlands. So tell me, Norn"—he used her by-name, given to her for her fair northern looks—"I would know if the rumors I've heard are true. Has your brother secured a match for you? Are you to be a Viking bride?"

She looked at him, her knuckles still tingling where he'd kissed her. "Kendrew does wish to find a husband for me. He's sent offers to a number of Norsemen, mostly lesser nobles in Orkney and Shetland.

"So far they've all declined." She drew a breath, keeping her chin raised. If she succeeded in trysting with a certain one-eyed Viking courier this day, she'd ensure another refused bid.

Hoping she'd yet spot the man, she squared her shoulders and held Alasdair's gaze. "I am not betrothed."

"I am glad to hear it." He looked away, into the crowd of fairgoers. Turning back to her, his face was shuttered. "You weren't meant to leave the glen. You'd be miserable elsewhere. Anyone born of this land would be."

"That I know." Marjory didn't blink, her tone as clear and proud as his.

But her heart dipped.

She'd hoped for a different response.

The one he'd given indicated he saw her as any clanswoman of the glen. That he'd touched her cheek and smoothed his thumb over her lips, heat in his eyes as he'd done so, only revealed his appreciation of females. A bonnie man, he'd always drawn their attention.

And it galled to know that a man who so enjoyed ladies and bed-sport could ignore the deep passion and true joy she was sure they would find if he weren't so thickheaded.

Yet, in many ways, Alasdair was more stubborn than her brother.

It was a truth that soured her mood.

Lest he guess, she gave him a dazzling smile. "I have no intention of leaving the glen." She twirled the blue ribbon through her fingers. "I've never felt a need to go journeying. Everything I desire is here."

"I could say the same, sweetness. Still, there are times when duty calls a man away." He gestured to the edge of the wood where a handful of MacDonald guards watched over a pile of salt barrels and sacks, goods meant for Blackshore Castle, the MacDonald stronghold at the southernmost end of the glen. "A clan chieftain cannae think only of his own wishes, howe'er he's tempted."

Marjory stiffened. "Were you tempted in the Hebrides?"

His gaze turned sharp. "What are you saying?"

"Folk spoke of you in your absence." She watched him carefully, gauging his reaction. "Talk of change at Blackshore, plans concerning you."

Alasdair shrugged. "Tongues aye wag o'er a chieftain's doings. My only plans were fetching my galley and"—his blue eyes glinted—"helping a friend, the MacKenzie chief, deal with a pack of rabid MacLeods bent on harrying Eilean Creag, the MacKenzie stronghold. Adding my new ship, and my fighting men, to a few sea battles is what delayed my return."

"I see." Marjory did, but she knew there was more.

There *had* been tales.

Chatter in Nought's own kitchens. Hushed words quickly silenced when she drew near, whisperings about Alasdair's men urging him to wed. One of the laundresses claimed she'd heard of a minor Mackinnon chieftain offering Alasdair his youngest daughter. The girl was famed as a great beauty, said to be sweet and biddable, and possessed of a singing voice to rival the songbirds.

Just thinking of such a fabled creature filled Marjory's mouth with the taste of bitter ash.

Not that she'd wish a cretin upon him.

On second thought, perhaps she would.

She also needed to know the truth.

So she took a deep breath and spoke her mind. "It is rumored you're to take a Mackinnon bride. That plans have been made and—"

"Is it now?" He looked amused. "Folk must've been mightily bored to spread such prattle. I'm wed to the glen, lass. Keeping peace is enough to occupy me. I've more to do than look for a wife."

"So it's not true?"

"Nae." He touched her face again, lifting her chin as he let his gaze slide over her, lingering just long enough at her amber necklace to show that he recognized the gemstones as belonging to his clan. Believed enchanted, the ambers had passed to her through Alasdair's sister, Catriona, and then by way of another friend, her brother's wife, Isobel.

"The ambers . . ." Marjory waited until he looked up. "I hope you don't mind I wear them?"

"Nae, I am glad that you do." He trailed his finger along the sensitive skin beneath her ear, his touch making her blood quicken. "I'd heard Lady Isobel gave you the ambers at her wedding celebration. They suit you well."

"I treasure them." She did.

"As you should." He looked at her, his expression unreadable. "They're a clan heirloom, no' a mere adornment."

"That I know." Marjory hoped her face didn't reveal that, to her, the stones were much more.

She and her two friends shared a secret pact, the amber necklace sealing their oath to foster peace between the three clans who shared the glen.

Catriona and Isobel had kept their vows. They'd each wed the chieftain of one of the other clans, erstwhile foes allied through nuptial bliss.

Marjory was the last, her part of the plan as yet unfulfilled. She'd hoped for a match with Alasdair, a union she'd been confident to achieve. Instead, he'd ignored her and then vanished.

He hadn't made it easy.

And now...

He'd returned a stranger.

Still a man who put duty above all else, and no less handsome than before, yet there was a new and hard edge to him, a boldness that hinted at a fierce will that she doubted would bend even for her.

"Some say the ambers are charmed." His voice held a teasing note, reminding her that he scoffed at such notions. "Whate'er you believe, they hail from the same ancient amber hoard as the stone in my sword pommel." He patted the blade's hilt, drawing her attention to the gleaming gold at its head. "My enemies swear the amber's powers aid me in battle. The truth is"—he winked—"any man's skill with a sword has more to do with muscle and long years of practice. Though I'll own Mist-Chaser is a fine brand." He hooked his thumbs in his sword belt, his pride evident. "Many of my bitterest foes have bloodied her steel. She's a thirsty lass when unsheathed."

"I've no doubt." Marjory felt a chill, once again struck by how much he'd changed.

He'd always been a fierce warrior, his reputation made by the sword.

Now he struck her as almost ruthless.

A man who'd let no one take what was his. And who'd gladly send his enemies to the darkest, coldest end of hell. But then his smile deepened, crinkling the corners of his eyes in a way that made her insides flutter.

He truly was the most dashing man she'd ever seen.

As if he knew, he leaned toward her and smoothed her hair back from her face, his touch unleashing a wealth of shivery sensation.

"I'm glad you have such faith in my skill." The look on his face said he meant something other than swordplay.

Something intimate, forbidden, and darkly exciting.

Marjory's heart raced.

Hope soared and she began to imagine him stepping closer, perhaps even lowering his mouth to hers for a kiss. His hands sweeping around her, pulling her against him as he—

"I owe my skill to my grandsire who put a wooden practice sword in my hand almost as soon as I took my first steps." His words shattered her burgeoning bliss, making clear that she'd misread him. "What he didn't teach me, I learned on the field. Often enough fighting Mackintoshes," he added, sounding pleased to remind her.

"Did you come here to fight us this morn?" She set her hands on her hips, straightened her spine.

He was well-armed. He wore his sword strapped low on his hip and a dirk winked from beneath his belt. A quick glance at his feet showed an extra dagger tucked into his boot.

He followed her glance. "Dinnae worry. I'll no' be lopping off anyone's head. But"—his voice hardened—"there are aye those who'd turn a fairground into a battlefield. The greater fool is a man who forgets suchlike are about."

"You mean my brother."

"I meant anyone who'd disturb the glen's peace. Such gatherings attract more than good hill folk and innocent wayfarers."

"You expect trouble?" She shot a glance at the Mac-Donald guardsmen near the wood's edge, noting that they'd followed their chieftain's lead. Steel glinted from beneath their plaids, proving they wore more arms than was appropriate for a harvest fair.

Marjory drew a tight breath. The Glen of Many Legends had seen enough bloodshed.

"This ground has run red more often than it should." She nudged the grass, a wave of protectiveness rising inside her. "It doesn't need another drenching."

Alasdair turned her to him, his hands on her shoulders. "The glen is quiet these days. So long as I have breath in me it will remain so. The arms are a precaution."

"Something is bothering you." She could feel it, see it in his eyes.

"Aye, that is true." He didn't deny it. "And it's naught to do with my hairy-legged kinsmen and how many swords they're carrying. It has to do with you." Gripping her elbows, he drew her into the shaded arch of a flower-covered bower. "See here, lass—"

"I see you're inviting trouble pulling me in here." Marjory didn't care for his tone, so gave him her airiest in return. A few moments ago, she might've welcomed entering a bower with him. Now…

She stood firm, not letting him maneuver her deeper into the shadows. "If Kendrew—"

"He is no' my master." His face hardened. "No man is that and any who thinks otherwise lives dangerously."

"He's in an ill temper of late."

"His mood will worsen if he crosses me." Alasdair set his hand on his sword hilt. "If he grieves you, he'll no' live to have a mood."

"He means well, even if I don't always agree with him. And I'm used to his bluster." She didn't say how good she was at outfoxing him.

There were some things men needn't know.

She glanced past Alasdair's shoulder at the three banners flying from Castle Haven's walls. Sited in the heart of the glen, Haven was a Cameron holding and hosted each year's early harvest fair and market. In olden days, only the Camerons' snarling dog pennant overlooked the festivities. Since a trial by combat settled glen disputes two years before, Mackintosh and MacDonald pennants were also raised.

The banners vouched for the clans' amity, declaring erstwhile foes were now allies, if not friends.

Her brother disagreed.

In his eyes, and despite the truce pressed on the glen by King Robert III, Alasdair remained a reviled and much-resented enemy.

Marjory felt otherwise.

She also knew she was the reason for her brother's growing temper.

If things continued as she hoped, his annoyance would only increase. Unbeknownst to him, she undid his every machination, employing wit and daring to ensure that each suitor he found soon withdrew his interest. She'd become adept at persuasion, flattery, pleading when need be, and offering coin when all else failed. Some were skills she wasn't proud of. But she wouldn't allow Kendrew to wed her against her will.

So she did what she must.

Fortune aye blessed the bold.

To that end, she couldn't miss meeting the one-eyed Viking who'd agreed to carry her own letter rather than Kendrew's to his master.

A decline she'd penned in Kendrew's name.

"I must be away." She moved to edge past Alasdair, back to the open space before the cloth stalls.

"No' yet, sweet." He didn't budge. Far from it, she'd swear he grew to fill the bower's arched entry. "I'll have a word with you, and then you can be on your way."

Marjory frowned. "We've already had words."

"No' the important ones." Stepping closer, he placed his hands on either side of her shoulders, backing her against the flowered wall and trapping her there. "The MacDonald ambers suit you." His gaze flickered to the gemstones. "You should wear them always."

"I do." Marjory lifted a hand to the necklace. The stones rested cool and smooth against her skin. A sign, if legend spoke true, that all was good in her world, no threat or danger imminent.

A pity the necklace didn't seem to warn of MacDonalds.

In particular, their chieftain.

Tall, powerfully muscled, and with a proud, open face, he'd captivated the first time she'd seen him. That'd been two years ago, several days before the trial by combat. Alasdair rode to her home, Castle Nought, to warn Kendrew of suspected treacheries, sharing his suspicions about strangers he'd seen in the glen.

Kendrew scoffed at the warning. He also ignored the famed Highland courtesy shown to guests, regardless of name. He would've set Alasdair before the door if Marjory hadn't intervened. Nought might be remote, perched on the stony cliffs that formed the glen's most rugged territory, but Marjory took care that all guests were well met. Alasdair's arrival merited lavish hospitality, including clean, warm bedding for the MacDonald party and hot baths before they'd retired. Willing kitchen lasses had provided additional comforts to those men desiring.

Kendrew had been outraged, his behavior barely civil.

Marjory lost her heart.

She'd never met anyone as compelling as Alasdair. No man had ever looked at her so heatedly, his smoldering gaze starting a fire that burned in her dreams for days and months after his visit.

Sadly, she suspected he'd allowed his gaze to devour her so boldly simply to rile her brother.

Here in the bower, he was eyeing her the same way. Only now she knew he couldn't help it. He surely looked at all women so hungrily. A shame his intensity still made her breath come unsteadily. Equally annoying, sunlight fell into the bower to gleam on his rich auburn hair. And like his isle-girt holding, the scent of the sea clung to him, along with a hint of cold wind and salt air.

A heady mix, it made her behave foolishly.

Unable to stop herself, hope beginning to flare again, she touched a finger to his plaid, tracing the detail of a soft, well-worn fold. "What is this important matter you wished to discuss?"

He leaned closer, his breath warm on her cheek.

Any moment he'd kiss her. A hot and ravenous kiss, full of passion.

Sure of it, she splayed her fingers across his plaid, aware of his warmth, the hard, steady beat of his heart. She moistened her lips in readiness, waiting. She almost closed her eyes, but didn't.

She wanted the triumph of seeing him lower his mouth to hers.

"I would ask you to send me word if ever you see anything strange at Nought." He spoke bluntly. He also gripped her wrist, lowering her hand from his chest. "Travelers who might not be what they seem or"—he straightened—"a shifting in shadows when nothing is there. I do no' trust your brother's instincts." He spoke briskly, all chiefly business. "I believe you'd notice a threat faster."

"I see." Marjory did. And she didn't like what she saw. She'd flattered herself.

Alasdair hadn't drawn her into the bower to kiss her.

He hoped to engage her watchfulness at Nought, the northernmost and least accessible corner of the glen. In Mackintosh hands since time beginning, it was a forbidding place of sheer cliffs and deep gorges. Strange outcroppings and ancient cairns known as the dreagan stones lent Nought an air of mystery and danger. Few souls dared to tread there save her kinsmen.

Many who did vowed they'd never return.

Now and then, broken men and other undesirables attempted to slip through Nought unseen. As they rarely emerged, it was rumored Nought's dreagans stalked and ate them.

Or so clan graybeards liked to claim, boasting that the stony-scaled beasties believed to sleep beneath the dreagan cairns wouldn't tolerate the passage of evildoers on sacred clan lands.

Just now Marjory wished a dreagan would fire-blast Alasdair.

She didn't want to be a useful set of eyes.

"I see no cause for such concern." She kept her tone as cool as his. "I walk Nought's battlements often and have seen nothing move except mist and falling rock. I know you send patrols into Nought. We all know it, even if you think we don't. So now you tire of the bother and would have me do the watching for you?"

"Sakes, nae." He gripped her shoulders, giving her a look that burned right through her. "I'd only know if you feel threatened. Don't ever put yourself in danger. Promise me you'll do nothing so foolhardy."

"I never do anything foolish." Marjory broke free, brushing her skirts. "I'm a Mackintosh." She raised her chin, speaking with pride. "We fear nothing."

"Mackintoshes are also known for their stubbornness." Alasdair swatted at his own sleeve, a muscle working in his jaw. "You're a thrawn folk. Stone-willed and unbending. Your brother is the worst. His wits don't reach past the head of his broadax." He paused, his scorn palpable. "Knowing him, he'd no' recognize—"

"Knowing me, you must be tired of life to stand so near my sister." Kendrew strode up to them, scowling darkly.

A big, rough-hewn man, he looked even more fearsome in full war gear, a sword at his belt and his huge war ax slung across his back. "Or were you just after having your bones trampled?"

"I owe you a scar, Mackintosh." Alasdair rubbed his left arm, his tone low and menacing. "Dinnae think I'll hesitate to give you a bigger one."

"You had your chance at the trial by combat."

"I'd sooner fight you one on one. Name the day. I'm ready now."

"Alasdair! Kendrew!" Marjory rushed between them to press her hands against their chests. "This isn't the place for a ruckus. You're already drawing eyes."

"Nae, you are." Kendrew scowled at her. "Consorting with a web-footed brine drinker, a man better suited to scrape barnacles off his leaky galleys than stain your name by pulling you into a bower."

"He didn't pull me anywhere." Marjory bristled. "I go where I please."

"You'll no' be lying to me." Kendrew's eyes narrowed. "He played the gallant, fetching your ribbon when you dropped it and even daring to touch your hair. Dinnae deny it. You know I have eyes and ears everywhere. And you"—he shot a look at Alasdair—"will be missing your fingers next time you—"

"Stand back, Norn." Alasdair drew his sword, whipping it up so the tip hovered at Kendrew's nose. "I could take off your face before you knew I'd cut you. Insult your sister again, if you dinnae believe me."

Kendrew reddened. "It's you insulting her, soiling her reputation with your unwanted presence. Leave her be. I warn you."

"I speak to whoe'er I will. Though I'll no' frighten her by fighting you here." Alasdair swept his blade downward, ramming the sword point into the ground. "We'll meet again on another day, that I vow."

"Alasdair, please..." Marjory stepped between them again. "He doesn't mean—"

"I ne'er say a word I don't mean." Kendrew kept his stare fixed on Alasdair. "I ken what's best for my sister. Aye, we'll clash swords elsewhere. When we do, you're a dead man, brine drinker."

"I'll count the hours." Alasdair yanked his sword from the ground, shoving it into its sheath. "They'll be few if the gods are kind."

"My gods will eat you and spit out your bones." Kendrew spoke loudly, grinning when the men behind him—his guards—snarled a few slurs of their own.

"Enough." Marjory threw a look at them, silencing them with a well-practiced narrowing of her eyes.

Kendrew grinned, apparently pleased by the ruckus.

Ignoring them all, Alasdair drew a coin from a pouch at his belt and flipped it to the gaping stall-holder. "For the lady's silk ribbon." He nodded at Marjory. "And any other trinkets she desires."

Turning to her, he took her hand and loosely wrapped the blue silk ribbon around her wrist. "Remember what I told you." He didn't bother to lower his voice, even bending to kiss her hand again.

Beside them, Kendrew snorted. "Forgetting you is what she'll be doing."

He would've said more, Marjory knew, but his wife, Isobel, joined them then, hooking her arm through his.

And—Marjory noted with appreciation—clamping her foot on Kendrew's booted toes.

The two women exchanged telling glances.

Catching the look, Kendrew frowned first at his wife and then at Marjory. "Dinnae think to try your scheming. I'll hurl every stone at Nought in your path if you do. No sister of mine will wed a MacDonald."

"There's no danger of that." Marjory took care to speak lightly.

She also spoke the truth, only wishing Alasdair could've heard how easily she dismissed the possibility.

But he was gone.

Already a good twelve paces away, he moved briskly through the crowd, leaving her to stare after him as he disappeared into the throng.

"Good riddance." Kendrew folded his arms, looking pleased.

Marjory and Isobel ignored him until he strode off in the company of his bearded, ax-carrying guardsmen.

"He'll never change." Marjory slipped the blue ribbon from her wrist, tucking it into her bodice.

"I hope he doesn't." Isobel's tone revealed how besotted she was with her husband.

Marjory glanced at her, feeling a pang to see that her friend actually glowed, her face softening as she watched Kendrew walk away.

"You really love him, don't you?" She put a hand on Isobel's arm.

"Madly, I do." Isobel beamed. "Wait until Alasdair comes round." She patted Marjory's hand, speaking with all the confidence of a woman well-loved. "Then you'll see—"

"I've seen plenty this morn." Marjory wished it weren't

so. "Alasdair is different. He's not the same man who left here a year ago. I scarcely recognized him."

Isobel's smile didn't waver. "He certainly recognized you."

"He is aye attentive to women." Marjory tightened her shawl about her shoulders, feeling a chill. "Any woman. In that, he hasn't changed."

"You are not any woman." Isobel glanced to where Alasdair had vanished. "Kendrew isn't the only one with eyes and ears everywhere. I saw how Alasdair watched you before he joined you at the cloth stall. And"—she tilted her head, her dark eyes twinkling—"I didn't miss the annoyance on his face when he walked away just now."

"To be sure he was annoyed. Kendrew provoked him beyond all reason."

Isobel lifted a brow. "Do you truly think a battle-hardened warrior would let a few angry words get to him? Is it not more likely that you turn Alasdair's blood to smoke, driving him to recklessness?"

Marjory considered.

Sadly, she disagreed with her friend. Isobel hadn't heard him ask her to keep an eye on Nought, informing him if suspicious wayfarers entered Mackintosh territory.

That was why he'd drawn her into the bower.

She'd been a fool to think otherwise.

"You know it is true." Isobel took her arm, leading her toward the cook stalls. "Alasdair wants you, and badly. He always has. He just needs to accept that truth. He will come for you when he does."

"You do not know him as I do." Marjory paused before a fish stall, eyeing a row of skewered herring, golden brown and sizzling over a bed of smoldering coals. "He won't forget I'm Kendrew's sister. If he does harbor such feelings, they'll only make him strengthen his defenses against me."

"Then you must tear them down." Isobel turned the most sensible gaze on her. "The way to do that is clear. You must tempt him."

For a moment, Marjory could only stare at her friend.

"I'm not a temptress." She wouldn't even consider it.

Isobel laughed. "Ah, but you can be if you wished." She nodded to the burly stall-holder, indicating she and Marjory would each take a spit-roasted herring. "You just have to use what nature gave you, that's all. You can begin the next time you see Alasdair."

"He's on his way to Blackshore. He'll be busy, having been gone so long."

"He'll be back. And sooner than you think, I'll wager. Or"—she produced a coin to pay for their fish—"did you not know it's impossible to chase a thirsting man from a spring?"

"I am not a spring."

"Nae, you're a woman." Isobel smiled brightly. "And that's even better."

Marjory just looked at her. "I do believe marriage has maddened you."

"So it has." Isobel had the audacity to wink. "In the very best way, I'll agree."

And as Marjory strove to keep a flush from blooming on her cheeks as she watched the stall-holder take their herring off the spits, she knew her friend's influence must be affecting her. Because even before the man brought them the fish, she knew what she had to do.

She'd seduce Alasdair.

The only question was how and when.

Chapter Two

❧

No one would ever make the mistake of claiming Marjory Mackintosh surrendered easily. In truth, she wasn't at all wont to do so. Not ever, if she had any say in matters. Regrettably, as she stood with her friend Isobel in the festively decorated ladies' bower at the harvest fair, she felt dangerously near to admitting defeat.

The possibility rankled. She'd never been thwarted.

Yet here she was, surrounded by chattering clanswomen, sipping watered wine and nibbling oatcakes when she should be plying her wiles on Alasdair. Enchanting him with her wit, seducing him with her womanly charm, as Isobel kept informing her. A wee wriggle of the hip and bounce of the bosom and he'd lose his head, her good-sister insisted.

Perhaps that was even so.

Isobel should know.

Hadn't she won Kendrew with the fine art of feminine persuasion? Now, after all was said and done, a soul would be hard-pressed to find a husband more ridiculously in love with his wife than her brother.

Marjory's heart squeezed, remembering how Kendrew had pulled Isobel to him, kissing her hard and fast when he'd left them at the ladies' bower. He'd also glanced back at her three times when he strode away with his men. No one could doubt how besotted he was. Or that his wife meant everything to him.

Isobel clearly understood men.

But could Marjory find success with her methods? Would a few glances from beneath lowered lashes and a brief but artful touch to her breast fire Alasdair's blood, winning his undying affection?

His love?

Marjory was skeptical, but willing to try her seduction skills on him.

Regrettably, he'd left the harvest fair hours ago.

He'd sauntered away into the crowd, surely putting her from his mind as easily as he tossed his plaid over his shoulder. His remarkably broad and oh-so-appealing shoulders. Marjory frowned, his image flashing across her mind, burning into her heart. Unlike her brother, Alasdair hadn't even looked back once.

Damn him for an arrogant bastard.

She wished a worse curse on Groat, the one-eyed, gold-earringed Viking courier who was also proving as scarce as winged sheep.

Waving away a serving girl's offer of more watered wine, she turned to her good-sister. "You're certain our friend said he'd be here?"

"Groat?" Isobel blinked.

"Shhhh..." Marjory lowered her voice, certain that

every woman in the bower just developed overly sensitive ears. "Of course, I mean him. I've searched everywhere and he simply isn't here. You spoke with him before he left Nought. Perhaps you misunderstood?"

"Oh no, I couldn't have." Isobel shook her head. "He made quite clear that he'd only hand over Kendrew's missive if you met him at the fair and"—a touch of regret flickered across her face—"gave him the sapphire ring he saw you wearing at the high table.

"He was adamant about the ring." Isobel linked her arm with Marjory's, leading her to a quiet corner of the garland-festooned tent. "Only then would he—"

"I already gave him enough silver coin to keep him in cows and women for years." Marjory flicked at her sleeve, her annoyance rising. "He promised to hand over Kendrew's letter of agreement when you slipped him my own parchment declining his overlord's terms for marriage."

Isobel looked uncomfortable. "I tried to reason with him. He refused after seeing your ring. He really wants it, so I'm sure he's about somewhere."

"I've worn tracks in the mud traipsing past all the booths and stalls. I even visited the horse market and the weaponsmiths. He wasn't anywhere to be seen and he's not a man to be overlooked."

"No, he isn't."

Marjory shuddered, remembering how the huge Viking had pulled slowly on his earring, his one good eye glinting wickedly at the young kitchen lasses who'd served him at Nought's high table.

He clearly appreciated women as much as he hungered for gold.

"I worried he'd demand a night with Maili." Isobel

spoke of Nought's most light-skirted, men-loving laundress. "She did wink at him a few times, until he noticed your sapphire ring and lost interest in her."

"Greed always matters most to such men."

"Even so, I think Maili gave him an itch. She's a comely lass and enjoys flaunting herself. She'll have stirred certain flames in him."

"His lusts scarce concern me." Marjory didn't care if he desired a thousand serving lasses. She only wanted him to hand over Kendrew's letter.

"Ah, but maybe his itch does matter." Isobel began tapping her chin. "Perhaps Maili started a fire he decided to quench here, at the market fair. There are other ladies' bowers at the festival. They're set back in the wood, away from prying eyes and very welcoming to men with certain needs." Isobel smiled. "I'm betting you didn't look there."

"To be sure, I didn't." Marjory felt herself coloring.

"I think you should." Isobel didn't appear at all adverse to the idea.

"What if someone sees me?"

"What if Groat is there and you don't go, missing him?"

"He'll make haste back to his ship and deliver Kendrew's agreement to his lord to spite me for not giving him my sapphire ring."

"That would be the way of it, I'm thinking." Isobel nodded slowly.

Marjory rested a hand over the small leather purse tied to her belt. She could feel the tiny, hard shape of her ring in its depths.

It was a precious keepsake that had belonged to her grandmother and her grandmother before her.

"I should gut him when he reaches for his payment." Marjory was tempted. Her father had taught her how to defend herself as soon as she was able to hold a child's dagger. She'd been a fast learner. "He should've been satisfied with the bag of coin I gave him."

"Aye, he should've been." Isobel took her arm again, this time urging her toward the tent's pinned-back entrance flap. "But he wasn't. And if you dirked him, his shipmates would only come searching for him, causing even more trouble than losing your ring."

They stepped outside where the crowd was thinning, many visitors making for the cook stalls and refreshment booths for their evening supper. Even so, Marjory cast a hopeful glance up and down the fair's main thoroughfare. Groat the Viking was nowhere to be seen.

She took a deep breath. "You'll have to keep Kendrew occupied if he comes for us before I return."

"Leave that to me." Isobel winked and gave her a little nudge. "You'll be the last thing on his mind, I promise."

Marjory didn't doubt it.

She also gave her friend a quick hug and then started down the thoroughfare, making for the dark line of trees at the far end of the market.

If Groat was there, she'd find him.

Even if she had to pry him from a joy woman's arms.

Fortune favors the bold. And, of late, she was feeling most daring.

Damn the lass.

And damn his clan's ambers for resting so sweetly against her smooth, creamy skin. Alasdair scowled as he rode at the head of the long column of his men. Traveling as swiftly as possible through the thick piney woods that, to his mind, clogged Cameron territory, he and his party were making good time. Castle Haven and its harvest fair well behind them.

Good riddance, in his view.

He didn't like how Marjory Mackintosh made a liar of him.

There wasn't anything sweet about how she wore the MacDonald ambers.

Provocative is how they looked on her.

Almost as if the gleaming gemstones, so rich and golden, wished to taunt him, drawing his attention to the lush swell of her full, round breasts. Worse, he could so easily imagine their pert rosy crests. That he'd yet to see, touch, and taste them struck him as a terrible injustice. That a Viking husband might soon do so made him murderous.

He should've kissed her in the bower.

She'd expected a kiss, even wanted one. He'd seen the desire in her eyes. Clearly availing her womanly wiles, she'd leaned her supple body into him, even lifting up on her toes and moistening her lips. Never had he burned more to seize a woman to him.

Only her name restrained him.

And now that a good length of miles stretched between them, and his blood still blazed with wanting her, he knew one thing only . . .

If she ever again tempted him so brazenly, he wouldn't be responsible for his actions.

Had he not given her good-day when he had, she'd be in his arms now. Like as not, beneath him, her long shapely legs wrapped soundly around his hips. Little under the sun could've stopped him from taking her.

And there'd be hell to pay if he did.

Too many good men of the glen, from all three clans, spilled their life's blood to satisfy the King's demands at the trial by combat. The freedom of every man, woman, and child in the glen, their right to remain on land they'd held for centuries, perhaps even their lives, depended on that fateful day, their willingness to abide by the King's truce.

Peace had come, but at a price.

Still, his feud with Kendrew went deeper, having roots that reached further back than the battle that had soaked the glen red two years before. Even the scar Kendrew carved into Alasdair's arm that wretched day was but a drop in the sea to their enmity.

Yet the bastard's sister...

Alasdair set his jaw, not wanting to think of her. But he saw Marjory so clearly before him. She invaded his mind, bewitching him. Everything about her made him crazy. Her shining waist-length hair swinging about her hips in ways that weren't good for a man. She carried more curves since he'd last seen her and they stood her well, making him itch to explore them. Even her eyes sparkled more than he remembered, their blue depths as clear as water and beckoning, almost suggestively.

Nae, indeed that.

She'd become a seductress.

Alasdair drew a tight breath, his mood worsening. Fury beat through him, his loins still painfully roused. Upon reaching Blackshore, he might forego a warm bath and take a bare-arsed dip in the loch.

And he'd thought his attraction to her had waned.

"Ho, Alasdair!" Wattie, one of his older clansmen, reined close. "Guid kens," he boomed, "the Mackintosh is a besotted fool, eh? Did you see him all moony-eyed each time his lady wife even looked at him?"

A low, rumbling chuckle rolled through the ranks of Alasdair's men, their mirth supporting Wattie's observation.

Alasdair resisted the urge to glare at them.

Instead, he shot Wattie the most expressionless look he could muster.

"Cannae say I noticed." He had, but Kendrew was the last man he wished to discuss.

He also didn't believe his worst enemy capable of any true feelings for a woman.

Save lust, of course.

"You missed a right fine show." Wattie hooted. "I'm thinking his bonnie lassie need only flick her skirts and he'll come running."

Alasdair snorted. "Aye, that I'll believe."

"Nae, nae." Wattie shook his head. "It's love that's addled him. Lady Isobel is more to him than a bedmate. Anyone can see—"

"He's daft, aye, but no' how you mean." Alasdair drew his horse to a halt and twisted round, facing Wattie full on. "You were along when his men ambushed us at Nought two years ago." The memory made the back of Alasdair's neck heat. "My sister, Catriona, rode with us. Yet he set his pack of ax-swinging wild men on us with no caring that a lady could've been harmed, much less killed. I'll ne'er forgive him for that." Alasdair leaned over, fixing Wattie with a long, hard look. "Dinnae tell me that bastard loves any woman, for I'll no' believe it. He cares only for holding on to his land. He'll sacrifice anyone and anything to do so."

"He said he didnae know Catriona was with us." Wattie tread dangerous ground. "There was so much mist blowing, have you forgotten? I dinnae think his men saw—"

"My sister could've been killed." Alasdair snarled the words, the blaze at his nape sweeping through him, igniting his temper. "Kendrew carries that shame."

"I didnae say I like him." Wattie looked embarrassed.

Alasdair felt like an arse.

Wattie was a good man, one of Alasdair's best. A fierce and fiery fighter in younger years, he still wielded a blade with terrifying skill. Now a widower, he deserved amusement where he found it.

"That I know, Wat." Alasdair reached over to clap his shoulder. "There isn't a redeemable bone in Mackintosh's body, so how could you like him?"

"I wouldn't mind breaking a few o' his bones." Wattie grinned, pumped a balled fist in the air.

The other warriors laughed. Not feeling so jovial himself, Alasdair looked down the line of men, glad for their levity. Two years of peace hadn't been easy on them. Hard and eager fighters, a wrong look or word could set them off. And once they'd drawn their steel, the first blood scented, there'd be no stopping them.

Alasdair eyed their swords now, knowing they'd serve him at a single nod.

Except...

One man's blade was missing.

And it wasn't just any sword. It was the one pried from the hand of the last MacDonald clansman to die at the trial by combat. A sword aptly named Honor that was now held in great reverence by the clan. Every time a party of warriors left Blackshore, one of them carried Honor rather than his usual brand.

And just now that warrior's sheath was empty.

When the man blanched beneath Alasdair's stare, clearly guilty of losing the precious sword, a snarling growl rose in Alasdair's throat. Anger almost choked him as he spurred down the line of men.

"Rory!" He jerked his horse to halt beside the warrior. "Where's Honor? Dinnae tell me you don't know."

"I-I . . ." Rory shifted in his saddle, his gabble answer enough.

Honor was gone.

Marjory's bravura waned the deeper she moved into the woods edging the market grounds. Although the sun still shone brightly over the harvest fair, it could've been after nightfall among the thick pines and moss-covered rocks of Clan Cameron's forest. The trees' green-black needle canopies hid the light, and the scent of resin, rich loamy earth, and wild orchids made clear that she'd left the crowded fair behind her, entering a dark and secret place.

Not that the forest frightened her.

A Mackintosh feared nothing, after all.

But she was also a lady.

And trees weren't the only things in the wood this particular day.

Pinpricks of yellow light flickered ahead, revealing the semicircle of garishly painted, flower-bedecked tents known as the other ladies' bowers. If she had any doubt, female laughter, a few telltale cries and moans, and snatches of bawdy song drifted on the air, leaving no mistake she'd almost reached her destination.

The place where men came to attend their manly cravings.

Marjory's breath hitched as she remembered how a certain part of her had warmed and tingled when Alasdair pulled her into the bower's shade, using his powerful arms to cage her against the flowered wall. She'd been so sure he'd kiss her, claim her lips in a bold slaking of passion. The possibility made her shiver with desire. When he didn't kiss her, she'd quivered with annoyance.

The tingles remained, taunting her.

But as she drew closer to the joy women's encampment, catching hints of ale and the ladies' heavy musk perfume, she also knew there had to be more to such pleasures than the furious couplings sure to be going on within the colorful, flower-draped tents.

When a naked woman burst from one of the bowers, dragging an equally bare-bottomed man behind her, then shrieking with laughter as she thrust him into the arms of another just as bare, she was sure of it.

She'd never share Alasdair with another female.

And she wouldn't have the opportunity to fret about such matters unless she retrieved Kendrew's letter from Groat the Viking.

So she nipped behind a tree, smoothed her hair, and brushed down her skirts. Then, straightening her back and shoulders, she stepped round beside the tree, allowing herself a good view of the clearing between the half-circle of tents.

Groat the Viking had to be there.

With luck, he'd emerge from one of the bowers any moment.

If need be, she'd call at the tents, asking for him.

Most of the joy women would be Rannoch Moor ladies, welcome at Nought's Beltane and Midsummer

Eve festivals. They wouldn't gossip about her, even if they guessed her reason for coming here. There were times when all women held together and this was one of them.

She hoped, anyway.

She also folded her arms, already feeling frightfully conspicuous.

She was just about to start tapping her foot on the needle-strewn ground when she heard, "A wench with such fine breasts shouldn't cross her arms unless she wants a man plumping and weighing them. Her teats, I mean."

Whirling about, she saw Groat sauntering toward her, a lecherous sneer on his blond-bearded face. He was also buckling on his sword belt, having just stepped out from one of the bowers.

Ignoring his jeers, Marjory held out her hand when he reached her, her tone as icy as she could make it. "I'll have the scroll you owe me."

"Perhaps I'll have something else in exchange for it?" His gaze dipped to her breasts, his one good eye glittering. "Thon wench"—he jerked his head at the tent he'd just left—"wasn't near as fetching as you."

"Touch me and I'll dirk you where it hurts most." Marjory whipped her lady's dagger from a fold in her skirts, aiming its tip at the bulge beneath his low-slung sword belt. "I've already considered doing the like, so you'd best not tempt me."

"Oh-ho!" He grinned but held up his hands and stepped back, away from the pointy end of her knife. "A shame you'll not be wedding my overlord. He likes his women with fire in their veins."

"I don't care what he likes." Marjory didn't lower her blade. "I will have my brother's letter."

"O-o-oh, Lord Thorkill would fancy you, he would." Groat pulled on his gold earring, eyeing her up and down. "So would many of us."

A big man, he had a shaggy mane of straw-colored hair and wore a sleeveless calfskin jerkin over a soiled tunic and loose trousers. His boots were old and muddied, and in addition to his sword, a Viking war ax hung from a belt slung over his shoulders. If he wished, he could knock the dagger from her hand with a puff of breath.

As if he guessed her thoughts, he stretched his arms over his head and cracked his knuckles.

"See here, Lady Marjory, I'm not looking for trouble." The smile left his face and he shook his head sadly. "Time was, I'd toss you over my shoulder and have you, your ring, and the coin you've already given me. As is"—he shrugged—"without both eyes, I'm only good for rowing oars and carrying messages. That's no work for a fighting man. So I pad my wages in other ways. Soon, I'll have enough land and wealth to settle down and keep my peace."

Marjory arched a brow. "Thanks to my monies and my sapphire ring."

He didn't turn a hair. "Yours, and such payment from others like you."

"Surely you know I have little choice."

"We all have choices. I'm not condemning you for yours, so don't rumple your nose at mine." An amused grin spread over his face. "Some would say your actions are as crooked as mine. You're tricking your brother, are you not? He desires a good marriage for you."

Marjory glared at him. "I see it otherwise."

He shrugged. "That's not my concern. Your ring is. You did bring it?"

"You'll have it after you give me my brother's letter." Marjory thrust her dagger back into its sheath and held out her hand again.

Groat sighed heavily. "Mayhap Thorkill wouldn't have been so pleased with you. You're too prickly to make a good wife."

"The scroll." Marjory wriggled her fingers.

The Viking fished inside his jerkin, producing a scrunched parchment. The red glob of wax that had been Kendrew's seal was broken. Marjory took the scroll and unrolled it, relief flooding her as she recognized her brother's boldly inked script.

Groat nodded as she re-rolled the missive. "See you, I keep my word."

"If that were so, we wouldn't be standing here. You were to give my brother's letter to Lady Isobel when you left Nought with my payment in coin. Instead, you demanded my ring." Marjory narrowed her eyes at him. "I'd say your word is only as good as your greed."

He had the audacity to grin. "A sharp tongue, too, eh?" His gaze turned shrewd, dipping to the small leather purse at her belt. "The sooner you hand over the ring, the sooner I'm away. I'll see that Thorkill believes what you penned. That his offer arrived too late and you're already wed to another."

Marjory flushed, her deceit, however necessary, embarrassing her.

Setting her lips in a hard, tight line that would've made her brother proud, she untied her purse strings and thrust Kendrew's letter inside. She'd burn it as soon as opportunity arose. That decided, she retrieved her sapphire ring and placed it in Groat's outstretched hand.

He stashed it away with lightning speed. "A pleasure doing business with you, my lady. If ever you need my services again—"

"I need you gone." Marjory bristled.

He laughed and bowed low. "As you wish."

When he straightened, he sauntered into the trees without a backward glance. Marjory stared after him until he disappeared into the gloom. She shuddered as the shadows claimed him, wishing she could scrub his taint from her skin.

Her meeting with him left a nasty taste in her mouth.

But as far as she knew, his overlord had been the last Norse nobleman on her brother's list of possible husbands for her. Ridding herself of Thorkill's acceptance of her as a bride was worth sacrificing her ring and coming to the other ladies' bowers to meet Groat.

Still...

Her heart was racing, her palms were damp, and her mouth had gone annoyingly dry. She could still hear Groat's mocking tone ringing in her ears, see the amusement on his bold, battle-scarred face.

Praise be, he was gone.

She'd be away herself as soon as she regained her composure.

Hoping no one at the tents had seen her, she cast a glance that way, her heart plummeting to her toes when she spied Alasdair ducking out of the tent flap of the largest, most gaudily decorated bower.

A half-naked woman stood in the tent's shadows, beaming after him.

Eyes rounding, Marjory gasped.

She took a fast step backward and lost her balance,

slipping on the pine needles as she tried to nip behind the sheltering trees. She didn't fall, but she did bump against low-hanging branches, dislodging a large, fat spider that dropped onto her shoulder.

"Agh!" She jumped, brushing at the spider.

It darted into her bodice.

She flung her shawl to the ground and tore at her gown's laces. The spider sped across her bosom, beneath the top edge of her gown.

From the corner of her eye, she saw Alasdair striding across the clearing, coming right at her. He carried a huge sword and looked furious.

She didn't care.

She did brush more frantically at her clothes, her efforts rewarded when the spider leaped to the ground, scurrying under the pine needles.

"Saints a' mercy!" She pressed a hand to her breast and heaved a great, shuddering sigh.

Her knees felt wobbly and she almost staggered. Her breath came ragged and her hair was mussed, her bodice loosened, the ties dangling.

Alasdair was almost upon her.

She turned away, fumbling at her gown, trying to right the laces. Before she could, Alasdair reached her. He stepped round to stand over her, tall and dangerously close. Even in the shadows, she could see his anger, the tight set of his jaw and the blaze in his eyes.

"Lady Norn." He spoke her name as if it pained him. Then, not taking his gaze off hers, he rammed the sword he carried so hard into the earth that its blade quivered. He looked her up and down, his expression hardening as he noted her dishevelment. "What's happened to you?"

Marjory bristled, not liking the suspicion in his voice. "A spider fell on me and—"

"That's why your hair is mussed and your gown opened?" He didn't believe her, doubt all over him. "I wouldn't have thought you so afraid of a wee spider—"

"It was huge."

"Och, aye, he will have been to undo your bodice."

"I did that myself." Marjory began retying the laces. "And my gown isn't undone, only a bit loose."

Alasdair leaned in, giving her a hard stare. "I can see your nipples."

"I don't believe you." She knew it was true. Heat swept up her neck, bursting onto her cheeks as she worked faster to close her bodice.

"Damn and blast, Norn, I saw a man leaving here." Alasdair spoke through clenched jaws. "He came from this direction and he looked most pleased."

"I saw no one." Marjory held his gaze, unblinking.

He gripped her arm, his hold like iron. "What were you doing here?"

"I told you." She jerked free, her own temper rising. "I was searching for someone."

She shot a glance at the colorful bowers, looking back at Alasdair when a peal of feminine laughter drifted from one of the tents.

"You haven't said why you're here. But that's easy enough to guess." She smiled sweetly.

"Dinnae rile me, lass." He took a step closer, his tone low. "If there's aught here I'd want, it isn't in thon ladies' bowers."

Marjory swallowed, her heart starting to beat faster.

Alasdair rested a hand on the hilt of the sword he'd

plunged into the ground. His own blade, Mist-Chaser, was sheathed at his side. And he was gripping the second sword so hard that his knuckles shown white.

"This"—he glanced at the sword—"is Honor, my lady. A brand that holds much meaning to my clan, as she belonged to the last MacDonald to fall at the trial by combat. Honor's value to us is immeasurable. Whenever we ride out, one of us carries her in respect of our fallen clansman and the others we lost that day. On this foray, the warrior carrying Honor forgot her when he visited one of the ladies here at the bowers." He paused, glancing at the tents. "I came to fetch the sword, wanting to give her the honor of being retrieved by her chief. Nor did I trust my kinsman to no' dally if he returned. He's a man who cannae resist temptation."

"And you can?" She could see him enjoying a dalliance, as he called such matters.

It shouldn't bother her if he had, but unreasonably, it did.

"I'm a man, Norn." His voice took on a disturbingly smooth, smoky quality. "No man can withstand all temptation all the time. No' if red blood courses in his veins."

He touched her hair, his fingers skimming the side of her face as he did so. "Sometimes the will to resist isn't as strong as the need. Did you no' ken that? You could tempt a man that way, making him forget reason."

Marjory lifted a brow. "How?"

"You only have to breathe." A muscle jerked in his jaw and his eyes went dark, smoldering like a deep-blue sea caught fire. She thought she heard him swear—she wasn't sure—but his entire mien changed, the transformation doing strange things to her insides.

"Och, lass…" He shook his head slowly, his gaze not leaving hers.

He lifted her braid, ran his knuckles down the side of her neck. Her skin prickled, deliciously. Sensation raced through her, her breasts tightening. She felt light-headed, breathless. His big, powerfully muscled body blocked the tents and even the nearby pines from view, casting them in their own seductive world.

She wanted to reach for him, touch his face, his hair. But her hand wouldn't move, her arm remaining motionless.

She could only stare at him, awareness beating inside her.

He looked fierce, intense in a way that made her body heat and her blood race. Her senses reeled, her earlier anger swept away by need. His caress, the portent behind his words, scorched the air around them.

"Alasdair…" His name was all she could say. She began to tingle again, *there* where she always did when she thought about him kissing her.

She should be shamed by such wayward yearnings.

She felt excited.

"Please…" She wasn't sure what she wanted, perhaps for his hand to stay on her neck. His touch gave her such pleasurable shivers.

He looked anything but pleased. Heat still simmered in his eyes. But it was different and darker now, infinitely more dangerous.

Behind him, someone must've lit torches in the clearing. The flickering light edged his outline, emphasizing his strong, broad shoulders. How the wind lifted his hair, making her ache to touch the rich auburn strands. She loved his hair, knew it was his pride…

She wished he'd smile.

Above all, she wanted him to bend his head and kiss her. Yearnings stirred inside her, making her bold. And frustrated because his face had gone so stony, so cold.

"I should be away..." She didn't want to go anywhere. Not now, not ever.

This was her chance.

Perhaps her only opportunity to seduce him.

She took a deep breath, began relacing her bodice again. Slowly this time. Isobel and Catriona had told her men go wild when a woman touches her breasts. So she willed him to be tempted, to fall for her seduction now, so long as her courage held.

"Norn..." He took a step closer, so near she could almost hear the hard beating of his heart. Warmth streamed off him, heady and enticing. But he still looked so angry, more annoyed than desirous.

"Let me help you, lass. You'll ne'er be done that way." He gripped her wrists, lowering her arms and refastening her gown with a speed and skill that proved how well he understood the workings of ladies' bodices.

Marjory stiffened, her seduction plans evaporating. "You shouldn't—"

"Och, that I ken, sweet." He reached for her, pulling her roughly against him. "A shame I cannae help myself."

He slanted his mouth over hers, almost crushing her lips. He thrust his hands into her hair, bracketing her face, gripping hard as if he'd never let her go. She leaned into him, sliding her arms up and around his shoulders, clinging to him as he kissed her deeply.

It was like no kiss she'd imagined.

Tantalizing sensations rushed through her, especially when he urged her lips apart and swept his tongue into her mouth, exploring her in a bold, sinuous melding of heat and breath that left her trembling. She twined her fingers in his hair, her knees weakening.

Little more than his plaid and her gown separated them. He kissed her with a fierceness that unleashed all her desires, fanning a delicious heat low in her belly. From somewhere, she heard a ragged gasp and hoped it wasn't from her. She feared that it was.

"Alasdair..." She gripped his shoulders, his plaid warm and rough beneath her fingers. Her skin tingled, awareness rippling along her nerves, exciting her, making her forget everything except being in his arms, his mouth ravishing her, their tongues tangling so deliciously.

It was almost more than she could bear.

She began to tremble, her senses and emotions alive, giddy with pleasure.

"Lass..." He deepened the kiss, pulling her tighter against him so she had no doubt how much he wanted her. She could feel the hard press of him, hot and rigid, straining against her. "See what you do to me."

Close by a twig snapped. A loud clearing of someone's throat followed almost immediately.

Breathing heavily, Alasdair tore his mouth from hers, looking round to glare at a tall, big-bearded man who stood less than a pace away.

"Rory!" Alasdair turned to him, stepping before Marjory to shield her from view. "You were to stay with our men."

Rory shuffled his feet, looking embarrassed. "I couldn't wait." His gaze flashed to the sword Alasdair had thrust into the earth. "I had to know you'd found Honor."

Alasdair nodded once, curtly. "Aye, so I did and no harm has come to her." He reached behind him, gripping

Marjory's arm, holding her still. "Nor do I wish any hurt to come of what you just witnessed, lest you hope to find yourself missing the tongue that rattled."

"I saw nothing." Rory held up both hands. "But . . ."

Alasdair took a step forward, his head angling as if he didn't trust what he'd heard. "Aye?"

"There be a party o' Mackintoshes in the wood, heading this way." Rory rushed the words, glanced into the gloom of the pines.

Following his gaze, Marjory saw nothing, but she didn't doubt him.

She did reach for Alasdair, tugging his plaid. "Kendrew will be looking for me."

"Aye, and so he should be." Alasdair turned, his face stony again, the passion gone. "And I should ne'er have touched you. I'll stay with you until your brother is in sight. This"—he jerked his head toward the bowers behind them—"is no place for a lady alone."

Marjory lifted her chin. "You seemed pleased enough to find me here."

"So I was, aye." His frown said otherwise. "More pleased than I should've been. So I'll give you warning." He stepped closer, taking her face between his hands. "Dinnae e'er think to tempt me again. Because if you do, there'll be no restraining me.

"A kiss"—he released her and stepped back—"will be only the beginning."

"I shall remember that." Marjory held his glare, her heart beating wildly.

He'd never know it, but his threat only encouraged her. She'd make sure they did kiss again.

And she'd welcome the consequences.

Chapter Three

❦

A kiss will be only the beginning. Alasdair's warning to Marjory echoed in his head, images of her accompanying the words each time they returned to plague him. Even here at the farthest edge of his own Blackshore territory, they dogged his every footstep, haunting him. Nae, she did. A sennight had passed since their encounter in the wood. Seven full days and nights, yet he could still see her opened bodice slipping off her shoulders, revealing the creamy smoothness of her skin, the lush swells of her breasts.

More irksome, he retained an excellent memory of her rosy nipples, pert, tight, and more tempting than he could bear. Even now, he ached to touch them, taste their sweetness. He also remembered how her braid came undone, her hair tumbling to her waist, her disarray making him crazy.

So roused, he'd forgotten himself.

He'd burned to seize her to him, never letting her go;

he'd burned more to turn on his heel and stride from the clearing, putting her from his heart and mind. The desire that, he knew, was so much more than the sharp pull at his loins each time he saw her.

Alasdair scowled, shoved a hand through his hair.

Damnation.

What in the bloody hell had made him warn her not to tempt him?

Every man with any sense knew better than to challenge a woman.

A lass with Mackintosh blood in her veins was worse than most. The clan's Berserker ancestry made the men fearless fighters and gave the women a bold, sensual heat that was nigh irresistible. They also had the skill and cunning to put such talent to use.

Norn was a born seductress.

He must've lost his mind completely to have gone anywhere near her.

Above all, he should never have allowed her to slide her hands inside his plaid, her fingers splaying across his chest so that she'd surely felt the hard beating of his heart. Aye sharp-witted, she'll have known the portent of such furious hammering. That his need for her went beyond the carnal, that he wanted to claim not just her body but her heart and soul.

It was a truth that could damn them both.

Yet she was unlike any woman he'd ever known. And now that he'd seen her again after a year, the feelings he'd hoped had lessened returned with a vengeance. Kissing her hadn't slaked his desire. Far from it, he now ached for her with a fierceness that could madden him.

Still frowning, he drew a tight, angry breath. He fought

back the curse rising in his throat, but he couldn't stop fisting his hands in sheer, terrible fury. If she were to appear before him again now, he'd not hesitate to possess her. Even though he knew the disaster that such folly would unleash on the glen.

He wanted her that badly.

He was doing his damndest to push her from his thoughts when he heard, "What was it like to kiss Lady Marjory?"

Ewan MacDonald, his cousin and general nuisance, strode up to him, wearing a cocky grin. "Was she good enough to put such a scowl on your face?"

"Have a care with your tongue, laddie." Alasdair narrowed his eyes at the younger man, his mood only worsening when Ewan's grin broadened.

"Aye, well..." Ewan hooked his thumbs in his sword belt, his mirth not diminishing. "To be sure, my tongue hasn't been having the fun yours has of late."

"God's eyes!" Alasdair snarled the curse he'd been stifling.

He'd do more when he confronted Rory. The lackwit should never have gabbled that he'd seen Alasdair kissing Norn at the joy women's bowers. Alasdair might even invite him to a round of swordplay, using the sharp edge of his brand to teach him to keep his lips sealed.

"I see she was better than good." Ewan employed his best efforts into ruining Alasdair's day.

It'd been a fine one until now. Ewan had clearly forgotten the reason they'd come up here. The training he'd sworn he was eager to participate in. He'd tagged along to make a nuisance of himself. And he'd chosen a damned irritating place to do so. Here atop one of the grandest cliffs in MacDonald possession, the sea breaking white beneath them and a polished silver sky stretching above.

Drangar Point was sacred to Clan Donald.

Alasdair's heart should be swelled with pride.

Instead, his pulse raced with annoyance and he could feel the heat spreading up his neck, a muscle jerking in his jaw. He bit hard on his tongue, not about to confirm his cousin's assessment of Norn.

A shame she *was* better than good.

The greater tragedy was that, now that he'd kissed her, he wanted her as he'd never wanted another woman. Even here at Drangar Point and in the midst of a training ordeal that should blur his mind to all but his purpose, his desire for her raged like fire.

Furious, he drew another long, tight breath. He focused on the sword hilt in his hand, the roar of the sea. Cold wind blew around him and the tang of brine filled his lungs. He was home on this high rocky crag, the world blue and gray, seabirds wheeling on the air currents, and long waves rolling in from the horizon.

He loved this place.

On such a day, there should be little that could diminish his pleasure in being here.

Sadly, Ewan enjoyed such power.

He stepped closer, joining Alasdair at the cliff edge. "Come, cousin. We all saw you drag Lady Marjory into the Lughnasadh bower. Why bother to steal a kiss if you willnae tell how sweet she is?"

Relief swept Alasdair, Ewan's babble revealing Rory hadn't betrayed him.

Ewan meant Alasdair's meeting with Norn at the

harvest fair's cloth stall. The few moments they'd had in the bower before Kendrew's arrival.

Still...

"I didnae steal a kiss from her." Alasdair spoke through gritted teeth, not about to say there'd been no need for thievery. She'd welcomed his attentions, even encouraging him, damn her.

"We had words, no more." He'd dare anyone to say otherwise.

Ewan snorted. "You were ne'er a good liar."

Alasdair clamped his jaw, not bothering to answer. He also kept his gaze on the sea, refusing to reward his cousin's badgering with a glance.

Suffering his blether was bad enough.

Indeed, it was becoming a worse agony than holding Mist-Chaser at arm's length, the sword's blade kept level above the sea several hundred feet below. His arm had lost all feeling hours ago. The rigorous training ritual, a trial he hadn't endured in years.

Making amends, he planned to stand there throughout the long, windy night. The drizzle just beginning to fall only strengthened his resolve. Each droplet that sneaked beneath his plaid to roll down his back only made him more determined to persevere.

If Ewan would leave, he'd achieve his goal.

But the bastard seemed unperturbed by the afternoon's chill wetness. Alasdair's foul mood wasn't serving to banish him either. Far from it, Ewan rocked back on his heels, seeming more ready than ever to keep peppering Alasdair with irksome observations.

It was a skill Ewan had honed to perfection.

Proving it, he leaned round to peer into Alasdair's

face. "Many men say such fair-haired, cool-eyed maids as Lady Marjory make the best lovers. When a cold wind blows, the fires burn the hottest." He winked, and then straightened. "I'll wager her kiss alone—"

"Have done, you arse." Alasdair shot him a dark look and then once more fixed his gaze on his sword, determined not to let Ewan vex him.

He was already annoyed enough for believing the long-nosed bugger's reason for accompanying him to Drangar Point, the highest headland along the MacDonald shoreline, was to join Alasdair in a sword vigil. The age-old clan ritual strengthened a warrior's prowess on the battlefield until no enemy could defeat him.

The vigil was a physically demanding rite and hard to do with someone blethering in his ear. When the babble also recalled images best forgotten, such a feat proved nigh impossible.

Not wanting to be thwarted, Alasdair threw a glance at the nearby Warrior Stones. Proud and ancient, they were two tall, upright rocks that stood close together near the cliff's sheerest drop. Once part of a stone circle now largely toppled, the stones speared heavenward, their wet surfaces shimmering in the afternoon's gray light. A hallowed site to the Old Ones, the Warrior Stones' rune-and-lichen-covered boulders still held an air of mystery.

The stones carried a touch of tragedy for the women of the clan, who called them the Sighing Stones. They insisted the wind that always wailed around the stone circle was the crying of a Selkie maid returned to the sea by Drangar, a half-mythical MacDonald forebear.

The clan women claimed Drangar broke the seal woman's heart. In her grief, she was said to have cast a spell of resentment, turning Drangar and his warriors to stone so that they would be forever doomed to stand at the cliff's edge, looking out upon the sea where Drangar banished the unhappy Selkie to an eternity of loneliness.

Alasdair tamped down a flare of irritation. The tales were nothing but romantic fancy.

If any strange sounds were heard at the Warrior Stones on dark, moonless nights, it wasn't the pitiful sobs of a despondent Selkie. It was the running footsteps of Mac-Donald fighting men as they raced past the stone circle on their way to defend kith and kin, protecting the home glen that meant so much to them.

That, Alasdair could believe.

Seal women...

Scowling more fiercely now, he shifted his feet in the rain-slicked grass and tried to ignore the unpleasant tingling in his sword arm. His shoulder burned and his fingers were beginning to cramp around Mist-Chaser's leather-wrapped hilt. Soon they'd go as numb as his arm.

Still, he wouldn't lower his sword.

MacDonalds didn't acknowledge defeat.

Even when Ewan spoke close to his ear. "I saw Lady Marjory trail her fingers down your chest."

Alasdair's sword dipped a full inch. "You mistake."

The glint in Ewan's eye warned that worse was to come. "She stood so close to you, I vow you must've felt the press of her bosom."

"Lady Marjory never came within several hand spans of me." Alasdair's body clenched on the lie, every inch of him recalling the warmth of her breasts, so soft and full. Her clean, heathery scent, and how she'd leaned into him so provocatively. "Your eyes are failing you."

"I think not." Ewan laughed.

"She's Kendrew Mackintosh's sister." Alasdair returned his gaze to the horizon. Unfortunately, instead of the cold, gray of the sea, he saw Marjory's large blue eyes. And for an unsettling moment, the crashing of waves sounded like the thundering of his heart.

He suspected that it was.

So he flashed a hard look at his cousin, his voice stern. "You'd be wise to remember who she is and curb your tongue."

"And you?" Ewan glanced at the darkening sky, his plaid snapping in the wind. "Is she the reason you wanted to spend the day out here with the Warriors, balancing on the cliff edge in the rain and gloom?"

"You know my reasons."

"Aye, I do." Ewan grinned. "The glen being quiet of late is only one of them."

"The glen is too quiet." Alasdair didn't share his cousin's levity. "It's an unnatural stillness and I dinnae like it. Did you e'er watch a cat before he pounces on a mouse? The cat freezes, no' blinking or moving a muscle as he eyes his prey. Then, in a blink, he attacks. The mouse is doomed before he sees the cat coming."

"So we're mice, eh?"

"Nae, we're MacDonalds. And we've held Blackshore for too many centuries to lose it because we allowed ourselves to be lulled into complacency." Alasdair looked to where the sea seethed around a few black-glistening skerries. The water foamed and churned there, clouds of spray catching the light. "No' all enemies come marching at you, clashing swords and spears against their shields and shouting war cries. Some foes slip up behind you on silent feet." Alasdair knew that well. Others didn't bother to hide, using harvest fairs or a courier's duty to excuse their presence. Alasdair stiffened, recalling the Norseman he'd seen leaving the joy women's clearing.

That one, he knew, had been up to no good.

Sure of it, he tossed another glance at Ewan. "Such foes bear watching lest the last thing you see is the flash of their sword as it ends your life."

"Or"—Ewan's grin didn't waver—"they see the glint of MacDonald steel, having done with them."

"True enough." Alasdair quirked a smile.

It was good when a man had faith in his kin.

He certainly did.

No greater race walked the Highlands than Clan Donald. Even their enemies knew it and respected them, with the sad exception of the Mackintoshes.

"So-o-o..." Ewan cracked his knuckles. "What are you going to do about her?"

Alasdair's smile faded. There was no need to guess whom Ewan meant.

He did adjust his grip on Mist-Chaser. He needed a distraction, tempted as he was to swing the tip to within inches of his cousin's belly. Just to wipe the smirk off his handsome face.

"Well?" Ewan goaded him even more.

Alasdair returned his gaze to the skerries. The current was running faster now, the water swirling around the rocks and sending up great plumes of spray. "I dinnae have plans to do aught with Lady Marjory. I did warn her to keep an eye on the shadows up Nought way. Not that I've seen or heard anything troubling, least of all from those remote bounds. Still, if the quiet hereabouts bothers me"—and it did—"it'll be deafening at Nought. She needs to be wary." And he needed his tongue cut out for voicing his concerns in a way that upset her. It ripped the heart out of him that he'd offended her. He could still see her face freezing over, feel the chill of the stare she'd turned on him. She'd thought he'd wanted her to spy for him, as if he'd ever imperil her.

Truth was, words didn't come easy in her presence.

She needed only to glance at him and the famed Mac-Donald charm left him faster than light vanished from a pinched candlewick.

Later, in the wood...

Allowing him to see her bared breasts, nipples wind-chilled and thrusting at him, had given him the rest, robbing him of his wits. Shattering his restraint until he'd lost his head, reaching for her...

Heat swept him. Not anger this time but raw unbridled need.

Hoping Ewan wouldn't notice, he turned his gaze once more on the horizon. Heavy clouds gathered there and a light mist was beginning to curl across the water. "See here, lad." He didn't look at his cousin. "If you dinnae wish to train, I'd sooner be alone."

"Och, I'll keep vigil with you." The scrape of steel against Ewan's sword sheath proved his vow. Stepping closer to the cliff edge, he raised the blade, aiming it like Alasdair's, toward the open sea.

"But I'm no' for staying the night on these cliffs." Ewan looked about, his levity gone. "No' anywhere near the Warrior Stones."

Alasdair laughed. "Dinnae tell me you're afraid old Drangar will appear."

"I saw him once, as well you know."

"You were all of eight summers. What you saw was sea mist drifting through the stone circle. Drangar, if e'er he existed, will have better to do in the Otherworld than float about these cliffs."

Ewan didn't answer.

A glance his way showed he could set his jaw as fiercely as Alasdair.

"We'll head back when the light fades." Alasdair knew some clansmen did believe in Drangar's bogle. And even though Ewan could annoy him more than a pebble in his shoe, Alasdair loved him too much to force him to suffer a dent to his pride when true fear was on him.

"There's no need to hold the vigil more than a few hours." Alasdair gave the concession gladly.

The tightness left Ewan's face at once. "I wouldn't mind being in the hall when Cook serves our supper." He glanced at Alasdair, his good humor restored. "Did you catch the smell of roasting pork when we passed the kitchens this morn? My mouth has been watering ever since."

"I noticed, aye." Alasdair returned the younger man's smile.

He just wished he could shake his certainty that the glen peace was about to be ripped apart. And in a way that meant a harder fight than ever before. His inability to sleep well in recent times and the increasing sensation that someone, somewhere was watching him only underscored his distrust of the ongoing calm.

Any man who lived near the sea knew that still waters often preceded the worst storms.

Men in coastal Scotland also knew one Viking never came alone. And the man who'd left the joy women's encampment so rapidly had been a Norseman. Alasdair could smell the bastards at a hundred paces.

A Highland woman in the clutches of such marauders would be doomed to a living death.

Worse, once they tired of her.

There were many fetching lasses at Blackshore. Also plenty of strong, older women and healthy children who would make good slaves. Clan Cameron had no less to offer. And at Nought...

Marjory's face flashed before him again, only now desire was the last thing on his mind.

He shifted his feet on the wet grass, squared his shoulders as if readying for battle.

Truth was, he hadn't just made this visit to the Warrior Stones because the age-old sword vigil was believed to give men strength, courage, and—when all else failed—a proud and noble death.

He'd wanted to take advantage of Drangar Point's wide-sweeping vistas. The high, fissured cliffs along this stretch of coastline offered excellent hiding for men planning raids into the Glen of Many Legends.

His gut told him such men were about.

And he always trusted his instinct.

Doing so made the difference between a simple fighting man and a good leader of men.

Alasdair took pride in being the latter.

For that reason, he'd make sure his men did more that night than enjoy Cook's savory roasted pork. As soon as they'd filled their bellies and quenched their thirst, he'd give them a warrior's task. Every MacDonald old enough to hold a sword would spend the night sharpening his weapons.

He just hoped such a precaution would prove for naught.

Sadly, he didn't think so.

Hours later, long after Alasdair and Ewan left Drangar Point and returned to Blackshore Castle where they were surely enjoying a meal of roasted pork and fine heather ale, another MacDonald warrior stood in the thin mist that blew across the high, windswept promontory.

The rain had stopped, but Drangar Point was colder now. Not that the warrior minded. A fierce-looking man, he was the sort who'd stare a winter gale in the eye, daring the wind to chill him.

Exceptionally tall, he had dark, piercing eyes and a black beard, carefully trimmed. He wore a coat of mail that gleamed brightly, a plumed helmet, and a long black cloak of finest wool that he valued as one of his most prized possessions. Humble despite the greatness he could claim, he was rather proud to know that his ene-mies quaked when he but touched the sword hanging at his side.

At least, that had once been so.

This night, as on so many others, he had greater cares than instilling dread in his foes.

He'd leave such pleasures to Alasdair.

He also shared the young chief's opinion that the glen was too quiet.

And that no Viking ever sailed alone.

Frowning, he stopped his pacing to stand with his feet apart, his hands braced on his hips as he surveyed the night before him. Moonlight silvered a broad path across the sea and cast shadows over the Warrior Stones. The two spearing heavenward shone wetly, the runic symbols carved into them, almost humming with life. The altar stone glowed white, retaining its dignity even though centuries of wind, rain, and lichen had rendered its runes almost indecipherable.

Not that it mattered now.

The runes belonged to a distant age.

Rolling his shoulders, the warrior sympathized. He felt his own years keenly.

He was also aware of a distant sound coming from the sea. A familiar noise that, though still faint, had nothing to do with the strong currents and huge tides brought on by the fullness of the moon.

It was the rhythmic pulling of oars and the hiss of water racing down the sides of a fast-moving galley.

Two galleys, if he wasn't mistaken.

And they were coming from different directions.

Intrigued, and eager to welcome action, if the truth were told, the warrior left the shelter of the standing stones and went to the bluff's far edge.

He saw the ships at once, recognizing them as Norse longships. Serpent heads topped their prows and the oar blades flashed, rising and falling at speed as they shot across the moon-washed sea. Even at a distance, mail glinted at the chests of the rowers, showing that they were prepared for battle. Or perhaps they simply wished to defend a precious cargo if another ship challenged them.

Still, in the cold wind on his craggy bluff, the Mac-Donald warrior frowned.

The Viking ships were gaining on each other fast, their long strakes sending up fans of white-glistening spray. And as always when he spied such mastery, the MacDonald's heart pounded, his pulse quickening. He missed the company of warriors. And even if the Norsemen had been his foes, he'd always admired their seamanship.

Yet something was different about these longships.

It was a peculiarity that chilled his blood.

If such a thing were possible, that was.

Still, he trusted his warrior's instinct now as ever. Though it pained him to know he'd have to unsettle the other MacDonald lookouts Alasdair kept posted on the cliffs. Those two men would have their eyes trained in a different direction than the racing longships. And something told the warrior it was important for them to see the ships' oddities.

Sadly, there was only one way to drive the men along the cliffs to where they'd spot the longships before they sped from view.

The warrior frowned, regretting what he must do.

Then he turned and made his way along the edge of the cliffs, his path taking him past the Warrior Stones. Only rather than skirt them as he usually did, in his haste he strode right through them.

The passage made his proud warrior's body shimmer. He had a deep connection to the stones, after all. The Old Ones might've placed them on the headland ions before his time, but he'd known the stone circle in days before most of the monoliths had toppled to the grass. He'd looked on them in wonder before the first lichen had dared mar their surface.

He'd carved their runes with his own hand.

He was Drangar the Strong, a warrior whose fame had once reached to every corner of the Highlands and beyond.

Even if some of his descendants, including the present

chieftain, Alasdair, doubted he'd ever existed, he certainly had.

In truth, he still did.

He was as real as he'd ever been, excepting certain annoying limitations.

Dismissing them, for he had no time for weaknesses, Drangar hurried on. With the exceptional senses of the deceased, he could already hear the low voices of the two MacDonald lookouts he planned to frighten into leaving their posts and hurrying farther along the cliffs.

He wished there was another way.

But at least he'd be making himself useful. Even if Alasdair scoffed at his existence, the lad had been right in one thing.

Drangar did have better to do in the Otherworld than float about like a curl of mist.

He was about to prove it.

Chapter Four

❦

Much later and far from Blackshore's Drangar Point, Marjory stood alone on the strand of a narrow, deep-sided inlet. Sheer, wave-beaten cliffs edged the bay and mist curled across the cold, gray water. A bitter wind came out of the north, stirring her hair and cloak. Mist swirled everywhere, trapping her between the plunging headland and the angry, white-capped sea. She was a prisoner to the darkness. A bleak, malevolent place where low clouds hid the horizon and even the cries of seabirds rang with malice.

"You should be honored to sail into the Otherworld."

Marjory started, hearing the older woman's words as clearly as if they'd been spoken in her ear. Both near and distant, the voice was strong and lightly accented. It also held a hollowed edge. Each word echoed in the chill air, at one with the darkness.

Yet she was alone.

Sure of it, she looked around, listened for a presence

she might've missed. Winter-born and raised on legends, she couldn't discount the passage of a ghost. Such beings would favor a place so forbidding.

She'd heard something.

Yet no stern matron leaned near speaking of the Otherworld. She blinked then, her breath catching as a strange luminance spread over the rock walls of the jutting headland. Waves battered the strand, and the air felt thin, so chilled that each breath burned her lungs.

Gooseflesh rose on her arms. Her nape also prickled. Almost as if cold, unseen fingers had slid down her neck.

Firm, strong fingers, as would belong to a sharp-voiced older woman.

She frowned, refusing to acknowledge that the touch also reminded her of the cold, bony hand of a harbinger of death. Such creatures were known to possess inhuman strength.

"You should rejoice for the privilege." The voice came again, stronger now and seemingly closer. "'Tis an honor without parallel."

Marjory's pulse quickened.

Something dreadful was near, however unseen.

She felt it and that was enough.

Her amber necklace was on fire.

Searing heat flashed around her neck and pierced deep inside her. A sharp, insistent pulsing that spread through her entire body like tendrils of flame. Oddly, the sensation wasn't unpleasant.

The heat didn't burn, only made itself known.

A rustle of movement came from somewhere. In that moment, the ambers' humming ceased. The stones cooled, stilling as if they'd done all they could and now held their breath, waiting.

Marjory peered into the gloom. Her eyes widened as a stout, hard-featured woman stepped out of the shadows to loom before her.

The look she gave Marjory was as icy as the wind.

"An honor, I said." The woman came closer, her voice as stern as before. "Your time of glory, do you not understand?" She gave Marjory the flicker of a smile. But it was the kind that didn't reach the eyes. "It will happen whether the act pleases you or not. To go unwillingly"— she paused, the smile gone—"will shame your name."

A band of women joined her. Younger, but each one looked as unfriendly as their leader. Big boned and sturdy, they stayed together, moving forward as one. Still more came out of the fog that rolled off the sea to drift along the strand. A few arrived from knife-edged paths cut into the cliff face, their steps as measured as the other women's.

They kept their gazes leveled on Marjory as they approached.

Soon, they'd surround her. Their intent stood clear on their faces.

They meant her ill.

Marjory met their stares. She kept her chin raised, refusing to run.

The women—and some girls—were tall and fair, with high cheekbones and startling blue eyes. Their hair hung in thick, looped braids. And their gowns were brightly colored, with flashes of blue and red showing beneath long woolen cloaks fastened by large, oval brooches. The brooches were worked with interlocking designs Marjory knew.

The women were Viking.

And although handsome in a fierce, stark manner, no

smiles lit their faces. And not a trace of warmth or welcome shone in their eyes.

They walked forward slowly, taking their places alongside the matron.

Marjory met their stares, challenging them. "What do you want?"

"You will meet the gods for our lady." The older woman turned her head to look down the strand. "You'll take her place at our lord's side in the Otherworld."

Following her gaze, Marjory saw nothing.

Only sheets of blowing mist, the dark cliffs beyond, and a glint of pewter-gray sea. To her relief, she didn't glimpse a deceased lord or any hint of the realm of the dead.

Still, the older woman's deep-set eyes glittered menacingly. She didn't look like someone to be thwarted. "You have been chosen." Her tone was matter-of-fact. "Your fate is writ."

"I think not—" Marjory broke off when the mist parted to reveal a slim young woman at the far end of the strand. No more than a wisp, she wouldn't reach Marjory's chin if they stood side by side. She had a regal air, her back as straight as if she'd swallowed a spear. A high lady, indeed, she clearly knew her status.

She wasn't Viking.

Her skin was a beautiful dusky shade. And her long ebony hair flowed free. The glistening strands rippled in the wind, the ends swinging about her hips. She wore a gown of cream linen and a blood-red cloak, edged with rich embroidery. Two large oval brooches winked from beneath her cape, each one glittering with inset gemstones. A golden torque gleamed at her neck, its ends shaped like serpent heads. Bands of bright silver and gold arm-rings lined her wrists and jeweled rings flashed on her fingers.

She was the most elegant woman Marjory had ever seen.

She supposed she was a Saracen.

Whoever she was, her grace was spoiled by arrogance.

It poured off her, thick as the sea haar drifting along the strand. Marjory couldn't tear her gaze from the tiny, raven-haired beauty. The kind of female her grandfather used to say should never have been born, for all the torment they caused good men. Until this moment, Marjory had never truly believed such she-devils existed.

When the Saracen turned her way, she knew her grandfather had spoken true. The woman's jet eyes could've been shards of frozen ice. More than a glacial stare, the look she gave Marjory was one of triumph.

And she was sure, pure unadulterated meanness.

Bristling, Marjory narrowed her own eyes, aware that her blue stare could frost the wintriest glare the Saracen might turn on her.

She wasn't called Lady Norn for naught.

So she straightened her shoulders, embraced the hint of color she felt blooming on her cheeks. She looked the other woman up and down, appraising her openly.

"Thon woman is capable of meeting her gods herself." Marjory turned back to the matron, making her tone as cold as the day.

The older woman's lips tightened to a thin line.

"You speak of Lady Sarina." She put a hand on Marjory's arm, gripping. "She is the second wife of our much-mourned lord, Rorik the Generous, who you will accompany into the Otherworld. Lady Sarina loved him greatly."

"Then why doesn't she go with him?" Marjory jerked free of the woman's grasp. She saw no need for tact. "I have no love for your lord."

The matron ignored her, looking past her to the exotic lovely in her cream-colored gown and blood-red cape. "Lord Rorik prized Lady Sarina above all else, even his fame and riches. As great-hearted as his name, he wished to spare her an end of cinder and ash, however noble."

Marjory didn't curb her tongue. "She looks most grateful."

Lady Sarina did appear appreciative. But in a wickedly feral way, as if she were a sleek black feline who'd just savored a bowl of cream.

Or—Marjory shuddered—as if she'd just been pleasured by a strapping, well-lusted man who cared only for seeing to her carnal needs.

The woman was a wanton.

Marjory was sure of it.

And she wasn't of a mind to journey anywhere with the vixen's departed husband.

"Lady Sarina is grateful," the matron hissed. "She's prepared a basket of the finest grave goods for you. You'll have bolts of wool, silk, and linen, along with finely patterned belts and furred rugs to warm you. She also selected the richest-woven eiderdown and feather pillows, combs, trinkets, and silver rings and brooches, even a jewel-rimmed drinking horn. You will enter the Otherworld with everything a lady—"

Marjory tossed back her hair. "I have no need of Lady Sarina's gifts."

The older woman sniffed. "The gods do not like mortals who scoff at honors bestowed on them."

"Then they must despise your lady." Annoyance began to pump in Marjory's blood.

The tall, large-boned matron glared at her. Marjory returned the woman's stare, refusing to be harassed.

"You speak of gods." She used her iciest tone. "I believe they do not know this place."

"Spleen will serve you naught. Destiny cannot be changed." The words spoken, the matron again looked to the Saracen. This time when their gazes met, Lady Sarina inclined her head ever so slightly.

The approaching women surged forward then, circling Marjory and the older woman. They pressed near, joining hands to form a ring of cold-eyed foes.

Marjory ignored their hostility.

But for all her bravura, threads of fear were beginning to coil deep inside her. They unfurled and spread, snaking round her chest and squeezing ever tighter until even the simplest breath burned her lungs.

Despite the pain, she inhaled deeply of the cold, salt-laced air.

Mackintoshes quaked before no man.

They certainly wouldn't quiver in the face of jeering women and girls.

Unfortunately, the band of women weren't the reason for Marjory's growing ill ease.

It was how the swirling mist parted just enough for her to catch glimpses of grim-faced Norsemen advancing out of the fog. Huge, bearded spearmen, they also wore swords or axes at their hips and carried colorfully painted shields. Behind them, fires burned brightly, showers of sparks leaping high to turn the day red

Marjory swallowed, her heart hammering even more

when the fog shifted again, this time revealing the burning mast of a Viking longship.

Her eyes rounded and a bead of moisture trickled between her breasts.

Everyone at Nought—loving Norse heritage and tradition as Mackintoshes did—knew the meaning of a torched Viking ship.

Such burnings had one purpose.

They were funeral pyres.

Steeling herself, she took a long, deep breath. Pride alone kept her from struggling against the matron's grasp, bursting through the crush of women, and sprinting down the beach. The approaching warriors were now calling on Odin and Thor, urging the gods to speed their lord's journey to the Otherworld.

As one, they chanted, beating their spear shafts against their shields as they came closer. Marjory knew with sickening surety that they were coming for her. As she stared, they formed two flanking lines, standing just far enough apart so the women could drag her past their ranks to the burning ship and the fate they'd planned for her.

She blinked hard, fisted her hands against her hips.

She would not show fear.

But her palms were dampening and she was fairly sure her knees shook. She couldn't tell because her pulse drummed so loudly, dulling her perception.

Or maybe she was just hearing the din of so many spears clashing on shields.

"See you"—the matron nodded once, her voice full of satisfaction—"even our hardest warriors do you honor this day."

A strange silence fell across the strand as the ranks of

spear-carrying warriors parted to allow one tall, stern-faced man to stride into view.

It was Alasdair.

Marjory's breath caught, her heart slamming against her ribs. Not since the Glen of Many Legend's trial by combat had he looked so fierce. Every inch a great warlord and hero, his hand rested on his sword hilt and he scowled his displeasure as he looked up and down the phalanx of Northmen. He'd clearly come to challenge them.

He'd slung his plaid over his broad, muscled shoulders and the day's pale light glanced off the amber pommel stone of his sword. He appeared as much a lover of battle as Kendrew, his cold eyes and hard-set jaw warning he wasn't a man to show mercy if pushed too far.

And this appeared to be such a time.

"Erred a bit far from your Highlands, eh?" One of the spearmen stepped forward, pointing at Alasdair with the tip of his spear.

"Or"—the man tossed a grin at the other warriors—"are you wishing to visit Valhalla?"

"Neither." Alasdair drew his sword with a terrible scrape of steel, thrusting her high so the blade flashed bright. "If one hair on my lady's head is harmed, I own your souls."

Then he brought Mist-Chaser down, thrusting her sword point deep into the sand.

"Bloodletting as you have ne'er seen will turn this land red." He grabbed the other man's spear shaft, gripping tight as his voice hardened. "Eternity wouldn't be long enough to still your screams."

Jerking the spear from the Norseman's grasp, he swung it round, leveling the spearhead at the two lines of warriors. "That I swear to you, in the name of my God and yours."

Beside Marjory, the matron sneered. "Scots bastard."

The other women and girls muttered their own curses and crowded around her, pressing in until she could no longer see Alasdair.

"Norn!" His voice swelled, ringing clear.

Marjory blinked. His words came from a great distance, hollow and fading away as the beating of spear shafts against shields resumed. And now another, more terrifying sound filled her ears.

It was the roar of a great, raging fire, its heat scorching the air.

The women began cheering, drawing back to again reveal the two lines of warriors, their spearheads and mail glittering red in the firelight. They raised the spears as Marjory looked on, thrusting the shafts point-to-point to form a long, deathly tunnel.

Lady Sarina waited at its end, her raven tresses lifting in the wind.

Marjory drew a breath, her gaze going past the Saracen to the circle of fire burning so bright behind her. The blaze was almost blinding, its leaping flares shooting heavenward, turning the sky a horrible flaming orange. Showers of soot and ash swirled everywhere, adding a pall of eerie blackness to the scene.

Alasdair was gone.

At the far end of the warrior line, Lady Sarina began working a silver arm ring from her wrist. The sight made Marjory's stomach clench, for she knew the bangle was meant as a parting gift.

Token thanks for taking the beauty's place on the burning longship.

The death pyre.

Marjory shivered. "No." She shook her head, vowing to shove the silver ring back on the Saracen's wrist if she dared thrust it at her.

For a moment, she remembered how Alasdair's eyes had burned into her own. The steel edge to his voice when he'd warned the Vikings against hurting her.

How could he have vanished so quickly? She pressed a hand to her stomach, feeling ill. She yearned for him, needing him so badly that her heart ached. The loss of him struck her like a physical blow.

Drawing on all the strength of her name, she glanced back at Lady Sarina, straightening her shoulders when the woman's dark eyes narrowed to slits. The silver arm ring dangled from her fingers, waiting.

A cold smile curved her delicate lips and she held out the bangle, wriggling it at Marjory.

It was the *wriggling* that unleashed Marjory's own Berserker blood. Fury rose inside her and heat raced through her veins. She felt its power, the terrible strength surging, deadly and ancient.

Lady Sarina jiggled the arm ring again.

"No o-o!" Marjory stomped down on the older woman's foot, twisting free when her captor yelped. Taking advantage, she kicked the woman in the shins and then leaped back, bloodying one young woman's nose with a swift, hard-fisted punch when she tried to grab her.

"Come near me at your peril." She kept her fists raised, glaring at the gaping women. Beyond them, the spearmen eyed her, some with amusement, most with cold, impassive faces. None of them moved, as if they knew she had nowhere to run. She did straighten to her full height, summoned her haughtiest tone. "I'll not be part of such madness."

"The gods have chosen you." One of the women started forward, her steps slow and measured. "Your fear dishonors them."

"I'm angry, not afraid." Marjory wheeled, ramming her elbow into another woman's ribs when she tried to sneak up on her from behind.

Another lunged at her, earning a cracked lip from Marjory's other elbow. A wicked backswing she'd learned while hiding in Nought's bailey shadows as a child and watching Kendrew and their cousins train to fight.

Setting her hands on her hips, she tossed back her hair and glared round. "I'll be leaving here now." She spoke as levelly as she could, hoping that only she heard the pounding of her heart. She abhorred fighting. But she loved living more. "Your lord can make his death journey without me. One step and I'll bite off the nose of anyone foolish enough to stop me." She'd do no such thing. But the threat appeared to stay her enemies. She let her eyes flash, knowing she looked like a Valkyrie. "I might try an ear as well, be warned."

"You will save your spirit to amuse Lord Rorik in Niflheim." A deep voice spoke behind her, one of the spearmen.

His words chilled her, proving they meant to send her into the Viking realm of death, a cold and misty place full of darkness, where those who died of age or illness were sent to languish, away from the warriors' mead halls of Valhalla.

"My *spirit* is not your concern." Marjory spun about to face a huge man with a plaited yellow beard.

He just looked at her, not seeming to hear.

He grabbed her by the arms, hauling her off the ground and returning her to the hard-faced matron. "She needs your herbs and charms to quiet her."

He set her on her feet before the woman and then frowned when she dusted down her skirts. "The gods chose unwisely."

"Leave her to me." The woman spoke to the spearman but locked her gaze on Marjory, her face unsmiling. "The fires have turned the minds of others, when they know they'll soon bathe in them."

The older woman grasped Marjory firmly by the jaw. "Flames of glory will speed you past the pain. Drink this"—she pressed a cold metal cup against Marjory's lips—"and you'll be whisked straight to Niflheim with the master. Open your mouth and accept—"

A great cheer cut off her wheedling.

Marjory pressed her lips tightly together, refusing the foul-smelling brew. She also narrowed her gaze, as much to stop the smoke from burning her eyes as to show her tormentor that she wasn't afraid.

Regrettably, she was. A sick feeling spread inside her. All around her, the smoke thickened as the fires raged, terrifying now with hot bursts of flame and burning ash. Yet the cold was equally biting. Bone deep and more arctic than any chill she'd ever known, it made Nought's worst winter feel like a spring morning.

Her fingers and toes were numb. She could no longer feel the tops of her ears. And they hurt from the roars of a crowd as the thunder of spears clashing against shields worsened, the sound now deafening.

"They do you tribute." The matron clamped her fingers around Marjory's chin, forcing the cup between her lips. "Drink and find courage."

"Pah!" Marjory refused to swallow.

The woman hissed something, but her words were lost in the din.

Marjory pulled away from her when the woman again tried to tip the drink into her mouth.

She'd had enough.

Her patience was grinding to an end.

She took a deep breath, her fists clenched. She wasn't called Lady Norn for nothing. When the good men of Nought believed she wouldn't hear, they swore she was as formidable as a Norse frost giant. Others praised her wit, boasting that she wielded her tongue as deftly as Mackintosh men swung their axes.

She took those observations as compliments, priding herself on standing tall, always.

Mackintosh women were bold.

Daring ran in their veins, letting them fear nothing.

Even so, she didn't believe her courage needed testing by flames.

Death by fire didn't appeal to her.

Yet the women crowded round her, bustling her past the twin rows of fierce-eyed spearmen until the Viking longboat loomed before her, its proud length pulled up on the strand. A dragonship, it was huge, terrible, and every bit as awe-inspiring beached as riding the waves. Festively dressed scaffolding rose along the ship's sides, hiding the great bonfires set beneath and within its hull.

Marjory's breath caught, her pulse racing. The women pushed and pulled at her, driving her onward, closer to the waiting ship. She knew it would burn.

Other, smaller craft already stood in flames. Their presence signaled the status of Rorik the Generous, whose mortal remains rested in honor upon a high bed of furs inside the dragonship.

Like the lesser ships, the warship would soon blaze,

carrying the noble in style to the Otherworld. Beyond the spearmen, other men held fiery torches, ready to ignite the bonfires that would guide their lord's departing soul from the mortal realm.

On Marjory's approach, the men began tossing their brands into the dragonship, the crowd cheering when the huge sailcloth burst into flame. The serpent-headed prow glowed red, orange-black sheets of fire swiftly engulfing its proud curving neck.

"No-o-o!" Marjory twisted and turned, fighting the hands that held her so tightly.

The infernos' roar filled her ears and smoke stung her eyes. Her throat closed, the ash-filled air choking her. Terrible heat leaped at her, tongues of fire to scorch her flesh and char her soul. Wind whipped the flames closer, sending them higher until even her hair caught fire. Sparks whirled around her, lighting on her skin, burning and marring her, hinting at what was yet to come.

She bit down hard on her lower lip, refusing to scream.

Dignity was all that remained to her.

Behind her, the clashing of spears on shields grew louder, a dreadful rhythm that echoed through her like the death knell it was. Then the women poking and prodding her toward the burning ship stopped for a moment, once again urging her to sip from the cold, metal cup.

"The flames won't bite as hard if you drink." The matron pinched Marjory's chin, prying her mouth open. "One sip—"

"Never!" Marjory reared back, snatching the cup and dashing its contents into her tormenter's face.

"Gah!" The woman jumped, swiping at her eyes as the younger women lunged for her, arms outstretched, fingers curled into talons.

It was then that the clanging worsened and the wind swung round, blowing spray from the surf into Marjory's face. She lifted a hand, wiping her eyes and finding her cheeks damp with icy droplets.

Rain.

A storm that no longer buffeted the cliffs but drummed on Nought's tower walls, also the rhythmic banging of a shutter blown open by the wind. Sitting up at once, she recognized her surroundings, relief sluicing her.

She saw not spear shafts on shields but her bedchamber's loose shutter. Just as the cold film of moisture on her cheeks was only windblown rain and not sea spray from a distant, foreign strand. She felt the brush of her bed curtains, tossing in the damp gusts coming through the window.

Everything was as it should be.

Even her tiny dog, Hercules, still slept at her feet, snoring softly. Across the room, all that remained of her earlier fire was a trace of soot and ash, a thin haze of peat smoke lingering in the air.

Nought was as quiet as always in the small hours, the stronghold at rest.

Marjory took a deep, steadying breath.

She could still feel the fires heating her skin. And she couldn't banish the feeling that Lady Sarina and the older woman and all the others had really been there, pushing and pulling her toward the burning longship.

Or that Alasdair had come to save her.

It'd been so real.

Yet...

Shaky, she eased her feet from beneath Hercules and slipped from her bed. Once she'd refastened the clanging shutter, she'd be able to sleep in peace. Forget the night's strange and unsettling dream. But she'd taken only a few steps across the damp, rush-strewn floor before her foot collided with a small metal cup.

Looking down, she saw that it was on its side. The darkening of the rushes around the cup indicated it'd been knocked over when full, its contents spilling out across the floor.

The only problem was there hadn't been a small metal cup in her room.

She was sure of that.

And—she blinked—there wasn't one here now either. For when she bent to snatch the cup into her hand, her fingers closed around one of Hercules's discarded toys. A crescent of smooth, well-chewed wood boasting two rounded balls on each end, carved for him by Grim, one of her brother's most trusted warriors and a great animal lover.

Marjory dropped the toy as if it'd bitten her.

She turned in a circle, searching the room, where moonlight poured in through the open shutter, casting a silvered wedge across the floor. She also peered into the gloom of corners and beneath her bed where dark shadows might conceal a plain metal beaker.

She saw nothing.

The cup was gone.

If it'd even been there, which she doubted.

Her mind was playing tricks on her. Kendrew's plan to see her wed to a Viking nobleman was wearing on her. She hoped that was the only reason for such a disturbing dream.

She didn't want to think about what would happen if such a dream was a portent.

She'd been weaned on Norse folklore and custom.

She knew fire burials existed.

Blessedly, she also knew that Kendrew had exhausted

his list of potential suitors. At least, she believed Groat's overlord was the last Viking lord to offer for her. She'd paid dearly to avoid such a union, even sacrificing her grandmother's heirloom sapphire ring.

She was safe.

Taking comfort in that knowledge, she went to the window and closed the shutter, securing its latch with a strip of hide. Then she pressed her hand to the small of her back and stretched, recalling the names of all possible husbands and how she'd successfully thwarted each bid for her hand.

Isobel had helped her.

Together, they'd cleared the path for Marjory's seduction of Alasdair. He wasn't exactly cooperating, but she was making headway. That he desired her stood without question. She only needed another opportunity to convince him that he could never have enough of her. That she was everything he could wish for in a lover, a wife.

Soon, he'd come around.

Her fearing dream meant nothing.

Yet...

Why did she feel a tingling in the back of her neck? Worse, why did the air in her room still hold a tinge of smoke? Not the earthy-sweet hint of cold peat ash from her bedchamber's hearth but the sharp, acrid bite of burning wood and something else.

Something she didn't want to ponder.

She did cross the room and fling back her bed curtains, tying them to a bedpost. If anything else came to her this night, in a dream or otherwise, she'd face the intrusion head-on and with her eyes wide open.

She'd be ready.

Chapter Five

❖

"The devil ravening." Alasdair snarled the curse, certain Marjory's fresh, heathery scent still wafted beneath his nose. Would that he could grasp her face, let his gaze roam over her, then lean near until he could feel the soft warmth of her skin, breathe her in. Kiss her once more. Need clawed at him, hot and fierce. Resisting her in the wood had cost him all his strength. If she tempted him again, he wouldn't have a shred of restraint left to summon.

She should be glad the whole of the glen now stretched between them.

He should also be pleased.

Instead, he stood at one of the tall arched windows of his colorfully painted solar and tossed back the *uisge beatha* he'd poured himself. He needed the fiery Highland spirits, hoped its bite would curb his temper, keep him from smashing his fist into a wall. Here at his own Blackshore Castle, a proud loch-girt stronghold on the southernmost bounds of the Glen of Many Legends, he shouldn't feel Marjory's presence so strongly.

Thinking of her so late at night was especially dangerous. But he didn't trust Kendrew and wasn't sure the bastard wouldn't persist with his quest to find her a Norse nobleman as a husband.

The possibility set his blood to boiling.

He closed his eyes for a moment, his entire body tightening.

He didn't care if her prospective husband was a Viking or a Scot. He simply couldn't bear the thought of her in the arms of another man.

The notion gutted him, caused a sharp, stabbing pain in the region of his heart.

Wishing that weren't so, and damning her because it was, he almost reached to slosh more *uisge beatha* into his cup. Unfortunately, his head was already beginning to ache. So he slapped the cup onto the window ledge and took a long breath of the cold night air.

It *was* a fine night.

He shouldn't spend it imagining how many ways he'd enjoy making love to the delectable, entirely too irresistible sister of his greatest enemy. The King might've pressed the glen clans into a truce, but he and Kendrew had a festering history of bad blood that went too deep to ever be forgotten. Forgiveness was beyond them both.

The scar on his arm pulled then, as if the old wound—carved by Kendrew's hand—agreed with his refusal to see Kendrew for anything but what he was: a true Highland scoundrel.

Praise God he only lusted after the bastard's sister.

If he loved her—

Alasdair pulled a hand down over his face, not about to even consider the possibility.

He did lean against the edge of the window to glare out at Loch Moidart. His mind should be filled with clan pride in such moments, naught else. Dark mists curled across the water and chill wind whistled past the ramparts. It was a good night for sleeping and his men took advantage, most sprawled on pallets in the great hall. Only a few torches yet burned and the air still held a hint of the evening meal, roasted pork and rich onion gravy. Some might catch a waft of old dog and spilled ale. If so, no MacDonald would complain.

Dogs were welcome at Blackshore, aging beasts being particularly honored.

And ale...

MacDonalds were famed for serving up the finest.

They were also known for the worthiness of their leaders. Proud men who didn't just protect kith and kin, guarding the land through the skill of their sword arms, but who were also good, honest, and fair. Wits served them as well as arms, a truth that demanded respect from all who knew them, friend or foe.

A shame his good sense had abandoned him.

There could be no other reason he'd kept himself up so late when every muscle in his body ached from the sword vigil on Drangar's Point. Why else would he allow his loose-tongued cousin Ewan and Malcolm, his uncle and the most querulous MacDonald of all, to invade the night peace of his solar?

Peace that the other two men seemed determined to shatter.

"I could've told you knuckle kissing would sour your

mood. No' that I believe you stopped at kissing Lady Marjory's hand. I wouldn't have." Ewan shifted on Alasdair's best chair, stretching his long legs to the remnants of the hearth fire. "A pity you didn't ask me how to handle her. I know much of women."

"Did you sharpen your sword earlier?" Alasdair didn't rise to the bait. "I ordered every man to do so. I don't recall seeing you tend yours."

"My blade is aye ready." Ewan grinned, winking broadly.

Across the room, Malcolm snorted. "It'll come back a stump if you're for swinging it in the same direction thon laddie's gazing so furiously."

"I'm watching the loch and the hills beyond." Alasdair shot them both an annoyed glance. "The rain's stopped and the mist is thinning, but it's still too quiet for my liking."

"Humph." Malcolm took a greedy bite of a pork rib. One of a large tray of ribs that he balanced on his knees as he sat on a three-legged stool, shunning the solar's more comfortable furnishings.

A great-uncle a time or two removed, Malcolm had been a formidable warrior in his youth, not even giving up his sword after a Mackintosh war ax had sliced deep into his hip. The blow also snatched two fingers from his left hand and spoiled his swagger, leaving him with a limp he refused to acknowledge to this day.

A proud man, he sat so straight on his stool only those who knew him would know one of his legs was bent and his back would be crooked if he allowed. No one but Alasdair was aware that the floor of his fine-painted solar boasted a luxurious covering of sheep- and deerskins because Malcolm's bad leg was less apt to slip on furred rugs than on the herb-strewn rushes that decked most of Blackshore's flooring.

The aged warrior enjoyed spending his hours in the little room with its dazzling colored walls, every inch and cranny filled with life-size murals of fanciful Celtic beasts and pagan deities.

Just now, moon-silvered light from the windows lit his weathered profile, and not for the first time Alasdair wished for Malcolm's dignity in age. He wore his gray hair pulled back into a thick plait that fell just below his still-broad shoulders and was fastidious about keeping his salt-and-pepper beard well-trimmed. Alasdair's dog, Geordie, a beast surely as old as Malcolm in canine years, sat hopefully by his side, his milky eyes trained unerringly on the tray of thickly sauced pork ribs on Malcolm's knees.

It was a familiar sight and one that usually warmed Alasdair's heart.

This night, the cagey glint in the old man's eyes was only irksome.

"Coira Mackinnon would make you a good wife." Malcolm tore off a bit of pork for Geordie, offering it to the dog on an outstretched hand. "She is known to be comely, has hips—"

"Lady Coira's hips do not interest me." Alasdair clenched his fist against the window ledge.

"They should." Malcolm leaned forward, his expression turning even more annoying. "From what I hear, she carries a broad enough spread to not split apart the first time she slips a bairn for you." Sitting back, he looked pleased by the prospect. "The same cannot be said for

Marjory Mackintosh. She's much too tall and lithe to breed well. And"—he gave Geordie another bit of rib meat—"Lady Coira doesn't have tainted blood in her veins."

"Lady Coira's bloodlines mean even less to me than her girth." Alasdair shot a glare at Ewan, who was rubbing his chin to keep from laughing. "Lady Marjory's is none of my concern either," he lied. "And she has a fine, shapely form if you haven't seen her lately. She'll give strapping sons to the man lucky enough to wed her."

A man he'd love to tear apart with his hands.

"As for Lady Coira, I thanked the Mackinnon for his generous offer and told him I am no' looking for a wife." Alasdair hoped the finality in his tone would dissuade his uncle from pursuing the matter.

"Such a maid as the Mackinnon lass would bring high honor and great wealth with her dowry." Malcolm proved his persistence. "You needn't love her."

"We have riches and glory enough." Alasdair turned fully to the window, splaying both hands on the cold stone of the ledge. "I needn't wed to increase either."

Across the room, Malcolm mumbled something unintelligible. Any further grumblings were stayed as he munched noisily on another pork rib. Ewan shifted on his chair before the fire, for once knowing when to hold his tongue.

Ignoring both men, Alasdair kept his gaze on the loch.

The night *was* too still.

And the same ill ease that sent him up to Drangar Point that morn plagued him still. The sensation sat deep, riding the back of his neck. Shrugging it off wasn't easy.

Nor did he think he should.

He also didn't care for the dark mist slipping down from the high moors to drift across the loch. It was an unholy mist, sure as his name was MacDonald. Stepping closer to the window, he trained his gaze on the hills edging the far side of the loch. He also watched the long curving strand at their base and the low stone causeway that ran from the shore to the castle gates, an access dependent on the tides.

When the loch rose, the causeway vanished.

Only a fool—or someone unaware of the speed and strength of the currents—would dare to cross to Blackshore until the waters receded.

Just now, silver-glossed wavelets were beginning to lap at the causeway stones.

Nothing else moved except the shifting tendrils of fog.

It should've been a bright night. The moon had risen early, hanging full and clear over Drangar Point and the long, indented coastline that marked the Glen of Many Legends' southern boundary. Still wet from the rains, the land had gleamed in shades of silver and black.

Yet the mist came as swiftly, turning the night uncanny.

Now, the shadows among the rocks on the foreshore were dark and deep. And they were worse atop the high moors. There, the rolling mist blurred the familiar landscape, giving innocent outcrops the look of crouching beasts and letting clusters of thorn and broom appear menacing, like a gathering of ghouls waiting to pounce.

More like the Viking from the harvest fair, along with his bloodthirsty, grasping friends.

Hoping he erred, Alasdair caught a whiff of the sea on the incoming tide. Soon the causeway would sink beneath the water. The moment wouldn't come too soon.

He was sure strange shapes moved in the mist.

Forms that drifted rather than walked as a flesh-and-blood man would do.

"Looking for Drangar, eh?" Ewan joined him at the window. "I knew this was a night he'd be about."

"He isn't anywhere except in the songs of the storytellers." Alasdair wasn't about to admit he'd imagined black shapes floating along the cliffs. "Drangar the Strong is a fable."

"Say you." Malcolm challenged him.

"I do." Alasdair met his belligerent stare.

Malcolm made a great show of setting down his tray of pork ribs, leaving the remainder for Geordie. Straightening, he wiped his hands on the linen napkin he'd spread across his knees.

"Say what you wish." He leaned forward again, his eyes gleaming in the glow of the dying fire. "I say Drangar walks on nights that are chill and damp."

"Then he'll have no rest, for that's how most nights are hereabouts." Alasdair kept his gaze on the loch, the dark shoreline beyond.

He knew what was coming.

"I saw him myself when I was nine summers." Malcolm didn't disappoint. "Up in the high passes behind the Camerons' Castle Haven, it was," he began, telling the old story Alasdair had heard a thousand times. "I earned my first battle scar that day. I'd snuck into Cameron territory hoping to catch a glimpse of that clan's Maker of Dreams, Grizel and Gorm. But instead of finding the legendary Bowing Stone said to mark the magical entry to that pair's hidden moor, I found a band of rowdy Cameron lads several years my senior." He paused, rubbing Geordie's ears as the dog chewed a pork rib. "They were armed with dirks and short swords. And each one was double my size in muscle."

"Indeed?" Alasdair pretended he was hearing the tale for the first time.

Ewan shot him an amused glance, proving he was still a bit too young to know when tact mattered more than denting an old man's pride.

"Aye, so it was." Malcolm's voice rang sage.

Alasdair bit his tongue to keep from arguing that a Drangar the Strong visitation seemed to herald all Mac-Donald youths into manhood.

Only he had been spared.

It was a lacking that didn't concern him.

Malcolm appeared bitter earnest. Pushing to his feet, he crossed the solar, his gait as swift as any man three times younger than his own redoubtable age.

Joining Alasdair and Ewan at the window arch, he rested a hand on each of their shoulders. "You'd be wise not to doubt me, laddies."

"No one does." Ewan spoke for them both.

Alasdair held back a denial.

Appeased, Malcolm closed his eyes, reminiscing. "It's so clear in my mind it could've been this morn." He released his grip on them and opened his eyes. "I'd been foolish and paid the price. Standing my ground against the Cameron lads, I stepped into a rabbit hole, snapping my ankle. Thon devils could've ended me then and there." He leaned in, indignation sparking. "They drew their blades, came in for the kill."

"It was then that Drangar appeared, eh?" Ewan nudged Alasdair with his elbow.

Thankfully Malcolm didn't notice.

"Aye, so he did." The old warrior stood straighter, his chest swelling. "Came out of nowhere he did. One moment I was alone, glaring down a band of bloodthirsty Camerons with naught but a dirk to have at them with, and the next, there was Drangar the Strong, looming before me in all his battle glory."

Alasdair pulled a hand down over his chin. "He would've been impressive."

"That he was." Malcolm nodded. "His eyes blazed like hot coals and the long sword that hung at his waist screamed when he whipped it free as the first Cameron darted forward and drew blood, slashing my arm."

As he always did at this point, Malcolm rolled back his sleeve, displaying the thin slivery scar halfway between his elbow and wrist.

"It was then that Drangar raised his blade. The fury on his face was terrible." He gave Alasdair a quick glance, as if he expected him to naesay him. "He stepped before me, guarding me when my leg buckled and I went down on one knee. He kept his sword aloft, holding it high above his head as if to strike any Cameron who dared to take advantage of an injured foe."

"But they didn't." Ewan grinned, leaving the window to pour a measure of ale. "Ran like all good cowards do, eh?" He tossed back the ale and then wiped his mouth with his sleeve. "Camerons were aye—"

"Camerons are now our staunchest allies." Alasdair shot his cousin a warning look.

"Aye, right." Ewan shrugged. "So long as the wind blows fairly."

Alasdair ignored him.

Camerons, at least, could be trusted. Kendrew and his Mackintosh Berserkers were an entirely different kettle of fish. A pack of unpredictable wild men who loved blood-letting more than peace and order, they kept their wits in the well-sharpened blades of their war axes.

"I did see Drangar that day." Malcolm reclaimed his stool, the set of his jaw showing he wouldn't argue his claim. "Of course"—he stretched his arms over his head, cracking his knuckles—"if he hadn't come, I would've beaten the Camerons on my own.

"I couldn't do that once he'd appeared." He lowered his arms, slapped his hands on his knees. "One must aye respect an elder."

"To be sure." Ewan grinned.

"Indeed." Alasdair turned back to the window, fighting his own smile.

It was good that Malcolm didn't see himself as aged. And it was equally fine that his oft-told tale took Alasdair's own thoughts in another direction. Namely away from Marjory as he'd last seen her in the wood at the Harvest Fair, her eyes sparkling and her cheeks flushed by the cold. How she hadn't resisted when he'd deepened their kiss, even welcoming the sweep of his tongue into her mouth. He absolutely refused to recall her nipples. Aye, he should thank his uncle for putting other images in his head. Myths and fables that wouldn't steal his sleep and make him crazy.

Except—his eyes rounded—there *was* something moving on the foreshore.

"Look there, a rider!" He gripped the window ledge and leaned forward, his gaze on the lone horseman silhouetted against the dark bulk of the cliffs.

The man was bent low across the horse's neck, his plaid billowing out behind him as man and steed raced along the strand, making straight for Blackshore's soon-to-be-submerged causeway.

"Thon's a fool—or else his arse is on fire." Ewan nudged Alasdair aside, craning his neck to peer round the tower wall when the rider thundered onto the causeway, sending his horse splashing into the rising water.

"Nae, thon lad is Gowan." Malcolm spoke from behind them, demonstrating that his eyesight was still sharper than any other man's.

"Gowan's on watch no' far from the Warriors." Alasdair shook his head. "He's up there with Wattie. They're our best spearmen and most trustworthy guards. Neither one would leave his post—"

The blare of a horn signaled that the rider was indeed one of the lookouts.

"There'll be trouble." Alasdair flashed a look at Ewan and Malcolm as they left the solar, Alasdair striding ahead to reach the hall door. He threw it open to see Gowan spur his horse the last few yards through the tossing waves and into the arched gatehouse. Riding into the walled courtyard, the guard reined in just feet from the hall's low steps.

"Norse longships, lord!" Gowan swung down from his panting beast. "Two of them, and huge. I'd say twenty-four oars each, maybe more." Coming forward, he stopped before Alasdair and bent forward, bracing his hands on his thighs. "Came from different directions, they did. We thought they'd clash, fighting each other. But they raised oars at the last minute and flashed up side by side before tearing off alone again.

"One went south"—he paused, taking a long, deep draw of air—"and the other shot inshore, passing our loch's entry but skirting the coast, more than suspicious."

Alasdair waited until the guardsman straightened and then slung an arm around his shoulders, drawing him into the warmth of the hall. He nodded to Ewan, indicating he fetch Gowan a mug of ale.

"Longships are aye about in these waters." Alasdair led Gowan to a bench, settling him at a table near the fire. A few women were still about in the hall and he didn't want to alarm them. "Our own galleys often ply the coast, as do those of Hebridean chieftains and a few from the scattered Norse enclaves still in the Outer Isles. They could've been from anywhere." Alasdair didn't believe it.

The way Gowan shook his head proved him right. "Nae, I dinnae think so." He was adamant. "Not these longships. They were up to no good, sure as I'm sitting here."

"Were they armed, arrayed for battle?" Alasdair frowned, again seeing the big, scar-faced Norseman who'd been at the joy women's encampment.

He'd known the man was trouble.

"Nae, that wasn't it." Gowan nodded thanks when Ewan brought him a cup of ale. "The ships were black."

"Black?" Alasdair looked at him.

"Aye." Gowan drained the ale in one long gulp and then tossed aside the cup and dragged the back of his hand across his lips. "The devils must've painted pitch on their hulls and even the oar blades. Far as we could tell, the sails were black as well. And"—he shook his head, his brow creasing—"so were the men in the ships, every last one o' them. We saw their black mail and cloaks by the light o' the moon, no mistaking. Even their helmets were dark."

"Black Vikings?" Malcolm folded his arms, his voice doubtful. "Such fiends haven't been seen hereabouts in years, not since Clan MacConacher banished them some"—he paused, scratching his beard—"fifty years or more ago, it must've been. The Black Vikings sank the *Merry Dancer*, a merchant cog that was carrying a daughter of the House of MacKenzie. The great Duncan Mac-Kenzie's eldest girl, I believe."

He looked around, seeming satisfied when a few men nodded, showing they remembered. "Darroc MacConacher found the lass washed ashore on his isle and saved her, even making her his bride. His vengeance on the Black Vikings who rammed her ship is legend. Bards still sing the tale.

"The MacConacher made sure the last Black Viking was swept into the bowels of hell. Those who didn't perish beneath his sword or meet a watery grave were forced to flee to Brattahlid in distant Greenland, a frozen wasteland beyond the Ocean Called Dark, as the Vikings call those northern seas." Malcolm spoke with authority. "I remember MacConacher's wrath. He vowed to rid these waters of Black Vikings, and did. That I say you," Malcolm lifted his voice, making sure everyone heard him.

"I ken what I saw." Gowan stood his ground. "Wattie will tell you the same when he comes down from Drangar Point in the morn."

"Humph." Malcolm set his mouth in a hard, tight line, saying no more. He also curled his hand around the finely tooled leather belt slung low about his hips, where his sword would've been if he'd worn one.

Alasdair's frown deepened. Vikings weren't welcome in these waters. Not with Kendrew offering Marjory's hand to any Norse warlord willing to bid on her.

Shoving back his hair, he strode away from Gowan and the men who'd gathered round him, badgering him with questions.

He couldn't think with their babble in his ears.

He did hear Gowan mention Drangar.

Whipping back around, Alasdair closed the space between them in three swift strides. "Dinnae tell me you saw Drangar. If you do"—his voice was low, deadly earnest—"I'll wonder if you and Wattie were into your cups rather than keeping watch."

"What you think won't change what was." Gowan spat into the floor rushes. "Why do you think I rode so fast to get here? No' because the two Viking ships flashed round to attack our coast, be sure. It was because old Drangar swooped at us from the mist, his long black cloak flying behind him like a shroud and his spear shooting flames from his spearhead. His eyes shone, too. Red as coals, they were." He shuddered, rubbing his arms as if chilled. "And his scowl—"

"Was no more than the rainclouds sweeping in from the sea. The shooting flames will have been lightning. There was thunder earlier." Alasdair looked up at the smoke-blackened rafters, praying for patience. "And Wattie? Was he no' too frightened to stay on the cliffs alone?"

Gowan touched an iron charm that hung around his neck. "We drew straws to see who'd stay up at the Warriors, watching to see if the Black Vikings returned. Wattie lost."

"Humph." Alasdair went to one of the hall's arrow

slits, looked out at the weird mist still curling across the loch's gleaming surface.

He'd seen the alarm on the faces of some of his younger warriors when Gowan burst into the hall, ranting about heathen Vikings and then, almost in the same breath, announcing the clan ghost was shrieking along the cliffs. If he didn't squelch such blether swiftly, his most promising fighters would be reduced to quivering women.

"Drangar is a legend, no more." He raised his voice, not hiding his annoyance. "The next man who claims he's seen a bogle shall scour the cesspit until it shines brighter than his arse."

"Aye, lord," his men answered as one.

The silence that followed held more than a few grumbles.

Alasdair pretended not to hear.

Highlanders were a superstitious lot. Much to his regret, MacDonalds held an unpleasant penchant for trusting in charms, omens, and myth. The magic of the amber in his sword's pommel was different, of course. Mist-Chaser was an exceptional blade.

Still, it was the strength of his sword arm that gave Mist-Chaser her true power.

And perhaps the blood that sometimes covered his arms to the shoulders after a good day's warring.

A foe's blood was known to strengthen a sword.

Such truths existed.

Bogles and Black Vikings...

The first was discounted easily. The second almost as quickly, as bards far and wide still sang the praises of Darroc MacConacher for chasing the Black Vikings from the Hebridean Sea. And after he'd wed Arabella

MacKenzie, harnessing his own fierce reputation to the fame of the maid's much-vaunted father, the Black Stag of Kintail, no Black Viking wanting to keep his head would dare near Scotland.

Not even after fifty-some years.

Unless...

A chill swept Alasdair. What if the black-painted long-ships hadn't been Black Vikings at all? He could imagine some men taking such measures if they didn't wish to be seen. Kendrew and his men were known for smearing soot and peat muck onto their skin and their weapons when they crept up on unsuspecting strongholds. They loved surprising their enemies in nighttime raids. Everyone in the Glen of Many Legends knew it. Kendrew boasted of his skill at such attacks.

Alasdair rubbed the back of his neck, thinking.

Kendrew could employ such a ruse to attack Blackshore, putting the blame on Vikings. It would be just the sort of underhanded ploy he'd use to rid himself of Alasdair.

He had the means to commit such a perfidy.

There was a narrow inlet known as the Dreagan's Claw cut deep into the northernmost bounds of Mackintosh territory. A bleak, stone-walled access said to have been carved in distant times when a dreagan's foot slipped, one of his claws rending a tear in the earth. The inlet was barely wide enough for an oared ship to enter. Nor did it lead anywhere, ending soon enough in a rim of fallen rock beneath Nought's steepest, most impassible cliffs.

To Alasdair's knowledge, the Mackintoshes ignored the inlet, deeming it useless as submerged rocks, huge and jagged, clogged the dark, uninviting waters. Nor did the Mackintoshes possess galleys.

Or did they?

Nothing Kendrew did surprised Alasdair.

His gut warned that the black-painted longships had nothing to do with the Black Viking raiders of old and everything to do with the Mackintosh.

Indeed, he was sure of it.

He could smell the scoundrel's trickery on the wind. He did *not* see another furtive movement in the mist across the loch, a stirring now accompanied by a faint bluish glow. Turning away before his tired eyes fancied a shape in an innocuous shaft of moonlight, he headed back to his solar.

There was no such thing as mist shapes drifting along the lochshore. As for black-painted longships, they were a matter he'd address.

It was just a shame that doing so would mean journeying to Nought.

In the same moment Alasdair entered his solar, the mist stirred on the far side of the loch as an otherworldly being peered across the water at Blackshore. The being—a ghost, many would call her—knitted her brow as she drifted closer to the loch's edge.

Stopping there, she hitched her filmy skirts, not wanting her hems dampened.

Once, she'd been known as Seona.

But her name no longer held significance.

Those who would've—or should've—cared for her were no more, their mortal bones fallen to dust as fine as, if not finer than, her own.

What did matter was that she existed in some form still. Not a very substantial one, all things considered. But she did possess the ability to focus her gaze on the torch-lit window arch that had given her a glimpse of Alasdair. He'd been in a foul temper, she was sure.

And as little happened in her world, curiosity prickled all through her.

She'd have enjoyed a better look at him.

He'd stared her way long enough, after all.

Not that he'd seen her. Like all mortal men who saw what they believed and nothing more, he'd have noted only a shimmering in the night mist. If he'd been caught off guard, he might've spotted her tall, slim form limned by the silvery glow that always surrounded her.

Those who did see her often mistook her for moonlight.

Even so, she took pride in her appearance. She might not have possessed enough beauty to keep the love of the man who broke her heart centuries ago, but she'd always taken care to move with grace, listen with interest, acquiesce when need be, and praise always.

It hadn't been enough.

She'd been set aside, abandoned before she'd had a fair chance to prove her worthiness.

Now...

She shivered, rubbing her wispy arms against the chill wind that threatened to *whoosh* her farther along the strand from where she now hovered, much too near the seaweed-draped rocks that had brought her such grief in life.

She enjoyed flitting about them now.

It was almost a challenge.

As if returning to the scene of her greatest heartache could erase her sorrow, yet when she manifested at the rocks, nothing bad ever happened.

She didn't hear haunting songs beckoning from the sea.

If any seals tumbled in the waves, they stayed where they were, only looking at her with innocent curiosity and never recrimination. They rolled in the surf, their dark dome-shaped heads bobbing as they watched her. They didn't torment and chastise her.

And why should they?

She had lost, not them.

So she came here again and again, reclaiming the narrow stretch of shingled strand and showing the loch-kissed rocks of doom that she still had her pride.

She was Drangar the Strong's lady.

His rejection of her, and even her ultimate demise, couldn't change that.

Once, she'd believed they'd belonged together.

He'd dropped to one knee before her, after all. Looking deep into her eyes—eyes he'd admired for their unusual smoky-gray color—he'd vowed unending devotion and love. Then he'd stood, pulling her into his arms and swearing he'd never gaze at another if only she'd be his.

She'd given herself willingly.

Letting him have her on this very strand, so near to the rocks of doom.

Then...

She drew a long breath, more from habit than necessity, and took her gaze from Blackshore's mighty walls. She flittered nearer to the rocks, not caring that now, at high tide, only their jagged, black-glistening tips peeked above the water.

Of the broad, tangle-covered ledges where fair Selkie maids might perch, preen, and lure a mortal man was nothing to be seen.

Yet she knew the ledges were there.

So she did the only thing her pride allowed her to do and tapped into her precious energy to make sure that her long black hair still held the sheen of those long-ago years. She also glanced down at her insubstantial form, grateful that the luminosity that marked her as otherworldly also flattered her smooth, pale skin.

Her soft silver-blue gown and her cloak of dove gray could've been spun of moonbeams and star shine. The ethereal raiments allowed her to slip about like the shadow she supposed she was.

One thing she wasn't, was a sigher.

She hadn't been the sort to bemoan her tragedies in her true life.

And she wasn't about to start wailing now.

She didn't even spend time at the Sighing Stones. It peeved her too much that the women of Clan Donald had given the stone circle such a name.

She knew better.

It was beneath her dignity to even think about the place. This foreshore was where she belonged and it didn't matter if the clan knew she walked here or not.

She did, and that was enough.

She just wished that her heart wouldn't lurch against her ribs each time she looked at the rocks. She could still see herself sitting there, poised so straight-backed on their slick, briny ledges. She remembered the cold waters rising around her. How the waves had first drenched her skirts and then seeped into her skin, chilling her to the marrow. She'd shivered uncontrollably, her teeth chattering. Her chest tightened, making it hard to draw breath.

Yet even then, with the tide swirling around her, she'd

kept casting glances at Blackshore, expecting Drangar to come.

But he had not.

His heart had been stolen by another.

And just when she'd realized her folly and would've pushed away from the rocks to return to the shore, she found she couldn't. Her skirts had twisted around her, snagged by the rushing tide and trapped in submerged crevices in the rocks.

She was doomed.

And then she knew no more.

Chapter Six

❧

"A man must admire your bravery, MacDonald, coming to Nought where you ken you aren't welcome." Kendrew Mackintosh leaned back in his heavily carved laird's chair and eyed Alasdair down the considerable length of his high table. He raised his ale cup to his lips, taking a healthy swig as he watched Alasdair over the rim. "Aye, most men would be impressed. A shame I am no' ordinary man."

"That you aren't, I agree." Alasdair lifted his own mug in salute.

Kendrew's eyes narrowed, but then he gave Alasdair a tight half smile. "Truth is I wouldn't be awed if you walked on water."

"Kendrew." Lady Isobel, his wife, gave him a pointed look. She sat beside him and from the way Kendrew's brow furrowed at her tone, Alasdair suspected she also stepped on his toes beneath the table.

"Have a care, Mackintosh. I'm no' in the mood for such blether." Alasdair kept his own voice cold but civil.

He also glanced to where his men sat at a long table in the lower hall. Only a handful had accompanied him. His cousin Ewan and a few other stout fighters made up his party. Just now, they conversed in seemingly genial terms with a score of burly, big-bearded Mackintosh warriors. Alasdair's men were their equal in size and brawn.

Though not of Berserker blood, they were formidable with a blade in their hands. Each man was capable of cutting a foe to ribbons before he knew he'd been struck.

So sharp was MacDonald steel.

So good were the men who wielded it.

Yet all MacDonald swords and shields were stacked in a small room off the Mackintosh stronghold's well-guarded entry. If a scuffle broke out, it would be fisticuffs only. Alasdair and his men wouldn't be able to snatch their arms before they came to blows with their enemies.

At Alasdair's side, Kendrew's shaggy gray beast of a dog eyed him hopefully, even rested a paw on his knee. Called Gronk, the beast had trotted over to Alasdair the moment he'd entered the torch-lit hall. Dogs usually did flock to him, sensing his sympathy.

He'd made the mistake of giving Gronk a twist of dried beef from a leather pouch he carried on his belt.

Now the dog wanted more.

His begging was making Kendrew's enmity worse.

"Poison my dog, MacDonald, and the buzzards flying round Nought's peaks will be picking your bones clean before nightfall." Kendrew scowled at his dog. "Doubt me at your peril."

Alasdair ignored him, calmly taking a bit of dried beef from his belt pouch. Kendrew's face reddened when Gronk snatched the treat.

"I know fine what you're capable of." Alasdair kept his tone just short of an insult.

"Do you, now?" A slow deliberate smile spread over Kendrew's face. He glanced at his wife as if expecting praise. But Lady Isobel only looked annoyed, her back ramrod straight and her shoulders rigid.

"Why do you think I'm here?" Alasdair resisted the urge to rub his scar. The damned wound was paining him again, as if his arm knew he sat at the table of the man responsible for slicing into his muscle.

His temper rising, he shot a glance at the small storeroom near the hall's entry arch. He didn't care that his weapons were stacked away, out of reach. He'd relish setting upon Kendrew with his bare hands.

He wouldn't mind smashing the lout's nose.

He deserved worse.

"I'm waiting for you to tell me." Kendrew leaned back in his chair, folded his arms. His smile was gone now, his gaze turned sharp.

"My scouts reported two black-painted longships off Drangar Point." Alasdair waved away the serving lass who tried to refill his ale cup. "Some of my men believe they were Black Vikings, the marauders of old returned to menace our waters. Others claim the lookouts saw phantom galleys or were deep in their cups, mistaking mist for dark-hulled warships."

"That's no' what you think." Kendrew didn't blink.

"Nae, it isn't." Alasdair met his foe's stare, waiting for a flash of guilt or a spark of triumph. But there was nothing.

Kendrew might've been made of stone.

Around them, the hall was erupting in agitated mumbling. Men shifted on trestle benches, their expressions wary and suspicious. Not for the first time since arriving at the remote stronghold, Alasdair was glad that Marjory hadn't yet shown herself. Her presence would only serve to distract him and he was already wondering at the wisdom of having made the trek at all.

Nought was a wild and bleak land, full of rock and cold wind. Shadows and echoes prevailed, and the mists here were often impenetrable. Some of Nought's peaks soared so high and were clustered so tightly together that the sun never reached their stony feet. Equally damning were the mysterious dreagan stones, ancient cairns spread along the steep-sided vale that cut deep through the heart of Kendrew's rugged, mountainous territory.

A place better fit for rock-climbing, cloven-footed goats than men.

No one came here gladly.

And now that he was here, Alasdair wouldn't leave until he'd had his answers. Kendrew might not look guilty, but he also didn't invite trust.

So Alasdair slapped his hand on the high table, hard enough that ale cups jumped. "I think the black-painted ships were yours. It's no' secret you and your men call yourselves night-walkers, smearing peat juice and soot all o'er yourselves before you go raiding. Why no' do the same to a longship?" Alasdair leaned forward, his anger rising again. "It'd be a clever way to rid yourself of an enemy while putting the blame on others. If word reached the King that Black Vikings attacked my territory, he'd ne'er point a finger at you, wouldn't hold you responsible for breaking his truce."

"You're howling mad." Kendrew sounded amused. "And you've made a fool's errand. I dinnae have any galleys. And I know naught of Black Vikings. But if I did"—his smile returned—"mayhap I'd offer them my sister. Seeing as they'd surely have a braw leader no' averse to a fetching bride in good health and who'd come with a hefty dowry. If you haven't heard, I'm looking to arrange a worthy match for her. She's a real beauty." He lifted his ale cup, took a long sip. "She deserves the best husband I can find her. Wouldn't you agree?"

"I didnae come here to speak of your sister." Alasdair's voice was low and hard.

"I am glad to hear it." Kendrew leaned forward, his eyes like slits. "If you dared to try I'd have to cut out your tongue."

"Before you could, I'd pierce your gullet with my eating knife." Alasdair held Kendrew's stare and gripped his ale mug tighter than necessary.

Kendrew's taunts were getting to him.

To his surprise, the dastard laughed. "A shame you're a brine drinker, MacDonald. I vow I could like you if you weren't."

Alasdair nodded, doubting the likelihood.

Somewhere in the shadows of the hall, one of the Mackintosh warriors lifted his voice, repeating his chief's jest about Alasdair walking on water. Rapping his table, the man also suggested MacDonalds were born with webbed feet. Throughout the hall, men sniggered.

The MacDonald guards' faces darkened.

Kendrew's lips twitched. "Aye, well." He reached across the high table, clinked his ale cup against Alasdair's. "I like seeing my men in good spirits. I'll have to stop calling you brine drinker and say water walker."

"A good swordsman has no need to walk on water."

Alasdair returned his smile, making sure it didn't reach his eyes.

"Your steel would serve you naught if I knocked it out of your hand with my ax."

"You can try." Alasdair felt his blood rising, anger pumping through his veins.

He glanced at the MacDonald table in the lower hall where even Ewan looked annoyed. Unlike Alasdair, he rarely lost his temper. Other kinsmen shifted uncomfortably, some fisting and unfisting their hands. Not one appeared in the mood for such ribbing.

"None of us asked for this truce." Alasdair surely hadn't. "The King ordered peace. Now that we have it, we must all sup at the same bowl, however unappetizing. If you still wish to fight"—Alasdair used his strongest voice—"come at me full on and we'll clash steel. Dinnae hide behind a pitch-coated longship."

"I haven't hid since I left my mother's womb." Kendrew paused, looking pleased as his men went into whoops of laughter. "And I'm no' worried about royal wishes. I'd rather sink Blood-Drinker in your skull." He flashed a glance at the huge Norse war ax hanging on the dais wall. "Indeed, I dream of doing so."

Beside him, Lady Isobel colored. "Kendrew..." She set a hand on his arm, her knuckles whitening as she squeezed his hard muscle. "Alasdair is our guest."

"He's a bluidy pain in the arse." Kendrew leaned forward, Isobel releasing him. "A limpet-coated, salt-smelling brine drinker who came here to befoul Nought's air with fool accusations, when all he wants is to run to court and besmirch our good name, hoping to bring the King's wrath hammering down on us. The black-painted longships are no doubt his own, a scheme to wrest Nought into his grasp.

"Do you think"—he gave his wife a sharp look—"I'm no' aware of his plans to seize all the glen, even using my sister to do so?"

Lady Isobel sat up straighter, her dark eyes blazing. "Have done, Kendrew."

He glared at her. "He's worse than the King and his Lowlanders. I'll no' have him making Marjory a pawn for his greed. Think you I'm no' aware how he chases after her, or why he wants her?"

Alasdair's patience snapped, the edges of his vision beginning to redden. "Lady Marjory has naught to do with this." He almost reached for the dirk hidden in his boot. He did raise his voice so all would hear. "I should've known better than to come here."

"Aye, you should have." Kendrew spoke just as loud. "MacDonalds are ne'er welcome here."

"That I know." Alasdair tossed back a gulp of ale, fighting his temper.

Marjory might not be in her brother's hall, but wherever she was, she could appear any moment. Kendrew wouldn't be so agitated if that weren't so. He kept sliding glances to an arched doorway the far side of the huge, weapon-hung room. His edginess proved he expected her. If so, Alasdair wouldn't allow her to walk in and find him brawling with Kendrew.

He *was* tempted.

More than that, he now knew what else had been bothering him ever since Lady Isobel had greeted him and his men, ushering them into the stronghold's great hall, despite her husband's heavy frown.

Marjory wasn't the only one missing.

Kendrew's captain of the guard was also absent. The man wasn't easy to miss, huge and big-bearded as he was. His wild black hair and the silver warrior rings he braided into his beard, coupled with his storm-gray eyes and hard, rough-hewn face, made him notable. He was also one of Kendrew's most ferocious fighting men.

Tongue waggers claimed he could cleave a man in two with a single stroke of his ax.

Alasdair didn't doubt it.

He also knew that if Kendrew was going to send two pitch-coated galleys into the night, the battle-probed warrior was the man he'd choose to lead such a mission.

"Enough insults, Mackintosh." Alasdair spoke curtly and gestured toward the smoke-hazed hall beneath the dais, the crowded rows of long tables. "Where is your captain? The man called Grim? I do not see him."

"Grim?" Kendrew's brows lifted and for a moment he looked surprised. "He's no' out in a black-painted long-boat if that's what you're thinking."

"The thought crossed my mind." Alasdair was still suspicious.

"Grim is nowhere near your damty coast." Kendrew paused, a wicked glint coming into his eyes. "He'd be afraid of catching a rash o' barnacles down your way."

Along the high table, Kendrew's men chuckled.

Lady Isobel stood. "I agree with Blackshore." She used Alasdair's title, her voice strong and firm. "This ribbing must stop. Now, before the good name of our House of Mackintosh is sullied beyond repair."

"Ribbing?" Kendrew twisted round to look up at her. "Men who come uninvited can expect—"

"That isn't so." She dismissed his protest with a wave

of her hand. "If anyone disagrees"—she glanced about, her brows lifting—"I shall personally see that such rudeness is rewarded with an empty stomach. The next man to slur our guests will not receive dinner in my hall this night. And I do mean everyone."

She sent a pointed look at Kendrew before she took her seat again.

Silence spread across the dais and along the trestle tables beyond. A few grumbles rose here and there, a scattering of cleared throats. No one lifted a voice to challenge her.

Even Kendrew looked chastised, a faint flush staining his face. He speared a bannock with his eating knife, proceeded to smear the halved roll with butter.

Lady Isobel smiled, nodding pleasantly at Alasdair.

"My lady, you do honor to Nought." Alasdair used his most courteous tone, ignoring Kendrew. "Your husband is fortunate to have you."

"It's you I'll have, you briny bastard . . . your head on a pike," Kendrew mumbled around his bannock.

Or so Alasdair thought, though he couldn't prove it.

If Lady Isobel heard, she chose not to react, sipping her wine instead.

"My husband told you true, lord." She set down her drinking chalice, her gaze direct. "We do not have ships. Our strength is elsewhere. Perhaps in the bravery of our men, their skill at arms. And surely in the impassable peaks that enclose our territory. The cold, clean air that greets us each morn and helps us sleep well at night.

"And Grim . . ." She paused, ignoring the dark glance Kendrew tossed at her. "He is only seldom at Nought these days. Did you not know he stayed on at Archie MacNab's last year? It was after Kendrew and his men rescued

Marjory and me from the band of broken men who'd captured us. They took us to Duncreag, the MacNab stronghold in the next glen."

"Aye, I remember." Alasdair did.

It rankled to know Kendrew often received accolades for his heroics.

Tales still circulated of the night Kendrew had led his soot-and-peat-smeared warriors—night-walkers they called themselves—up to Duncreag's ramparts. They'd faced formidable odds, scaling a sheer rock face even steeper than Nought's worst cliffs. Bards praised the Mackintoshes, claiming no other men could've climbed to the inaccessible stronghold. Yet Kendrew and his warriors had passed through the night darkness unseen, gaining the gatehouse before the miscreants who'd overtaken the castle even knew they'd been set upon.

The slaughter that followed, and the rescue of the two women, was now legend.

Even some of the younger MacDonald warriors enjoyed hearing the tale.

Alasdair's ears would shrivel if he was ever again made to suffer through the telling.

If he'd known in time, he and his men could've hastened to Duncreag and saved the women even more swiftly than Kendrew had done. They would've also seen justice served for old Archie MacNab, ridding him of the miscreants who'd invaded his home and murdered his sons.

But Alasdair hadn't known.

Kendrew had. Always looking for glory, he'd stormed off to the MacNab's remote glen, rescuing Marjory and Lady Isobel almost singlehandedly.

The rankling in Alasdair's gut worsened, leaving a bad taste in his mouth.

Lady Isobel was still speaking. He'd barely heard a word.

"The broken men . . . ?" He seized the last scrap of her words.

"They were that, belonging to no clan." She glanced at Kendrew, but he only took another bite of his bannock, munching sourly. "Ralla the Victorious was the leader. He and his men killed nearly everyone at Duncreag, almost the entire garrison. They spared only a few children to be sold as slaves, and the old laird.

"They wouldn't have let him live much longer." She shivered, her gaze meeting Alasdair's. "There have always been rumors of treasure at Duncreag. Ralla hoped to force Archie to reveal the hoard's whereabouts."

"Bah!" Kendrew slid an annoyed look at his dog, his frown turning even blacker when the beast rested his head on Alasdair's thigh. "There aren't any riches at the MacNabs' and ne'er has been. Duncreag has more stone and wind than Nought. That's all a man will find there. It's a place for those who like thin air and cold, bare hills. Duncreag makes Nought look like a spring meadow."

Leaning forward, he held Alasdair's eye. "Their bards made up the hoard years ago because suchlike sounds good in a song."

Lady Isobel's brow pleated, but she continued. "Grim and some of our Nought warriors are there now. They're training the young MacNabs so Duncreag will have a new garrison." She paused, ran a finger around the edge of her wine chalice. "The MacNabs—"

"Are a clan o' poets and scribes." Kendrew's tone

revealed his opinion of such men. "Ne'er did have fighting in them. Why else would a craven like Ralla choose Duncreag to quarter his foul band?"

"Perhaps because the stronghold is nearly impregnable, sitting higher than an eagle's aerie?" Alasdair couldn't resist the argument.

Kendrew's scowl said he'd hit his mark. "Do you aye ken everything?"

"Nae." Alasdair dug another few bits of dried meat from his belt pouch and offered them to Gronk and two other dogs who'd joined him. "I'm good at thinking like my enemies. Or have you ne'er heard that a man should know his foes better than his friends?"

Kendrew snorted. "I ken all I wish of you."

"And I would hear more of you." Alasdair leaned back in his chair, ignoring Kendrew's pointed glance at the hall's main entry. "Such as"—he lifted a hand, examining his knuckles—"if you paid someone to harry my coast with pitch-covered longships? Seeing as you dinnae have any ships yourself."

"I already gave you my answer."

"I'm asking again."

"Howling at the moon is what you're doing. I might no' like you, but I aye speak true. I ne'er heard of black-painted longships. Leastways no' since that old tale the bards love to sing about Clan MacConacher of MacConachers' Isle. How one of their chiefs rid the Hebrides of Black Vikings and then sweetened his victory by marrying a daughter of Duncan MacKenzie, the Black Stag of Kintail. And that, my friend"—he made sure the last word sounded anything but genial—"was o'er fifty years ago. No such devils have been seen since, last I heard. If they are about, I've told you what I'd do." He sat back, grinning. "I'd find them and if their lord was braw and deep-pursed enough, I'd offer him my sister as a bride. If they proved to be blood-thirsty blackguards"—a wicked glint entered his eyes again—"then I'd send them your way. Though the reek o' so much brine might see them turning tail before—"

"Enough!" Alasdair stood, his anger flaring. "Call me what you will, but dinnae slur my folk."

"Dinnae come chapping at my door." Kendrew shoved back his own chair, rising. He glared angrily at Alasdair. "I keep the King's peace because it suits me. I can break it and still sleep easily. Especially with your head on a pike, high o'er Nought's walls. The ravens feeding on your gizzard—"

Lady Isobel's gasp cut him off. Alasdair's men jumped up and ran onto the dais, forming a half circle around the high table. Many of Kendrew's warriors joined them, others staying where they were but thumping the tables with their fists. Every man stilled when Alasdair snatched a two-bladed ax off the wall and swung it at Kendrew, let-ting the blade head hover a breath from his nose.

"I should take off your face. Now, while my blood's too hot for me to care." Alasdair held the ax shaft steady, its blade not wavering. "Unsay your slur or I will, even if your men slay me a beat later."

"I'll unsay naught." Kendrew didn't flinch, his gaze locked on Alasdair's. "Except that you're a dead man."

"So be it." Alasdair jiggled the ax, allowing the blade to glide along Kendrew's cheekbone. A bead of red appeared, rolling into his beard. "I cannae think of a bet-ter way to die than defending my clan's honor."

"And I'll no' have your corpse slumped o'er my table!"

In a lightning-quick move, Kendrew grabbed the ax shaft, using it to hook Alasdair behind his knees.

"Ompf!" The blow sent Alasdair sprawling onto the floor rushes.

"We'll fight proper another day, brine drinker!" Tossing aside the ax, Kendrew pounced, reaching for Alasdair's neck. "No' this one, no' here—"

"That we will!" Alasdair grabbed Kendrew first and they grappled, rolling across the rushes. The warriors who'd crowded onto the dais jumped back now, making room and widening their circle. Alasdair ignored them, only hearing Kendrew's curse when he plowed his fist into Kendrew's mouth, splitting his lip. "Where'er we meet, only one of us will walk away."

Alasdair stood, resisting the urge to plant his foot on his foe's heaving chest. "That I promise you."

Kendrew laughed. "I'll hold you to that, you arse." Grinning as if Alasdair had only tickled his chin with a feather, he pushed up on an elbow and dragged his sleeve across his bloodied lip. "When the time comes," he vowed, his amusement proving his love of fighting, "I'll crush you like an egg in my hand."

"You can try." Alasdair nodded as Kendrew pushed to his feet, brushing meadowsweet from his plaid.

"Dear heavens!" Marjory appeared on the dais steps, rushing forward as the warriors parted to make room for her. She looked from Alasdair to her brother and then back again. "What happened here?"

Alasdair frowned, shoved a hand through his hair. "Your brother and I had words."

"Say you." Kendrew shook back his own wild mane, blinked sweat from his eyes. "She sees fine what happened."

"You fought." Marjory folded her arms, her gaze narrowing on them both.

"We settled a matter, aye." Alasdair threw a dark look at Kendrew. His pulse still raced and his blood roared in his ears. The scar on his arm screamed, pulling as it did sometimes, the sharp pain demanding payment in kind.

Vengeance he burned to claim, but not in front of Marjory.

She roused entirely different emotions in him. Dark, unholy desires that twisted and writhed deep inside him, so close to breaking free.

"It must've been a matter of great import for you to come here. Something"—her blue eyes flashed—"you and my brother disagreed upon."

"We aye disagree." Kendrew folded his arms.

Alasdair just looked at Marjory, unable to help himself. Her hair was windblown and soft light from a nearby torch fell across her, making her feminine curves so apparent he could hardly breathe. He'd always found her beautiful, but now she had a sensual, provocative air about her that made him want to devour her. He could feel his eyelids lowering, his loins tightening. Her breasts rose and fell against her cloak, as if to taunt him. She came closer and he caught her scent, drinking it in, greedy for more. As if she knew, she touched her breast, watching him as if aware of his thoughts. Heat coursed through his blood, lust flaring. She shook her head slowly, more alluring than he'd ever seen her.

Never had he been more conscious of her.

He'd gone hard, the discomfort reminding him where they stood.

Her composure didn't falter. "Well? Her gaze flicked

to the mussed floor rushes, an overturned trestle bench. "Am I not to hear the meaning of this?"

Alasdair frowned, reached to right the toppled bench. He'd tell her true, seeing no reason to lie. "Lady, I—"

"The MacDonald thinks we have black-painted long-ships and are planning an assault on his stronghold." Kendrew stepped demonstrably before his sister. "He now knows that he erred."

"I know I dinnae trust you farther than the end of my sword, Mackintosh." Alasdair jerked a nod at his men, indicating it was time to leave. "This isn't over, be warned."

"Nae, it isn't." Kendrew came forward, slapped him on the shoulder. "That'll be the day I spit on your grave."

"We shall see." For once, Alasdair didn't care to exchange insults with his foe.

In one matter, Kendrew had the rights of him.

He had erred.

Ever since seeing Marjory again at the harvest fair, he'd forgone sleep to stare at the ceiling almost nightly, convincing himself she wasn't the woman he wanted. That lust alone made him ache for her. Pure carnal need he could slake with any jolly serving lass willing to air her skirts. That his worry he could never get enough of just touching her was because he'd gone so long without a woman.

And that the reason he'd not bothered had nothing to do with Marjory.

Now he knew better.

He would've preferred to remain oblivious.

Drangar the Strong would've sympathized with his young descendant's plight. Indeed, he did. He even felt Alasdair's frustration as his own. How could he not? If mortal men knew that a bond stretched across time between those who presently walked the earth and those who went before them, men in spirit form lived that truth.

Besides, didn't he know the pain of having loved in vain?

Drangar frowned and pulled on his neatly trimmed black beard. Even here, on the wildest, most bleak edge of Nought territory, his memories dogged him, snapping at his heels and biting hard.

He'd hoped to escape them.

If only for the duration of his business here, deep in enemy lands. Yet just as duty, honor, and loyalty had guided him through life and now the Otherworld, so did his regrets and longings also accompany him. Such things stayed with a man, whatever form he held.

But at the moment, other matters occupied his mind.

And they were much more serious than the sorrows of a wounded heart. His recollections of a woman's soft, warm body held close to his. The fullness of lush, naked breasts against his chest as he'd cradled his love's face in his strong, living hands, kissing her thoroughly. Or—his frown deepened—the wonder of rolling on top of her and then losing himself deep inside her, reveling in her silky, welcoming heat.

How he missed such pleasures.

How he ached to simply have her beside him again.

But he drew himself up, ever the fierce and invincible warrior.

That he was here at all was a triumph.

He should be glorying in this moment.

Tall and proud, he hovered at the top of a steep narrow path, looking down into the silver-gleaming inlet known as the Dreagan's Claw. He preferred thinking of the place as the devil's toehold on the glen, seeing as Mackintoshes claimed the wee sliver of a cove. Either way, it was something to be here. A remarkable feat and one he enjoyed. He didn't often venture into enemy territory. The last time was so long ago that he could scarce remember.

He did know that he'd had an army of MacDonald warriors at his back.

Now he stood alone.

Or he hovered, depending on the charity of one's viewpoint.

What mattered was that his warrior's instincts were still as sharply honed as ever. Centuries of ghostdom hadn't dulled his wits. And that was a grand accomplishment, something to be celebrated. As was his ability to negotiate the treacherous winds and dark mists that made the long journey from the Warrior Stones at Drangar Point to this bleak Mackintosh outpost so arduous.

Several times, the strong sea winds had almost sent him hurtling back to Blackshore.

Once he'd paused atop a particularly notable promontory, sure he'd reached the Dreagan's Claw, only to discover when the mists parted that he was nowhere near the hidden inlet so loved by Vikings and other sea raiders in his day.

He drifted nearer to the cliff's edge and peered down into the deep, steep-sided cove. Apparently the place was still appreciated.

As he'd suspected, the two black-painted longships moored there.

A handful of smaller boats had been pulled onto the shingled bank. Men gathered there, sitting round a fire. They clearly didn't know they were observed. Instead, they drank from mead horns, laughed, and conversed. Seemingly in highest spirits, their mood was congratulatory.

Still, their swords and spearheads shone through the mist. And although they'd coated their mail with pitch or black paint, a fool could see that each man on the narrow shore was dressed for battle.

Equally arrayed were the men who'd remained on the two longships.

Drangar only wished they could see him.

They could if he'd desired.

But his warrior instincts told him it was best to let them believe no one saw them.

So he pulled his long black cloak closer about his tall, well-muscled form—insubstantial, though it was—and clutched his leather-gloved hand tighter around his spear shaft. A shame he couldn't hurl the spear down at them. He'd love to pierce one of them, pinning the craven to the rocky ground. Doing so would've given him much satisfaction.

For with the capabilities he'd developed as a ghost, he heard every word to pass the men's lips.

And if ever such a skewering death was deserved, the miscreants below earned that and more.

Their plans also needed telling.

Unfortunately, along with exceptional hearing, Drangar's ghostly condition also brought limitations. He couldn't simply float into Blackshore's hall, sail over to Alasdair's high table, slam a heavy fist onto the boards, lift his voice, and announce what he knew.

But he could use his wits and warlord's logic to do what he could.

He'd seen Alasdair and his small band of men riding to Nought.

Knowing the Mackintoshes as he did, he knew their chieftain, Kendrew, would not welcome the arrival of the MacDonald party. He'd greet them curtly and quickly send Alasdair on his way.

But Alasdair had a sharp mind. He wouldn't miss a chance to visit the Dreagan's Claw, having ventured so deep into Mackintosh territory.

At least, Drangar hoped so.

Almost sure of it, he drew back from the cliff edge and settled in to wait. The men below would be leaving soon. That, too, he'd heard. But Drangar wasn't going anywhere. Leastways he wasn't until Alasdair and his men appeared. He just hoped they'd come soon.

The wind blowing in off the sea was strengthening. And a man did have his pride. Much as Drangar was adept at holding himself together, such powerful gusts as tore across these cliffs did tend to toss him about. Already the great plumes on his helmet were in danger of being blown away. And his gleaming black hair, always his pride, had been whipped into a snarl of knots and tangles.

When he returned to Drangar Point and the Warrior Stones, he'd have to spend longer than usual to wipe the sea salt off his coat of mail. He took care to keep its links well polished and he could tell the buffeting Nought winds were seeping through the wool of his cloak, the salt already dulling the sheen of his mail.

A warrior looked best when his armor shone.

Still, he knew that if any man saw him, he'd present a fierce and daunting image.

Doing his part to help his kin was worth a bit of discomfort and unpleasantness.

Feeling justifiably noble, he allowed himself a rare smile.

Ghostdom did have certain advantages.

Eager to make use of one of them, he sheltered in the lee of an outcrop, gathering the energy he'd need to do what he planned. He just hoped Alasdair and his men would notice and then act upon his message.

So much depended on them.

Chapter Seven

❖

Marjory could hardly believe she'd returned to the hall to find Alasdair at Nought. Or that having been taken so unaware, she'd barely had a chance to speak with him before he'd left. What didn't surprise her was her brother's satisfaction at Alasdair's angry departure.

She couldn't just let him go.

Her heart had leaped to see him. And when he'd looked at her, his face had been fierce, his eyes blazing with a fiery heat she knew was desire.

That and something else.

Something that quickened her blood and made her tremble with excitement.

He couldn't be gone already.

She hastened from the dais, glancing about, her pulse still racing as her gaze flickered over the hall's weapon-hung walls. Everywhere she looked, swords, spears, and axes seemed to stare back at her accusingly because she dared to search for a MacDonald in their midst. Kendrew's bearskin cloak hung above the high table, the thick black pelt glistening in the firelight. For two pins, she'd believe the cloak might come to life any moment, growling at her.

She didn't care.

Hurrying deeper into the hall, she kept searching for Alasdair. There were so many men milling about. She hadn't seen him go. She'd only caught the angry surge of warriors, Mackintoshes and MacDonalds, leaving the dais and heading toward the entry arch.

She pressed a hand to her breast, straining to see into the hall's farthest corners. Here and there, wall torches revealed red-painted wolf and bear skulls, hinting at the clan's claim of Berserker ancestry. Huge silver-rimmed bull horns and ancient, battle-damaged shirts of mail shone in the flickering light, testimony of a warlike past.

There were also a few bones. She shivered, knowing the hall's darker recesses held worse things. She avoided those relics from distant times when pagan worship and sacrifices were more than tales to amuse clansmen on cold winter nights.

Just now, she'd offer anything to catch a glimpse of Alasdair's broad shoulders in the throng of men near the door. She'd love to spot the glint of his auburn hair gleaming in the torchlight, or to hear his deep voice above the din, admire his plaid swirling about him as he strode purposely through the crowd.

But he was nowhere to be seen.

Nor were his clansmen. The MacDonalds had left the hall.

Before she could decide what to do, she felt a light touch on her arm. Turning, she saw Isobel standing beside her, looking flushed.

"This shouldn't have happened. I tried to keep them from each other's throats." Isobel slid a reproachful look at her husband. "My efforts were as helpful as tossing grease on a fire."

"Good riddance, eh?" Kendrew joined them, looking pleased as his guardsmen began filing away from the hall's great double doors. They'd trailed Alasdair and his men to the door, flanking them as if they were released prisoners. "Thon MacDonald bastard willnae be fouling Nought with his presence again for a while, I vow."

"He had reason to come here." Isobel challenged him.

"No' any good one." Kendrew leaned against a table edge, crossed his arms.

"Why does he think you'd attack Blackshore?" Marjory was sure he had another reason for visiting Nought. She hoped it was her. "Nor have we ever had galleys, certainly not black-painted ones. He knows that."

"So I told him." Kendrew shrugged.

"I'm thinking you said more than that." Marjory noted the blood flecks in Kendrew's beard, and then she glanced back toward the dais.

The hall's proud upper level stood in shambles.

Several chairs and a trestle bench lay toppled in the rushes. A platter of freshly baked meat pasties had been knocked off the high table, much to the delight of Gronk and the other castle dogs who'd pounced on the delicacies. Spilled ale and wine from broken ewers stained the snowy-white table linens and spread across the floor in strong-reeking puddles.

The smell would hang in the air for days.

"A bit o' bloodletting ne'er hurt any man." Kendrew rolled his shoulders, brushed a few sprigs of meadowsweet off his sleeve. "Could be I knocked some sense into him. At the least, he knows he's no' welcome here."

"He knew that before," Marjory reminded him.

"Did I no' say he's daft?" Kendrew strode over to the fire to warm his hands. "How can he no' be? Accusing us of sailing round in pitch-coated longboats, whetting our ax heads as we approach his shores. Black Vikings, come a-raiding. Speaking of the Norse"—he shot a look at Marjory—"why did you return so early? Weren't you with old widow Hella? Thought you'd be at her cottage all the day, listening to her blether. Or did you know MacDonald was coming?"

"She couldn't know that." Isobel went over to him, began dabbing flecks of blood from his beard with a napkin. "She—"

"I ken the two of you. Aye scheming, you are." Kendrew snatched the napkin and tossed it aside. "Dinnae deny it for you cannae."

Isobel hooked her arm through his, leaning into him. "Even if it's true, I've not heard too many complaints from you."

"Humph." Kendrew frowned. The kind of scowl he wore when Isobel maneuvered him into a corner. A place he apparently enjoyed, for he slid his arm around her, drawing her close. "I only want the best for my sister. The MacDonald is no' the man for her."

"To be sure, he isn't," Isobel agreed, sending a quick wink to Marjory. "We all know that."

Kendrew's frown vanished. "I'm glad to hear it."

"Of course, men can change..." Isobel smoothed back his hair, adjusted his plaid, her voice soothing. "Look how you "

"Dinnae compare me with a brine drinker." Kendrew's

voice hardened and he took his wife's wrists, lowering her hands from his chest. He turned to Marjory, suspicious again. "I'll hear why you came back so soon. If your visit to old Hella had aught to do with Blackshore, if it was a ruse, I'll—"

"Hella wasn't there." Marjory spoke true. "And she isn't old, just widowed."

"Could be I've forgotten." Kendrew reached down to scratch Gronk's head when the dog came to sit beside him. "That woman goes on so many rambles I scarce take note of her. I've no' seen her in ages."

Just then the hem of Marjory's cloak stirred and a tiny black nose appeared, quickly followed by a small white paw. Then the dog's entire brown-and-white face emerged, his friendly brown gaze honing in on Kendrew.

He looked down at the tiny dog, taking a backward step. "Dinnae think to do it, laddie. My boots aren't in need of watering."

Peering up, Hercules gave him a long, intense stare before disappearing once more behind Marjory's skirts.

"If you wouldn't glower at him, he'd leave you be." Marjory lifted her chin, her mind racing. Alasdair would soon be at the bottom of the cliff stair, riding away.

Kendrew kept grumbling about Hercules, his words seeming to come from a great distance.

Marjory heard only the thundering of her heart. Then the loud *thunk* as one of the guards dropped the door's drawbar in place, barring the hall from intruders. Unwanted guests like Alasdair and his men.

After such a fracas, Kendrew would watch her even more carefully. Her chances of meeting Alasdair alone, of seducing him, would diminish greatly.

Her insides went cold at the prospect.

Kendrew was still fussing about her dog. "You've trained the wee bugger to devil me." He flashed a glance at her hem where Hercules's little black nose was peeking into view again. "You, my only sister who ought to know I aye have your best interests at heart. Rather than thank me, you—"

"I'll take him to my room." Marjory had no intention of doing so. But she did scoop Hercules into her arms and head in that direction.

She just pushed through the crowd until she was sure Kendrew could no longer see her and then veered toward a certain shadowy corner. Once there, she set down Hercules and slid her hand beneath a moth-eaten wolf pelt on the wall. With outstretched fingers, she searched for a loose stone that, when pressed, opened Nought's least-used secret passage. It was the original cliff stair, ruined in a rockslide over three hundred years before.

Marjory doubted even Kendrew knew it existed.

She'd discovered the stair as a child when she'd enjoyed hiding behind the hanging wolf- and bearskins to spy on the late-night festivities in the hall. Her shoulder had accidentally bumped the access rock and the great stone door had groaned open, revealing its dark, cobwebby secrets. She'd learned the rest from an old clanswoman who'd been fond of her and, Marjory later discovered, had used the passage in her youth to tryst with her lover.

Marjory intended to do the same.

Alasdair might not be her lover, but she did mean to win his heart. Nor was she averse to doing whatever such a feat required of her.

Truth be told, she looked forward to such encounters.

His kisses only whet her appetite for more. And as her intentions were surely noble, she saw no shame in pursuing his attentions.

So she bit her lip, concentrating, as she felt along the wall. The stone was cold and damp, hard and not giving, until at last her thumb rubbed across the raised, rough-edged rock that was so different from the rest. Relief sweeping her, she pushed the rock.

A low groan rewarded her. The telltale grinding of stone on stone as the hidden door slowly opened, revealing the passage beyond.

"Come." Marjory whispered the command to Hercules as she stepped into the chilly darkness, the ancient stair so familiar she didn't need a torch.

Even if she had, ruined as the passage was, enough light trickled through cracks in the rock walls to allow anyone to descend the narrow steps without too great a risk of slipping.

Hercules bounded ahead of her, racing down the steps as if they were playing a game.

Marjory hurried after him, hoping only to catch Alasdair before he reached the guardhouse at the base of Nought's main cliff stair.

From long practice, she ducked cobwebs and slowed her steps where she knew fallen rumble made the stairs treacherous. She listened for the sound of trickling water, careful on the patches made slick by damp and moss. Then, just when she was sure the well-manned guardhouse would loom up before her, its back wall marking the end of the old passage, she caught the murmur of men's voices and the sound of masculine feet tromping down the main stair.

She quickened her own steps, recognizing one deep voice above the others.

Alasdair was just ahead of her.

And her timing couldn't have been better, for a long-forgotten niche loomed near, hewn into the rock wall of the old passage. Either an ancient storeroom or a wind shelter for erstwhile guards, the tiny room was well protected from the elements, and from prying eyes.

Marjory hastened down the last few steps and then paused to catch her breath.

She shivered badly.

But the prickling sensation was from excitement, not the cold.

If this was to be her only opportunity to be alone with Alasdair, she would do her damndest to make the best of it. Her very life and happiness hung on what she was about to do. She just hoped Alasdair would be receptive.

"Blackshore, wait!"

"Marjory?" Alasdair turned on the cliff stair, his jaw slipping to see her a dozen steps above him. Wind tore at her hair and although she clutched her blood-red cloak to her breast, he could see a hint of her bosom, the MacDonald ambers gleaming at her throat. Mist swirled everywhere and torchlight from farther up the steps cast a halo around her, revealing her shapeliness and letting her appear like a living flame, seductive and alluring. She beckoned him in a way that made his entire body tighten.

She was breathing hard, her breasts rising and falling beneath her cloak. Her eyes were wide, her lips parted.

Alasdair knew she'd only hastened from the hall, yet she looked as if she'd just risen from a mussed bed, still roused and excited from love play.

The thought set him like granite and he swore, ordering his men to remain where they were before he bounded up the steps to stand before her.

He gripped her shoulders, shaking his head as he looked at her. "You shouldn't have come after me. It was dangerous to do so."

He didn't say he posed the threat, knowing she'd assume he meant her brother.

"Kendrew thinks I'm in my room." She held his gaze, unblinking. "I had to speak to you, alone."

"We are hardly that, my lady." Alasdair didn't release her. As always, her scent bewitched him, the temptation of her nearness hitting him like a blow to the chest. His heart thundered and he'd wager anything that hers pounded just as fiercely.

It was all he could do not to kiss her again, their audience be damned.

There were onlookers, even if to their left, where the cliff path fell away into nothingness, little could be seen but thick whirling mist.

Elsewhere...

Alasdair didn't care. Lifting his hand, he trailed his knuckles along the softness of her cheek and then down the smooth line of her neck, noting how her pulse quickened beneath his touch.

"If you look behind and above you"—he stepped closer and leaned toward her—"your brother's guardhouse is well-manned. My warriors are but a few steps below us. I wouldnae say we're no' observed, sweet."

"We shall be in here." She drew him off the stair and behind a jutting rock that looked like part of the cliff face.

In truth, the outcrop hid a deep and narrow niche in the rock wall, forming an alcove that must've been used as a guardhouse or storeroom in earlier centuries. It stood empty now, the tight space filled with nothing but cold, the damp, and shadows.

It was a sheltered place, well shielded from the main cliff stair. The cavelike niche also offered absolute protection from prying eyes.

Alasdair's men wouldn't disturb them here.

Nought's guards hadn't seen them slip inside the secret place. Alarm horns would've blasted if they had. Marjory had spoken true.

They were alone.

Thick mist blowing past the opening did the rest, sealing them away from the outside world. Torchlight slanted in through a crack in the rock ceiling, casting a sheen on Marjory's hair. Each strand shimmered as if dusted with diamonds. Her eyes sparkled like sapphires. Her cloak had opened, offering glimpses of her pearly skin, stirring images of even more bared flesh. Her nakedness pressed hard against his own, their bodies entwined.

Alasdair drew a tight breath, his pulse racing. Just looking at her made him forget every reason he shouldn't desire her. Masculine awareness thrummed the entire length of him, warning that even if he did remember, he no longer cared.

The time for restraint had passed.

"This was no' wise, sweet." He moved closer to her, slowly shaking his head, his gaze steady on hers. "I warned you. Now it's too late." He placed his hands on the rock wall behind her and leaned in, trapping her within his arms. "I've run dry of warnings."

"Perhaps I do not need them?" She straightened to her full height, squaring her shoulders so that her breasts were displayed to advantage.

She also let her gaze glide from his face down over his plaid-draped chest and then to where his sword belt was slung low around his hips. It was a deliberate assessing that only fired his blood, stirring very wicked thoughts and causing his loins to throb.

As every time their paths crossed, her hair tumbled in fetching disarray to her waist. Her gown hugged the curve of her hips and her nipples were chill-tightened. They pressed against her bodice, an unbearable enticement. And her luscious, parted lips only served to remind him how thoroughly kissable she was.

Alasdair bit back a groan.

She remained perfectly still, almost daring him to admire her.

She tilted her head, her blue gaze seemingly innocent. "I wished only to speak with you."

"A man could think you wished to seduce him." Alasdair gave her a slow smile, knew heat burned in his gaze. The blazing passion she ignited in him, unleashed. "Is that it, Norn? Did you drag me in here with seduction in mind?"

Her eyes widened, and even in the dimness, he could tell her cheeks colored. But she kept her chin raised. She also didn't deny the suggestion.

She glanced at the billowing mist and then at him. "I know you didn't come here just to question Kendrew about black-painted longships. Everyone knows we aren't a seafaring clan. You had another reason. I'd like to hear it." She stepped closer, her breasts brushing his chest, the intimate touch making him want her desperately.

Before he could answer, there was a rustling at the hem of her skirts. A low *grrr* as her little dog, Hercules, crept from behind her skirts. A tiny beast with four white legs and a brown saddle and face, Hercules had floppy ears and seemed to enjoy baring his teeth. Yet despite his grumbles, he wagged his tail.

"Hercules." Alasdair looked down at him, glad for the distraction.

He did love dogs.

And he'd never met one who didn't take to him. He also wouldn't mind keeping this one occupied. Dogs were known to be protective and Hercules clearly loved his mistress. Alasdair was also fond of her. And just now, he didn't need interference from her four-legged companion.

Clearly of a different mind, Hercules lifted a lip and growled again.

"See here, laddie." Alasdair dipped into his leather belt pouch for a suitably small twist of dried meat. "I have something for you." Producing the treat, he reached down, extending the tidbit from his fingers.

"You shouldn't feed him." Marjory gripped his wrist, stopping him. "He—"

"He's a fine wee lad." Alasdair shook free, eyeing the dog.

"He is himself." Marjory frowned at her pet. "He just isn't used to those he doesn't know."

Alasdair tried to waylay her fears. "He has no reason to fear me. I love dogs and they aye know it."

Hercules took two steps toward him, indicating that

was so. Marjory stood as still as a pillar, watching him. She'd raised a hand to her lips, uncomfortable. Alasdair dropped to one knee, hoping to ease her mind as he again offered Hercules the twist of dried meat.

The dog came closer, pausing a few feet from Alasdair. Hercules kept his gaze on the treat, his expression intent. His tail wagged slowly.

Alasdair smiled, triumphant.

"Hercules!" Marjory cried out the instant Hercules shot forward, ignoring the treat to make a sailing leap for Alasdair's ankle.

The bite was swift. It stung more than it hurt. And it did draw blood.

"Oh no!" Marjory lunged for Hercules, but her fingers closed on air as he bolted away to dash in a circle around the little room.

"It's nothing," Alasdair lied, feeling as if someone was jabbing his lower leg with a fistful of fiery, razor-sharp needles.

Worse, Hercules streaked around Alasdair's still-kneeling form and attacked his other ankle. And this time he wasn't snapping.

The dog's cocked leg warned of a more devious intent.

"Whoa, laddie!" Alasdair shot to his feet, colliding with Marjory as she dashed forward to grab Hercules. But instead of capturing her pet, her arms slid around Alasdair. They knocked together, Hercules flitting away with the twist of beef that had fallen from Alasdair's fingers.

Alasdair gripped Marjory's waist, steadying her. "Are you hurt?"

"No..." She glanced down, her eyes widening at the blood on his ankle. "But Hercules bit—"

"He was playing." Alasdair excused the wee beastie. "It's a scratch, no more."

Marjory didn't look convinced. "You are generous."

"Sweet lass, you dinnae want to know what I am." His gaze slid downward to her breasts. Lush and ripe, her silken curves promised forbidden delights. Desire speared him, buzzing in his head, roaring through his veins. "Nor should you learn what you do to me."

She eyed him up and down, lifted her hands to cup his face. "And if I say otherwise?"

"You'd be asking for trouble." Alasdair already had his own with all thought of duty, honor, and loyalty vanquished by her sparkling blue eyes and the way her shining hair spilled about her shoulders. How her tightly cut bodice shaped her breasts, wicked and scintillating. Sensual, womanly heat poured off her, rousing him so thoroughly even his conscience fled. "A man is only so strong, lass."

She leaned in closer. "Is that why you're here? To prove your strength, to—"

"You heard why I came." Alasdair could hardly breathe, his heart thudding. Then she blinked and her eyes reminded him of his other reason.

He'd almost forgotten.

"There was another reason, aye." He stepped back and reached inside his plaid, retrieving a golden ring. He held it out to her, its sapphire glittering in the dimness. "I believe this is yours?"

"My ring..." Her brows lifted and she took the ring, closing her fingers around it, pressing it to her heart. "It was my grandmother's and her grandmother's before her. A family treasure. Where did you find it?" Her voice was thick, her fingers shaking as she slipped on the ring. "I lost it the day of the harvest fair." She looked up, seeming nervous. "How did you—"

"I took it from the man who had it." A muscle twitched in Alasdair's jaw, remembering. He burned to question her—he'd seen the Viking Groat leave the joy women's encampment—but her face had softened and when she turned her huge blue eyes on him he couldn't upset her. Seeing her so vulnerable did worse things to him than his desire for her. His chest tightened and a fierce wave of protectiveness swept him. That, a strange, unsettling ache inside him that he wasn't about to consider too deeply.

Whatever it was pained his heart.

And that bode ill.

"He was a wayfarer." He gave her the closest answer he dared to truth: that he'd tracked the man after he'd left her that day at the harvest fair. "A Norseman. I found him by a burn, admiring the ring. When I recognized it as yours, I questioned him. He claimed he found the ring in the wood, near the tents of the joy women." Alasdair didn't say they'd fought. That a slice of the Viking's ear had repaid him for taking what wasn't his. Alasdair didn't believe the man's tale, suspected he possessed nimble fingers for all his brute size. That he'd bumped against Marjory at the fair, slipping the ring from her finger, her unaware.

"I don't know where I lost it." She looked down, rubbed her thumb over the ring. Then somehow her hands were on his shoulders. "Now, having you return it, the ring will mean even more to me."

"Norn..." Alasdair tensed when she wrapped her arms around his neck, leaning into him. She held tightly and he swept his own hands around and down her back, gripping her hips, pulling her closer.

He couldn't stop himself. She felt so soft and warm against him that he couldn't release her. The silk of her hair teased his chin, almost maddening him. She smelled of spring meadows, the scent going straight to his head. Clean, light, and thoroughly feminine, the fragrance beguiled him as no other woman's scent had ever done.

He tried not to breathe and failed miserably.

She curled her fingers into his plaid, her touch only worsening the heat coursing through him. His desire flared, swift and demanding. He kissed her hair, then her temple, his lips skimming her cheek. Her mouth beckoned, urging him on with a fierceness he couldn't deny. Not now, with her so soft and pliant in his arms. He took one of her hands, pressing her fingers to his lips.

"Have a care with the ring, then." He kissed the bauble's stone and lightly nipped her fingers. "One should ne'er be parted with something so valuable."

Would she know he meant more?

That it would break him to walk away from her? That he no longer believed he could?

Touching her—letting her touch him—had been a mistake. They'd crossed a threshold and the rapid beating of his heart warned there'd be no going back. So he turned her hand over, kissing her palm and then lighting kisses across the soft skin of her wrist.

Tasting her, losing himself.

Outside the little room, the wind rose, blowing curtains of mist past the entrance. Chill air swept inside, intensifying the smell of cold, wet stone.

Somewhere within the dark, weathered rocks, water dripped.

Alasdair scarce noticed.

His world had slammed to a halt, contracting to hold only Marjory's intense blue gaze, the soft, warm press of her breasts against his chest. Above all, he relished the taste of her skin on the back of his tongue. An intimacy that had him setting as hard as granite.

He wanted more, needed all of her.

His entire body tightened, his pulse drumming in his ears. Tendrils of mist swirled into the room, curling across the floor and sliding up the walls so that the air shimmered around them, taking on a strange ethereal quality. Awareness flashed through him, igniting his senses. Every inch of him wakened, coming alive as never before.

She shone here, in the tiny stone-walled room, her light brighter than the stars. The mist's luminosity paled before her. And he was drawn to more than her body's curves and the glow of her eyes, the temptations hidden beneath her gown. Her heart and soul called to him, stripping away his resistance, branding him as her own. She intrigued, enchanted, and delighted him, as if the day's sun fell on her alone.

He admired her pride and spirit, her deep love of the wild, rugged territory she called home.

Her passion...

He started to speak, to tell her they must leave here, but she touched her hands to his lips, stopping him. "The love of a man and woman is worth more than any gold." She rested her hand against his cheek, her touch so warm. "True loss is to have one's desire so near and yet—"

"Damnation, Norn. Dinnae speak so." He splayed his hands over her bottom, digging his fingers into the plump flesh, pulling her closer until she couldn't doubt what she did to him. "You will bring me to my knees."

"I will do what I must." She held his gaze. "And not a whit of it is damning. To me, this is a wonder."

She leaned up on her toes, nipped his lower lip, and then kissed him lightly.

"Nae, it is madness." Alasdair knew that well. He also went rigid, sensation racing over his skin, heating his blood, making him want to devour her.

She shook her head. "Madness is to deny one's heart. The pity is when we turn from what could be, refusing pleasures offered. The comfort of shared bliss, even stolen—"

"Say no more, lest you push me too far." He already verged on his limits. Her hips and breasts moved against him, tantalizing him, hurtling him into a fire he couldn't begin to douse. Flames already scorched him.

He frowned, certain she knew it.

Saints help him, but he could live a thousand years and he'd still desire only her.

Was this what love did to a man? Could his feelings for her be more than mere lust?

Deep inside, he knew that was so.

She was watching him closely. She didn't blink, only looked at him with her remarkable blue eyes, breaking his heart and stealing his soul.

He silently cursed her brother, damned his entire rash, hotheaded race.

He railed at himself more. He'd lost the battle by allowing her to drag him into such a close, hidden space. It would've been so easy to shake off her grip, continue down the stair, putting her from his mind.

He bit back a harsh laugh.

Truth was he'd follow her to the ends of the earth. To

hell and back, even the Norsemen's dread Niflheim. He'd leaped at the chance to enter this hidey-hole with her. Now that they were here...

He brushed the hair back from her face, the strands so smooth beneath his fingers. He let his gaze sweep over her, hungrily.

Her blood-red cloak had fallen completely open and her breasts touched his chest. Her nipples were hard, twin crested peaks that thrust against him, taunting and tormenting. Equally bad, her skirts clung to her, revealing the shapeliness of her thighs and hinting at the sweetness of her woman's mound, the rich femininity he ached to explore.

More than that, he wanted to claim her.

Sweep her into his arms, lower her to the bare stone floor, and then push deep inside her, sink into her hot, silken heat.

"We should leave here." His voice was strained, proving he didn't want to go anywhere. Yet he had to give her this chance, needed surety before...

He drew a sharp breath. "It may already be too late."

He knew it was.

She smiled, looking almost victorious.

"I know you want me." She reached to stroke his face and then stepped back, letting her cloak slide from her shoulders. It pooled around her ankles, a sea of deep, shimmering red. "I've known your kiss and can see your desire. Truth is"—her gaze dipped to his groin—"I have felt it."

He couldn't deny it, his arousal more than apparent.

"Walk away if I'm mistaken." She untied her bodice laces so that her gown slithered down her body, joining her cloak on the cold stone floor.

She stood before him near naked, her undershift clinging to her curves. The wispy material was thin and almost translucent, revealing far more than it hid, as if crafted by a fiendish hand. Someone who understood a man's desires and wished to exploit them.

Alasdair set his jaw, hoping he didn't begin to sweat.

Marjory's eyes smoldered, an unspoken challenge.

"Damn you ..." He stared at her, his heart hammering. "Have mercy, lass. Cover yourself."

She didn't move. "So I did err?"

"Och, nae." He pulled her to him then, drawing her hard against his chest as he slashed his mouth over hers, kissing her with a ferocity that astounded him. He gripped the back of her neck, thrusting his fingers into her hair, holding her in place as he plundered her lips. He swept his other arm around her, locking them together.

She clung to him, wrapping her arms around him, running her hands up and down his back as she parted her lips beneath his onslaught, returning his kiss with equal fervor. She even angled her head, allowing him to deepen the kiss, welcoming the glide of his tongue against hers, the sweet intimacy of the warm breath they shared.

"Norn..." His voice was deep, ragged. "I didn't want this."

But he couldn't stop, knew he could never get enough of her. He brought his hand down over the wisp of cloth covering her breasts, his pulse racing at the feel of her soft feminine warmth, her tightly puckered nipples. She took his breath, maddening him so that all he knew was that he had to possess her, make her his.

They kissed hungrily, their bodies sealed together, their hands sliding everywhere, claiming and exploring, the world around them forgotten.

Need and want crashed through Alasdair, the pleasure

like a flood tide. He pressed his knee between her thighs, nearly spilling when she gasped and rubbed against his leg, her passion as great as his own.

"Oh, dear..." She shivered when he tore his lips from hers to kiss his way down her neck and then on to her breasts. He closed his mouth over her nipple, sucking gently, licking her flesh.

"I have wanted you, Norn, have aye desired you." His voice was ragged, his breath hard and fast. "I would make you mine, here, now."

Somewhere in the distance thunder rolled, loud and booming.

Alasdair paid no heed.

Nought and its soaring Mackintosh peaks and the whole of the world could crumble to dust. He wouldn't care. Nothing mattered except claiming Marjory's lips again, kissing her hard and furiously. He tightened an arm around her, crushing her to him as he ran his hand over her breasts, letting his fingers brush her nipples. She melted against him, supple and intoxicating. Need for her flared, hot and demanding. His manhood throbbed, rigid and aching.

Thunder cracked again, the cold wind howling.

Alasdair ignored the storm's wrath.

Marjory swayed against him. "I knew it would be this way between us." Her voice was husky, her eyes dark with passion. She twined her fingers in his hair, broke their kiss to press her head against his chest as if to hear the fierce beating of his heart. "I—"

"You were unwise to follow me, but I'm glad you did." He captured her wrists, lifting her arms over her head and backing her against the wall. "I want you, lass. I dinnae think I can e'er have enough—"

The loudest burst of thunder yet cut him off, the boom accompanied by the *hiss* of a boar spear speeding into the room, cracking against the wall mere inches from where they stood.

"Thor's bleeding eyebrows!" Kendrew burst in on them, his broad chest heaving. "You'd be skewered if you weren't holding my sister." He grabbed his war ax, tossing the heavy-bladed weapon from hand to hand. "Release her and fight, the King's peace be damned!"

"Kendrew!" Marjory stared at her brother.

Alasdair stepped round in front of her, shielding her.

He glared at Kendrew. "Only you would throw a spear with a woman anywhere near," he snarled, a red haze blurring his vision as Lady Isobel rushed forward, pulling Marjory into a corner of the room.

Alasdair drew his sword, Kendrew already charging him, ax swinging. Alasdair raised Mist-Chaser and lunged, ready. Outside, the wind shrieked, and across the room, Marjory and Isobel cried for them to stop, but neither man paid any heed. Sword and ax clashed hard, the force of the first blow racing up Alasdair's arm.

One of them would die.

The thought only made Alasdair's blood boil the more. He also swung his sword with greater purpose. He wasn't leaving this world. Not after coming so close to claiming his heart's desire.

He'd do whatever he could to keep her safe, protect her good name.

Even if doing so would make her despise him.

Chapter Eight

❦

I warned you no' to touch her!" Kendrew tossed aside his ax and charged Alasdair, hurtling him against the stone wall. In the small room, brute strength served better than unwieldy steel. "No threats now, brine drinker! You'll ne'er sully—"

"She's no' sullied," Alasdair snarled, dropping his sword to grab Kendrew's arms. They grappled, banging into a corner. "I didnae—"

Kendrew roared. "You say she offered—"

"She is innocent." Alasdair tightened his grip, fury almost choking him. "I'll cut the tongue from any man who says otherwise."

Kendrew jerked free, his face darkening. "You admit forcing yourself on her?"

"I admit kissing her, touching her." Alasdair caught a glimpse of Marjory, the horror on her face, her hair tumbling free, bright as the sun. For a beat, he felt as if he'd run into a wall, his chest squeezing, the breath leaving him. He turned back on Kendrew, spoke terse. "By God's grace, I'll no' deny what happened, that I wanted her."

"You tore the clothes from her!" In a blur of speed, Kendrew snatched Marjory's gown off the floor, balling it in his fist before he flung it aside. "I should pare the skin off you, inch by bluidy inch."

"You can try." Alasdair's dare echoed in the small stone-lined room.

Kendrew's eyes narrowed, his Thor's hammer pendant shining in the dimness. "No man defiles my sister."

"I wouldn't dare."

"You did!"

They started to circle each other, both in fighting stances. Each man flexed strong fingers, their gazes locked. Somewhere Hercules barked madly and the men crowding the door opening shouted encouragement. Warriors of each clan cheered on their hero, raucous, eager for blood. In the corner, Marjory and Isobel clung to each other, yelling for them to stop, their cries drowned out by the ruckus, the howling wind, and the distant boom of thunder.

Alasdair kept his attention on Kendrew. Raising a clenched fist, he stepped nearer, still circling but closing the space between them.

Kendrew did the same. "Have you e'er seen a man who's been skinned?" He gripped the dirk hilt rising from beneath his belt, came closer. "The sight would make you think twice before soiling a lady."

"He didn't," Marjory cried out, starting forward. Isobel grabbed her arm, pulling her back into the corner. "It wasn't his fault. I—"

"She tempted me, aye." Alasdair lifted his voice over hers, loathing what he was about to say. "Any half-fetching female would've done." Anger seethed in him at the lie, the red haze swirling round him intensifying, almost alive. Like Kendrew, he reached for the dagger at his belt, leaning in so they stood beard to beard. "I was away nigh a year, without a woman all that time." He growled the words, knowing he had to speak them to spare Norn's name. "Will you deny the urges that rise in a man? Could you go without ease so long?"

"I'd have taken a lusty kitchen wench."

"And so I should've." Alasdair stepped back, chest heaving, bile in his throat.

He could feel Norn's stare without looking at her, knew he'd cut her to the quick. But now men would speak angrily of him, putting all blame on his shoulders. No one would accuse her of scandalous behavior, though some might look on her with pity. Unless...

With lightning speed, he whipped out his dirk, closing his hand tightly around the blade as he thrust his fist toward Kendrew. "I'll wed your sister, Mackintosh. We can end this here and now."

"No' that way, we won't." Kendrew ignored his outstretched hand.

Alasdair cast his dirk aside and held up his hand, displaying his bloodied palm. "Come, man"—he glanced at Marjory and Isobel—"there was a time you'd have sworn ne'er to marry a Cameron. And I ne'er believed I'd offer for a Mackintosh."

Kendrew tightened his lips, saying nothing.

Alasdair extended his dripping fingers. "A blood vow to seal the betrothal, our continued peace. We'll agree—"

"We agree you're a bastard!" Kendrew knocked away his arm and drew his own dirk, jabbing the tip at Alasdair's belly. "My sister willnae be a peace token. And the only piece of you I want is your guts spilling to the floor. Forget a truce and fight!"

Tossing aside his dagger, he lunged, hurling himself at Alasdair. They crashed together, the impact slamming them into the wall. They grappled fiercely, beating each other with their clenched fists until they toppled to the stone floor. Somewhere, women's screams rose and Hercules's shrill barks were even louder as the little dog leaped into the fray, jumping and snapping at them both.

When Hercules thrust his furry face between them, almost taking a blow, Alasdair pushed to his feet, hauling Kendrew with him. "I'll no' fight with a dog darting—"

"Then out here." Kendrew smashed his fist into Alasdair's jaw, knocking him through the door opening and into the whirling mist of the cliff stair.

Reeling, hot blood welling in his mouth, Alasdair almost plunged down the steps. He righted himself at the last moment and flew at Kendrew, hammering him with his own fists until he felt Kendrew's nose crunch beneath a wild, anger-driven blow. Blood sheeted down Kendrew's chin, but his eyes lit, as if he was enjoying himself.

Hair wild and still on his feet, he grinned, proving it. "Your blows faze me less than chaff in the wind." He glanced round at the men lining the steep steps, all armed with swords and axes. "Can you do no' better?"

Some of the men snickered. Others looked back at him hard-faced as they reached for their sword hilts, their grips white knuckled.

Warriors of both clans, they stepped back, making

room on the narrow stair, waiting. At a nod from either chief, chaos would erupt.

More blood would spill, men would die.

Cold wind gusted across the steps, the blowing mist blurring edges. Only Nought's high walls, the orange haze of torches, and the shadowy forms of men could be seen. But Alasdair knew a sheer drop loomed near. One false move, and he and Kendrew would plunge to their deaths. Their ends decided not by steel but by Nought's jagged rocks.

He didn't care.

He did resent Kendrew's taunt. Rolling his shoulders, he took a deep breath of the cold air, ready to knock Kendrew's smugness out of him.

"I'm waiting, briny." Kendrew raised his arms, cracking his knuckles.

"No need." Alasdair drove his fist into Kendrew's ribs, rained blows on his head when he grunted and bent double under the onslaught.

"No' good enough," Kendrew huffed, straightening to hurl himself at Alasdair. He started punching him with equal might and they wrestled, lurching ever closer to the stair's abrupt drop-off.

One of them—Alasdair wasn't sure who—lost his footing and they toppled over, slamming against the hard and slippery steps. But they rolled together, not missing a blow as they hammered each other with clenched fists. Men leaped aside, making room and stamping their feet, roaring encouragement to their leader.

"Stop them!" Marjory's voice rose above the din. "They'll kill each other."

"Enough!" Isobel called out, equally loud.

And then both ladies were upon them, grabbing at arms and plaids, dragging them apart. When their efforts failed, they dropped to their knees, beating on them with their own fists.

"Odin's balls!" Kendrew jumped up, gripping his wife by the elbows, lifting her with him. "If I'd known you'd no' let a man fight, I'd have ne'er—"

"You've both fought enough." Isobel shook herself free, dusted her skirts. "This must end here and now."

"Indeed, lady." Alasdair stood, reaching to help Marjory, but she pushed up on her own. Ignoring him, she clutched her blood-red cloak about her. Alasdair stiffened, aware that she was near naked beneath it. He turned to Isobel, shoved a hand through his hair. "Your husband and I will settle this another day."

"I think not." Marjory stepped forward, her chin raised. Wind whipped her hair and high color stained her cheeks. Her eyes were narrowed, cold shards of deepest blue. "Killing each other will serve naught. And"—her gaze flicked between the two men—"I'll not have you fighting over me."

Kendrew's brows snapped together. "You'll no' be wedding him." He flashed an angry look at Alasdair. "I may no' have found a husband for you yet, but I'll be putting together a new list soon. MacDonald willnae be on it. He—"

"I've no wish to wed a Norse noble." Marjory's tone was as chilled as the wind. "Nor will I marry Alasdair," she added, her voice even icier. "No harm came to me this day and I prefer to forget what did happen."

"Norn . . ." Alasdair started toward her, but she raised a hand, shaking her head.

He strode forward anyway, catching her by the waist, holding her gaze. "My offer stands, lass. It was given—"

"I know why you made it." She stiffened in his grasp, her eyes narrowing even more. "I bid you to leave."

Alasdair looked at her, wanting to say so much. Yet he wouldn't cause her embarrassment before his men or, worse, her own kinsmen.

He did release her, hard as it was.

Even surrounded by men as they were, Isobel's hovering presence, and Hercules racing around them, yipping shrilly, he wanted her badly. He could still taste her kisses, feel the silky-smooth warmth of her bared skin beneath his fingers. His awareness of her was painful, a physical ache far worse than the cuts and bruises her brother had given him.

He clenched his hands at his sides, ignoring the dull throbbing, a need that stemmed from his heart as much as his loins.

He was also sure he'd grab her and carry her away, her brother and their truce be damned, if he didn't turn and leave anon.

So he straightened, flung his plaid back over his shoulder. He ignored the blood trickling down the side of his face from a cut in his temple. With luck no one would guess his labored breath and heavy scowl came from wanting her so fiercely. The rage, and hot desire, that ate at him like a living, scorching flame.

Marjory certainly didn't know.

Never had she looked at him with such loathing. "It grows late. I asked you to go."

"As you wish, my lady." He made a slight bow, not taking his gaze off her.

"I do." Her voice was clipped.

Beside her, Isobel frowned, bent to scoop Hercules into her arms.

Kendrew grinned, dragged the back of his arm over his bloodied beard. "You heard her." He glanced at Alasdair's men, jerked his head at the downward steps. "Be gone before I crave more blood."

"We'll meet again, Mackintosh." Alasdair turned to his foe, nodding curtly before accepting his discarded sword and dirk from one of his men.

"Ladies." He looked again at them both, letting his gaze linger on Marjory, glancing briefly at her sapphire ring. He knew there was more to the tale of her losing it. The thought of her being accosted by anyone, even a simpleminded, fair-going thief, made his blood boil.

Stepping past Kendrew, he leaned close to her, spoke with all the command of his chiefly status. "You are aye welcome at Blackshore. Remember that."

"I shall not forget anything that transpired this day." She spoke coolly, her face now void of emotion.

Isobel started to say something, but Marjory took her wrist and pulled her away before she could. In a blink, they were gone, the massed bulk of the Mackintosh guards blocking their retreat from view.

"You've lost her." Kendrew's taunt was muffled by the edge of plaid he was using to swipe at his bleeding nose. "She doesn't want you. And I'm tired of brine tainting fine Nought air."

"A shame, for it's a reek hard to banish." Alasdair smiled and stepped forward to grip Kendrew's arm. "Dinnae say you weren't warned."

Then he and his men left swiftly, no further words spoken, the mist swirling round them.

*   *   *

"Did you hear him?" Marjory shot an annoyed glance at Isobel as they descended the dimly lit steps from Nought's great hall to the kitchens and cellars. Unlike the turnpike stairs elsewhere in the stronghold, this one was long, narrow, and steep. Full of gloom and shadow, despite air slits cut into the walls and the placement of iron-bracketed torches at regular intervals.

Just now, the darkness suited Marjory.

Spears of light from the kitchen fire cast an orange glow across the foot of the stairs, the sight always making her think of the entrance to hell. Even the tantalizing cooking smells didn't chase that impression. The fire's roar also sounded ominous, like grumbles of angry demons.

She wouldn't mind joining their discourse.

She'd sooner suffer suchlike than be trapped at the high table listening to Kendrew's booming account of his fight with Alasdair. It was bad enough that his men's rumbling voices and Kendrew's words echoed in the stairwell.

Alasdair's words also followed her, sluicing over her like icy water. The shock had been as startling. Stunned fury had taken her breath. Now she just felt ill. Her eyes stung and her throat was tight, burning.

She would not cry.

She *was* angry.

"Did I hear who?" Isobel stopped on the steps, looking at her. "Kendrew? Saying he craved more blood? He was going on like a beast—"

"Not my brother." Marjory met her friend's gaze. "Alasdair." She spoke his name quickly, not liking the intimacy on her tongue. The memory of how she'd clung to him, returning his kisses, wanting so much more. "He said he'd

been alone too long, without a woman's ease. And that"—
she bristled, a stab of jealousy piercing her heart—"any
half-fetching female would've drawn his attentions."

"His kisses?" Isobel lifted a brow.

Marjory took a breath, her ire rising. "He did more
than kiss me, as everyone saw." She pulled her cloak
tighter about her shoulders, painfully aware of her hast-
ily donned gown, her mussed and windblown hair. "To
think I believed I'd seduced him. That he'd succumbed
because he wanted me, desiring me above all others. That
he might—"

"Love you?" Isobel's dark eyes glittered in the dimness. "I dare say he does. Or that he's very near to doing
so if he doesn't already."

"And I say you're mistaken." Marjory glanced down
the steps. They were almost at the bottom. She didn't
want anyone to hear them. "He doesn't love me or any
woman." She brushed her hair off her face, frowning. It
was so hard to keep her voice low. "Lust drove him to kiss
me. The base urges that plague all men."

"Pah!" Isobel took her arm, urging her into the smoky
warmth of the vaulted kitchens. Several serving lads
glanced their way, acknowledging them before returning to their work at a heavy oak table in the center of the
room.

"I'd tell you true, Norn." Isobel paused as a light pat-
ter of claws announced that Hercules had caught up with
them. She looked down, smiling at the little dog before
turning back to Marjory.

"I've seen Alasdair look at you." She led Marjory
along the wall, toward an archway in a quiet corner of the
kitchen. "Just now, after the fight, his gaze was so intense,

so heated, I'm surprised he didn't scorch you. He was caught in your spell, a man torn by passion."

"He did singe me." Marjory could still feel his stare. It lingered like bold, strong hands on her skin, exploring her secrets, making her shiver even now. Furious that was so, she waited as a gust of wind whistled past one of the tall, narrow windows. "And I wanted to sear him, entice and seduce him. I was prepared for anything. Then Hercules bit his ankle and"—she glanced at her dog, remembering—"I grabbed for Hercules just when Alasdair also bent. We bumped heads as we straightened and then—"

"He kissed you." Isobel spoke softly, glancing again at the lads cutting onions. She also looked to the far side of the kitchens where Cook stood before the huge double hearth, stirring a delicious-smelling meat broth. "For truth, I am sorry Kendrew spoiled such an opportunity. One of his men noticed the open door to the secret passage.

"You couldn't have closed it securely because Gronk and a few of the other dogs were sniffing about behind the tapestry that hides the ruined stair." She switched her gaze from Cook back to Marjory. "Kendrew saw the dogs and guessed what you'd done."

"He would." Marjory's head was beginning to pound. She glanced at her hand, hoping he wouldn't have noticed her ring had gone missing a short while.

She wore it always.

She rubbed her thumb over the ring's gleaming blue stone, again feeling Alasdair close his fingers over hers, warning her to take care.

He spoke with a deep resonance, rich tones that stirred incredible longing. She wanted to hear him again. Relive how she'd felt when he'd leaned near, his gaze locking with hers. The delicious shivers his voice sent flowing through her, melting her.

She frowned, curled her fingers into the soft folds of her cloak to keep from glancing at the ring again, remembering and aching.

She did step around Isobel to open the door to Nought's walled kitchen gardens. Isobel followed her outside, closing the door behind them. She took Marjory's wrist, lifting her hand to peer at the sapphire ring.

"Do you think Alasdair believed you lost the ring at the fair?" Isobel's gaze was sharp. "Or that he accepted Groat's tale of finding it in the wood?"

Marjory slipped her hand from Isobel's grip. "At the time, I did think something bothered him. Now..." She flicked at her sleeve, resenting the unpleasant tightness coiling in her chest. She'd been prepared to risk everything, do anything to win his heart.

She'd trusted he felt the same.

"Everyone knows what was irritating him." She looked at Isobel, unable to keep the bitterness from her voice. "His manly needs, as he plainly said."

Isobel tsked. "You are being unfair."

Marjory felt a bump against her leg. She bent, reaching down to pet Hercules as he leaned into her, making small rumbling noises. He understood her vexation and sympathized even if Isobel didn't.

"I have had my eyes opened." Marjory straightened. "Though I'll admit it hurts to see I allowed my heart to choose unwisely. I'd so hoped I wouldn't break our pact. My confidence rose after Kendrew fell so hard for you. Who would've believed he'd abandon his wild ways and wed you, a lady? He'd sworn never to touch a woman of gentle birth. Then you came to our Midsummer Revels and—"

"He couldn't help himself." Isobel smiled, her face softening. "Just as Alasdair couldn't resist kissing you in the old guardroom—"

"He seized advantage, aye." Marjory's chest squeezed again, her annoyance making it hard to breathe.

"That wasn't the way of it. He was overcome by desire at being alone with you."

"Humph." The throbbing in Marjory's head worsened.

So did Isobel's smile. "Denying the truth won't change it."

"Nor will twisting what happened into something it wasn't." Marjory started down the path through Nought's walled kitchen gardens. "Alasdair kissed me because it's been ages since he's sought his ease with a woman," she declared, taking a deep breath of the cold, herb-scented air.

Isobel walked beside her, Hercules trailing along.

"Alasdair is keeping himself for you." Isobel glanced back at the closed garden door behind them. She lowered her voice. "No other woman interests him. Anyone can see that. He needs—"

"All men have needs and he hasn't been tending his." Marjory squelched the dash of hope stirred by Isobel's words. "He is a well-lusted man. His behavior had nothing to do with me."

Isobel slanted a glance at her, her eyes twinkling. "Say you."

"I do." Marjory looked away, not wanting to recall how she'd felt pressed so intimately to Alasdair. Their bodies almost seamed together, her breasts crushed against his hard-muscled chest. How his hands had gripped her hips, pulling her closer. Or her pulse began to race, the sinuous glides of their tongues as they'd kissed. The hot breath they'd shared, her excitement. She'd melted, desire sweeping her.

Then...

She turned her face into the wind, toward Nought's peaks. Massive and jagged, they soared above the garden walls. Mist still wreathed them, but it'd thinned in places, allowing the mountains' granite to wink in the lowering sun. The rain clouds had moved on, taking the thunder with them. But the wind brought the distant rush of Dreagan Falls, a waterfall hidden deep within Nought's heart.

Marjory straightened her back, squaring her shoulders.

She would've loved to stroll the garden with Alasdair, showing him Nought's beauty as few have ever seen. Instead, she was here with Isobel, following a pebbled path through the well-ordered beds of herbs, onions, and garlic.

The pungency hung in the damp air, along with the scent of wet stone. It was a smell all Nought's own, and that always made her heart beat faster.

Just now, she scarcely noticed.

She couldn't forget how good Alasdair smelled. Almost sinfully wicked, his scent was a heady blend of cold leather and peat smoke, a hint of brisk, clean wind. She'd wanted to breathe him in, drench her senses so she could always feel near him. Now, she only felt bereft.

At the garden well, she turned to face Isobel. "I do not wish to speak of Alasdair. Especially here, so close to the kitchens."

Nearly every wall at Nought had hidden spy and listening holes. So Marjory hooked her arm in Isobel's and led her toward the back of the herb beds.

Nought's stone garden stretched beyond, a sanctuary of flagged paths, polished granite arcades, and benches. A scattering of lovely, reflective ponds set among fanciful groupings of rocks lent tranquility. Created by a past Mackintosh lady who must've loved Nought as dearly as Marjory did, it was one of her favorite places. Hercules also loved the stone garden and Marjory often walked him along the curving paths.

He bolted ahead now, waiting for the women at the gate. New and beautifully crafted of iron, it proudly bore the letters *K* and *I* intertwined inside a heart at the gate's center. The design was Kendrew's and bespoke his devotion to Isobel.

A pity his heart wouldn't expand enough to allow his sister to follow her own dreams.

Of course, now she knew the folly of her hopes.

"I think we should speak of Alasdair." Isobel reached around her to open the gate, stepping aside so Marjory and Hercules could enter the stone garden. "You will see him again anon. You ignite fires inside him. He isn't resistant and stubborn like Kendrew. Nor is he like my brother James. Alasdair—"

"I'm not comparing him to Kendrew or James." Marjory started along the broad flagstone path through artfully placed groupings of large, polished stones. "Indeed, I thought I knew him well. There was such a spark between us when we met." She stopped to draw her cloak tighter. Here, in the open space of the stone garden, the cold wind was biting. "You know how it was. Catriona knows, too.

She was with Alasdair when they came here. I felt almost feverish, my breath catching when I stepped into the hall and saw him." She started walking again, her pace brisk.

"There was an intensity of feeling I'd never before experienced. He consumed me, chasing reason like a swift, flooding tide I couldn't resist. I believed we were meant to be joined." She glanced at Isobel, willing her to understand. "When we made our pact, after the trial by combat, I was sure he was the man I would wed. If he resisted, I trusted I could seduce him."

"You did." Isobel smiled encouragingly.

"Perhaps so"—Isobel looked again toward Nought's peaks—"but with disastrous results."

It'd been the hope of all three women to win their men's hearts. Only so did they believe to end the years of strife between the three clans that called the Glen of Many Legends their own. They'd forged a plan better than any King's writ. Forced amity can be given token acceptance but will shatter at the first ripple of dissent. Peace born of marital and blood bonds can heal all wounds if the hearts involved loved true.

James Cameron was utterly devoted to his wife, Catriona MacDonald, Alasdair's sister.

Kendrew was clearly besotted with Isobel, James's sister.

Only Alasdair proved disinterested in pursuing matters of the heart.

He'd left the glen, vanishing for a year. And he'd returned a different man. No longer the honor-and-duty-bound chieftain Marjory once knew, he'd become a lust-driven rogue who cared only for quenching his manly needs.

Perhaps he'd always been such a blackguard?

Marjory shut her eyes for a moment, listened to the wind racing through the stone garden. Frustration wound inside her, annoyance heating her cheeks.

It didn't help that she'd relished every scandalous touch Alasdair had given her. Their scorching kisses and his hands on her breasts...

Her plans were doomed.

Her heart aching.

"I erred, don't you see?" She glanced at her friend and then went to one of the low-walled reflective pools, watched the wind ripple the shallow water. "Alasdair might be easy to seduce, but he isn't prepared to give his heart to any woman. I was foolish to believe he would fall in love with me."

"You are foolish to doubt him." Isobel joined her at the pool. "He offered to marry you, did he not?"

"What else could he do? Besides, he knew how Kendrew would react. He felt safe offering, hence his bold words." That truth was a knife jab to Marjory's heart. "It would seem our pact might not be completed. Although"—she took a step closer to the pond, nudged its stone rim with her toe—"I am not ready to concede defeat."

"I am glad to hear it." Isobel moved out of the way of Hercules, who was running back and forth along the edge of the pool, barking at his reflection. "All is not yet lost. Kendrew was a much harder man to catch. I also had Catriona aye trying to persuade me to abandon my heart's desire and forget him.

"You"—she turned back to Marjory—"have me encouraging you with Alasdair."

"I know, and I love you for it." Marjory darted a glance

at the path they'd come along, making certain they were still alone. "But even you cannot conjure feelings Alasdair doesn't have. Gorm and Grizel, your clan's dream spinners up on the high moors, could surely work a charm for me. Yet they only guide and nudge, never really interfering in mortal affairs. The great Devorgilla of Doon... Now she'd be one to help me." Marjory couldn't keep the wistful note from her voice. "If I knew how to summon her, I would. She's said to have a heart for ill-starred lovers. She might—"

"The legendary Devorgilla will be away in Kintail or other far-off bounds, aiding those in true need of her help." Isobel smiled. "You don't need her meddling. You must only step over your shadow and not be waylaid by doubt."

"I appreciate your support, truly." Marjory did.

Sadly, there was another reason she'd asked Isobel to accompany her into the stone garden. Something that had nothing to do with Alasdair and that she wished had little to do with her as well.

Unfortunately, she suspected otherwise.

So she rubbed her arms against the cold and fought back a shiver. Then she lifted a hand to touch the smooth amber stones at her throat, knowing that she couldn't deny their portent any longer.

"I'm worried, my friend." She spoke plainly. "When Alasdair said his lookouts reported black-painted longships, my ambers nearly burned my neck. Just like in that horrible dream I had not too long ago. You'll remember, where I—"

"Saw yourself at a Viking ship burial, being led to the dead lord's funerary pyre?" Isobel's brows knit. "How could I forget?"

"I can't either." Marjory shuddered, curled her fingers around the now-cool ambers. "The sensation earlier, in the hall, was the same. I'm certain there's a connection. We both know the ambers are enchanted. They don't lie. They're telling me of coming danger. And"—she spoke in a rush—"I'm sure it isn't Alasdair and his kisses. He only gave a name to the peril. The ambers are warning me of Vikings."

"So it would seem." Isobel began to pace, walking between the reflective pond and a group of tall granite obelisks, each one formed by nature. Dubbed Thor's thunderbolts by the Mackintoshes who'd collected them, the unusual spears of rock had been gathered over time, whenever one broke away from the higher peaks.

"The question is..." Isobel paused beside one of the thunderbolts, resting a hand on the stone's curved edge. "How can a Norse ship threaten you now? Black-painted or otherwise, there aren't any Vikings coming to claim you. That fright is behind us."

"Can we be so sure?" Marjory was anything but.

"Of course, we can." Isobel glanced back at Nought's torch-lit bulk and then looked again at Marjory. "I've spent long nights badgering Kendrew to learn his plans for you. I've used methods I am not proud of, pressing my advantage when he was"—her face colored—"shall we say, a bit vulnerable? Each time, he swore the same truth." Her expression turned serious. "He's exhausted his resources. We heard him say as much to Alasdair when they fought. Every Norse warlord or noble he's offered your hand has declined the match. Groat's overlord was the last. The few remaining are, according to Kendrew's spies, either too old and infirm for you or known to be cruel. Much as we both wish he wouldn't have tried to wed you to a Viking at all, he does love you dearly. He wouldn't see you sent to a dotard who'd dribble in his beard or a coldhearted fiend who'd beat you."

Marjory drew a long breath, knowing her friend spoke true.

Even so...

"We also heard him say he intends to find more suitors." Marjory wasn't sure how long, or how efficiently, she could thwart such attempts.

"Bluster, I'm sure." Isobel made light of her worries.

"I hope you're right." Marjory straightened her back, her gaze on the stark black peaks beyond the stone garden's walls. "Do you truly believe the MacDonald ambers have magical powers?"

She hoped Isobel would say no.

Instead, Isobel looked unhappy. "Catriona believes so, and she will have heard all the tales, having been raised at Blackshore. My experience with them says they speak true. If they heat and tremble against your skin, they're telling of danger."

"Then I must take heed." Marjory stood straighter, not sure from what corner a threat could strike her. She was certain the danger came from the black-painted longships and her frightening dream.

She knew only one way to find answers.

Regrettably, the woman who could help her wasn't at her cottage each time she made the journey to the humble dwelling deep in a birchwood between Nought and the clan's famed dreagan stones.

Still...

"I must speak with Hella." She hoped Kendrew wasn't

sending the widow on pointless errands to keep her from catching the older woman at home.

He'd been angry with Hella ever since the outspoken Norsewoman upbraided him for attempting to foist an unwanted marriage on Marjory.

Twice widowed and happily married both times, Hella lost her first husband when his Norse merchant ship sank in the treacherous waters just offshore from Nought's Dreagan's Claw. It was a tragedy that left few survivors. Most young oarsmen returned to Shetland whence they'd come. Hella was too badly injured to make the journey home to that far northern isle. She'd stayed on at Nought, eventually falling in love with the Mackintosh warrior who'd pulled her from the surf. The pair married, enjoying many good years until her husband succumbed to a fever.

Rather than return to Shetland, Hella remained at Nought, the home she'd come to love as her own.

She also loved Marjory, treating her as the daughter she never had.

Of late, Kendrew scolded that Hella was stirring discontent in the clan. Almost as if he knew that Hella...

"Kendrew doesn't trust Hella." Isobel spoke Marjory's mind. "He suspects she had something to do with a few of the declines for your hand."

"She carried only a few of my messages to Norse couriers when I was unable to slip past Kendrew's nose." Marjory looked at the pool's black-glistening water. "My brother has men who'd die for him in battle. He cannot blame Hella for standing with me."

"He shouldn't, but he does."

"After I speak with Hella, I'll make certain she has

enough peat and victuals to allow her to stay away from
Nought until Kendrew is in a better mood." She'd also be
sure several of the guards loyal to her watched over the
older woman's cottage.

If the black-painted longships posed a danger, the men
in them would be an even greater threat.

Unlike ships, men could climb steep cliff paths and
find ways through tight mountain passes. A remote
thatched cottage wouldn't protect a lone woman if a war
band of rough-hewn men happened upon her.

Hella was still an attractive woman.

Tall, blond, and strong, she could've been long remar-
ried to any of the Mackintoshes' older fighters, if she'd
wished such attentions.

She chose to live alone in her cottage.

"And you?" Isobel sounded concerned. "Will you
heed the ambers' warning?"

"I will if Hella gives me the answer I'm expecting."

"And what is that?"

Marjory hesitated only a moment. Isobel knew every
detail of the dream. "I want to know if there are Saracen women in Norway. If so, if she recognizes the names
from my dream."

"And if she does?" Isobel made the sign against evil.

Marjory gave her a reassuring smile. "I'll be forewarned."

Chapter Nine

❦

Ne'er have you made a greater arse of yourself."

Alasdair considered ignoring his cousin Ewan's remark. Having ridden away from Nought at speed, they were now crossing Mackintosh territory's higher ridges, making for their own Blackshore Castle in the south. A cold north wind accompanied them through the rocky, inhospitable terrain. Sadly, for all the wind's strength, it didn't blow powerfully enough to carry away Ewan's quip. Alasdair clearly heard the amusement in the younger man's voice.

So he drew rein and turned in his saddle, fixing the lad with a long, hard look. "Be glad MacDonalds aren't led by a feeble dotard, afraid to bloody his fists. I didnae do so poorly that Kendrew's bones willnae be aching this night. Heed that well and know you'll be less a tongue if you say another word."

To Alasdair's annoyance, Ewan grinned. "Did you see Kendrew's nose?" He glanced round at the other men, chuckling. "It'll be bigger than his ax blade come morning. And you look—"

"I have a wee scrape, no more." Alasdair knew he carried an egg-size swelling at his temple. His head hurt worse than if he'd downed a barrel of bad wine. But he welcomed the throbbing pain.

It took his mind off what really weighed on him.

Marjory.

They were a good distance from Castle Nought. Even the ancient cairns known as the dreagan stones were now well behind them. Yet Marjory continued to torment him. He'd almost believe she'd bewitched him. He could still feel her silky hair, the smooth warmth of her breasts, so full, round, and tempting. The taste of her lips and how she'd welcomed the thrust of his tongue. The frustrating knowledge that if they hadn't been disturbed...

He scowled, aching to settle his mouth over hers now.

More than that, he wanted to take back the words he'd said to her. Hoped she'd known why he'd done so. Regrettably, her face as she'd bid him to leave left no doubt that she'd not grasped his intent.

In that regard, Ewan was right.

He had been an arse.

But he was sure he was right about Kendrew. The bastard had to have something to do with the black-painted longboats seen off Blackshore's coast.

Alasdair didn't trust him past the end of his sword.

"So when will you claim Lady Marjory?" Ewan leaned over and punched his arm, his smile not slipping. "We all ken you want her."

Alasdair glared at him. "I want many things. One is for you to stop blethering."

"Dinnae care for the truth, eh?" Ewan straightened, looking smug. "I'd be for setting the heather ablaze, telling everyone. If I'd lost my heart to such a fine lass as Marjory Mackintosh, that is."

"If I have, it's no one's concern." Alasdair glanced at his other men, annoyed to see they'd also edged nearer. Each man's ears appeared turned his way, flapping like ship sails as they strove to listen.

His ire rising, Alasdair lifted his voice. "What should concern you is the reason we rode to Nought."

"Aye, so you could see Lady Marjory." Ewan looked him in the eye. "We all know it." He waved a hand at the other men. "Will you be denying it?"

"I say you're mad." Alasdair kneed his horse, spurring forward.

Ewan raced after him, catching him swiftly. "I'm no' crazed enough no' to ken that grief will come of the ruckus you caused at Nought." His mirth gone now, Ewan spoke earnestly. "If the King hears, he'll declare our oaths broken. He'll call us hotheaded heathens and send his armies to banish us from our land. They'll come like a tide, making good his threat to ship us to the Isle of Lewis."

"You think I'm no' aware of that?" Alasdair rubbed the back of his neck, frowning. "Kendrew knows it, too. That'll be why he's sent galleys to harass us. He'll have ordered them to provoke us until we sail out in challenge. When the King cries foul, the longships will beat away, ne'er to be seen again. Mackintosh will point the finger at us, ridding himself of a hated foe and"—anger heated Alasdair's nape—"no doubt accepting Blackshore when the crown offers him our lands as a reward. He's a crafty bastard—"

"I dinnae think he has galleys." Ewan's voice held doubt. "Even Lady Marjory said—"

"She'll no' ken what he's about." Alasdair was sure of it. "Like as no', Kendrew doesn't have longships. But he can aye hire a few."

"Ahhh..." Ewan nodded.

"Indeed." Alasdair leaned toward his cousin, heavily aware of their age difference. "There isn't much that cannae be bought for a handful of silver. Galleys and a crew to man them can be had easily."

And he'd fallen for the bait, losing his head.

Putting his clan, and everything he cared about, at risk.

The knowledge rode him in a worse way than Ewan or any of his men could guess. He just wasn't of a mood—yet—to release the fury boiling inside him. He felt too raw. Stripped bare and bleeding, as if someone twice his size and strength had whipped him with a steel-tipped flail, taking whacks until not a shred of resistance remained.

His soul had been dredged, his very heart wrung by the hands of a woman. And if he only lusted after her, as he'd been trying to tell himself, why did he have the worst urge to leap from his horse and smash something?

His cousin's head, for one. Or an inviting slab of hard Nought stone. Anything would do, as long as it stemmed his rage.

Whatever he felt for Norn was slaying him.

Kendrew's blows hadn't fazed him.

He'd enjoyed pummeling the bastard. Warriors who didn't regularly fight grew old and fat, their sword arms useless. Once-sharp wits went dull. When a real battle came along, they were worthless. They'd face their foes as shadows of what they'd been, quickly finding their guts slit, their blood drenching the ground.

In such a light, the scuffle with Kendrew had been a gift.

Now he was primed for battle.

"We'll none of us be going to Lewis." Ewan guided his horse around a spill of broken rock and pebbles. "That island's beyond the edge of the world. Men say it's a dark place with worse cold and mist than the blackest winter here in the Glen of Many Legends. Our men have wives and families at Blackshore." He glanced to the warriors just riding up to them. "They're no' for riling the King and—"

"The King can sleep easily in his royal bed." Alasdair drew rein again and stopped beside a tumbled mass of rock. Even in the slanting sun, the outcrop held an air of menace. Little grew here except stunted hawthorns, heather, and a bit of straggly whin. Circling hawks were the only life they'd seen since reaching the higher ridges.

Looking round, Alasdair resisted the urge to spit against evil. He turned back to Ewan before he did. "Our people needn't worry," he vowed, determining to make it so. "No MacDonald will give Robert Stewart cause to send his armies marching on us. Though I cannae speak for Mackintosh. He's aye a scoundrel."

"He's a good man to lord it over these godforsaken peaks." Ewan glanced to where the ground fell away from one side of the path, disappearing into a narrow, dark-shadowed ravine that appeared bottomless. "Kendrew is mad to dwell here."

"He would say you diffcrently." Alasdair adjusted his plaid against the knifing wind. "For all his bluster, he does love this place."

"I still say he's crazed. Did you see the bull's skull on the wall of his great hall? The bones hung about as trophies?"

"They were animal bones, not from men." Alasdair secretly appreciated Kendrew's upholding of the old ways. But he kept his expression cleared, not about to let on that he admired aught about their enemy.

"Did you believe Mackintosh about the ships?" one of his men called from the rear of their party.

"I considered it." Alasdair spoke true. "His surprise appeared great, his anger as well. He's also a braggart. If he had such ships, he'd surely boast of them, no' deny their existence."

"Then why are we on this bleeding goat track rather than riding straight to Blackshore?" Another warrior raised his voice, sounding irritated. "If our horses don't slip on these damned rocks and send us plunging to our deaths, the wind will soon blow us away."

Alasdair silently agreed.

A cold, strong wind raced through these high passes, and at each twist in the path, the land grew wilder. The shifting of the stony ground made every step treacherous. His kinsman had put words to what surely nagged them all.

Men died gladly in battle.

No one went happily to his grave because of a fool's errand.

This was anything but.

So Alasdair swung his horse around to face his men. He understood their annoyance. They'd been riding two abreast for the last hour, following a steep, rough path through the worst of Nought's most savage heights. The air was thin here, the cold bone-piercing.

There was also rain on the wind, like as not sleet.

Alasdair sat straighter in his saddle, hoping he hadn't brought his men here in vain.

The looks on their faces said they saw it that way.

So he took a breath, cleared his throat. "Why do you think we brought along spears only to leave them hidden near the dreagan stones while we called at Castle Nought?" He lifted his voice so every man could hear him. "We did so because even if those two black-painted longships don't belong to the Mackintoshes, they could've been hired by Kendrew. Mercenaries paid in coin to harry our coast and provoke a sea fight with us. That, my friends, is what I believe. And"—he patted the long, steel-tipped spear tied to his saddle—"what place along this coast offers mooring so hemmed by sheer-sided cliffs that the land presents an impassable barrier? The ideal spot to strike a foothold if a shipmaster wished to appear and disappear at will?"

He looked hard at each warrior. "Think, men, and tell me."

"Drangar's Point offers many hidden caves and little-used coves." Angus, a heavily built man with a bold, square face, surveyed the towering rock faces pressing so close to them. "We needn't scour this arse-end of Nought to find a hidey-hole for ships no' wanting to be seen."

"Aye, we must." Alasdair disagreed. "Kendrew, or any foe, might send a warship beating along our coast, but they'll no' camp there. It's known we keep lookouts. Well-armed men able to flash down our cliff paths and be on them in their sleep, slitting throats and burning shelters before they even wakened. That will deter them." Alasdair waited as rumbles of agreement went down the column of riders. "So we'll have a look at the Dreagan's Claw."

"Dreagan's Claw!" several men spoke as one.

"No fool would camp there." Angus frowned, shook his bearded head.

"A fool, nae." That was what worried Alasdair. "A highly confident shipmaster with a skilled crew would attempt the like."

He didn't say how that spoke for Norsemen.

Kendrew kept strong ties to Vikings. He wouldn't have trouble finding a Shetlander or Orkneyman willing to lend him two longships. He could also have sweetened the price by tossing Marjory's hand into the bargain.

Having failed in procuring her a noble husband, he might be that desperate.

Shipmasters held high rank in northern lands.

Alasdair set his jaw, his hands white-knuckled on the reins, anger tightening his chest.

"And so"—his voice hardened—"we're riding for Dreagan's Claw."

"No man can ride there." Ewan leaned near, reached to grip his arm. "The men speak true. We'd end up on the rocks, adding to the grim tales about the place. There isn't even a path that way."

"Aye there is, and we're on it." Alasdair pulled free of his cousin's grasp. "A goat track, for sure. But it'll lead us to the cliffs overlooking the access. If anyone is camping there, we'll see them."

"And then?" Ewan didn't look happy.

"We line the edge of the drop-off and raise our spears, letting them know we're aware of them." From the corner of his eye, Alasdair saw Angus nod approval. "A small show of strength to warn that we also watch these shores, that we cannot be easily surprised."

"These are Mackintosh's bounds." One of the men at the rear spoke what Alasdair knew could be a problem.

"The land is still part of the Glen of Many Legends." It was Alasdair's sole argument, without mentioning his burning need to protect Marjory. "We send patrols into Kendrew's territory nigh every sennight, as well you know. Perhaps we haven't ridden as far as the Dreagan's Claw, but"—he used his most firm tone—"we are going there now."

His men looked at him, saying nothing.

"My gut says the black-painted longships are using the inlet as a halting place." Alasdair was sure of it, as certain as if someone whispered the truth in his ear.

Indeed, about an hour ago, he'd have sworn someone *had* leaned close and urged him to ride on to the Dreagan's Claw. He'd heard the words at his ear, clear and urgent, annoyingly unmistakable.

Alasdair fought a shudder.

He knew plenty of Highlanders who claimed they heard voices. Some, like his guardsmen, Gowan and Wattie, even swore they saw bogles.

He wanted nothing to do with ghosts.

So he pushed the memory from his mind, determined to keep such a mystery to himself. He hoped with equal fervor to never experience the like again.

"One look and we'll have our surety." He curled his hand around the shaft of his spear, glad he'd ordered them brought along.

"And if the longships are gone?" That from Angus, who was still scowling.

"We'll see that they've been there." Alasdair raised a hand when his men grumbled. "That's enough for this day. We'll ride home thereafter."

"We could be halfway there now," one of his men argued.

"Hear, hear," others agreed.

"Thon inlet is tight as a mouse's ear. All say it's clogged with jagged rock." A big-bearded man near the front of the column looked round at the other riders. He nodded, clearly pleased when they growled agreement. "We've heard the tales. The submerged rocks are fiendish, able to rip the bottom of any boat. We'll spy nothing there but wreckage, if anything."

"No' if the ships are Norse." Alasdair spoke his worry. "They are such good seamen, they could take a ship through the eye of a needle."

The man clamped his jaw, unable to argue.

Alasdair's other men went equally stiff-faced, each one letting silence voice his displeasure.

But a short while later when they reached the jutting promontory known as the Dreagan's Claw grumbles were heard. The rugged path they'd been following ended abruptly in a tangle of rock neither man nor beast should attempt to scramble over. Twisted tree roots, ancient and fossilized, showed that once, long ago, thick woods covered this high, windblown place. Worst of all, gaping black crevices left no doubt that one wrong step would send a soul hurtling into the sea that pounded the rocks far below.

Alasdair looked round, assessing.

Horses were useless here.

Nor would he risk allowing them any closer to the sheer drop-off.

He did glance at his warriors, nodding for them to dismount. "Stay with your beasts. Keep them calm and away from any gaps in the rock. I'll go to the edge on my own.

If I see ships or signs of men, I'll signal. We'll then line the cliffs with our spears, showing them—"

"Cousin..." Ewan strode forward to grip his arm. "We aren't—"

"I prefer my bruises from battle, lad. No' because you keep pinching my arm." Alasdair freed himself, turning to block the younger man's access to the rocks. "I'll no' have you any closer to thon drop-off. Stay back unless—"

"We aren't alone." Ewan slid a look at the end of the promontory. "There's a man there, crouched among the boulders."

"A man—" Alasdair narrowed his gaze at the cliff's highest point where a large outcrop spurred toward the horizon. He saw the warrior at once for he was just then standing, looking their way.

The man's face was strong, his expression fierce.

Huge, with a wild mane of black hair, he'd braided warrior rings into his beard. War trophies made of silver taken from the swords of fallen enemies, the rings chinked as he moved, giving him a rough, heathen air.

Dressed in full war gear, his mail shirt gleamed in the lowering sun. A battle sword hung at his side, but he didn't reach for the weapon. Even so, the suspicion in his smoke-gray eyes warned that he'd draw it if provoked. A wolf pelt slung round his shoulders, as his Viking war ax marked him as a Mackintosh.

He was Grim.

Kendrew's captain of the guard. He was also a man noted for his blood thirst and savagery.

Alasdair cracked his knuckles, welcoming a clash with the stony-faced giant. He'd fought toe to toe with the man at the trial by combat. They'd been a good match.

Alasdair had put a keen sword slice into the man's left hip, a cut that had surely bit deep. In return, the Mackintosh champion had given Alasdair such a whack on his head that his skull had reeled for days after the battle.

He was sure the bastard remembered.

"Ho, Grim!" Alasdair raised a hand, watching the warrior across the rocky expanse.

"MacDonald." Grim nodded curtly, the terse greeting making Alasdair resent the warrior kinship they'd shared at the trial by combat. Rather than fighting on, they'd each stepped back, moving away to challenge others.

A parting spurred because they'd fought so close to the King's royal entourage, both warriors catching the eager looks on the Lowland courtiers' faces as they'd stared down at them from the spectators' viewing platforms.

When they began shouting for carnage, hoping to see the warriors tear each other apart, Alasdair and Grim ceased being enemies.

For a beat, they were simply Highlanders.

And so they'd exchanged swift nods and whirled to disappear into the melee, sharing the triumph of thwarting the pleasure of a common enemy.

Now...

No Lowland lofties stood watching them, roaring for blood. Nothing buffered the old enmity that ignited so quickly when MacDonalds and Mackintoshes came together.

Trouble could flare in an eye blink.

The look on Grim's face warned he had the same thoughts.

Behind Alasdair, seabirds wheeled and screeched, as if crying for a fight. As this was Nought land, he had a good guess whose blood the screaming birds hoped to see spill onto the rocky ground.

Alasdair felt the urge to please them like a fire in his blood. His heart began to pound, his gaze flicking across the broken, lichen-covered boulders that littered the promontory. Cold wind flattened the stunted bits of heather that grew here. And from far below came the pounding crash of the sea against the rocks.

The Dreagan's Claw would make a good place to die.

And the barren ground would drink deeply of Mackintosh blood, welcoming its own as nourishment. So easily it could be done.

The fingers of Alasdair's sword hand began to itch.

His men stirred, growing restless.

Then Marjory's face flashed across his mind. Her blue eyes chilled with even more dislike than she'd shown him on Nought's cliff stair.

"Damnation." Alasdair curled his hands to fists, willing her from his mind.

She'd driven him to enough madness this day. So he clenched his fists tighter, forcing himself not to think of her. He did recall his suspicions about Grim acting as shipmaster on one of the longboats.

And here the bastard was, right where such nefarious dealings would put him.

Alasdair felt his blood heating. His sword hand itched worse than ever. Grim strode forward, looking as if he suffered the same malady.

That suited Alasdair fine.

Miles away, on a shingled strand at the southernmost bounds of the Glen of Many Legends, Seona paused near a seaweed-draped rock. A legend herself, or so many believed, she lifted a wispy hand to her shimmering breast. She kept her gaze on Blackshore Castle, rising so proudly from the middle of Loch Moidart. The stronghold glistened with recent rain and soft yellow light shone in some of the tall, arch-topped windows. Men would gather there, warming themselves before the fire, sipping ale and telling tales.

No doubt a few such stories would be about her.

She didn't much care for being a legend.

A fable, good for little more than giving MacDonald children shivers. And perhaps, if the tall tales came even close to the truth—which she doubted—acting as a warning to the young women of the clan.

Hoping it was so, she began drifting along the water's edge again.

It would please her if even one innocent lass were spared the heartache she'd suffered.

Torment and anguish she still endured.

Sorrow of her own making.

Men's hearts were fickle, while women loved true. And hurts didn't fade over time. They worsened, digging deeper into one's soul the longer such pain must be borne. Those were the truths she knew.

Would that she'd known them then...

In the distant past when she'd walked, not floated, along this strand. She'd been so young, her heart pure and trusting. No one else could've enjoyed such happiness. Or—she shivered, her long black hair rippling in the wind—no other maid could've been so in love.

Resenting her foolishness, she quickened her steps, almost flitting down the strand now. At least she could appreciate that her feet didn't touch the cold, wet ground. No icy wavelets would dampen her slippers. Far from it, her soft silver-blue gown and her cloak of dove-gray shimmered flatteringly about her, looking as always as if they'd been spun of moonbeams and star shine.

Even ghosts took pride in their appearances.

What pleased her more was the thick mist blowing in from the sea. Swirling and iridescent, the billowing fog blurred contours, hiding the great hills rising behind her and even obscuring the dark bulk of Blackshore, lurking out on the loch as it did.

Sometimes she wished it wasn't there.

It hurt to gaze upon the stronghold that had once meant so much to her.

Now the mist and darkness were her friends, shielding her from memories that had the power to break her. She who'd been known for her gaiety, the laughter Drangar the Strong had likened to an angel's song.

She couldn't remember when last she'd laughed.

An eternity ago didn't seem long enough.

Wishing that weren't so, Seona paused again, this time casting a sad eye on the rocks of doom. Their black-glistening tips were just visible above the tide. Beyond them, deep inside the whirling mist, she imagined she saw a dark coracle bobbing in the surf.

But when she looked again, it was gone.

As well it should be, for she'd only let her heart conjure a memory.

In her time, the fine stone causeway that stretched from the strand to Blackshore hadn't yet been built. True, Drangar the Strong had started it, but the work wasn't completed when she'd met her fate.

Again, she touched a hand to her breast, her heart remembering.

She could see the past so clearly, as if it all happened but a moment ago.

How Drangar had braved the worst tides to join her when she walked the strand opposite his mighty stronghold. Most times he'd row a coracle across the loch, claiming it strengthened his warrior arms to battle the waves. Now and then, he'd swim, coming to her wet and naked from the water, uncaring if he was seen.

He'd laugh, declaring that his love for her was cause for joy and never shame.

Then he'd wink and say the only souls who'd resent such passion might be graybeards no longer capable of raising such desire. And as he'd make such claims, his nakedness revealed that he was more than able—and ready—to prove his need of her.

Seona blushed, the memory of Drangar's prowess making her shimmer brightly.

Recalling how he'd look at her before pulling her into his arms set her heart aflutter.

Knowing that for a time he'd loved her stilled the world around her. The mists trembled and then parted, showing the strand as it'd been on a fine, windy morning so many years before. Seabirds wheeled and dove, and the loch sparkled, foaming white onto the shingle. She'd stood on the cliffs, watching Drangar's approach, only coming down when he'd jumped into the surf and pulled his coracle ashore.

She'd hurried then, laughing as she raced down the cliff path. At the bottom, she'd shed her clothes, leaving only her light linen undergown. Then, feeling most wanton, she'd undo her hair. Wind then tore at the long black strands, letting them stream behind her. In a playful mood, she'd run along the strand, deliberately dashing past her love to plunge into the water.

After a quick glance at Drangar, she'd dive deep, disappearing beneath the waves. Then she'd surface again, sea foam clinging to her like pearls. She'd twirl and tease, proud she could swim so well.

The loch was cold, so very cold.

But she didn't notice, her joy warming her.

As did the heat in Drangar's eyes when she'd returned to the strand. She'd known her sea-wet gown molded to her like a second skin, leaving no secrets while offering just enough mystery to tempt her lover.

Well-lusted, indeed, he'd torn off his clothes faster than the wind.

His face would darken then, his eyes narrowing with desire as he stood naked on the strand, his arms opened wide. She'd run to him, one hand clutched to her breasts, much as she pressed a hand there now.

Only unlike now, he'd been there for her.

He'd catch her to him, lifting her in the air and twirling her round and round. When they were both dizzy, he'd lower her onto the warm, dry pile of his shed clothes. The magnificent black woolen cloak he always wore.

They'd made love there on the strand, their bodies writhing on his mantle. Long sea winds had kissed them as he'd vowed his love, the words potently seductive in the soft morning light.

She'd always loved his voice, so deep and richly burred.

That long-ago day, he'd spun beautiful tales for her,

making her heart sing in anticipation of the wondrous life he claimed they'd enjoy together.

He'd stroked her hair and smoothed his hand over her bared skin. Pulling her close against him, he'd warmed her with the heat of his warrior's body. He'd nuzzled her neck, gently nipping the soft skin beneath her ear as he murmured Gaelic endearments.

Love words that slid through her like honeyed wine, melting her soul.

And, she now knew, declarations so false she should never have believed him.

How sad that she had.

But she'd not suspected his betrayal. She'd never have believed he'd spurn her. That he'd leave her to meet her end on the rocks of doom.

Seona straightened, standing as tall and proudly as she could, all things considered. She took a deep breath of the chill salt air and smoothed her shimmering silver-blue gown. She also adjusted the fall of her dove-gray cloak. Little things to occupy her, taking her mind off her memories.

It pained her to remember, but the truth was that he had abandoned her.

He'd cast her from him so that, at the end, there was no one but the seals to watch her breathe her last.

They alone had seen the waves swirl higher and higher around her. And the seals were there when the white tumbling surf finally claimed her, welcoming her into their cold, watery realm. Drangar the Strong hadn't come for her as she'd secretly hoped he would.

It was foolish to even consider such a possibility.

But she'd been so in love with him.

What a shame she still was.

Chapter Ten

❧

High atop the rock-bound promontory known as the Dreagan's Claw, Alasdair watched as Kendrew's best friend and companion-in-arms strolled toward him. A low grumble of menace rose from his men, but Alasdair gave Grim a brief nod. His expression could say the rest.

If that failed, other tactics could be employed.

One false move and the Mackintosh warrior would have to cut his way through a wall of MacDonalds if he wished to return to Nought Castle.

The King's writ be damned.

Certain his men agreed, Alasdair flashed a glance at Ewan. "That's Grim. He's Kendrew's captain of the guard. And"—he turned back to watch the man's approach—"it appears he's no' over at Duncreag, helping Archie MacNab rebuild his slaughtered garrison."

Somewhere behind Alasdair, a scrape of steel revealed that one of his men had pulled his sword. Others quickly followed suit, the whisper of blades, chill and deadly in the cold, thin air.

"Ho, Grim!" Alasdair lifted his voice as the warrior drew near.

"MacDonald." Grim didn't break stride, crossing the broken ground as easily as if it were a smooth, well-swept floor. "Looks like Nought bounds aren't good for you," he returned, his gaze flicking to the lump at Alasdair's temple. "Or have your men grown so unruly they've taken to knocking their chief about the head?"

Alasdair ignored the slurs. He did touch the hilt of Mist-Chaser, knowing Grim would notice. "Word is you bide o'er in the next glen these days. That you're now Archie MacNab's man. What brings you—"

"I am aye Kendrew's man." Grim stopped where he was, placing one foot on a large rock, proprietarily. "Why are you here? You, a MacDonald, so far from your own waterlogged Blackshore?"

"We had business with your chief." Alasdair kept his hand on his sword. "A matter that makes me wonder at finding you here of all places."

"Och, aye?" Grim cocked a brow, looking skeptical.

"So I said." Alasdair straightened, damning the wind for whipping his hair into his eyes.

He itched to unleash his sword, the urge almost tugging his lips into a smile. Instead, he kept his face stony, his gaze hard.

A clash with Kendrew's captain wasn't wise.

Alasdair and his warriors outnumbered the Mackintosh champion. The outcome would be sealed before steel struck steel. Mackintoshes weren't the only fighters in the Glen of Many Legends. And a MacDonald riled, his temper ignited, was a force no man would wish to face. But Grim's reputation as a champion was well-known. And as chieftain, Alasdair wasn't of a mind to lose three good men, perhaps more, just to quench his simmering anger.

Fury that, he knew, had as much to do with Marjory as her brother.

So he drew a tight breath before her face could rise before him again, spurring him to rashness. Why just the thought of her sent his wits flying and caused him to lose all control, was a mystery he didn't care to examine too closely. Leastways, not at the moment. He did square his shoulders and step forward, placing himself before his men. If Grim had any sense, he wouldn't push him.

Grim folded his arms, eyeing Alasdair coldly. His silence spoke louder than words. He clearly wanted Alasdair and his men gone, off Nought lands.

"There can be no business to bring you here. I'm thinking you followed the length of your nose." Grim's words proved his enmity. "This is Mackintosh territory."

"So it is. And that's all the more reason for my interest, see you?" Alasdair flicked a look at the stumps of smooth, age-darkened wood that littered the ground. He then aimed a pointed glance at the twist of fossilized root in Grim's hand. "Gathering stone roots, are you?"

To his surprise, the big man looked embarrassed. "Foul things clog this headland." Grim cast aside the root as if it'd turned into a snake. "They can trip up a man or a horse." He glanced at the MacDonald garrons. "The stone roots make it hard to patrol these cliffs. Even your hill ponies, surefooted as they are, could take a fall." He shifted and the sun came from behind a cloud, catching his broad-bladed war ax. "I'd no' see a beast hurt on Nought ground. No' even one of yours."

"So you're on watch, eh?" Angus strode over, his tone unfriendly. "Looking for anything in particular?"

"If I was, it'd be naught to you." Grim eyed Angus up and down. "I've no' wish to cut down a man double my years. Be gone before I change my mind."

Angus spluttered, his face reddening. "I'm no'—"

"You could be my father." Grim stepped forward and set a hand on Angus's shoulder, gripped once, and released him. "Be glad I have other cares on my mind this day."

"Humph." Angus brushed at his plaid, looking nowise placated. Far from it, he fixed Grim with a rude, unblinking stare.

"Have a care, graybeard." Grim held his gaze, spoke easily. "Still, you command a good share of your Blackshore territory. I'll no' have it on my shoulders if you suddenly find yourself holding no more than the earth packed round your moldering bones."

A dangerous glint entered Angus's eyes. "See here, you—"

"Enough." Alasdair stepped between them. He nodded at Angus and then glanced to where the land dropped down to the sea before turning to Grim. "Longships interest me, naught else. Black-painted war galleys. I'm thinking you'll know of them."

Grim arched a brow. "How so?"

"Mayhap you steered such a vessel?" Alasdair voiced his suspicion.

"Why would I do that?"

"Could be that's what I'm waiting to hear."

"Then you may well spread your plaid on the rocks for

the night as you'll be waiting long. No' in all thon broad waters did I see such craft." Grim swept an arm toward the sea. "If I did, mayhap I'd no' tell you."

"That would be a mistake you'd rue." Alasdair followed Grim's gaze, his own narrowing on the horizon.

The light was fading, but the coast's splendor still took a man's breath. Beyond the cliff's edge, the air was filled with wheeling, screaming seabirds. But the eye was drawn farther, toward a vast, open vista of rolling sea and countless islands, rocky islets, and black-glistening skerries. Gleaming white sand ringed each island, some low and grassy, others boasting jagged, mist-topped peaks. Some marked themselves through sheer, beetling cliffs, black and forbidding. But even those soaring rock faces opened here and there, offering glimpses of welcoming coves where the last of the day's sun sparkled like jewels on the water.

Alasdair's heart squeezed at the beauty. No Highlander could stand in such a place and not be moved, deeply so. If such land were his own, his pride would know no bounds. If the land belonged to another, his soul would weep. Alasdair set his jaw, not about to do so. He also understood why the land-greedy Norse returned so often, aye seeking to make the Sea of the Hebrides their own.

He could even sympathize with Kendrew, wanting all the Glen of Many Legends.

Whatever it cost him to bring his nefarious plan to fruition.

At the thought, Alasdair leaned menacingly toward Grim. "My lookouts saw such ships off Blackshore's coast. Hull and sails, black as pitch."

"Perhaps your men saw seabirds?" Grim didn't blink.

He'd stepped closer to Alasdair, his pride evident as he again surveyed the great, watery expanse before them. "In certain light, any bird can look black. Or"—his tone held a trace of humor—"mayhap your men were in their cups? I'm just off those seas and have seen no such ships." He clamped his lips then, apparently regretting his admission.

"You were sailing?" Alasdair glanced at his men, suspicion racing through his veins.

One of his warriors spat on the rocks. Others peeled their eyes on Grim, their stances aggressive, faces hard.

"Speak, man." Alasdair held up a hand when his men started to move forward. "I believe your chief sent the ships to provoke a fight, a sea battle. It would serve him well to see me break the King's peace."

"Bah! If Kendrew wanted to challenge you, he'd come overland, no' by water." Grim shook his head, making his silver warrior rings jangle.

Alasdair pressed him. "If you came here by sea, where is your ship? The crew? Have you birds' wings strapped to your back to cross water? Or"—his voice hardened—"did Kendrew lie when he swore Mackintoshes dinnae have galleys?"

"Kendrew spoke true," Grim defended his master.

"Then it's you telling a tall one." Ewan sauntered over to them.

Alasdair shot him a look. But Grim offered Ewan a crooked smile, for a beat, transforming his rough-hewn face. He looked almost congenial.

"I like a man who speaks his mind." Grim glanced back at the sea, drew his hand down over his chin. "No Mackintosh tells tales. Save the ones we enjoy before our fire of a long, dark winter night. Truth is, an Irish galley set me ashore no' far from the mouth of the Dreagan's Claw. I climbed up the cliff path and hadn't been here long before you arrived." He looked at Alasdair, his eyes narrowing. "If aught was amiss hereabouts, I'd have noticed. To my mind, it's you out of place here."

Grim hooked his thumbs in his sword belt, his face unfriendly again.

Alasdair didn't blink, not moved by the unspoken threat.

"You were on an Irish ship?" Alasdair wasn't sure he believed him. "Is Kendrew now seeking to wed Lady Marjory to an Irish kinglet?" The words sprang from his tongue before he could stop them.

"Nothing the like." Grim looked at him for a long moment, his gray eyes sharp. "Archie MacNab's business took me to Ireland. I'll be returning to Duncreag after I've spent a few days at Nought."

"I see." Alasdair still didn't trust him.

Angus, Ewan, and the rest of Alasdair's men exchanged glances, looking equally doubtful.

It was Ewan who spoke. "You saw no sign of an encampment below the cliffs?"

Grim shook his head. "If I had, I'd no' be here. I'd have made haste to Nought to warn my chief of trespassers. When you arrived"—he spread his hands—"I was enjoying the view, see you?" His words didn't ring quite true. "It's no' oft that we of Nought can gaze upon the sea. You'd do best to savor it as well." He stepped back, adjusted the wolf pelt slung about his shoulders. "Your own Blackshore cannae offer such magnificence."

The taunt spoken, he turned and strode away, not looking left or right at the gathered MacDonalds. In a blink, he was gone, disappearing down the same goat track Alasdair and his men had climbed to reach the promontory.

"Thon's a great hairy bastard." Angus stared after him, glaring.

Ewan shrugged. "He saved us from having to creep over to the cliff edge."

"No' so fast." Alasdair thrust out an arm, catching Ewan by the elbow when he made to hurry back to their horses. "I'll still be having a look."

"You're mad." Ewan jerked free, tossed a glance at the jumbled rocks everywhere, the dark-shadowed crevices and the tangle of stony tree roots. "Only a fool would go any closer to thon edge."

Secretly, Alasdair agreed.

But the tight bands of ill ease clamped so fiercely about his chest had little to do with the risk of tumbling off a cliff. They did concern his suspicion that Kendrew was using the Dreagan's Claw cove to hide hired long-ships and their crews. The alternative...

That the Norse ships brought a new suitor for Marjory was even more troubling.

Worse, the nagging sense she was in danger.

Alasdair frowned, rubbed the back of his neck. He could feel menace in the air, strong as the long, cold wind blowing in from the sea.

"One look"—he reached for Ewan, gripping his elbows—"and we'll be away."

"I dinnae like it."

"Nor do I, but—"

"Smoke! Look there." One of the men ran over to them, pointing at the cliff edge. "Threads of smoke, as if from a guttered fire."

Alasdair and Ewan turned, following the man's outstretched arm.

Alasdair saw nothing.

Ewan's shrug said he didn't either.

"That's sea mist, Farlan." Alasdair was sure his kinsman had seen a coil of the ever-drifting mist that hung
about this coast. Or perhaps a large breaker had crashed
against the rocks, sending up a plume of spray.

The like happened. Blackshore's cliffs were aye fanned
by sea foam.

"Nae, it was smoke." Farlan shook his head, vigor-
ously. "I saw it plain as day. The MacDonald hasn't been
born who can't tell the difference between smoke rising
from a doused fire and sea haar. As for sea spray..." Farlan spat, showing his disdain for the suggestion that he
wouldn't recognize such a commonplace sight.

Alasdair gripped his chin, knowing that was true.

When he started to say so, Farlan shouted again.
"There it is!" He leaped up on one of the boulders, pointing. "It's bigger now. A great swirl from a smoking campfire, I say you."

Alasdair and Ewan looked, both men searching the
long rocky rim of the drop-off.

Nothing stirred there except screaming seabirds.

Even the mist had been blown away by the strong,
gusting wind.

"There's naught there, Farlan." Alasdair regretted the
look his denial put on his kinsman's face.

"I ken what I saw." Farlan swelled his chest, thrust out
his jaw. "There be a fire down there. Leastways, there was
one. Taking a Mackintosh's word o'er mine won't change
what is. I have good eyes, I do."

"That I know." Alasdair did.

Farlan could spy a ship on the horizon before the sail crested the earth's rim.

Nor was he given to falsehoods.

Alasdair lifted a hand to his brow, looking more closely. He still saw only seabirds. He turned to Ewan, also known for his keen eyesight.

"And you?" Alasdair challenged his cousin.

Ewan hesitated and then sent an apologetic look at Farlan. "I saw naught that reminded me of smoke."

"Then you both have your eyes turned backward." Farlan wheeled about and stalked to the horses, muttering as he went.

Alasdair again glanced at the maze of rock, stony tree roots, and crevices that stretched between where he stood and the promontory's drop-off. Swirling mist suddenly blew in from nowhere, making it difficult to choose a safe path to the cliff's edge.

The chill that swept his spine told him it was an uncanny mist.

Not that he wanted to accept the possibility.

He did regret announcing he'd peer down into the Dreagan's Claw. Doing so now might mean his end and he'd much prefer to finish his life on someone's sword blade. Falling off a cliff was as shameful as dying in one's bed.

Yet Grim had scaled the rock face and strode about the promontory's uneven ground without batting an eye.

That he'd done so left Alasdair no choice but to do the same.

He couldn't return to the comforts of his hearth fire at Blackshore only to have his men complain that their chief refused to go where a Mackintosh had trod with such ease.

So he straightened and threw back his plaid. "I'll have a look o'er the edge, Farlan," he called to his sullen-faced kinsman.

Farlan nodded once, some of the annoyance slipping from his face.

"I'll go with you." Ewan started forward, but Alasdair waved him back.

"Nae, all of you wait here." Alasdair was already striding purposely through the whirling mist, taking a path right over a tangled growth of fossilized roots. Carefully picking his way, as would've been more prudent, was out of the question. "I'll return anon."

But when he reached the cliff edge and lowered himself to his knees, peering down into the narrow inlet, the first thing he saw was a great black-cloaked warrior staring up at him. Tall, and with a dark piercing gaze that held his own, the man wore polished mail and had a neatly trimmed black beard, showing he wasn't a Viking.

He didn't look friendly.

He clasped a long spear, its end resting against a low mound of rocks. A sword hung at his side, while his plumed helm marked him as a lord.

Alasdair's blood chilled as he looked down at the man whose great black cloak billowed in the wind. Most astonishing, the warrior glowed. He shone like a ray of sun against the gloom of the cliffs.

His stance proved him a proud man. The kind of fighter worth a hundred men in battle.

Alasdair felt his eyes rounding, his jaw slip.

By all the fireside tales he'd heard, the warrior fit the description of Drangar the Strong.

Yet Drangar didn't exist.

And neither did the warlord on the inlet's tiny strand. Alasdair blinked and the man was gone, a swirl of sea mist in his place.

That, and a faint smear of black across the rocks nearest the water.

Edging closer to the drop-off, Alasdair held fast to the sturdiest rock of the same outcrop where Grim had knelt. He leaned forward, peering at the inky stain.

The tide was out, revealing wet-glistening shingle and a dark ribbon of seaweed that marked the waterline. Traces of black remained, looking suspiciously like a trail left by a boat that had been dragged ashore.

Not a Norse dragonship, but a small coracle.

The kind of lightweight, skin-sided craft carried by larger ships so their crews could go ashore in inhospitable waters, places like the tight, rock-strewn inlet known as the Dreagan's Claw.

And in this instance, the coracle appeared to have carried a coat of pitch on its stretched-hide hull. If such a cockleshell had been employed, and Alasdair believed that was so.

Sure of it, he leaped to his feet. "Dinnae come after me," he called to his men. "I've spotted something on the rocks."

Then he nipped around the outcrop and over the cliff edge, taking the barely discernible path down to the strand before anyone could follow.

He went faster than was wise. But if he slowed his feet, he'd think too hard on the recklessness of chasing down such a steep, slippery track.

Sometimes a man had to act first and think later.

This was such a time.

His instincts proved right when, upon reaching the strand, the smear of black along the tideline looked even more like pitch than from above.

Certain it was, he headed for the largest smear, leaping from rock to rock to get there. His suspicions were confirmed as soon as he dropped to one knee beside a tide pool and trailed his hand along the dark-stained shingle. His fingers came away black.

"Damnation." He stood, surveying the narrow strand. Nothing stirred here now. All was still save the slapping of the sea on rock, the freshening wind. For sure, no ghost haunted this bleak inlet. He'd mistaken the tarry smears for the warlord's black cloak.

He hadn't seen Drangar.

Besides, even if his much-sung ancestor existed, he had no reason to visit Nought's Dreagan's Claw.

Living men who wished to remain hidden, their business unknown, were another matter.

There could be no doubt that at least two pitch-coated coracles had been dragged ashore here. And that knowledge churned in Alasdair's gut. A gnawing ill ease that made him go cold inside.

Again, his mind wandered to Marjory, so he lifted a hand to his brow, turning his gaze on the open sea beyond the cove's rock-strewn opening. Long lines of rollers, huge and white-crested, stretched as far as he could see. Nowhere did he glimpse a sail. There wasn't even a fishing boat anywhere near Nought's bleak and jagged bit of coast.

And no wonder.

The seas here were hostile, the currents strong and deadly.

Still...

He shook his head, lips pressed together. He narrowed his eyes, staring at the horizon as if by sheer will alone he could peer beyond its edge.

See the evil he was sure lurked there.

Black-hearted men who'd tread this rocky skirt of beach, up to no good, he was certain.

Wishing he knew who they were, he turned away, eager to scramble back up the cliff path. Once at Black-shore, he and his men would decide what to do. Starting forward, he cast one last look at the tarry stains on the rocks. They were nearly washed away now.

Perhaps he was mistaken...

He knew he wasn't.

As if to prove it, the wind changed, swinging round to carry a trace of smoke past his nose.

Old smoke, stale and faint, but notable enough to stop him in his tracks.

It was then he remembered the low mound of rocks where the bogle-he-hadn't-really-seen had jammed his spear butt against the ground. There, where the pitch stain was the largest, letting him imagine that the smears were Drangar the Strong's billowing black cloak.

Except Drangar didn't exist, and neither did his long, dark mantle.

But there was a slight heap of stones.

And the rise appeared manmade, put together by someone's hand and not nature.

"Damnation," Alasdair muttered again, retracing his steps to reach the mound.

Once there, he knelt on the cold, wet shingle and tossed aside the rocks. They'd covered a doused campfire, the charred wood and ash still damp. Frowning, he thrust his fingers into the sticky mess, not surprised when fresh, inky soot clung to them.

Standing, he crossed to a tidal pool to wash the smeary ash from his hand. As he did, a whirl of images flew across his mind. Clear as day, he saw Marjory claimed by a savage Viking lord, the man's bearded mouth plundering hers, his hands ripping the gown from her, his ship carrying her away to his distant northern lands.

Just as ominous, if not as personal, he caught a flash of Kendrew pouring silver coins into the outstretched hands of a greed-driven shipmaster, the lout's equally scrupulous men crowding round, their eyes alight as they silently counted their newfound riches.

"No' so long as I breathe," Alasdair snarled, looking about the strand once more. A muscle jumped in his jaw, hot anger beating inside him. He put his hand on Mist-Chaser's hilt, the day now edged in red.

His suspicions were confirmed.

He just hoped that his concern for Marjory proved less valid. If such a fate awaited her, whatever he did would result in disaster.

For do something he would.

There'd be hell to pay if harm came to her.

This day, he and his men hadn't required the long spears they'd brought along to the Dreagan's Claw. But in his mind's eye, he could see those killing shafts in his men's hands, the steel-tipped heads dripping blood.

The image was as real as the cold mist damping his face, the rhythmic wash of the sea against the stony ground beneath his feet.

He could almost smell death in the air.

He knew such a day was coming.

Soon, the blow would fall. A tide of men bearing swords, spears, and axes would flood his beloved glen. The hot, red glow of raid fires would stain the sky, while thick, acrid smoke choked the life from those who didn't perish beneath the bite of steel.

Alasdair rubbed his mouth with the back of his hand, the thought unbearable.

Most damning of all, if events unfolded as he suspected, he'd be responsible.

As if the fates agreed, the voices of strangers came from the mist curling round Alasdair's home on its rocky islet in the southernmost corner of the glen. Low and guarded, the grumbles would've been the men's death knells if Alasdair had heard them. Truth be told, fury would've boiled the blood of any warrior of the glen.

But the speakers apparently didn't know the dark sea winds of Blackshore drifted far. Or that even mist sometimes had ears. They only knew their greed. And the burning lust that some men can't control...

"I could've done with some fine, womanly heat," Troll, a huge, one-eyed Norseman groused as he pulled the oars of a small, black-sided coracle. His war-scarred face darkened as he cast a look over his shoulder to where the waters of Loch Moidart broke on the curving strand at the far end of Blackshore Castle's causeway.

The woman he'd spotted at the loch's edge had slipped into the shadows.

He frowned, annoyed that his companion, Bors, hadn't been willing to beach the coracle, "We could've had her and been away before she could even scream."

Bors didn't answer him.

Troll didn't care. He did peer across the loch again, trying to see where the woman had gone.

It'd been too long since he'd aired the skirts of such a beauty.

Even through the mist, he'd recognized her worth.

She'd practically glowed.

Wanting her badly, he turned back to the other man in the coracle. Bors puzzled him. Big, brutish, and just as hot-blooded as he was, Bors wasn't a man to pass on the chance of a good tumble.

Yet he had, arguing that Troll's goings-on about the woman would be heard by the guardsmen on Blackshore's battlements. He didn't want to alert them of their presence. Troll tamped down a bark of laughter.

As if the MacDonald guards had such sharp ears.

Morelike, Bors was worried about angering their leader, Ivar Ironstorm.

Ivar frowned on dallying unless he'd given his men leave to enjoy such pleasures. Most times he concerned himself only with gaining land and gold. Slaves he could trade or sell. Women, when they brought an advantage.

"We could've taken her, there on the shore. I can see her with her skirts high, her legs spread wide. She'd thrash and writhe..." He gripped the oars tighter, his arm muscles bulging. "I'm still hard for her."

Bors snorted. "All that ails you is that your good eye is going as blind as the missing one." Leaning forward, he fixed Troll with a narrow-eyed stare. "There was no woman on that strand."

"I say there was. And she was a beauty." He dropped the oars for a moment, sketching a shapely form in the air. "Long black hair and fine features, smooth creamy skin, white as fallen snow. Her gown clung to her, a slip of silvery-blue. And she wore a fine gray cloak I wouldn't have minded taking back to Norway for my mother. She was a lady, no doubt." Troll licked his lips, his grip on the oars now white-knuckled. "Just think how sweet her—"

"I'm thinking Ironstorm will thrash you to bits when he hears you were ogling mist and calling it a woman. Our task was to learn the strength of Blackshore's walls." Bors snarled the words, rowing with all might now, as they swept round the headland known as Drangar Point and entered deeper, rough-tided water.

Bors grimaced when a large fan of sea spray blew across the little boat, drenching them. "Your good eye should've been searching for weak spots in the walling, nothing else. If all goes as planned, we'll add to our gains by filling our holds with Blackshore amber. Slaves to sell in Dublin..." He dragged a quick arm across his brow, dashing the sea water from his eyes. "*Mist wenches* won't bring a coin."

"She was there, sure as you're an ugly bastard. Even Ironstorm would've wanted her. He likes breaking ladies." Leaning forward, Troll's tone went conspiratorial. "Word is MacDonald women are fiery. And"—he licked his lips—"the taste of them headier than mead."

Bors scowled at him. "Ivar has only one female on his mind these days and she isn't a MacDonald."

"The Mackintosh maid isn't his yet." Troll pulled hard on the oars, straining.

"She will be." Bors grunted as they fought the drag of the current.

"And then we'll all enjoy her." Troll increased his own

oar-work, the two of them turning the tiny craft toward the fierce-prowed dragonship they could just make out through the mist. Half-hidden behind a craggy islet a good way offshore, only someone who knew where to look would've seen the craft's black-painted hull and high, single mast, its large, square-shaped sail as dark as night. "We'll treat her to the honor of our prowess before—"

"You'll not be a part of the ceremony if Ivar cuts off your balls." Bors said that with satisfaction. "When I tell him how your cry about a mist woman echoed round the loch, risking the attention of the Blackshore guards, he'll—"

"Say a word and you'll find your throat slit as you sleep." Troll gave an equally smug smile, knowing he'd won.

His face might not be pretty, but he was silent on his feet, his dagger hand swift and deadly. More than one man who'd vexed him breathed no more. And—Troll dug his oars into sea, victory sweet—those sorry fools had ended their lives in their beds, no sword or ax in their hand, guaranteeing a welcome at Valhalla.

Thor's mead hall was closed to warriors who died in their sleep.

And the soured look on Bors's face said he knew he was in danger of meeting such a fate.

"Something else, friend . . ." Troll rowed happily as they neared the anchored dragonship. "When the day comes, I take my turn at the Mackintosh maid before you."

Bors grunted, the tightening of his lips agreement enough.

"Don't look so grieved," Troll taunted as the coracle bumped aside the ship's black-painted hull. "You won't know the difference anyway. All cats are the same in the dark, even fine Highland ladies."

Still, Troll just might enjoy Marjory Mackintosh twice, if possible.

He'd be doing her a service, after all.

Women sent to Viking funerary pyres burned more contently if well-sated beforehand.

Chapter Eleven

❖

Three days later, Marjory and Isobel made their way through a birchwood near Nought's most formidable peaks. Wind funneled down from the highest passes to whistle through the trees and send fallen leaves skittering along the path. The women walked briskly, their cloaks drawn against the cold afternoon. Marjory just wished her mantle would also shield her from certain mind wanderings.

"You're not fooling me." Isobel hitched her skirts to step over a patch of mud-slicked ground. "You're thinking of him, aren't you?"

"Who?" Marjory pretended not to know.

"Blackshore, of course." Isobel glanced at her, her gaze so perceptive Marjory's face heated. "You're yearning for him. Especially now, after he's practically made love to you. Any woman would—"

"You're mad." Marjory shot her a look of annoyance. "Angry, is what I am. I'm certainly not dwelling on what happened in the old guard room. Or better said, what didn't. Truth be told, I'm glad nothing came of it." She spoke the lie as boldly as she could. "I only regret I was so naïve to follow him, expecting…"

She couldn't finish, irritation making her throat hurt.

She did set her jaw, not wanting to acknowledge that even now she felt the powerful force of him. Pure sensual heat poured through her, prickling her skin and stirring memories of his touch, his kisses. Need and desire as strong as if he stood before her still. She inhaled sharply, resenting the damning pull, undiminished by her aggravation.

"Such folly." She swiped her hair behind her ear. "How could I have—"

Isobel tsked. "Seducing the man you love is never folly, dear heart. Some men need a bit of prodding." Her lips curved in a reminiscent smile, her eyes softening. "I know that well, trust me."

"Alasdair is not Kendrew."

"To be sure." Isobel stepped over a fallen log. "Yet they are more alike than either would care to admit. Both are proud men, leaders of their people, and with a long history of clan feuding and personal grievances between them. They are fierce warriors. And"—she smiled again, this time knowingly—"the kind of men who make the best of husbands once they settle down. The finest of lovers—"

"Isobel!" Marjory flushed so hotly she could hear the blood roar in her ears. "You know we didn't—"

"A mere trifle." Isobel's smile didn't falter. "As for seduction, I'll own you only had to stand before him to send all thoughts from his mind save wanting to ravish you there and then."

Marjory just looked at her, her pulse thundering.

She was sure the truth stood on her face. That had been the way of it.

"See? I knew it." Isobel sounded so pleased. "You only fueled the fires already burning. You weren't just anyone there in the shadows with him. You were the woman he desires above all others."

"He wanted a woman. Any half-fetching female in a low-cut gown and with fluttering eyelashes would've served." The words tasted bitter on Marjory's tongue. "He said as much. Did you not hear him?"

"I heard him say words that damned him and saved your honor."

"Pah!" Marjory didn't believe it.

Much as she'd been wrestling with just such a possibility for days.

"You think so, too. I see it all over you."

"I don't know what I think."

"And so you've been slipping away every morn, telling Kendrew you're off to visit Hella when what you truly hoped was to catch Alasdair on one of his patrols through our territory." Isobel made it sound so logical. "You need to look in his eyes, search for answers—"

"I need to put him from my mind." Marjory didn't deny that she *had* hoped to encounter Alasdair.

Not that she knew what she'd do if she did.

For truth, she'd almost swear he'd used some kind of witchy magic on her.

How else could he invade her every thought?

Even now, she could see him. His clear blue gaze steady on hers, and how in certain light, his eyes gleamed with the most delightful golden flecks. How wide of shoulder he was, or how proudly he wore his MacDonald plaid over his broad, hard-muscled chest.

She stiffened, not wanting to recall how her hope had crumbled on his stinging rejection, her joy slipping away like sand spilling between her fingers.

It'd been days, yet the hurt sat deep.

She glanced up at the racing clouds, wishing they'd swoop down to chase him from her heart. Undo how she couldn't forget that his lightest touch could make her skin warm, even sending fiery heat whipping through her so that she tingled clear to her toes.

Trickery he surely used on every female who crossed his path.

That damnable knowledge put such a scowl on her face that she glanced aside so Isobel wouldn't see. With any luck, her friend would think it was the shadowy birchwood that made her frown.

"I have been searching for Hella." She lifted her voice as a sharp wind whistled through the trees, tossing branches and rattling leaves, lending to the wood's eeriness. Deep and almost impenetrable, the thickly growing birches crowded a fast-running burn halfway between Castle Nought and the clan's famed vale of the dreagans.

"Aye, and just where we know Alasdair often sends his patrols." Isobel glanced at her. "Men he often accompanies, if our own scouts are to be believed."

"You know I have good reason to speak with Hella." Marjory refused to allow Isobel to maneuver her into further discussion of Alasdair.

She did pull her cloak even tighter as the wood drew in around them.

This part of Nought *was* a bit unholy.

Little visited because of the thick mist that often hid the wood from view—fog many Mackintoshes held for enchanted—the birchwood was a place where the veil that separated the living from the dead had worn thin, allowing easy passage between the worlds.

Or so clan bards claimed.

At gloaming, strange blue lights sometimes glimmered through the trees. Eerily glowing orbs many believed were men who'd lost their way. Wretches who'd become forever trapped in the wood's murky depths.

Marjory peered into the shadows, glad she'd never seen the lights.

She didn't doubt their existence.

She could almost feel their stares now.

No, not their stares, Alasdair's. He was watching her. She blinked, losing her breath at the sight of him. She could see only his face in the whirling mist, but that was enough to set her heart thundering. The air between them shifted, the swirling mist almost coming alive, even seeming to crackle as their gazes locked. His intensely blue eyes narrowed, carrying a challenge, daring her to come to him.

She started forward, her pulse quickening even more.

Norn... She was sure she heard him call to her, his voice deep and smooth, the intimacy of his tone making her insides flutter.

The mist stirred and she caught a better glimpse of him, saw that he held out a hand to her. She took another few steps, hurrying now. Sheer, primal need drove her, female desire she couldn't deny.

"Botheration!" Isobel cursed, and hastened after her.

Marjory hitched her gown higher, preparing to leap over a narrow burn.

But then a gust of wind shook the trees on the far side of the water and she realized her mistake.

Alasdair wasn't there.

A quick glance at Isobel proved it. Her friend was hopping on one foot while shaking the other, clearly trying to dislodge a pebble from her shoe.

Had Alasdair been there, sharp-eyed, ever-alert Isobel would've known. Yet she looked wholly unconcerned, entirely occupied with her errant shoe.

Marjory pressed a hand to her breast and took a deep breath, waiting for the tingles of awareness to recede. Even now, knowing she'd erred, she could still feel the excitement that had swept her. The powerful pull of Alasdair, reaching to her through the cold mist, a bold smile teasing his lips as he waited for her.

Yet...

He wasn't doing anything of the like. He wasn't there at all.

Nothing was.

The wood was playing tricks on her.

Or she'd seen an *an cu glas,* the fairy dogs also rumored to roam this part of Nought. Thought to have interbred with mortal dogs, the fairy beasts were usually reported as green, though some folk insisted they'd seen blue *an cu glas.* Either way, the creatures were known for seeking companionship. Unfortunately, if they barked three times and a man heard them, his certain death was said to follow.

Marjory had other cares.

Isobel slipped her now pebble-free shoe back on her foot and dusted her hands. "Did you hear that?" She tilted her head, looking in the opposite direction from where

Marjory thought she'd seen Alasdair. "I think it was a dog, a large brute—"

Marjory listened, but heard nothing. "It was the wind."

"Say you." Isobel turned in a slow circle, peering into the trees. "It wasn't that long ago that two of Kendrew's men swore they'd seen a fairy dog near the dreagan vale. They said he was huge and as bright as green fire."

"And they lived to tell the tale." Marjory reached out to halt her friend's turning. "If there are *an cu glas* about, they'll be lonely and glad for our company. I never did believe they bring doom.

"We're safe here." She stepped back, assuming her most confident mien rather than alarm her good-sister by admitting that the wood was uncanny. She was also glad to steer the topic away from Alasdair. "Truly, the threat of a Viking funerary pyre disturbs me much more than whatever creatures might lurk in a mist-haunted wood."

"I did hear something." Isobel still wore a vague frown.

"You heard our feet scrunching on the rocks." Marjory was sure as they'd just reached a stretch of path covered with gravel.

"I thought you believed in Highland magic."

"I do." Marjory kept walking. "Just now I want to see Hella more."

Isobel looked at her sharply. "Let's hope we don't regret her answers."

"We'll know soon enough." Marjory quickened her pace.

Hopefully, they'd find Hella at home at Skali, her thatched cottage in the wood's deepest, darkest heart. Named for the main room of a Viking longhouse, the communal area where sleeping benches lined the walls on either side of a central fire, Skali Cottage allowed the widow to retreat into what she called the comfort of candlelight and peat smoke.

Hella appreciated solitude.

Marjory touched the amber necklace at her throat, saying a silent prayer. Something—an instinct, her ambers, or just plain good sense—told her that she needed the truth about her dream before it was too late.

Commonplace dreams vanished upon waking.

Her dream stuck to her like a burr, clinging and sharp, minding her of its presence.

She could still see the sheer, iron-gray cliffs and the frost on the rocks. At times, she even caught the smell of cold Arctic air and the deep-blue waters of Nordic seas. In those moments, the acrid bite of burning wood and strange herbs haunted her, while her skin felt smeared by sea spray and ash. Flying soot that rode a fiery wind and came from flames meant to roast her alive.

"There's that noise again." Isobel put a hand on Marjory's arm, gripping tightly.

"I heard nothing." Marjory angled her head, listening, but the wood was still.

Unfortunately, her pulse was skittish.

And she needed her wits.

Even Nought born and bred as she was, it wasn't easy to find Skali Cottage.

The birchwood protected those it welcomed into its embrace. When Hella claimed the cottage's ruined shell, restoring the erstwhile shepherd's hut to its earlier soundness and naming it Skali, the birches began growing more closely about Skali's thick white-washed walls. The cottage soon became as much a part of the wood as the trees and mist.

Skali could be passed unnoticed if one didn't know where to look.

Blessedly, Marjory did.

At least, she'd always thought so.

Now...

She stopped, resting a hand against her hip. "I'd swear the path keeps changing." She glanced at Isobel, seeing the same frustration on her face. "It's leading us nowhere, circling round as if someone cast a spell of concealment on the track's stones."

"The *an cu glas* could work such a trick." Isobel glanced about, into the shadows, as if expecting a pack of the fairy dogs to appear.

"Pah." Marjory made a dismissive gesture. "I have a good idea what the problem is."

"Grim?" Isobel sounded doubtful.

"Just because we haven't spoken of him doesn't mean he isn't trailing us. We've both known it for hours."

Annoyed, Marjory glanced over her shoulder, pretending not to see the big black-bearded man who followed them. As a good Mackintosh warrior, proud of his Berserker blood, Grim wore a wolf's pelt slung over his mail-clad shoulders and carried a bright, broad-bladed war ax strapped across his back. His tread was silent, for all Mackintoshes could move easily on swift, soundless feet.

Isobel lowered her voice. "You think the wood is throwing him off our track?"

"It's possible." Marjory stood straighter and brushed her skirts. Grim's presence wasn't wished, however much he meant well.

"Hc's keeping his distance." Isobel leaned close, her gaze on the spot where a hint of silver revealed Grim's hiding place. "He has a good heart. He won't come near enough to press his ear to Hella's door."

Marjory bit back a laugh. "He's a Mackintosh. He'll do as he pleases. And he is my brother's man."

"He helped us when Kendrew was courting me. It was Grim who—"

"You didn't need help." Marjory studied the path before them. She was certain it should curve to the right, yet the pebbled track wound to the left. She frowned upon noting a second path, choosing to follow its mud-slicked stones into the deepest part of the wood.

Isobel hitched her skirts as they left the pebbled trail for the muddied one. "Grim only wants to be sure we're safe."

"We are. There's nothing here that would harm either of us."

"Hearthside tales say otherwise."

"Such stories are meant to entertain."

"Yet each one holds a grain of truth." Isobel's pretty face went serious. "Don't forget I saw one of your dreagans, along with his master, the night Kendrew rescued us from the broken men who seized Duncreag Castle from old Archie MacNab. Kendrew and I were up on Duncreag's battlements, looking toward Nought. It was then that he asked me if I wished to return with him to his home or be escorted back to my own, Castle Haven. I told him my choice was Nought.

"He grabbed me then, pulling me into his arms. He kissed me and in that moment"—her voice took on a confiding tone—"I saw the great dreagan Slag and his master, Dare. It was storming and they were on the ledge of a nearby mountain. I saw them clearly."

"I believe you." Marjory did, wishing she, too, had seen the fabled beast and his keeper. "I didn't say I doubt there are wood sprites or fairy dogs in this wood, or that the mist might be enchanted.

"I meant we have no reason to fear." She cast another glance behind them, noting that Grim had again slipped from view.

"Then why is it taking us so long to reach Hella's cottage? We should've been there hours ago."

"I know." Marjory didn't like the thick mist drifting through the trees. It was denser now and almost luminous, seeming to pulse around them. "But I'm sure we're on the right path."

Isobel changed the subject, voicing the one question Marjory couldn't answer. "What will you do if Hella confirms your dream?"

She touched her ambers. The stones proved cool and smooth.

If she was in peril, the threat wasn't in this much-maligned corner of Nought that she loved so dearly. But even as she acknowledged her relief, her fingers caught a faint vibration deep within the necklace.

A fleeting stir, little more than a flicker.

She took a breath, her awareness quickening. "If Hella knows of a Viking lord named Rorik the Generous, or a Saracen woman called Lady Sarina, I shall take care never to cross their paths. No matter what Kendrew might say or do if he tries to foist such worthies on me."

"He won't." Isobel slid her gaze away, as if seeing her husband's face before her. "Even if he wished to see you wed to a Viking lord, he wouldn't offer you to any man as a second wife. He loves you too much to suffer you such a fate."

Marjory scarce heard her.

More shivers were racing up her spine. And this time they were making her scalp prickle. Her palms were also dampening and her pulse raced.

Something was afoot.

And it wasn't the whirling mist.

As unobtrusively as possible, she lifted a hand to her ambers again. Oddly, the necklace wasn't humming. The stones were cold and completely still. So she swung around, narrowing her eyes to peer into the birches at the last spot she'd sighted Grim.

He still wasn't there.

"We've lost Grim." She turned back to Isobel. "He's not behind us anymore."

"He wouldn't just disappear."

"That's what worries me."

"Perhaps he stepped aside to. . ." Isobel's blush revealed her thought.

Marjory shook her head. "Wherever he went, he's not near the path. I don't like it."

"The noise I heard earlier." Isobel stepped closer. "Do you think—"

"I don't know what I think." Marjory took one deep breath, then another. The shadows were darker now. And the pearly luminescence of the mist seemed alive, shimmering around them. An eerie quiet had descended so that the only sound was the wind and the rushing of the nearby burn.

Until a crunch on stone revealed the approach of determined footsteps.

It was a man's tread.

And it wasn't Grim's.

Marjory knew who was coming. And the knowledge hit her hard enough to punch the air from her lungs. Turning, she saw Alasdair emerge from the mist. This time there was no doubt it was him. His stride strong and purposeful, he strolled toward her as if he owned the birchwood. As if he possessed her as well. His gaze swept from the top of her head to her toes and then back up again as he approached, the look in his eyes making shivers race all through her. Her breath came short and fast, her entire body heating. And this time her discomfort, the chills flashing along her skin, had nothing to do with the uncanny wood.

It was him.

Alasdair.

She could only stare at him. Words wouldn't come no matter how hard she tried to think of something to say.

From the corner of her eye, she caught Isobel smiling at him.

"Alasdair," her friend gushed. "What brings you to Nought territory?"

Alasdair gave Isobel a slow smile that, for all its politeness, set Marjory's nerves jangling. "I'm here to—"

"He's stalking about where he has no business." Grim stepped out of the trees to stand beside Alasdair. He clutched his war ax in his hand and his expression was dark, doing his name justice. "He brought a score of men with him, trespassers all."

"That depends on one's view. I wouldn't call them thus." Alasdair's gaze flickered from Grim to the trees where his men appeared on their horses. "Nor did I come here to dent my sword on your thick skull."

He reached out with lightning speed then, snatching

the ax from Grim's hand and spinning it several times before thrusting it back to him, haft first. "Think hard before you pick a fight with a man who comes in peace."

To Marjory's irritation, Grim only grunted and rammed the ax into its strapping.

Marjory narrowed her eyes at both men. "I know why you're here, Grim." She lifted her chin when he looked ready to argue. "But you"—she fixed her iciest gaze on Alasdair—"have no reason to be here."

"Ah, but I do." He came closer. "If thon guardsman of yours"—he flashed a look at Grim—"hadn't interrupted, I'd have told you I came to see a lady."

"That's a pity because I have no wish to see you." Marjory held his gaze. "You aren't welcome here."

"Indeed?" His eyes warmed with amusement. "Who said I came to visit you?"

Marjory backed out of his reach, too stunned to answer.

She did arch a brow.

"Have a care, Norn. With such ice in your eyes, a man could think you care for him." A slow smile spread across Alasdair's face. "As is..." His tone was almost teasing. "You aren't the only lady hereabouts, or are you?"

Marjory hoped her gaze would freeze him. "If you've come to see my good-sister, Kendrew will show less restraint with his ax than Grim."

"Lady Isobel isn't the reason for my journey." He turned aside then, taking Isobel's hand and dropping a kiss on her knuckles. "All the same, it's always a pleasure to see her. Lady Isobel's brother James and I are good friends. A man needs trustworthy allies."

Marjory bristled at the unspoken dig to her brother

"Such alliances wouldn't be needed if clan boundaries were respected."

Alasdair's smile faded. "Lady, as chief of my people, it is aye my duty to see invaders kept out of this glen."

"Yet you are trespassing now."

"The Glen of Many Legends belongs to us all. Or have you forgotten that the King deemed it so?"

"I've forgotten nothing." Marjory tried to ignore the heat surging through her.

He'd come so near that her heart almost stopped beating. She should turn and walk away. He deserved no better. Instead, he had the daring to step even closer. His gaze locked on hers, smoldering in a way that made it impossible for her to glance aside.

She could see the pulse at his throat, a muscle twitching faintly in his jaw. The golden flecks in his eyes shone, reminding her how easily she could drown in his gaze. His voice, so deep and deceptively soft, slid over her like sun-warmed silk, battering her defenses, completely unnerving her.

It'd be so easy to recall his kisses, his mouth slanting over hers, ravishing her...

Fortunately, she remembered his hurtful words.

Any half-fetching female would've done. I was away nigh a year, without a woman...

Marjory stood straighter, squaring her shoulders.

Alasdair's quip, spoken so lightly, helped her regain her composure.

She gave him a hard look. "Whatever brought you here, it'd serve you better to leave."

His face darkened. He stepped closer, reached to grip her chin. "Those who are wise know that things aren't always as they appear, my lady." He leaned in, lowering his voice so only she could hear. "If you look into your heart, you will know that is so."

"I'm sure I don't know what you mean."

"I say you do." His eyes took on a dangerous gleam and for a moment she thought he'd kiss her. Instead, he stroked his thumb over her lips. "Remember it, sweet, for I will not remind you again."

"I don't need anything from you. Not reminders. Not kisses. Not even lost baubles." She glanced at her sapphire ring and then flashed a look at Isobel who'd opened her eyes very wide, sending her silent warnings.

Marjory ignored them.

"Nothing at all," she finished, breaking free of Alasdair's grasp.

His face was stony. "So be it."

"Indeed." Marjory flicked at her sleeve.

"I'll be on my way." He nodded to Isobel and Grim. Then he turned back to her, bowing slightly. "My men and I would've escorted you back to Castle Nought, but"—he looked again at Grim—"you're in good hands with Grim."

Grim mumbled something unintelligible.

Isobel appeared pained. "You are always welcome—"

"To ride Nought's boundaries," Marjory allowed. "This birchwood lies at Nought's heart. As such, it is land you've no reason to tread."

A muscle twitched in Alasdair's jaw. "Dinnae push me too far, lass."

"I would say you drew your own line in the sand." The finality of her tone made Marjory's stomach knot.

But her heart was beating so rapidly she feared she'd

die any moment. If, she worried, it was possible to perish from a man's mere proximity.

If so, Alasdair would be the end of her. She could think of nothing except how disastrous it was to desire him so much, to love and want him as she did. How ghastly it was that, for the remainder of her life, she'd have to content herself with one toe-curling, bone-melting encounter with him.

Kisses and caresses he would've given any ready female, by his own damning admission.

She had every reason to be wroth.

And she'd no choice but to hasten him on his way.

To speak to him coolly, ensuring he understood she didn't wish his attentions. Even if he'd made it plain he'd come to Nought territory to see someone other than her. Her chest tightened on the thought.

She closed her eyes, half certain death was imminent.

Then she heard horses moving through the wood and realized Alasdair and his men were leaving. She opened her eyes at once, hoping to glare at him one more time before he was gone.

But he already was.

The mist billowed around him and his men, hiding them from view. Even their horses' hoofbeats were fast fading into the distance.

She should be glad.

She felt bereft.

Isobel appeared at her side, a reproachful look on her face. "That could've been your last chance to speak with him. He may never come back now. You should've found out what he was doing here."

"He told us." Marjory's mind spun. She couldn't think

straight. "It involved a woman, so I'm sure I don't want to know."

"Yes, you do." Isobel signaled to Grim who came grudgingly closer. "Tell Norn what you told me while she was speaking with Alasdair."

The big man pulled his beard braids, looking uncomfortable. He said nothing.

"If you don't tell her, I shall." Isobel gave him her most persuasive smile. "What did he say he was doing here?"

Grim furrowed his brow. "Carting fish o'er the hills. Herring for Hella. From his loch, caught fresh, was the excuse he gave."

Marjory blinked. "Are you sure?"

"So he said." Grim kicked a pebble on the path. "I'd have whetted my ax blade on his bones otherwise."

Marjory's heart started pounding again. "Did you see the herring?"

"No need." Grim's nose wrinkled. "One of his horses had a cart with barrels. The smell could only be brine."

"Why would he take herring to Hella?" Marjory glanced at Isobel, but she looked equally puzzled.

Grim shrugged. "I wouldn't know, my lady. He saw you and strode off before I could ask. He and his men were riding south, so he must've been to Skali and was already heading back to Blackshore when I challenged him."

"I see." Marjory glanced at the wood where Alasdair had disappeared.

Taking herring to Hella.

She'd been so unsettled to see him that she'd forgotten the widow.

The moment he'd mentioned a lady, she'd felt the earth tilt beneath her feet. The most unpleasant wave of dizziness had swept her. Jealousy—it could've been nothing else—had overwhelmed her, chasing reason.

Now he was gone.

And that was surely best because whatever had taken him to Hella's couldn't undo what happened between them in the old guard room.

She was better off never seeing him again.

What a shame that truth didn't make it any more bearable.

Chapter Twelve

❧

"Are you sure that's Skali?" Isobel's brow furrowed as she peered through the trees. The wood was darker now, almost ominous. A deep, high banked burn ran beside the path, its rushing water loud in the stillness. "I don't remember a burn near Hella's cottage."

"It's nearly gloaming." Marjory knew that said everything. "This wood changes after dark."

Isobel tsked. "Burns can't alter their courses."

"This is Nought. And we're in its heart." Marjory glanced about, studying the wood's gloom and shadows. "Anything can happen here."

"Something almost did. Or would have if you'd let it." Isobel made it sound so simple. "Didn't you see Alasdair's face when he walked up to you? His eyes blazed and the passion rolled off him, almost scorching the air. I wouldn't have been surprised if he'd seized you to him, ravishing you whole."

Marjory flicked at her sleeve. "Alasdair MacDonald

would pounce on any female who chanced to cross his path." She spoke sharply, regretting the words as soon as they left her tongue. She was especially sorry when sympathy flickered across Isobel's face.

Pity was the last thing she wanted.

She also had other concerns than a roguish chieftain who only needed to look at her sideways to set her pulse to leaping. When he touched her, she felt dazed and giddy, excited. His kisses...

Marjory frowned, annoyed that he held such power over her.

She should revile him.

She should—

She froze, raising a hand to warn Isobel as a magnificent white stag stepped onto the path before them. Huge and with the dignity of great age, he stood perfectly still, watching them with his peaty-brown eyes, his gaze unblinking. Mist swirled and sparkled around him, the strange luminosity leaving no doubt that he was no ordinary creature.

"*Laoigh Feigh Ban.* The white stag." Isobel gripped Marjory's arm, her voice low and reverent. "He's enchanted, the pet of Grizel and Gorm, my clan's Makers of Dreams. His name is Rannoch."

"I know." Marjory spoke as softly as Isobel. Her heart thundered, blood roaring in her ears. This was the third time she'd seen the fabled stag in recent days and the first time he'd come so close. "Everyone in the Glen of Many Legends knows of Rannoch."

Isobel edged closer. "He rarely leaves Grizel and Gorm's high moors. He'll have a reason—"

Isobel tightened her fingers on Marjory's arm. "Dear

saints!" The stag's eyes were changing color, turning from deep brown to rich, glowing gold. "Do you see—"

"I've seen him do this several times of late, never so close." Marjory couldn't look away from the stag's steady golden stare. Her skin tingled, the fine hairs on her nape lifting. "Until now, I thought I'd imagined him, especially the changing of his eyes."

"I wonder—" Isobel broke off as the whirling mist brightened and closed in on Rannoch, spinning ever faster around him and then vanishing, taking the enchanted stag back whence he'd come.

The path before them stood empty.

Rannoch was gone.

Marjory could hardly breathe. She turned to face her friend, hoping Isobel's thoughts weren't her own. "Gorm's prophecy, do you remember it?" She saw in Isobel's eyes that she did. "Your brother James went to the Makers of Dreams just before the trial by combat, hoping they would tell him the outcome of the battle. Gorm gave him a prophecy instead, telling him that—"

" 'Peace will be had when innocents pay the price of blood and gold covers the glen,' " Isobel finished for her, proving that she, too, knew the ancient's words by heart. "I haven't forgotten. I doubt anyone has. Though"—she gave Marjory a smile of encouragement—"many believe the prophecy was fulfilled after the battle. Innocents did die that day. And"—she glanced to where the stag had vanished—"the trial by combat took place in autumn, gold covering the glen."

"I believed that, too. I no longer do." Marjory rubbed the back of her neck. Her pulse still raced. "Not since I've been seeing Rannoch in the wood. I think the changing of his eye color is a warning. That perhaps the gold in Gorm's prophecy wasn't the autumn coloring of the glen, but that he meant"—she could hardly voice her suspicion—"the Vikings who will swarm the glen to seize me if my dream comes to pass."

Isobel blinked. "Vikings?"

Marjory nodded. "Norsemen are known for their golden hair. Look at me . . ." She patted her own hair, well aware of its sunlike brightness. "The dream was so real, Isobel." She lowered her hand, hoped her friend wouldn't notice she was trembling. "Then Rannoch's strange appearances, how he's fixed me with his odd golden stare. Now you know why I must speak with Hella." She hoped her voice sounded firmer than it did to her. "I haven't just been traipsing about in the wood hoping to catch glimpses of Alasdair."

She *had* hoped to see him.

But she'd sooner eat a plate of bog moss seasoned with stone dust before she'd admit it.

"Come, it's growing late," she declared before Isobel could question her further.

Isobel had a suggestion every time she mentioned Alasdair's name and, at the moment, she didn't want to speak of him.

She wished she'd never met him.

Annoyed, she hitched her skirts and started down the path. Her braid had come undone, the wind tangling her hair. She was sure she looked a fright and didn't much care. All that mattered was reaching Hella's cottage. A flash of crimson through the trees and a smudge of blue peat smoke against the sky revealed that Skali was close.

The cottage's red-painted door was unmistakable.

"Not a word to Hella about Rannoch or Alasdair." Marjory brushed back what was left of her braid, irritated that she'd lost its ribbon. "I don't want anything distracting her from my questions about her homeland."

Isobel glanced at her. "Rannoch isn't a problem. But if I don't mention Alasdair, Grim will."

"I think not." Marjory felt a twinge of guilt. "He'll be away in the wood for longer than we'll need to speak with Hella."

"Oh?" Isobel arched a brow. "What did you do?"

"Nothing. I didn't have to." Marjory glanced at her. "Grim loves animals. All creatures great and small, even mythical ones that might not even be there."

"You think he'll see Rannoch?"

"I doubt it." Marjory shivered. "Laoigh Feigh Ban's message is for me, I'm certain."

"Then... ahhh." Comprehension lit Isobel's eyes. "That's why you told Grim you thought you saw an *an cu glas* drinking at the burn."

Marjory flicked a twig off her sleeve. "When he reaches the burn and the fairy dog isn't there, he'll search for the creature. If I know Grim, he'll keep looking for a while."

"He did believe you." Isobel glanced to where the big man had slipped into the birches.

"No harm done." Marjory turned back to the path to Skali's door. "This evening, he'll weave a fine tale of almost tracking down a fairy dog. The men in the hall will hang on his every word, applauding his daring in chasing after such a dangerous beast. Grim will be a hero." Marjory wouldn't have sent him on such a goose chase otherwise.

She loved Grim dearly.

But she didn't need his hulking presence at Skali.

"Come, I believe Hella is home." Marjory was certain, for a glimmer of candlelight shone through the cottage's two small windows.

A rowan grew at one side of Skali, lending protection to the cottage. At their approach, one of Hella's cats leaped off a bench beside the door. Moving fast, the cat streaked past them into the wood.

Hurrying as well, they followed the last bit of path to the cottage. With its rough stone walls and heather thatch, Skali could've belonged to another time. Long-ago years when the ancient magic was strong. Many believed such powers lingered in the Glen of Many Legends.

Somewhere in the mist, another of Hella's cats gave a loud, high-pitched wail.

Hella's pets were the reason Marjory hadn't brought along Hercules. He didn't care for cats and was especially suspicious of the Norsewoman's. Just now, when another glowing-eyed cat appeared out of the mist to fix them with a long, unblinking stare, she almost understood her dog's objections to the creatures.

Hella's cats were a bit uncanny.

"Do you believe the tales that claim Hella has certain powers?" Isobel leaned in, whispering in Marjory's ear. "The cats—"

"Hella's cats are her companions, not her familiars. They're spoiled, not wicked."

"Her familiars?" Concern pleated Isobel's brow. "So she does have powers?"

"Pah!" Marjory dismissed the notion. "No more than any woman who bathes her face with Beltane dew and hopes to gain youthful skin all her days. Or"—she eased her arm from Isobel's grip—"the girls who hide yarrow beneath their pillow, believing they'll see the face of their future husband in a dream."

"I've done both." Isobel sounded embarrassed.

Marjory smiled. "There you have it. Hella is no different than any of us, save that she's borne two great tragedies and earned wisdom from her sorrow. It cannot be easy to be twice widowed."

"Men do speak of her—"

"To be sure, they do," Marjory kept her voice low. "Age hasn't diminished her beauty and her rejection of their suits leaves them no choice but to look for other reasons than the truth."

"That she still loves her two late husbands too much to desire another?"

"So I believe."

Isobel sighed. "No man could replace Kendrew either. He—" She broke off when Hella appeared in the doorway.

"Ladies..." Smiling, she came forward with her arms outstretched in welcome. A tall, strongly made woman, her face carried only a few faint lines around her eyes. Her flaxen hair hung in a thick braid to her waist, the strands still bright and silken. She wore a light-gray gown and a silver clasp held a deep-blue shawl about her shoulders. The colors, combined with the fairness of her hair and skin, were reminiscent of a clean Nordic wind blowing across the cold, deep waters of her distant homeland.

A silver Thor's hammer amulet rested against her breasts, her only adornment.

"You do me honor." She glanced at Isobel and then looked back to Marjory. "What brings you to Skali on such a chill, misty day?"

Marjory smiled. "Who at Nought doesn't relish a walk in such weather?"

"True enough." Hella ushered them through her doorway, into the cozy warmth of her cottage. "Yet something tells me there's another reason?"

"You are perceptive as always." Marjory spoke true. "But it is aye a pleasure to visit you at Skali."

And it was.

In keeping with her home's name, Hella had arranged cushioned benches around the cottage's main room. Peats glowed on the central hearth and the stone-flagged floor was well-swept and spotless. Hella's sturdy oaken table proved equally clean, its surface scrubbed and gleaming. Two small chairs and a low, three-legged stool offered further seating, while the quiet smoldering of the peat fire and the wind through the thatch lent to the coziness.

Bunches of dried herbs hung from the ceiling rafters. And a string of plump, golden herring stretched across one wall, the fish drying in the earthy-sweet haze of peat smoke that filled the little room.

Marjory jerked her gaze from the herring, her heart giving a sharp lurch at the proof that Alasdair had been there.

Isobel moved to the fire to warm her hands. "M'mmm…" She sighed appreciatively. "Such lovely herring, Hella. Wherever did you fetch them?"

Marjory drew a tight breath, felt heat sweep her nape.

For two pins, she'd look murder at Isobel.

Instead, she kept her gaze on one of Hella's cats, a small gray tabby, sleeping on a window ledge. Two other cats, one entirely black and the other tri-colored, played with a heather sprig in a corner.

They were a welcome distraction.

Even so, Hella's enthusiastic response reached her. "The herring are fine, aren't they? The MacDonald chieftain brought them by a while ago, a gift from one of his clanswomen for an herbal concoction I made for her."

"How was the MacDonald?" Isobel wriggled her fingers in the fragrant smoke rising from the peats. "Is he well?"

"Better than I've ever seen him." The admiration in Hella's voice made Marjory grit her teeth. "He's a bonnie man. And he's a good one to come all this way to bring provender to my humble door."

Marjory tightened her fists against her skirts.

Any more praise for the lout and she wouldn't be able to breathe.

"I've heard he declined Laird MacKinnon's bid for his daughter's hand in marriage." Hella tsked, wonderingly. "Lady Coira is said to be a beauty. Her dowry would've been immense. I was surprised he rejected the offer."

"Perhaps he desires someone else?" Isobel's dark gaze slid to Marjory.

"I've wondered." Hella lifted a hand, tapping her chin with a finger. "I've seen the fairest maids vie for his attention, yet he pays them scarce heed. I suspect his heart is given. Perhaps to someone he met when he was away so long?"

Marjory stiffened, pretending not to hear.

She did feel a pang, standing in the Norsewoman's cottage, listening to her speak of Alasdair.

More than once, she'd wished she could live as Hella did at Skali.

Her day's work would have been harder. She'd have

faced constant toil that left a woman with reddened, cal-
loused hands and an aching back.

But life would've been so much easier.

Her heart, and her hand in marriage, hers alone to give
as she chose. Of course, even then she'd find happiness
only if Alasdair happened to be a shepherd and not chieftain of an enemy clan.

No one would have objected to their union.

They could have lived in peace, caring for the land,
raising strong, strapping sons and bonnie daughters, and
enjoying evening songs by their hearth fire. And when the
embers died, they'd turn into each other's arms and spend
the long dark hours of the night loving.

Although...

Even some shepherds were known to be notorious
charmers.

Bold, laughing-eyed men who kissed any woman who
happened across their path, simply because they could.

The image struck her like a slap in the face, sending
the homey idyll she'd envisioned spinning away.

A rogue was a rogue, whatever his station.

And Alasdair was the worst of such blackguards.

"Come, you must be hungry." Hella's softly accented
voice startled her.

Marjory blinked, shamed to see that the older woman
stood before her with a tray of freshly baked oatcakes and
cheese. She was also waiting for Marjory to take the chair
she'd drawn closer to the fire.

Isobel was already seated on one of the benches, sipping a cup of ale. Hella's tri-colored cat had jumped up
beside her, purring for attention.

"I made the oatcakes just a while ago." Hella glanced

to where another batch baked on a griddle above the fire. A bubbling kettle of savory stew hung there as well, the tempting aroma filling the air.

Hella offered the oatcakes again. "I know you have a good appetite. And"—she beamed—"the MacDonald even praised them. Wasn't he kind?"

Marjory nearly choked.

But she took one of the oatcakes as she settled herself on the chair. She didn't want to offend her friend. Hella's oatcakes truly were the best in the land.

Unfortunately, eating was the last thing on her mind.

Rich auburn hair and piercing blue eyes invaded her thoughts, as did Alasdair's powerfully muscled shoulders and his strong arms that could pull her so tightly against him. The subtle but heady scent of the sea that clung to him, dashed with the briskness of cold clean air. His hands holding her face as he kissed her, long, deep, and intoxicating.

Marjory shifted on the chair, aware of her skin flushing, the heat sluicing her veins. She felt breathless, her chest tightening with a painful, burning ache that was beyond maddening.

So she reached for another oatcake, carefully avoiding Isobel's knowing stare and Hella's searching one. Unseen eyes watched her, too. A haughty black gaze that pinned her from the realm of dreams as the Saracen beauty rose in her mind, her cold face blotting all else.

"You're shivering." Hella swept behind a plaid curtain where Marjory knew she slept upon a down-stuffed pallet. Returning as quickly, she slid a soft woolen shawl around Marjory's shoulders. "Now, my lady, tell me why you're really here," she urged, taking the chair across the fire from Marjory's.

"She had a dream." Isobel leaned forward, speaking earnestly. "We think you can help her find answers to what she saw."

"What kind of dream?" Hella turned to Marjory.

"I saw a Viking fire burial." Marjory smoothed her skirt, refusing to acknowledge the bile rising in her throat.

Instead, she sat straighter on the rough-hewn chair, her gaze steady on the Norsewoman as she described the dream. The words flowed, coming as if from true memory, as she recalled the hard-featured Viking woman who'd taunted her and tried to tip a bitter-tasting brew past her lips. She also spoke of the other women, how they'd appeared as a group to crowd and jostle her, jeering the while. She shivered when remembering Lady Sarina, the cold-eyed Saracen.

She left out no detail, however small. She told of the huge, bearded spearmen who'd advanced on her so menacingly, beating their spear shafts against their shields as the bright, leaping flames of burning burial ships colored the sky behind them.

So slowly, they'd come for her, each man's harsh, grim-set face revealing his deadly intent.

Vaguely, Marjory noted that one of Hella's cats was weaving in and out of her chair's legs, brushing against her, purring.

She reached down to stroke his back, taking comfort in his silken warmth as she shared the dream's final scenes. How the spearmen formed a double ceremonial line so the women could poke and prod her past them, leading her to a Viking lord's funerary pyre.

A great dragonship, dressed with scaffolding to hide the bonfires beneath its hull.

Death fires that would be lit as soon as she'd joined the

dead Norse warlord she was meant to accompany into the Otherworld.

Somehow she'd finished the small cup of heather ale Hella had poured for her. And with the grace that Marjory so admired, the older woman had moved quietly to her side and now took the cup from her hands, setting it on the little oaken table beside her.

"I must know"—Hella smoothed Marjory's hair back from her brow and rested a hand on her shoulder—"did you enter the flaming dragonship?"

"Nae, praise be." Marjory couldn't keep the relief from her voice. "A Highland warrior appeared on the strand, arriving out of nowhere. He looked so fierce, battle ready in all his war finery, fury rolling off him. He drew his sword and rammed the blade into the sand. Then he stared round, glaring at my tormentors."

Marjory ignored the look Isobel shot her, pinning her friend with a warning glance of her own.

She wasn't about to tell Hella that Alasdair was the hero in her dream.

"This Highlander rescued you?" Hella slid a disturbingly knowing look at Isobel.

"He did." Marjory brushed oatcake crumbs off her knees, pretending she hadn't caught the women's exchanged glances.

She had the most uncomfortable feeling that Hella knew the dream hero was Alasdair.

Marjory cleared her throat, rushing on before Hella could ask her. "One of the Norsemen challenged the Highlander and he grabbed the man's spear, leveling it at them all. He warned them not to harm me. I don't know how he came there."

"He came from your heart, dear one." Hella tucked a strand of hair behind Marjory's ear. "A hero to brave wild seas and wind, even defy hard-fighting Norsemen to champion you. He will be the man destined for you."

Marjory bit her tongue rather than say something she'd surely regret. All Alasdair would do to her heart, if she allowed, was stomp on it.

She hardened her jaw, pushing him from her mind.

Fortunately, Hella didn't seem to notice her discomfort.

"We Norse have a saying and it is true." Hella stepped back, looking down at her fondly. "Fate is inexorable, my dear."

"I told her the same." Isobel folded her hands in her lap, looking pleased. "Such a hero would tear apart a mountain to keep his lady safe."

Marjory stiffened. "He wasn't really there. It was a dream."

Hella shook her head. "As a Nought Mackintosh, you have enough Nordic blood in your veins to know that dreams are where our souls wander paths that once were, or where we will someday find ourselves walking."

Marjory inhaled deeply, wishing Hella hadn't reminded her of what she knew so well.

What a shame the man she knew was her destiny was a greater scoundrel than her brother.

"Did the Highland warrior carry you away with him?" Hella returned to her seat, lifting the cat who had claimed it onto her lap. "He saved you?"

"He disappeared, vanishing as if he hadn't been there at all." Marjory wasn't surprised by that part of the dream. "I fought the women holding me. I even tossed the brew they wanted me to drink into their faces. But there were so many of them. They fell upon me from all sides, dragging me to the burning ship, a great dragonship that the men had set alight with torches.

"I felt the flames, even choked on the whirling soot and ash. And then"—she tamped down a shudder, took a grateful sip of ale—"the banging of my window shutter wakened me. It was raining hard, a cold, wet wind gusting into my bedchamber. And yet..."

She glanced at Isobel, appreciative of her friend's nod of encouragement. "When I went to close the shutters, my foot knocked a small metal cup like the one in my dream. The beaker of some foul-smelling brew that the first woman tried to force me to drink, but—"

"When she looked again"—Isobel leaned forward, finishing for her—"it was only one of Hercules's wooden dog toys. That would've been the end of it, but Marjory's room smelled faintly of smoke. And not from the smoored peats on her hearth but the acrid reek of burning wood and things best not mentioned in gentle company."

"The dream and everything you experienced on waking was that vivid?" Hella paused in taking a sip of her ale.

"So it was." Marjory nodded.

Hella's brow furrowed. "You are afraid this will come to pass?"

"I'm concerned, aye." Marjory stood, began pacing the small, bench-lined room.

Terrified was a better description, but pride wouldn't allow her to acknowledge the fear.

"I wish I hadn't been away so much these last days." Hella set down her ale cup, her gaze flicking to the clusters of herbs hanging above them. "Some of the glen women pay well for certain cures. It was Maili, the laundress at

Blackshore, who sent the MacDonald here with herring for me. I'd given Maili a salve to soften her hands. And Beathag, the cook's wife over at Castle Haven"—she flashed a look at Isobel when she mentioned her home—"sent word that she needed my special tincture for a toothache."

Marjory heard only one word.

Blackshore.

She couldn't allow Isobel to use Hella's mention of Alasdair's stronghold to bring up his name again.

The determined glint in Isobel's eyes said she was about to.

"Hella..." Marjory didn't give her the chance. "I've been wondering about your northern homeland."

Hella twisted around to look at her. "What do you want to know?"

Marjory stopped as far as possible from the string of MacDonald herrings. She took a deep breath. "Are there Saracen women in Norway?"

"Slaves?" Hella blinked. "To be sure, there are some. My people have always traveled far and wide, often taking strong children and young, beautiful girls as captives to be sold or traded. See here..." She lifted the plaid curtain to her sleeping corner again, disappearing to return with a length of shining silver coins. "This is a belt-chain made of dirhams, Arab coins from distant lands beyond the known horizon. My first husband, Lars, crafted the belt for me not long after we wed. He was a trader and often spoke of the mysteries of the strange places he visited."

She set the belt on the table and the silver coins gleamed red in the firelight. "It's very fine, isn't it?" A soft smile curved Hella's lips as she looked down at the gift. "Lars spoke of the beauty of the women in those lands. He said they smelled of exotic spices and their silky black hair shone like moonlight on a deep, dark sea. Their eyes"—she shrugged, lifting her hands—"he swore a man could sink into their depths, so rich and beguiling were they. Indeed, if I hadn't known how much he loved me, I would've fretted each time he set sail." Her face brightened then, her smile deepening. "If I'm honest, worry over those dusky-skinned lovelies was the reason I took to accompanying him on many of his journeys."

"I wouldn't want Kendrew around such females either." Isobel gave a delicate shudder.

Marjory resisted the urge to roll her eyes. Her brother didn't know any women except Isobel existed. A more besotted man didn't walk the earth.

Alasdair...

Marjory drew a tight breath, an unpleasant rush of heat sweeping her. How could she have given her heart to a man who was drawn to women as easily as bees swarmed to a honey hive? Annoyance shot through her and she was sure her cheeks were glowing.

Blessedly, if Isobel or Hella noticed, they didn't say anything.

"Any woman would have good reason to keep her man from Saracen females." Hella was nodding at Isobel. "They are known seductresses. They're said to move in ways that steal a man's reason."

Marjory cleared her throat. "Do great Norse lords ever marry such women?"

Hella shrugged. "Such men can do as they please. If a slave girl was exceptionally attractive..." She let the words trail off, reaching to pet the cat that chose that moment to lean against her ankle.

Marjory forced herself to speak calmly. "Have you ever heard of Lady Sarina, a Saracen beauty wed to an aging Viking warlord named Rorik the Generous?"

"Not that I recall. Although"—Hella began tapping her chin—"there was a popular young fighter named Rorik the Bold who was known for his love of dark-haired, dusky-skinned slave girls."

Marjory's mind raced. "Are you sure he wasn't called 'the Generous'?"

"Nae, I would have remembered." Hella went to the door, opening it for one of her cats who'd been crying to go out. "He was Rorik the Bold. Many were the hearts he broke because he wouldn't look at any of us." She turned back to the room, lifting her flaxen braid. "He didn't care for our sun-colored hair and blue eyes. Only dark beauties would do." She let her braid fall, her smile wistful. "He sampled every slave girl who landed on our shores. Loving them as he did, he could well have made one his wife in later years."

"Could his name have also changed in age?" Marjory had to know.

Hella considered. "If he did something truly remarkable, perhaps. A deed his men might wish to honor with a more appropriate by-name."

Marjory nodded, not caring for the answer.

Something told her Rorik the Bold had become Rorik the Generous, the dead Viking warlord from her dream.

Lady Sarina remained a puzzle.

Until a short while later, when Marjory and Isobel left Skali Cottage to wait by the path for Grim's return from chasing fairy dogs.

"By the gods, Isobel. I know why Hella hadn't heard

of Lady Sarina." Marjory rushed the words before the tightness in her chest could rise to close her throat. "Hella has been here for years. She wouldn't know if Rorik Whoever-He-Was took a Saracen bride."

Isobel blanched. "That could be so."

"I fear it is." Marjory took a deep breath, closing her eyes.

"That isn't all you should worry about." Isobel gripped her elbow, squeezing.

Marjory snapped open her eyes, seeing at once why Isobel sounded so concerned.

Deep in the wood ahead of them, the mist had thinned just enough to reveal a group of horsemen. Big, well-armed warriors in plaid and steel and leather, they thundered through the trees as if bent on murder.

Alasdair led them.

And Marjory had a good idea who'd incurred their wrath.

"They're after Grim." She grabbed Isobel's hand and started running after the horses.

"Grim can take care of himself," Isobel said, panting beside her. "It's you I'm worried about."

"Me?" Marjory flashed a look at her.

Isobel pressed a hand to her side as they dashed along the path. "No man wears a look that dark unless a woman put it there."

"Indeed." Marjory almost stumbled.

"Love does that to a person." Isobel had the nerve to laugh. At least, she gave a gasp that could be taken for laughter.

Marjory just kept running.

If Alasdair was in a temper—and he'd looked to be in

a fine one—his anger would have nothing to do with her, she was sure.

But her heart was hopeful.

If she could stir him to fury, she could also inflame his passion.

Seduce him. And she'd do so properly this time.

Such a gain was only half the battle, yet it'd bring her much closer to victory.

How sad she was no longer sure she wanted to win.

Chapter Thirteen

❧

All Mackintoshes are mad men."

Alasdair muttered the slur as he spurred his horse through the birchwood, his disbelieving gaze on Grim. He rode as fast as he dared, plunging through the thick-growing trees. His men followed close behind, a tightly packed group who surely thought his wits had left him.

Perhaps they were right.

Why else would he have reined round so abruptly to pound after Grim when they'd spied the big-bearded Mackintosh warrior striding along a burnside, bending low to peer into bushes and behind trees.

Grim's follies were his own.

It was nothing to Alasdair if the man was feebleminded.

He should slew his horse about and lead his men back home to Blackshore before Grim noticed them barreling down upon him.

But he rode on.

A fury such as he'd seldom known raged inside him and he wouldn't have any peace until he'd addressed the matter, and swiftly.

Norn and Lady Isobel were who-knew-where in the wood, unescorted. Dark clouds filled the sky and a light rain was beginning to fall. And it was cold, the mist thickening by the minute.

Yet Grim was poking about the burn as if he hadn't a care in the world.

The man was addled. Not worthy of protecting a louse in his beard.

Alasdair might kill him.

Bending low to the ground as the bastard was, it wouldn't take more than one swing of Mist-Chaser to lop off his irresponsible head.

A snarl rising in his throat, Alasdair whipped out his sword.

His horse shot forward in a burst of speed, the well-trained beast sensing Alasdair's need for blood.

Grim straightened as Alasdair thundered up, reining close. "Still about, brine drinker?" Grim didn't flinch, even thrust out his jaw, inviting a blow. "Did you no' hear my lady tell you to be away from here?"

"I go where I please." Alasdair leaped down from his horse before the big man could blink. Still holding his sword, he went toe to toe with Grim. "Where is she?"

"Nowhere that concerns you." Grim narrowed his odd smoke-colored eyes and swelled his massive chest.

Alasdair saw red. "Tell me, you bastard."

Grim just glowered at him.

"Curse you!" Alasdair rammed his sword into the ground and plowed his fist into Grim's face, sending him reeling. Staggering, Grim wheeled his arms, catching himself before he tumbled backward into the burn.

Some of Alasdair's men laughed.

Surprisingly, so did Grim.

Looking almost pleased, he rubbed his bearded jaw as he looked round at Alasdair and his mounted warriors.

"That was a fine blow." Grim lowered his hand, shaking his head at the blood on his fingers. "It's been a while since anyone dared."

Alasdair didn't return the lout's low chuckle. "I could've taken your head off." He glared at Grim, his hands on Mist-Chaser's still-vibrating hilt. "Be glad I'll no' strike a man with his back to me."

"So I turned and earned your fist?" Grim wiped more blood from his mouth, still appearing amused.

"If that wasn't enough for you, draw that damnable ax of yours." Alasdair held Grim's gaze, his own as cold as he could make it. "We'll end this here and now. After I hear where Norn is."

Grim's face shuttered, his levity gone.

"You'll no' give orders on land that isn't yours, is what you'll do." He leaned toward Alasdair. "Lady Marjory"— he stressed her title—"is at the widow Hella's cottage. Lady Isobel, likewise. No' that it's aught to do with you."

"The weal of all the glen's womenfolk is my business." Alasdair's fist itched to punch Grim again. He'd defend any female in need. It was a matter of honor. The only difference with Marjory was that the thought of harm coming to her turned his world red.

It made his head pound and squeezed his chest so badly he was sure his lungs had caught fire.

That Grim, a Nought guardsman, had let her out of his

sight, putting her in possible danger, sent rage pumping through him.

"You forget your duties." Alasdair stepped closer, resisting the urge to grab his plaited beard and twist hard.

Grim's face hardened. "I made it my duty to follow the ladies through the wood. If I wasn't prepared to watch o'er them, I would've stayed at Nought where a fine, plump kitchen lass was making moony eyes at me just when the ladies crept from the castle."

Alasdair didn't sympathize. "You weren't looking out for them strolling along thon burn, peeking into bushes and behind trees."

"Skali Cottage was ne'er out of my sight." Grim folded his arms, belligerent. "Nor are they in danger. No one goes near that cottage. Folk hereabouts fear this wood and keep their distance."

"My men and I rode here." Alasdair glanced at his warriors, still mounted. He didn't say they'd been trying to leave the wood for hours but the trees kept closing in on them, the path twisting in wrong directions. "If we entered these blighted birches, others could as well."

Grim clamped his jaw, his mouth setting in a tight, thin line.

"Ho, Grim!" One of Alasdair's men edged his horse near and then leaned forward over the beast's neck. "What were you looking for in the bushes along the burn? Naked water sprites?"

Grim said nothing.

Alasdair narrowed his eyes at him, furious. "What kept you from standing guard outside Skali?"

"I did." Marjory stepped out of the trees to stand

beside Grim. Eyes blazing, she stood as straight as if she'd swallowed a sword, her clipped tone chilly as the air.

Alasdair stared at her, seeing only her damned kissable mouth. Even frowning, she took his breath, made his entire body tighten with wanting her. Heated images flashed across his mind, all the ways he burned to possess her, show her how much he desired her.

Before she could guess, he lifted his gaze from her lips, met the icy blue of her stare.

"Lady Marjory." He nodded curtly, returning her scowl.

"Blackshore." She lifted her chin, his title cold on her tempting lips.

Several of his men sniggered.

Alasdair ignored them, seeing no one but the beautiful, indignant woman before him. Pure sensual heat poured off her, charging the air between them. Her braid had come undone and her shining hair spilled to her hips. She was breathing hard, her lips temptingly parted. She'd been running, but she looked bed-mussed, flushed, as if freshly sated, her pleasure still rippling through her. She tantalized him beyond reason. Her eyes were opened wide, blue fire snapping in their depths, high color staining her cheeks.

He'd never seen her more magnificent.

And rarely had he felt such a fury.

"This wood is no place for women alone." He shot a glance at Lady Isobel, just emerging from the trees. Every bit as mussed as Marjory, she didn't come close to firing his blood as did the angry vixen still glaring at him as if she hoped her stare would set him aflame.

Striding over to her, he curled his hand around her

wrist, his grip firm. "You, especially, aught know that, my lady." He lifted her hand, flicking a look at her sapphire ring. "There are aye men about in any glen. Brigands and rogues you dinnae wish to meet."

A deep rumbling sound came from Grim's chest and he took a step forward, balling his fists. "That'd be you, to my way of it."

Ewan and some of Alasdair's men crowded Grim, forming a snarling wall of plaid, steel, and muscle between their chief and Marjory. An argument ensued, voices raised and curses sworn, also the sound of a scuffle.

Alasdair scarce noticed.

He released Marjory's arm, unable to bear the feel of her skin beneath his fingers.

Every inch of him burned to grab her and kiss the breath from her. He ached to be inside her. Kindle her fury into a raging, fiery heat that would consume them both until nothing remained but smoking cinders.

He looked her up and down, need searing him. She'd been running hard because her cloak had come askew, the edges gaping to reveal the blue woolen gown beneath. The soft material clung to her curves, showing how well-suited her body was for loving. She was made to be naked in a man's arms, to writhe and moan in the throes of deep, sinuous pleasure. And he was the man who should introduce her to such carnal delights.

Nae, he was the *only* man she should know so intimately.

He fisted his hands, not from anger but to keep from grabbing her to him. He stepped closer to her, almost toe to toe.

"You'll regret this meeting, Norn." His voice was low,

dark. His need was a fierce drumming in his blood, almost excruciating. But her nipples were chill-hardened, thrusting right at him.

Begging attention...

He caught her hand again and brought it to his mouth, kissing her knuckles, nipping the tips of her fingers. Behind them, his men were arguing with Grim. He didn't care. Her skin was smooth, the taste of her nectar on his tongue. Hunger for her seized him, her soft gasp and the warm, feminine scent of her driving him wild.

"You should ne'er have left Nought's walls." He threaded his fingers with hers, turned her hand to kiss the soft underside of her wrist. "There are dangers in these parts, see you? And you've run right into the worst of them."

"That I know!" She jerked free, stepping back to glare at him.

"You know naught." Alasdair caught her by the waist, held her fast. "If you did—"

A strange roaring in his ears cut him off and he blinked, not sure if the sound was the thunder of his own blood or Grim shouting at him.

Then Grim loomed before him, his beard rings clacking. "Unhand her or—"

"Stay out of this." Alasdair thrust out an arm, splaying his hand against the bastard's mailed chest. "You neglected your duties—"

"He did not." Marjory inserted herself between them, grabbing his wrist and lowering his hand with surprising strength. "I sent him into the wood. I'd seen a large dog near the burn and feared for Hella's cats. Grim left us at my bidding."

"Indeed?" Alasdair didn't believe a word. He let a slow smile curve his lips, hoping to irritate her into telling the truth.

But she only put back her shoulders and pinned him with another icy stare. "Grim knows his duty. A pity you don't have the grace to heed a lady's wishes." She lifted a hand, dashed a raindrop from her brow. "I made clear you aren't welcome here."

Alasdair's temper snapped. "I go where it pleases me, lady. But I'll own that we were on our way to Blackshore. We didn't get far because every track in this devil-damned wood runs in circles."

Marjory smiled, threw a look at Lady Isobel, almost as if they'd conspired for the wood to vex him.

Almost, he could believe it.

"If you can't follow a track through the trees, you shouldn't have come in the first place." She drew her cloak tighter, briskly brushing its folds in place. "Someone else could've delivered Hella's herring."

Alasdair couldn't argue with that.

It was true.

"Why did you come here?" Marjory's gaze held his, her blue eyes sharp.

She knew he had other reasons.

He did. But he wasn't about to share them.

Leastways he had no intention of telling her he'd use any excuse in the world just to see her again. It didn't matter if such a meeting took place in anger. Or if the circumstances made him look a fool.

There wasn't much a man wouldn't do when he wanted something badly enough.

And he wanted Marjory.

Worse, he desired her so fiercely that his need to be near her overrode his good sense. He should've sent one of his men with the widow's herring. That same man could've journeyed on to Nought to question Kendrew about the tar he'd seen on the strand at the Dreagan's Claw. His suspicion that one of his guards hadn't seen a sea beastie in Loch Moidart but a black-painted coracle.

The forerunner of men he was sure wished to provoke a fight.

Men he believed were acting on Kendrew's orders.

Now...

He'd struck Kendrew's captain of the guard with such force that the man's head had snapped back and his split lip was already swelling. Marjory was in a temper, clearly protective of her oversize watchdog. And after he'd fallen upon her, kissing her wrist and even biting her fingers, she no doubt held him for an ill-mannered craven.

Alasdair frowned and rubbed the back of his neck.

Had he ever made a greater mess of things?

Truth was, his wits fled whenever Marjory was near. She was speaking now and he hadn't heard a word she'd said.

"I asked why you're here," she lifted her voice, narrowing her eyes at him so that he half believed she'd read his thoughts. "I don't believe it was to deliver herring."

"We did take herring to the widow." It was all he could think to say.

She *did* fuddle his wits.

Somewhere not too distant, thunder rumbled then. And the wind was picking up, bringing the sharp wet chill of an imminent downpour.

His men's soured faces said they knew it.

Very shortly, they'd all be drenched. And if Marjory caught an ague, he'd never forgive himself.

"So you won't tell me?" Her voice held an edge. The wind brought her scent closer, teasing his senses with a light, clean freshness reminiscent of a spring meadow. "I'll give you no peace until you do."

"I am well warned, my lady." He almost laughed.

At last, a way to bind her to him.

Instead, a rusty old-dog bark drew his attention to the herring cart where Grim now stood. Alasdair frowned, knowing his favorite dog, Geordie, slept in the cart. Geordie was old, lame, and fond of any excursion outside Blackshore's walls. He deserved his rest without being accosted.

His blood heating, Alasdair strode toward Grim. "Touch my dog and I'll have a new sword belt from your hide. He's no' the wild beast you were searching for along the burn. Geordie wouldn't—"

"I ne'er hurt animals." Grim whipped around to face him, the twist of dried meat in his hand showing he'd been about to give Geordie a treat, not harm the dog. He patted a leather pouch hanging from his belt. "I aye carry food for dogs with me."

Alasdair just looked at him, keenly aware of his men sniggering again.

Only this time they were laughing at him.

Geordie took the meat twist from Grim's hand. He gulped it down with relish. Then, with surprising speed for his age, he snatched a second treat from Grim's fingers. To Alasdair's horror, Geordie then braced his front paws on the side of the cart and stretched to slurp Grim's bearded face.

The big man grinned, reaching down to rub Geordie's bony shoulders as the old dog swished his tail.

Alasdair felt heat sweep him, his chest tightening as he stared at the spectacle.

It was beyond acceptable.

Equally annoying, some of his men were swinging down from their horses, joining Grim beside the wagon.

One of the bastards took his hip flask from his belt and offered Grim a swig. Alasdair knew it was finest uisge beatha, fiery Highland spirits that a man didn't generally share with a foe.

"I told you Grim is a good man." Marjory appeared at his elbow. Her eyes glittered in triumph. "You haven't told me why you're truly here."

Alasdair turned his back on the men—they were now passing round the whisky—and set both hands on Marjory's shoulders, gripping tightly.

"I hoped to see you, lass. I want you." He told her true. A great mistake, because as soon as the words left his tongue, her expression closed, turning frosty. He stepped back, shoved a hand through his hair. "I'd thought—"

"What?" She lifted a brow, her gaze twin shards of sapphire ice. "Did you wish to catch me unawares, slake your manly needs again?"

"Nae, that was no' my intent. I did wish to see you, aye. I'll no' deny it. No' more. But I had other reasons as well. Suspicions I hoped—"

"About my brother?" Her face went even colder. "All know you can't abide him."

"Sweet lass, I…" The words snagged in his throat. She was standing so near, the wind lifting her hair so the silken strands teased against him. He couldn't breathe without inhaling her scent, an intoxication so feminine and entirely her own, its freshness maddening him. His heart slammed against his ribs and his head began to throb again. Another part of him also pounded as desire sluiced him, pouring like a fever into his blood, his loins.

He frowned. He was sure his need for her stood blazing on his forehead.

The soft clearing of a throat saved him. Relief, and something else, an indefinable emotion, flashed across Marjory's face as she turned to her friend Isobel. The other woman stood a few feet away, watching them with a bemused smile.

"I, too, would hear what brought you here?" Isobel's smile deepened as she came forward to hook her arm through Alasdair's. "If your concerns have to do with the Glen of Many Legends, we at Nought should hear them."

Marjory shot an annoyed glance to where Isobel's hand rested on Alasdair's arm. "He brought his worries to Nought's hall not long ago. I cannot imagine he has anything of greater import to tell us now." She looked at Alasdair, challengingly. "Unless he is again in need of—"

"Norn!" Isobel stepped away from Alasdair, her eyes rounding. "You forget yourself—"

"She is right to be wary." Alasdair's voice was rough, his emotions warring inside him. Half of him wanted to pull Marjory in his arms, haul her over his shoulder, and ride with her to Blackshore. The other half of him knew he had a duty to protect every man, woman, and child in the glen.

Torn, he glanced toward the herring cart where Grim had hitched himself onto the cart's bed and was rubbing Geordie's ears.

"Ho, Grim!" Alasdair called to him. "A word with you."

The big man grunted and pushed to his feet, giving Geordie one last ear rub before he sauntered over to Alasdair, suspicion all over him.

"Aye?" He hooked his thumbs in his sword belt.

In the herring cart, Geordie whined. Worse, the sound of his tail thumping against the cart's side proved that the dog liked Grim.

The thought made Alasdair's stomach twist.

Grim cocked a brow, waiting.

"The other day at the Dreagan's Claw, after you left..." Alasdair glanced at Marjory and Isobel, hoping his words wouldn't frighten them. Then he told Grim everything he'd seen on the little beach, from the smears of pitch at the tide line to the smoored campfire that someone had taken such care to hide behind a low mound of stones. The only thing he left out was that he'd thought he'd seen his ancestor, Drangar the Strong, staring up at him from the strand moments before he'd hastened down the cliff path.

Grim didn't need to know everything.

Besides, Alasdair didn't believe in ghosts. He'd seen mist and nothing else. But the pitch on the rocks and the cold campfire had been real.

"I didn't see anything the like when I was there." Grim didn't believe him.

Or he was lying.

"Men see what they expect to see." Alasdair watched him closely. "I looked more carefully because I suspected something would be there."

"And if there was?" Grim's eyes narrowed.

"Then someone has been using the inlet to hide." Alasdair was sure of it. "I'll wager they're up to no good, whoe'er they are."

He didn't say he suspected they could be mercenaries paid by Kendrew.

Grim was shaking his head. "The Dreagan's Claw is nigh inaccessible. If the currents don't sink a ship that comes too close to those cliffs, the rocks will rip the bottom out of any boat that tries to enter the inlet. Only a shipmaster bent on destruction would—"

"Vikings could pass those rocks with ease." Alasdair spoke his worst concern. "Their shipmasters can take a ship to hell and return unscathed, no' a scratch on the hull and nary a man lost."

"Vikings?" Grim grinned, touched the heavy silver Thor's amulet hanging round his neck. "Fear the Northmen, do you?"

A few feet away, Marjory and Isobel stood close together, their hands clasped tightly. Both women had gone pale and Alasdair wished there'd been a way to speak of the matter without alarming them.

"I fear no man." He kept his gaze on Grim. "But I'll no' have unrest descend on this glen. You'll no' deny the Northmen aye bring trouble."

Grim folded his arms. "I'd suggest you let Nought men deal with trespassers on our shores. If such intruders have even been here. If they harry you at Blackshore, then you can make them your business."

"They have been at Blackshore." Alasdair's blood chilled at his suspicions. He was sure the two black-painted dragon ships had been sent by Kendrew. Worse, that they had something to do with Marjory.

Grim appeared unconcerned. "Ships passing your coast, howe'er they're painted, say naught."

"They were also in my loch." Alasdair heard Marjory gasp and his heart clenched. "No' dragonships"—he glanced at her—"but a black-painted coracle, slipping along beneath my stronghold's walls. One of my men saw the boat from the ramparts."

He didn't say that his guardsman swore he saw a long-necked humpbacked sea serpent, steam blowing from the creature's nostrils.

Alasdair knew a black-painted coracle, a round cockleshell of a two-manned boat, could be mistaken for such a beast on a cold, dark-misted night. The *steam* would've been the luminescence of spume, stirred by the dipping of oars into the water.

In his mind, Alasdair saw his great-uncle, Malcolm, sitting ramrod straight on his stool in Alasdair's painted solar. *The truth, lad, varies depending on the direction of a man's viewpoint,* the aged warrior loved to say. *Ne'er forget that and you'll do well in life.*

It was a lesson Alasdair had taken to heart.

Steam-spewing sea beasties weren't swimming in Loch Moidart.

But his man had seen something.

Grim didn't turn a hair. "Did you see the coracle?"

"My man's word sufficed."

"I'll tell Kendrew." Grim's tone hinted at what he'd say. He'd make Alasdair sound like a raving madman.

Alasdair nodded curtly. He didn't care.

He did have another point. "It would be like him to send a paid crew to Blackshore, stirring trouble, hoping to goad me into a sea fight."

Grim snorted. "We have better to do at Nought than pull such pranks."

As if the heavens agreed, thunder cracked closer than before and a gust of wind shook the trees, bringing a flurry of cold, spitting rain.

"Come, ladies." Grim took both women by their elbows and began steering them away. "We'll wait out the storm at Skali. Hella will—"

"Nae, we must return or Kendrew will be furious." Isobel dug in her heels, balking. "He thinks we're in the ladies' solar, working on new wall hangings for the great hall."

"If we hurry, we can be back before he notices." Marjory turned, already making for the trees.

Alasdair frowned as Grim and Isobel hastened after her. They disappeared into the wood, thick mist hiding them like an eager conspirator.

"Wait!" Alasdair strode forward, catching them in several swift strides. "I have horses. My men and I will take you back to Nought. We'll have you there before the worst of the storm breaks." He ignored Grim, looking only at the women. "Kendrew won't know you've been away."

Grim's eyes took on a stubborn glint. "I think not—"

"An excellent idea." Isobel took his side, gracefully disentangling herself from Grim's hold on her arm. She started forward, smiling. "We shall be in your debt."

"You don't have extra horses." Marjory didn't move.

Alasdair smiled. "Grim can ride in the herring cart with Geordie. I've rigged an oiled sailcloth to cover the cart for Geordie. The brine smell might be a bit sharp, but they'll be comfortable enough."

Grim said nothing.

He was looking at Alasdair as if he'd grown two heads and a tail.

"You, Lady Isobel, can ride with my cousin Ewan." Alasdair felt a stone fall from his heart when she beamed, her gaze lighting on Ewan as the lad swung down from his horse and made her a bow.

"I shall be pleased." She hitched her skirts and went to join Ewan, no doubt hurrying before Grim or Marjory could argue with her.

"That leaves me." Marjory turned a cool blue gaze upon him.

"She stays with me." Grim stepped between them. "Or"—he lifted his hands, flexing his fingers—"are you thinking otherwise?"

"No' at all." Alasdair pushed past him and swept Marjory into his arms. "The matter's settled. She rides with me."

Grim roared and blocked his path. "I'll no' allow it."

Alasdair stepped around him, carrying Marjory across the little clearing. His men were already riding forward, Ewan leading his horse. Lady Isobel was mounted behind him and Alasdair would've sworn she winked at him as they rode closer.

Behind him, Grim muttered curses.

But after tossing one last furious glance at Alasdair, he swung himself into the herring cart with Geordie, quickly pulling the oiled sailcloth into place as if to blot the view of Alasdair and his men.

It was then that Isobel slipped from Ewan's horse, falling hard onto the mossy ground.

"*Owwww!*" She rolled onto her side, clutching one

ankle. She made no attempt to stand, her dark eyes round
and full of pain. "I've hurt my foot," she cried, not looking at Alasdair or Marjory.

Alasdair did glance at Marjory, not surprised to see
her frowning.

Isobel wasn't injured, he was certain.

But something was amiss.

Before he could figure out what, Grim leaped from the
cart and ran over to Isobel.

"My lady—dinnae move!" The big man knelt beside
her, sliding an arm beneath her shoulders. She turned
toward him, pressing her face against his neck, moaning
pitiably. "Be still," Grim advised again, this time reaching for her hem. "Let me see your ankle."

"No-o-o!" She grabbed his hand, shoving it aside.
"Don't touch it, please!"

"Lady, you can ride in the cart. But first you must let
us see—" Alasdair started forward only to stop when he
caught a glimpse of Isobel's face.

She was smiling.

There could be no mistaking.

"I don't think I could stand the jarring." Isobel's voice
lifted, the words muffled because she spoke against
Grim's shoulder. "I'd rather stay a while at Hella's." That
was much clearer. "Grim can carry me there."

"I will, my lady," Grim quickly agreed.

But he threw a look at Marjory, his bearded face suspicious. "You should return with us to Skali, lady. You cannot ride on with MacDonald—"

"Oh, but she must." Isobel spoke without lifting her
head. "If she reaches Nought swiftly enough, she can join
Kendrew in the hall at supper, telling him I'm feeling poorly

and have retired early. He aye comes abovestairs late, after making his rounds of the castle. By then"—she paused and Alasdair would've sworn she was struggling against laughter—"Grim and I can be back at Nought and—"

"No one will be the wiser," Marjory finished for her.

"It's for the best." Isobel threw them a glance, not looking at all pained.

Alasdair was mightily so.

He now knew what exactly had bothered him when Isobel's fall put a frown rather than worry on Marjory's face.

Lady Isobel hadn't slipped from Ewan's horse at all. She'd staged the fall. And there could be only one reason she'd done so.

She wanted to give Marjory time alone with him.

And—his lips twitched, his mind racing—he intended to take full advantage.

Far be it from him to disappoint a lady.

Hours later, another proud MacDonald stood tall and straight at the edge of Blackshore's most rugged headland, the sheer cliffs known as Drangar Point. It was because the promontory bore his name that Drangar gave his best efforts to hover erect and not let the wind make a mockery of his once-intimidating posture.

It helped that the night had turned so still.

Fine silver light spilled down across the sea each time the moon slid from behind the clouds. And hardly a ripple broke the water's black, glassy surface. A tenuous mist hid the horizon and thicker fog curled around the Warrior Stones, the twin monoliths that speared heavenward only a few paces from where he hovered.

Drangar glanced at the stones, so still and cold. Even

the altar stone, toppled onto the grass these long centuries, appeared to be holding its breath, waiting. Runes and lichens covered the stones, aged markings as silent as the mist-shrouded night.

Once, in the distant past when he'd carved the runes, he'd believed their magic would guard Blackshore and Clan Donald for all his days and beyond.

Now, he suspected his vanity might've angered the Old Ones.

The stones were sacred before he'd touched them, after all.

His runes probably weren't needed.

Yet the gods had given him a gift that required safekeeping. At the time, it never crossed his mind that he'd already possessed something so precious that its worth was immeasurable. He'd simply accepted the gods' benefice.

Then, as he should have known, he'd paid the price.

Drangar stood straighter, adjusted the fall of his fine black cloak.

How pathetic that just touching the soft woolen folds hurt him more than if someone thrust a dagger into his heart.

Yet he wore the cloak always.

A reminder of all he'd lost.

How over the years, he'd learned what truly mattered in life. Such as taking pleasure in the small joys and accomplishments, and that it wasn't victory that made a man great but the courage to step upon the road that would take him there.

He frowned, wishing one road was still open to him.

But just as in their earthly lives, ghosts made their own paths. And the woman he'd loved then, and still loved now, had barred the way to her heart.

He couldn't reach her.

Even as he'd failed to save her when they'd lived. He tried, pounding across the strand and plunging into the cold, tossing sea, swimming out to the tidal rocks that had stolen the life from his love.

All his power and might availed nothing.

And in the end, only they remained.

He'd been colder, his earth life more empty than these long years beyond the grave.

So he took a deep breath—or did as if—and stood as tall and proudly as he could, grateful for the things he had achieved.

He also thanked the gods for causing the wind to drop.

Maintaining his dignity proved easier when he wasn't buffeted about as if he possessed less substance than a wisp of bog cotton.

How sad that the description fit.

Yet he had every right to keep his head lifted. Despite his limitations, he'd managed to attract the young chief's attention at the Dreagan's Claw. He might not have the solidness he'd once kept so hard-muscled and battle-ready, but his wits hadn't deserted him. Some things stayed with a man, even in the Otherworld.

Love didn't leave a man either, as well he knew.

Or the sorrows that could still weigh down on a man's shoulders, making his heart ache with a fierceness to rival any living man's tragedies.

If young Alasdair was wiser than he'd been, he'd be spared such heartache.

Drangar hoped it would be so.

Perhaps he should even pay a call to Blackshore and do what he could to talk sense into the lad. To be sure, he wouldn't be able to sit him down in his painted solar and lecture him as he'd like to do.

But he still had ways.

Unfortunately, just as he made to wish himself into Alasdair's presence, his ever-sharp eyes caught a glimmer on the water that wasn't moonglow.

His warrior instincts snapping alert, Drangar peered out across the sea to where a faint reddish glow in the sky revealed the night lanterns of a moored ship. A high dragon-headed prow rose black against the darkness, revealing the ship's Nordic origin.

Whoever the Vikings were, they felt safe enough to light a fire.

Men so bold meant trouble.

Drangar frowned, forgetting his own cares. Almost, he wished himself out across the open water so that he could see the men for himself. Take his measure of their strengths and weaknesses, make a battle plan.

Only one thing held him back...

His fine black mantle.

Even after so many years, he hadn't mastered how to *whoosh* across great distances without his cloak slipping from his shoulders. Its fine Celtic clasp, so secure in life, was now just as insubstantial as he was.

Once, while attempting to whisk across a patch of marshland, the cloak had fallen into a bog.

It'd taken him forever to retrieve it, and twice as long to clean the hand-spun wool.

Had anyone other than his beloved Seona crafted the cloak for him, he'd risk crossing the waves to reach the moored dragonship.

But if he lost his mantle to the sea...

It was all he had left of her.

The wife he'd hurt so badly.

And who'd refused to believe that he regretted his one-time dalliance with a Selkie maid. And that all the comeliest seal women of the seas could have swam ashore and he'd have walked past them all, seeing, desiring—and loving—only his precious wife, Seona.

Instead, she'd reviled him, despising him so fiercely that she'd taken her life.

The truth of it was *he'd* killed her.

It was a sorrow he'd borne for eternity.

A regret he could never undo.

And so he did what he could and stood guard on the cliffs, leaving the Vikings to Alasdair. Sometimes a man's greatest moments came when he was pressed against a wall.

That, too, Drangar had learned.

If he'd failed at his own hour of reckoning, when he'd realized where Seona was and what she intended, he knew Alasdair would triumph.

He wouldn't arrive too late, unable to prevent tragedy.

Love was strength.

And even if the lad didn't yet know it, the Mackintosh lass loved him enough to see him through greater battles than any Vikings could pitch.

What a shame his own lady hadn't loved him with equal fervor.

How he wished she had.

Chapter Fourteen

❦

With the cold wind buffeting them, Alasdair and his men thundered across Nought's most bleak and empty bounds. Marjory shared Alasdair's horse, her arms wrapped tightly around him, her face pressed to his plaid-draped shoulder. He spurred his horse to great speed, his riding style bold and aggressive. As if he owned these wild, windblown lands and not her family, as they'd done for centuries.

"Please, slow down! This is no place to ride like a demon." Marjory lifted her head, raising her voice above the wind so he'd hear her.

If he did, he gave no sign.

He did send his horse sailing over a rushing burn.

"You're crazed." Marjory hissed the words between her teeth.

"Aye, that I am!" he called over his shoulder, proving he had heard her.

But he said no more.

And rather than slow his beast, he gave the animal his head, letting him careen with them across ground many at Nought swore had been hewn by the devil's own hand. Marjory curled her own hands tightly around Alasdair's sword belt. Her fingers brushed the rock-hard muscles of his abdomen, an intimacy that sent warmth spooling through her belly. But instead of sighing with pleasure, as well she could, she tried to ignore the melting deliciousness. The tingles rippling so sweetly across her most intimate places.

She'd seen Alasdair's face when he'd glanced back at her.

His expression was hard and fierce. Never had she seen him look so angry.

He clearly couldn't wait to reach Nought, to be rid of her.

Why else would he ride at such breakneck speed?

Marjory blinked, her eyes stinging from the cold wind. Her hair streamed out behind her, a skein of tangles, she was sure. And still they barreled on. Sheer stone walls, Nought's fiercest peaks, edged the narrow vale they were racing through, the granite heights seeming to glower down at them. Jumbles of rocks were everywhere, the broken ground treacherous, while the air was thick with the wet smell of imminent rain. More threatening was the rigidness of Alasdair's back, the stark displeasure pouring off him.

Whatever had sizzled and burned between them in the clearing was gone.

He'd withdrawn from her, his stony silence chilling her more than the rain beginning to spit down at them from the dark and angry sky.

Stung and confused, Marjory clung to him, refusing to allow pride to make her loosen her grip on his belt. Unlike Isobel, she wasn't an expert horsewoman. And she had no wish to fall to the rocky ground.

She wanted to live for another day.

If only to look Alasdair in the eye, keep her chin lifted, and show him he couldn't hurt her.

How sad that just a short while ago she'd believed everything would be right with them.

She'd felt so close to triumph.

Even though she'd not dared to show it, hope had bloomed, her heart soaring. She'd seduce him properly this time, if not with skill then with all the passion burning inside her. And he'd succumb, falling in love with her at last, never again desiring the other women who so easily caught his eye. He'd be hers alone.

And she'd be his.

Her pact with Catriona and Isobel would be fulfilled, her heart even more joyous.

Truth was she'd want Alasdair even if he was a sheepherder and dwelled in a humble cottage like Skali.

Nothing would matter except their love, which would burn brighter than all the stars in the night sky, their passion dimming the sun.

She'd been so certain. At the clearing, she'd felt the truth so strongly. Her heart had swelled, her spirits lifting. Fortune was hers, Isobel's trick fall paving the way for her. The rain would do the rest, demanding a halt.

Now...

She tightened her grip on Alasdair's belt, bit her lip against the hot pain in her throat. Angry, she swallowed against the thickness rising there.

Mackintoshes didn't cry.

But what a fool she'd been!

Riding away with Alasdair had shown her the real truth. He'd gone more distant with each heather mile they crossed. Her hopes crumbled, her budding excitement disappearing like a snuffed candle. Frustration bit deep, her hard-won confidence fleeing.

Not about to let him know, she forced herself to sit as stiffly as he did. To pretend her arms weren't wrapped snug about the man she loved so dearly, and wanted so badly. She ached for him with primal need, the woman in her not caring about pride. She'd have given him her virtue. She'd have done so gladly, if this ill-starred race across Nought hadn't revealed his indifference.

But all wasn't lost.

Soon they'd reach her home. She could walk away in dignity, not looking back.

Forgetting the dreams he'd shattered.

Until then, she'd return his cold silence and not think of anything else.

About the same time, but far out to sea, a Viking dragon-ship rode the night at anchor. The glow of an oil lamp illuminated the ship's tall, serpent-headed prow and the large square sail was furled. A heavy iron-and-stone anchor secured the twenty-oared warship against the tide.

Here, so distant from the far peaks of Nought, the night was still. Nothing stirred except the water along the hull and the creaking timbers. What wind there'd been had died hours ago and the sea shone like polished black glass. Darkness hid the moon, though now and then its wan light slipped through the clouds to silver the coastline where, even on such a windless night, waves broke white against the rocks.

Some might say the Glen of Many Legends was showing its teeth.

A Viking would laugh and smash those teeth, proving that bold men with swords and axes wouldn't be stopped by Highland bravura.

Plenty of Norse fighting men crowded the dragonship *Storm-Rider.* Fearless men with good, strong faces that folk of weaker blood might liken to the devil's own spawn.

The shipmaster, Ivar Ironstorm, had handpicked each oarsman. He'd chosen them for their brute strength and daring. Their willingness to swear him allegiance was also of great importance. Almost as crucial as the number of coins in the two heavy leather sacks at his feet just now. Wealth he'd been counting until Troll, his one-eyed oarsman, ruined his concentration by belching.

A fastidious man, Ivar was offended by crudeness.

Even if their night's meal of old bread, cheese, and ale wasn't the sumptuous fare Ivar preferred, he expected his men to eat like the lords he'd make them once his aging overlord succumbed to his ailments and Ivar reaped the riches he so rightly deserved.

Troll might not live to receive his share.

His mood souring, Ivar stood and left the sheltered steering platform where he'd been enjoying the cold weight of silver in his palms.

"Troll!" He strode down the aisle between the rowing benches, his hand unfastening his leather clout from his sword belt.

"You belched." He struck Troll hard in the face with

the switch. The blow would have the lout biting his tongue before he'd emit another such peace-stealing noise into an otherwise quiet night.

"I didn't." Troll's good eye glittered with rebellion and he leaped to his feet, thrusting a thick arm toward the darkened coast. "I said, *look there,* I did. There was a glow on the cliffs by Drangar Point. A bright flare, it was, as if from a balefire.

"Could be the MacDonalds have spotted us and are lighting fires in warning." Troll glanced round at the other oarsmen as if hoping they'd concur.

Snores or blank stares answered him.

Ivar tapped the clout slowly against his thigh. "Blackshore's coast is dark. There's not a glimmer of light there. You're lying." His voice took on a dangerous softness. "Aren't you?"

"I saw the light, too." Bors, who sprawled near a pile of oilcloth-covered weapons, pushed up on his elbow to defend his friend. "It grew and spread along the cliff top. I saw it plain as day. Could be there was even a man on the cliffs." Bors touched the hammer amulet at his neck, shuddering visibly. "A tall man in a dark cloak, he was. I saw his shadow lit by the glow, even from this distance." He curled his fingers around his talisman, gripping tightly. "He was looking out to sea, staring right at me."

"You were asleep." Ivar turned a stern eye on him. He took a step closer, aware that the light from the ship's lantern would glint off his arm rings and give his pale, unbound hair a godlike sheen. Many said he had the looks of Thor and he enjoyed using the likeness to keep his men respectful. "If you don't wish to sleep forever, think hard before you lie to me."

All down the ship, men swiveled their heads, watching the exchange.

Ivar folded his arms, pleased by their interest. "Well?"

Bors slid a regretful look at Troll.

He said no more.

Ivar nodded. He also made a silent note to lose both Troll and Bors in the sea before they sailed back home to his beloved Trondelag in Norway. A fine place of wild, rolling seas and cold winds where mountains and rivers of ice were kissed by snow that fell from clean, white skies. The Trondelag was also where he'd soon rule supreme, the most alluring temptress in the land at his side by day and in his bed at night.

Lady Sarina.

His overlord's wife. And Ivar's lover.

Ivar's loins tightened at the thought of her. He inhaled sharply and turned on his heel, striding back up the aisle to the steering platform before his men could see the bulge straining at his breeches.

Even here, so many sea miles away, he could smell the exotic musk of her perfume. Her taste lingered on the back of his tongue, dark, heady, and intoxicating. His lust for her maddened him every waking moment he didn't have her seductive little body pinned beneath him, writhing in ecstasy. When he slept, he felt her fingernails scoring his shoulders, could hear her cries of pleasure as she met his every thrust each time he drove into her hot, silky heat.

"Thor's steaming seed..." Ivar hissed the curse as he sat back down before the two sacks of silver coins. Closing his eyes, he took a long, ragged breath, willing away the images of his lascivious, dusky-skinned wanton.

Much as he desired her, riches mattered more.

Land, power, and men to serve him.

So he plunged his hands into one of the coin sacks, letting the cold weight of the silver chase the painful pounding between his legs.

When the agony lessened, he turned his attention to another sack.

A bulky leather pouch crammed beneath a nearby rowing bench. The sack held deliberately dirtied travelers robes. Scruffy shoes with holes at the toes that would give the impression that the men who'd worn them had made a long and tedious journey. Filthy garb that two of his craftiest men had donned when they'd climbed the cliff path leading up from Clan Mackintoshes' convenient Dreagan's Claw inlet and paid a call to Kendrew of Nought who, he'd heard this very night, had been most pleased to greet them.

Their news exceeded his expectations.

Hoping to enjoy their tidings again, Ivar looked down *Storm-Rider*'s aisle, searching for Dag or Skring. He spotted Skring first, pleased to see the man sitting against the hull, whetting his ax blade.

"Skring." Ivar jerked his head when the man looked his way, knowing the warrior would come to him at once.

And Skring did, setting aside his ax and pushing to his feet to join Ivar on the steering platform.

"You wish help counting the coin, lord?" Skring squatted beside him, his surprisingly guileless face splitting in a grin as he eyed the heavy pouches.

Ivar returned his smile.

He valued a man who could pass for a hapless mendicant friar or a pilgrim yet could delight in dancing in a foe's spilled guts an hour later.

Who would suspect that such a courier carried false messages?

Ivar clapped a hand on Skring's shoulder, hoping to show his appreciation. He rewarded such followers well and Skring would soon be a rich man.

They all would, if everything went to plan.

So Ivar took a silver flask and two small silver cups from a niche in the ship's hull and poured two measures of fine birch wine.

He gave a cup to Skring, proving his favoritism.

Not many men were worthy of his private stock of birch wine.

"I'd hear again your assessment of the Mackintosh chieftain's reaction." Ivar clinked his wine cup against Skring's and then turned his gaze on the black line of coast that was the Glen of Many Legends. "You're sure he'll be satisfied with only one bag of coin?"

It didn't seem possible.

All men thirsted for land, sinuous hot-blooded women, and coffers of gold.

Silver, in this instance.

"We can't risk him declining my lord's offer." Ivar wouldn't consider failure.

Skring tossed back his birch wine, thrust out his cup for more. "Mackintosh has everything most men desire," he reported as Ivar refilled his cup. "Land aplenty. And by all accounts, he loves his wife and lusts after no other."

"And wealth?" Ivar arched a brow.

Skring shrugged. "His hall is grand and Dag and I were feasted like kings. I'd say he suffers no dearth of coin. He doesn't need the second sack of silver. We didn't even mention it." He cocked a brow, following Ivar's gaze to the coast. "We thought that would please you."

"It does." Ivar could scarce believe his good fortune.

No one would guess that Kendrew hadn't received the full bride price for his sister.

If any of his men dared say a word, they wouldn't live to speak another.

A fact they knew well.

Still...

"The Mackintosh." Ivar rubbed the back of his neck, frowning. "He has pride, I've heard. And he's rumored to care for his sister. Why would he accept so little for her hand?" He turned back to Skring, truly puzzled. "Surely he would bargain for more?"

"Not Kendrew Mackintosh." Skring drained his wine cup again, dragged his arm over his mouth. "He's proud of his family's ties to the northlands. He even claims descent from Berserkers."

"Ahhh..." Ivar rubbed his chin, his lips quirking. "So he wishes to strengthen blood ties to the old homeland?"

Skring snorted. "That's why he's accepting the offer as we made it. You, lord"—he leaned forward and tapped his cup to Ivar's again—"are the prize. We told him your overlord is dying and that his greatest wish is to see you, his most powerful warlord, settled and wed before he breathes his last, leaving all to you."

"Settled and wed to a Scotswoman of Nordic blood?" Ivar's doubts were beginning to ease. "A Scotswoman who, upon Lord Rorik's passing, will be the wife of the greatest noble in the land?"

Skring nodded. "So it is, lord."

"Mackintosh wants his sister to marry into Norse

nobility." Ivar felt a slow smile curving his lips. "And"—
he slapped his knee—"that she shall! A pity she'll only
enjoy my new status for such a brief time." Ivar's loins
began to throb again. Skring and Dag had reported that
Lady Marjory was fair, yet said to be quite attractive.

Women with hair the color of moonbeams didn't stir
him. But he'd still relish a tumble or two with her.

She was no doubt a virgin.

Her sheath would be tight and slick, a reward for his
trouble in fetching her.

Best of all, it would drive Sarina to fits of jealousy if he
rutted with the Scotswoman before they sent her to take
Sarina's place on Rorik's funerary pyre.

Sarina in a rage would be a rare delight.

Ivar could almost spill himself now, just imagining
taking her when she was in a temper.

"You are a good man, Skring." Ivar reached again for
his prized birch wine.

Skring grinned and held out his cup.

And at the other end of *Storm-Rider*, Bors and Troll
kept horror-filled gazes on the long dark coast that was
the Glen of Many Legends.

The pulsating glow on Drangar Point was back again.

And this time there could be no mistaking that a tall,
cloaked man stood in the middle of the strange, otherworldly light.

Regrettably, no one else on the ship seemed to see him.

Bors and Troll knew in their hearts that he was there.

Yet when they exchanged worried glances and then
looked to the coast again, the man and the eerie light
around him were gone.

But they knew what they'd seen.

And with all the saga-telling of their homeland, they knew they were doomed.

"By all that's holy!" Alasdair slewed his horse around, reining sharply when a flooded burn loomed before them out of the rain and mist. The rock-strewn cataracts roared, the splashing torrent sending up fans of spray to rival the wind-driven fog. "Ne'er have I seen a more godforsaken place." He twisted round to glare at Marjory. "Is there naught hereabouts but stone and water?"

"This is the Thunder Vale, named for Thor." Marjory spoke as coolly and calmly as she could, trying hard to ignore how the wind whipped her hair, tossing the wet strands across her face. "Some say it's called so because of the noise of the rapids. They often overrun their banks."

"Indeed." Leaping down, Alasdair reached for her, sweeping her off his horse before she could blink. "We'll have to circle back." He set her on her feet, his face darker than the stormy night. "I won't send the horses through such raging water."

"That is wise." Marjory lifted her chin, no longer trying to ignore her windblown hair, but how her skin tingled from where he'd grasped her waist. She glanced at the foaming burn, her emotions in equal turmoil. "I could've told you—"

"Why didn't you?" Alasdair's face darkened even more, a muscle now jerking in his jaw. "I wouldn't take a horse across such a devil's cauldron in the best of weathers."

"We could try." Ewan rode over to them, managing to look amused despite his rumpled plaid and wet, dripping hair. He glanced at Marjory, grinning boyishly. "First

man to reach the other side wins a kiss from the lady!"
He leaned down, punched Alasdair's shoulder. "What
say you?"

"That your wits have flown," Alasdair snarled, reaching for Marjory's arm when she stepped away. He pulled
her close to his side, glared at his young cousin. "Since
when does a bit of wind and rain turn you into a buffoon?"

"That wouldn't be me." Ewan's grin flashed even
brighter. The merriment in his eyes made the accusation
he didn't put in words.

"You'll not have a stramash over me." Marjory
straightened to her full height, standing tall even if she
couldn't break free of Alasdair's iron grasp.

"Och, lady, we're aye fighting o'er you." Ewan turned
his full charm on her, his blue eyes twinkling. "My cousin
willnae say it is so, but you've only to ask the men and—"

"Have a care, lad." Alasdair's face hardened. "You
dinnae want to rile me."

"I don't have to." Ewan laughed, unconcerned. Swinging down from his saddle, he stood before them. "You've
been in a black mood since we left the clearing. I say we
all know why." Ewan tossed back his wet hair, threw a
glance at the other men, the fast-flowing rapids behind
them. "Mayhap a good dousing in thon burn would chase
the meanness from you? Then you'd admit—"

"I admit I should've ordered you to stay at Blackshore
and clean the cesspit." Alasdair's arm was rock-hard
against Marjory's back, his hand flexing against her hip.
"You're a gangling, ill-mannered—"

"I'm ill-mannered?" Ewan staggered backward,
clutching his heart, his eyes wide with mock astonishment.

Marjory bit her tongue, not wanting to laugh.

She liked Ewan.

How she wished Alasdair had a bit of the younger man's levity. Instead, his face had gone stonier than ever. And his arm about her waist now felt like a tight, steel band. The heat of his powerfully muscled body warmed her through the wool of his rain-splattered plaid. She also felt his surging anger, each agitated breath he inhaled and exhaled. Shocks of awareness shot through her each time his chest expanded, bringing their bodies even closer together.

She shivered, deliciously.

He released her at once, striding away as if she'd bitten him. "Lady Marjory is cold." He went to the herring cart, lifted the oiled sheepskin rigged to keep out rain. His dog, Geordie, appeared at the rail, rheumy eyes eager, as if looking for a treat. "Ewan, the rest of you"—he dug in a leather pouch at his belt, fished out a twist of dried meat for the dog—"take off your plaids and pile them in the cart," he finished, already unclasping the heavy Celtic pin that held his own plaid at his shoulder. "Once we've made the lady comfortable and warm, we'll head back the way we came. Then—"

"This is the most direct way to Nought." Marjory felt a spurt of confidence, pride in her home's savage fierceness. It was also time to play her final option.

The reason she'd held her tongue when Alasdair and his men turned into the Thunder Vale.

Her womanly wiles had failed her so far.

Seduction wasn't her best talent.

But Nought was magnificent, triumphant in all ways, never letting her down.

She squared her shoulders, took a deep breath, and

sent a silent prayer to the ancient gods of stone, wind, and wild weather.

Then she cleared her throat, looked straight into Alasdair's eyes, and pointed to the great granite peaks guarding the rock-bound vale.

"We can shelter up there, in the Thunder Caves," she said, taking some pleasure in Alasdair's startled expression. "There's no need to disturb your dog. Or"—she smiled at his men—"for anyone to give up his plaid. Everything we need is in the caves."

"The Thunder Caves?" Alasdair stared at her.

"So we call them." Marjory smiled, pride in her voice. "Like the vale, the name hails from Thor. It's also appropriate because of the storms known to rage here, the thunder of the rapids, and the rumbling of stone when a rockslide hits now and again. Our men use the caves as lookout hideaways." She felt a blush coming on, didn't care. "That's how Kendrew knew you were riding to Nought the day we met. His scouts spotted your party from the Thunder Caves."

Alasdair frowned. "I ne'er heard of them."

Marjory shrugged. "Nought has many secrets, my lord."

Ewan slapped his thigh, laughing. "Ho! Leave it to the Mackintoshes to pull one o'er on us."

The other men joined him, chuckling as they refastened brooch pins and adjusted the near-waterproof folds of their heavy woolen plaids.

Only Alasdair crossed his arms, standing as still as stone in the spitting rain. His gaze was on the cliffs, his expression unreadable.

"I see no caves up there." He lifted a hand to his brow,

narrowed his eyes. "Nor can I make out a path up to them, if they're there."

"Oh, they're there." Marjory went over to him, her heart beating hard at her daring. "You can't see them because they're so well hidden. Look there..." She pointed to an odd-shaped cluster of rocks at the base of the nearest cliff. "Do you see the rowan growing from the side of that outcrop? The tree marks the start of the path to the caves."

"How many are there?" He was looking at her, not the outcrop and its rowan.

"More than anyone can say." Marjory could hardly speak anyway. Alasdair's tantalizing male scent, combined with the heady smell of rain and fresh, cold air, was getting to her. The look in his eyes unsettled her even more. He still appeared tense, but in a different way from during the ride from the clearing.

Truth was, his expression excited her.

Something shifted when she mentioned the caves. His gaze was fierce now, his entire focus on her. As if the wind and rain, his men, the caves, nothing else existed except the two of them.

And that could mean only one thing. The old gods had heard her. Nought was giving her the chance she needed.

"Your people don't know how many caves are up there?" Alasdair was looking at the cliffs now. But he'd put his hand on the small of her back, his fingers splayed, the touch possessive. Bold and claiming, and doing the sweetest things to the lowest part of her belly.

Marjory swallowed. "Nought is mysterious, see you?" She glanced at him, finding him looking right at her again, his gaze so intent, her breath caught. "The caves have been counted many times and always a different number is given. Most are small with room enough for one or two men to comfortably spend a night of guard duty.

"One"—her pulse quickened when he curled his fingers around her hip, his thumb rubbing slow circles as she spoke—"is larger than the rest. It's the highest cave ever found and is mostly used for storage. Provender is kept there, also dry plaids and piles of wolf and bear skins for bedding. Kendrew sends someone there every fortnight to make sure the cave is clean, the floors well swept. He—"

"He shall receive my thanks—someday!" Alasdair leaned close and lowered his voice. "We shall seek shelter there now, my lady. We have unfinished business to attend. Something that's been a long time in coming and that"—he straightened—"can wait no longer."

Marjory's heart leaped.

But he couldn't mean what she thought.

"There is room enough for us all in the large cave." She glanced at the cliffs, not wanting to see his face if she was wrong. "The path winds back and forth up to the caves. High rock walls hide the ascent and overhanging ledges block the wind and rain. It's an easy climb, even Geordie can make it. Or someone can carry him—"

"My dog and my men will use the lower caves." Alasdair gripped her chin, turning her face so she had to look at him. "You and I will go up to the high one."

For a moment, Marjory couldn't speak. Her mouth went dry and her heart knocked against her ribs. Her hopes and desires came winging back to her.

"And your men?" She glanced at them, not surprised to see that most of them were busying themselves with something. A few fussed with their plaids. Two were refastening the oilcloth on Geordie's cart. And another appeared to be removing a pebble from his shoe.

She looked again at Alasdair, her knees already weakening. "There are so many of them. Will they not—"

"They are well trained." He aimed a dark look at Ewan who was leaning against the herring cart, watching them with amusement. "Even those who aren't will no' speak of this night. They are loyal."

"And you?" She had to know.

He pulled her closer, his gaze locking on hers. "That I am, aye. I'm also a man. And you, sweet"—he skimmed his thumb over her lips—"are about to find out why I warned you in the wood."

"Why you warned me?" She blinked, not remembering.

It was impossible to think with him so near.

He stepped back and extended his arm. The look on his face showed that he wasn't asking her to take it. He expected her to, without question. When she did, his smile flashed.

"I said you'd regret coming to the clearing." He was already leading her toward the outcrop with the rowan, the start of the path to the Thunder Caves. "You're about to find out why."

"Then I am most curious." Marjory bit her lip, quickening her steps to keep pace with him. She already knew what he meant.

He thought to seduce her.

She bit her lip harder, stifling the smile she didn't want him to see.

It finally was a night for seduction, hers and his.

She couldn't have planned it better.

Chapter Fifteen

✤

Iₜ's like the world drops away here, isn't it?"

Marjory paused on the cliff's zigzagging path. Pride beat through her, but also a bit of trepidation. Never had a man sought to seduce her and her last attempt to entice Alasdair had ended in disaster. So she kept her back straight and turned to peer through a hand-chiseled spy hole in the soaring rock wall that kept the cave path from being too treacherous to climb. She breathed deep of the cold air racing past the opening and then glanced at Alasdair. He stood a few steps behind her on the narrow, tunnel-like track.

"Look, you can see straight down to the burn where we left the horses." She spoke as brightly as she could, not wanting him to guess how vulnerable she felt.

Or how embarrassed she'd be if she'd read him wrongly.

He *had* changed since she'd mentioned the Thunder Caves.

She just hoped she hadn't erred in her assessment of his tenseness, his taut expression. And—she felt almost light-headed with excitement—the way he kept touching her, standing near or even pulling her close against his big, strong body.

He was looking at her fiercely now. He'd stopped in the middle of the rocky path, his intent gaze holding hers as she watched him.

Faith, his eyes burned so hotly, she wouldn't be surprised if the clothes melted from her.

"I ken where we left the horses." He didn't move, but the wind brought a hint of his tantalizing male scent and she felt a sudden tingling between her thighs, an ache she knew was pure feminine desire. "They'll be fine. I dinnae need to peer down at the beasties."

Marjory scarce heard him. The blood was roaring in her ears, her mind whirling. Now that the seduction, if it indeed happened, was so near, she didn't know what to do to initiate the proceedings.

Something told her Alasdair would take charge.

It was a thought that both thrilled and terrified her.

She needed these last few moments to build her courage. So she gripped the edge of the spy hole, glad for the stone's support.

She stepped closer to the opening, pretending to admire the view.

"Come see." She didn't look at Alasdair this time. "If you lean out a bit, the whole of the Thunder Vale opens up before you." She waited for him to join her, her belly fluttering when he slid his arm around her, pulling her tight against him. She took a breath, her excitement mounting. "On fair days, we can see clear to—"

"Sweet lass, all I wish to see is here beside me." He smoothed back her hair, letting his fingers drift down the side of her neck. "Though I'll own there remains much I wish to discover."

His voice was deep and low, so husky that a cascade of sinuous heat slid through her.

He dipped his head, nuzzling the sensitive flesh beneath her ear. Marjory inhaled sharply, the rocky path seeming to tilt under her feet.

"Aye, there is much I wish you to show me." He flicked his tongue across her skin, dropped kisses along her shoulder. Straightening, he brushed the backs of his fingers down her cheek, his mouth curving in a slow smile. "Beautiful, enticing treasures to be savored and cherished."

She swallowed hard, not wanting to speak until she was sure her voice would be steady.

The way he was looking at her made her feel as if she'd caught a fever.

"The Thunder Caves are a treasure." She took his hand and led him away, around the last bend of the path to where a solid wall of granite appeared to end the track. "Tucked around here is the entrance." She pulled him past a tall, jutting edge of rock, beaming at his astonishment. "Now you see why we are so proud—"

"Your caves aren't what I meant." But still, he stopped and stared.

Marjory was sure his jaw would've slipped if he weren't so stubborn.

The Thunder Caves were awe-inspiring.

Pride of Clan Mackintosh, the largest and loftiest of the caves was a broad, high-ceilinged wonder of glistening stone kissed by the ever-present roar of wind. Better yet, even on the darkest nights, slanting cracks in the domed roof allowed shafts of silvery moon- and starlight to fill the cave's huge central chamber. The angle of the crevices kept out the worst of any rain.

Marjory stepped closer to Alasdair, touching his arm. "My grandmother used to say the moonbeams are trapped fairies, pursued by princes of star shine. My grandfather would then laugh and claim..." She stopped, pressing a hand to her lips as hot color flooded her cheeks.

"Aye?" Alasdair looked at her, one brow lifted. "What did he say?"

"That..." She glanced away, looking quickly into the cave's silver-shot depths. "Ach, well, you'll see for yourself soon enough. He liked to tease that the gods called down the moon and starlight to distract clan women so we wouldn't see the cave's true purpose."

"And what is that?" Alasdair crossed his arms, his lips twitching. "Did your ancestors sacrifice virgins here?"

Marjory's flush deepened. "Not exactly, but..."

She took his elbow, pulling him to the far side of the cave's entrance where a low, naturally formed bench ran the length of one wall. She stopped before an iron-bound chest covered with a sheepskin. Opening its lid, she retrieved candles, steel, and flint. She handed them to Alasdair, smiling apologetically.

"I'm not good at lighting fires. But if you can get these candles to burn, there are brackets in the walls."

"Now you are the teasing one," he countered, quickly doing as she bid. "Or did you truly no' guess why I went so quiet on the ride from the clearing? You are well-skilled at lighting fires, a true seductress. You make me burn, lass. You have aye—"

His jaw dropped. His hand stilling as he set the first candle in its iron holder and the flame illuminated the cave wall.

The gleaming stone was carved with ancient runic symbols. Norse runes, by the looks of them. More notable were the bold drawings etched near the cave's sloping roof. Naked men and women cavorted everywhere, forming a lascivious circle of men and women coupling in a great variety of positions. The carnal scenes were painted red and black, each carving stark, vivid, and shocking.

Alasdair's brows rose. Then he started laughing. "So that's what your grandfather meant. I vow he was right!"

"I have always believed so. He never said." Marjory's face flamed hotter. "I do know Kendrew refuses to allow watchmen to use this cave. He says the drawings would keep them from their duty."

"Spying on MacDonalds?" Alasdair sounded more amused than concerned.

Before she could answer, he crossed the cave to slip a lit candle into another of the wall brackets. The flickering light drew attention to his sure, confident stride, his powerful build. His rich auburn hair gleamed, the ends just brushing his broad, plaid-draped shoulders. He wore his sword belt slung low on his hips, the amber pommel stone bright in the cave's dimness. Marjory waited as he lit and placed other candles, awareness of him and how alone they were, prickling her skin. Rarely had he looked more striking. And never before had his actions been so bold, his every word and glance making her hot inside, letting her believe...

Could he indeed care for her?

She straightened, clasping her hands before her. She

didn't want him to see that her breath had grown ragged, her pulse racing with hope.

"Our men have aye kept watch for MacDonalds." It was all she could think to say.

"And your women?" His voice deepened, spooling through her like heady wine. "What do they think of Blackshore men?"

"They've reviled them, for centuries."

"And you?"

"I..." She couldn't speak. He was coming toward her, the intense look on his face making the secret place between her thighs tingle again. Her palms were dampening and her breasts felt heavy, achy.

"So you cannae tell me?" He stopped before her, lifted a length of her hair, fingering the strands. "A pity that, for I'm of a mind to hear what you think of me, Norn. I know your good-sister, Isobel, is attempting to throw us together." His smile flashed. "She didn't fall from Ewan's horse. She slid off deliberately, claiming an injury so I'd ride off with you."

"She wouldn't do that." Marjory knew she had.

"You're no' a good liar." He dropped her hair, angling his head as he looked at her, his gaze searing. "There'll be a reason she went to such trouble to trick me. I'd know what it is?"

Marjory lifted her chin. "Is that why you were so angry on the journey? You believed we—"

"So you knew she was pretending?"

"I guessed." Heat scored her cheeks on the admission. "She meant well. And she was clearly misguided in thinking—"

"That I'd enjoy carrying you away, having you alone?"

He let his fingertips glide over her cheek. "I'd say she was clever."

His words fired her blood, encouraging her. His nearness made her daring. "It could be she feels a match between us might work well for the weal of the glen." That was as close as she'd go to revealing the pact she'd made with Isobel and Alasdair's sister, Catriona. "After all, Isobel is now wed to Kendrew and Catriona married James, the Cameron chieftain. It could be she believes—"

"She should know better." His face hardened. "Kendrew is a scoundrel. He's wild and crazed, totally unpredictable. He's much too thrawn, the most stubborn man I know. Any match between you and me would end bloody." He touched her again, caressing her cheek, fingering her hair. "Your brother and I would fight and one of us would die. Or he'd provoke me in other ways, calling down the King's wrath o'er the broken truce. Blackshore would be seized, my people exiled to the Isle of Lewis." He looked at her, his expression fierce. "Kendrew would greet such a tragedy. Indeed, I believe he plots one."

"And I am his sister." Marjory held his gaze. "He does love me. I return that love with the whole of my heart." She wouldn't lie. "He has his faults, but we all do. He is a good man."

Alasdair's jaw clenched and he looked aside, his gaze on a nearby pile of bear- and wolfskins.

Marjory stood her ground. "You didn't say why you were so wroth during our ride." Her heart raced, her need for surety a throbbing ache in her chest. "Is my name the reason? Were you angered because I am your enemy's sister?"

"I wasn't angry, leastways no' with you." He shoved a

hand through his hair, whirled to face her. "Sweet lass"—
he gripped her waist, his gaze sweeping over her—"I was
furious at your godforsaken, wind-ridden home. Your precious Nought and its comfortless, stone-clogged bounds,
so wild and barren—"

"I don't understand." She didn't. "You're not making
sense. Nought—"

"Nought was thwarting me with every rocky mile we
thundered across."

"The land?"

"Aye, every stony inch of it." He circled his arms
around her, pulling her tight against him. "I was sure I'd
once seen a shepherd's hut near the birchwood, yet there
was none. The farther we rode, no others appeared, only
more rock and your damnable rapids."

"If you hadn't ridden into the Thunder Vale, we'd have
come to a shelter." She could hardly speak. She was too
aware of her disarray. Her damp and clinging gown, her
hair tumbling loose, and—she took a breath—the wild
desire beating inside her. She'd felt the hard slabs of his
muscled chest and abdomen on their ride. She'd rested her
head against the proud strength of his broad shoulders.
Now she wanted to see and touch those wonders, run her
hands over him.

Enjoy his kisses again, lose herself in the sweetness...

"I saw no other resting place. For sure, I was looking!"

"We have refuge now." She glanced at the mound of
furs, half wondering if the gods of seduction caused the
cave's shafts of moon- and starlight to spill across them.

Almost, she could believe it.

She was also melting. Pure, feminine need gathered
inside her, chasing all thought except the irresistible

urge to lean even closer against Alasdair. His arms were already like iron bands around her, holding her tightly against him. She could feel the solid strength of his chest, the heat of his powerfully muscled body, and—sweet, purple heather—she was acutely aware of the hard, thick length of his arousal pressing against her belly.

There could be no mistaking his desire.

And she wanted him badly, consequences be damned.

She moistened her lips, knowing something momentous would happen as soon as she took her gaze from the pile of bear- and wolfskins.

"Were you concerned I'd catch a fever from the storm?" She kept her attention on the furs, so near, so beckoning. "Is that why you sought a shelter?"

"You know why." He gripped her face with both hands, holding her fast as he kissed her roughly, his mouth plundering hers.

She clung to him, thrusting her fingers into his hair as he deepened the kiss, his tongue gliding against hers in long, sinuous sweeps. She trembled, her entire body aflame, the most delicious heat spreading through her. Her breasts felt heavy, her nipples tight and aching. And still he kissed her, each bold swirl of his tongue against hers sending sweet molten fire rippling across her most intimate place. Her need, all her female desires exalted, reveling in the delicious tingles, the exquisite throbbing, so urgent and intense.

"Now do you see? How it is with me?" Alasdair broke the kiss, jerking away from her. He cupped her chin, staring down at her. "What you do to me? What you've aye done to me?"

Releasing her, he shoved a hand through his hair. "I

told you once no' to push me, to ne'er tempt me again. I tried to leave be, did my damndest to forget you, even stayed away for a year. And ne'er in all that time did I even look at another woman. It was you I wanted, Norn. It's only ever been you."

Marjory pressed a hand to her cheek, her heart thundering. Her eyes stung and a vein in her throat was beating wildly. "Oh, dear saints..."

"The devil more like!" He reached for her again, gripping her hips and pulling her close, against his groin, his straining arousal. "Only he would torment a man so." He kissed her, hard and fast. "When you stormed into the clearing, all indignant and beautiful, I could resist you no more. I had to have you. Nae, I must have you." He unbuckled his sword belt, tossing it aside. He whipped off his plaid with even greater speed. "I've wanted you since the first day I laid eyes on you. And I'll defy your brother, the Scottish crown, and even the gods themselves if they try and keep me from making you mine."

"Alasdair..." Marjory could hardly speak past the lump in her throat. Her vision blurred, her eyes swimming with stinging heat.

Alasdair—*her beloved Alasdair*—stood naked before her in the Thunder Cave, light and shadow dancing across his tall, strapping body. He set his hands on his hips, making no attempt to hide his maleness, so roused and magnificent. There could be no doubt that he wanted her. Or that he intended to mate with her here, this night.

Only one worry rose through the haze of desire.

So she stood tall, as proud as she could. "You didn't say you love me. Or that you wish to wed—"

He frowned. "I would no' be here if I didn't love you."

He was on her with three swift strides. And somehow, he had her out of her cloak, her gown, before she realized what was happening. When only her shift remained, he hooked his thumbs beneath the shoulder straps. His gaze burning into hers, he ripped the gown off of her, rending the linen with a loud tear. The sound echoed through the cave as her ruined shift fluttered down her legs to pool around her ankles.

She gasped, feeling vulnerable as the cave's chill, damp air hit her exposed skin.

"You take my breath, lass." His gaze drifted over her, hungrily. "More beautiful than I'd dreamed."

She shivered when he ran his hand down her arm, trailed the backs of his fingers across the top swells of her breasts. Something in the deepest, most womanly part of her clenched, liquid heat swirling low by her thighs. Her excitement rose, spinning out of control.

Her knees felt weak, unable to support her.

This was the fever Isobel and Catriona had told her to expect.

The bright, all-consuming desire that fired the blood, blazing with the heat of a thousand suns—until quenched by a man's loving.

"So you do love me?" She needed to be sure.

"I love you more than my own life." He gripped her wrists and held her arms to the side. He looked her up and down again, his eyes darkening as he surveyed her nakedness. "I have dreamed of you nightly, ached to see you so, burned to take you in my arms, hold you close, skin to skin, claim you as mine. Again and again, for I know I'll ne'er have enough of you. So, aye, I love you." He lowered her arms, stepped closer. "I love you more than my land, my clan, and my word to a King. And, aye, I will wed you." His voice was rough, his roused manhood nudging her hip. "I'll prove my love to you this night. Then I'll speak with my council. We'll leave the glen if such is deemed necessary. In a few years, Ewan can step up as chief. Until then, the elders will guide him."

"You'd leave Blackshore? The glen?" Marjory touched his face, tracing his jaw with her fingertips. "You would do that for me?"

"I would slay dragons for you," he vowed, sweeping her into his arms and carrying her to the mound of bear- and wolfskins. "I'll even speak with Kendrew, though I cannae see good coming of that!"

"He will—"

"Mind his peace, if he is wise." His voice took on a hard edge, his steely resolve sending shivers through her. He met her gaze, holding it as he knelt on the furs. Settling her into their softness, he smoothed his hands down her sides and back up again, possessively. "Nothing matters except you. This night and always." He stretched out beside her, his gaze hot and fierce. "I've waited too long to make you mine."

"Then do." She turned in his arms, curving her hand around his neck and pulling him to her. "I've waited no less." She blinked, not wanting him to see the tears burning her eyes. "I have loved you all the while, ever hoping, yearning for your return—"

"Marjory..." He slanted his mouth over hers, kissing her long and deep. She leaned into him and he curved his hand around her hip, drawing her even closer. Their tongues stroked and swirled, the sharing of their breath so intimate she melted from the pleasure.

He broke the kiss, easing back to look at her. "You know what is about to happen?" He slid a hand over her breasts, kneading them gently, brushing the tips with his thumb. "It willnae be easy, but I can stop now. You must tell me if—"

She pressed her fingers to his lips before he could finish. Smiling, she shook her head. "The Thunder Caves were my last hope," she admitted. "I believe the gods caused you to veer in to the Thunder Vale. I could've warned you that the burns would be flooded, but I didn't want to risk one final chance to see if you—"

"Would fall under your spell?" He took her hand, pressing her palm to his chest. "Do you feel my heart?" When she nodded, he brought her hand to his lips, kissing her fingers. "Its pounding should tell you I am yours and aye have been. You didn't need your Thunder Vale and its caves. Though I am glad we are here!"

"It is a grand place." Marjory glanced at the slanting star- and moonbeams dancing about the cave, silvering the floor and walls. Candlelight flickered across the ancient drawings, giving them life so the entwined couples appeared to move, writhing in passion, unaware that they were observed. Shivering, she reached to twine her fingers in Alasdair's hair. His earthy male scent filled her senses, thrilling her. She looked back at him, her heart beating wildly, so many longings swirling inside her.

"I thought to seduce you here." The truth slipped from her lips before she could stop them.

"I told you, sweet, you did that long ago." He smoothed his hand down her side, shaping every dip and curve, slowing his fingers perilously near the part of her that rippled with pure molten heat.

"You were gone so long." Those words, too, fell before she could stay them. "You said there were many—"

"So I did, and there were. But no' many women as you were about to say." He laughed, the sound low and dark in the cave's vastness. But then the levity left his face and he sealed his mouth over hers, kissing her deeply. When he pulled away, he caught and held her gaze. "Many were my thoughts of you, great was my need. When I slept, I saw your face, dreamed of you. If I walked through Inverness and spotted a woman's fair and shining hair, my heart would leap. Then I'd see she wasn't you and I'd feel like someone punched me in the ribs. On the nights I lodged at a friend's hall and his lady sat beside him at the high table, my heart ached because I wished you graced my side at Blackshore."

"Alasdair..." Marjory slipped her hand down his shoulder, gliding her fingers along his hard-muscled arm. "I never knew, though I'd hoped."

"I did try to forget you. I finally believed I had." He captured her hand, placing it back on his chest. "Yet there were times, especially sailing home through the Hebrides, when the moonlit nights were so beautiful and I'd ache to hold you, kiss and touch you everywhere. Then I'd remember all the reasons I shouldn't love you, damned good reasons, and I'd want nothing more than to smash something. Or"—his smile flashed—"to kill your brother."

"You may yet have the chance." Marjory was sure that was so.

But she didn't want to worry about Kendrew now.

She wanted...

"Oh my!" She froze. Alasdair *was* touching her everywhere.

Somehow he'd wrapped an arm around her, drawing her even closer to him. And his knee was now between her thighs. His hand was also there, gliding ever upward, his fingers drifting oh so lightly over the part of her that thrummed so deliciously. Holding her gaze, he stroked her even more intimately, circling his thumb over a spot that sent bolts of intense pleasure spearing through her.

She caught her breath, arching into his hand, wanting more of the exquisite sensations.

A shimmer of embarrassment flickered through her mind, but then all thought spun away. All that remained were the wondrous feelings whispering across her flesh. Sensations more thrilling than anything she'd ever experienced. When he slipped a fingertip inside her, his thumb and other fingers still working such magic, she tensed, digging her hands into the bearskin's thick pelt.

"My precious." Alasdair's voice was deep, coming as if from a distance.

"Kiss me." She wanted his kisses badly.

"I will," he promised, glancing at her. A wicked smile tugged at the corner of his mouth when, instead of kissing her, he leaned back to look at her breasts. He cupped and rubbed them, rolling her nipples between his fingers. "I shall kiss you here."

"What?" Marjory's eyes rounded.

"You'll no' be denying me the pleasure," he vowed, splaying his hand across the full rounds of her breasts. "I have craved the taste of you for long. I'm done with the waiting."

From somewhere—his chest?—there came a low rumbling, almost a growl. Then he rolled over her, his big, strong body seamed to hers as he kissed her breasts, opening his mouth over her tightened nipples to lick and draw on them. With his hand, he kept on cupping and kneading her, the pleasure almost unbearable. And still he stroked and teased the damp, swollen flesh between her legs.

"Please..." She squirmed against the furs, certain she'd break apart from the maddeningly sweet sensations. "I can't stand it."

He stopped at once, looking up at her. "Enough? Shall we leave now? No more touching? Are we done kissing already? Shall I no'—"

"Yes!" She pushed up, reaching for him. "I mean no, I don't want to stop. I've waited long, too." She rushed the words, her cheeks heating to admit her desire. "I want you to love me."

She now knew that he did, with his heart.

She meant his body.

"Och, lass, I shall." He spoke low, his gaze burning into hers, leaving no doubt he'd understood. "As soon as you are ready, I will—"

"I am now." She was certain. "I know of such things. Isobel and Catriona have instructed me. And"—she hoped only she heard her voice waver—"I have seen beasts at Nought. Horses and cattle—"

"Indeed." He arched a brow, his hands spending such magic, his gaze amused.

"Yes." She hissed the word through her teeth when he slid a second finger inside her, his thumb now circling with even more deliberation.

"So I see." He slid his fingers through her intimate curls. "Then tell me, sweet, if your Nought beasties do this..."

Leaning forward, he nipped and sucked on her lower

lip before moving down her body to settle himself between her legs. "I would know the truth," he challenged, holding her gaze. He eased her knees apart and lowered his head, nibbling and kissing his way up the inside of her thighs. "I promise that no creatures at Blackshore are so skilled," he teased, his face now only a shiver away from that place.

Marjory stared at him, torn between begging him to stop and urging him on. "You can't mean to..." She felt herself blushing, also felt his soft, warm breath on her most intimate flesh. "Dear saints!"

"Indeed." He gave her a wicked smile, his gaze locked on hers as he opened his mouth over her, licking deep.

"O-o-oh, no..." Her hips bucked and she gripped the bearskin so tightly that her knuckles whitened. Her entire body tensed and then fell apart, pleasure such as she'd never imagined, streaming out from where he licked her, tasting her so intimately.

"I see you like this." He paused, watching her intently. "But you'll no' be enjoying it as much as I am. You, my love, are a succulent treat to be tasted to the full, savored deeply." As if to prove his words, he lowered his head again, circling his tongue over the same incredibly sensitive spot he'd rubbed with his thumb.

And this time she truly couldn't bear the pleasure.

"Alasdair, please..." She grabbed his shoulders, trying to pull him away.

"Nae, sweet, no' yet." He started licking her again. Long, leisurely sweeps of his tongue across her hot, tingling flesh. With his thumb, he once again rubbed the place that spent the most intense pleasure. "Only when you truly melt will I touch you."

"You are touching me and"—she arched into him,

desperate for more, something she felt hovering just at the edge of her reach—"I am melting!"

"No' yet," he argued, lifting away from her. "But you soon will be. I dinnae wish to hurt you." Still watching her closely, he reached down and dragged his fingers across her wet and sensitive flesh. Then, as her eyes rounded, he circled the long, thick shaft of his arousal, damping his own flesh with the moisture that glistened on his fingers. Her *woman's dew* that Isobel and Catriona had told her about, swearing it would ease her first time lying with him.

Even knowing what it was, her face heated to look on as he finished and then stretched out on top of her, his manhood hot and heavy against her hip. And then—his eyes darkened, masculine triumph flaring—as he reached between them so that his arousal nudged at her. He curled his other hand around her neck and slanted his mouth over hers, kissing her fiercely, plunging his tongue deep into her mouth as . . .

He thrust the hard length of himself inside her, claiming her at last. Fiery pain shot through her and she gasped, gripping his shoulders. At her cry, he stilled as her body tensed and tightened around him. But the sharp stinging eased quickly and before he could pull away, she reached to cradle his face, kissing him deeply. She rocked her hips, encouraging him with all her womanly instincts to keep on, to make her his now and forevermore.

"Norn . . ." He raised up on his elbows, his eyes glinting so darkly she'd think they were black if she didn't know otherwise. "I'm sorry, sweet. Ne'er would I cause you pain."

"I'm fine." She spoke true, the hot pinch she'd felt

insubstantial to the rush of happiness sweeping her. The joy of lying so closely, skin to skin, intimately joined with the man she loved so fiercely. "I knew there would be some pain—"

"Hush, lass." He silenced her with more kisses, used his thumb to circle that special place again. Gentle touches, each careful rub sent pleasure rippling through her. Then, sure and with determination, he began to move his hips, pushing deeper into her, inch by slow inch.

"My precious..." He raised his head, closing his eyes as the hard, thick length of him stretched and filled her. Veins stood out on his neck, his body tensing above her. She saw a muscle jerk in his jaw and then she knew little more because the sweet circling of his thumb was sharpening her need. She trembled as the sensations grew, drawing her closer to a glittering edge of delight where the pleasure was almost beyond bearing.

Then he opened his eyes, looking at her with such smoldering heat she almost slid right over that tempting, beckoning release.

But there was something so glorious, so right, about locking gazes with him, looking so deeply into each other's eyes as they were joined so intimately.

"My heart, I love you so." She smoothed the damp hair at his brow.

"Norn." His voice was rough, the sweetness of it making her heart ache. "You are mine." He caught her wrist, lifting her arm above her head, linking their fingers. "I will ne'er let you go. No' ever."

"You won't have to." She looked past his shoulder to the cave's domed ceiling. The naked cavorting pairs no longer embarrassed her. Now, the way they seemed to move in the candle glow encouraged her, urging her to rock her hips more sinuously.

Gripping Alasdair's hand, her other arm wrapped around his shoulders, she matched his rhythmic thrusts as he deepened his strokes. His body's claiming of her as binding as his words of love.

So why was one of the etched figures looking at her with such pity?

Marjory blinked, narrowing her eyes at the red-and-black drawing of a voluptuous female riding astride an equally well-built man.

The painted couple did appear to be alive, the candles' dancing flames giving them substance, life.

They did seem to be moving, the woman lifting up and down atop the male. Her head was thrown back as if in ecstasy, her hair wild and free, flowing down her back. But she was no longer peering down at Marjory, a world of sorrow in her darkly etched eyes.

Nor had she looked at Marjory at all.

Her pleasure, the excitement and her carnal bliss, were playing tricks on her.

Still, despite the heat swirling around her and Alasdair, she felt a chill in the air that hadn't been there before. But then his thrusts deepened even more, his hips moving ever faster as he tensed above her, his hold on her hand strong and tight.

"Norn!" He stilled above her as he threw back his head, his eyes closed and jaw clenching. Stinging heat filled her even as he pressed his thumb down hard on that intensely sensitive spot, circling fast now, the sensations spiraling until everything around her spun away. The star-and moonbeams blended with the dancing light of the candles as she split apart, losing control, as she sped over the brink into womanhood.

Slowly, she sank into the soft bed of bear- and wolf-skins. Sated, dazed, and wondrously happy, she opened her eyes to see Alasdair stretched out alongside her, the most glorious smile on his handsome face. Braced on an elbow, he reached out to smooth his hand down her side before resting it possessively on her hip. The look on his face, the triumph, chased any feelings of awkwardness that might've risen.

"I'd rather this happened at Blackshore." He stroked her lightly, his voice still roughened by passion. "But I took you knowing you'll be my wife. Dinnae you forget that after I leave you tonight. I meant what I said. You are mine. No one will e'er come between us again."

"My brother will try." It had to be said.

Kendrew would be furious if he knew. He'd challenge Alasdair, and whichever one of them was killed, she'd bear the responsibility.

She bit her lip, not wanting to think of such a tragedy.

Not now, when such glittering, all-consuming pleasure still warmed her and the beautiful haze of their loving buoyed her so sweetly.

Yet...

She did have to return to Nought. This night, and very shortly lest Kendrew noticed her absence and sent out a party of men to search for her.

She sat up, glancing about for her clothes. "We must be away, now before it is too late."

"Hush, sweet." Alasdair curled his hand around her wrist, pulling her back down again, wrapping his arms around her. He smoothed the hair from her face, kissed her brow, the tip of her nose. "I'll see you safely to Nought, and at speed." He glanced toward the cave's entrance where a wedge of the night sky could be seen.

The wind had died and a sparkling scatter of stars shone against the clear, black heavens, the storm now gone.

"I will handle your brother." He turned her in his arms, cradling her back against his chest. "Dinnae say aught to him until I've had the chance. That is all I ask of you. I dinnae trust him."

"He won't do anything to me." Marjory defended him, knowing in her heart that Kendrew wished only the best for her.

But his idea of good was different from hers.

And so she reached to where Alasdair's hands were clasped over her abdomen and placed her own hands over his, squeezing tightly.

"The only danger for me has been his plan to see me wed to a Viking lord. That threat no longer exists. There's nothing—" She jerked, her amber necklace trembling, white-hot against her throat. Her eyes flew wide, the shocking heat almost scalding her.

The sensation passed in an eye blink.

Even as she lifted a hand to the necklace, the stones were cool to the touch, the ambers still.

But the chill she'd noted when Alasdair had made love to her was back. The storm may have passed, but the cave had turned icy enough to raise gooseflesh on her skin. It was all she could do to keep her teeth from chattering. Yet Alasdair didn't seem to notice.

And that could mean only one thing.

The warning was meant for her.

Wanting nothing to do with it, she twisted around in his arms. She took his face in her hands, kissed him deeply. She poured all her love and passion into the kiss, her heart soaring when he tightened his arms around her, returning the kiss with equal fervor. Such kisses, such abandoned and pure loving held power. The greatest magic on earth, she was sure.

If trouble came, she'd be ready.

With Alasdair's love to protect her, nothing could harm her.

He'd said so.

Still, she wouldn't look again at the ancient painted woman up near the cave's ceiling.

She'd sooner trust in Alasdair's promise.

She silently made one of her own to bring him happiness all his days.

Chapter Sixteen

❦

Her fortune had turned at last.

Reliving every beautiful moment she and Alasdair had enjoyed in the Thunder Caves, Marjory settled deeper into her bath. She wished they could've spent the night in each other's arms. But she'd understood Alasdair's need to return to Blackshore. Nor did she wish to rile her brother unduly. Much better to bide her time and let Alasdair confront him, man to man. When he did, she secretly hoped Kendrew would accept their union, perhaps even be happy for them.

It wasn't likely, but she'd do her best to make it so.

Considering her options, she leaned her head back against the wooden tub's padded edge, relishing the warm, scented water. Her emotions were still ragged. Her ride with Alasdair across Nought had taken her from the darkest depths of doubt and despair to the most wondrous heights of bliss she could imagine. She'd thought he was lost to her, only to learn that he'd carried her in his heart all the harrowing while. Her own heart swelled, so full she wondered it didn't burst with her happiness. She did dip her washcloth into her jar of lavender-scented soap and scrubbed her breasts and then her arms, remembering Alasdair's touch. His hot gaze devouring her, the kisses they'd shared.

His loving and how she'd never believed a carnal mating could be so intense, almost rapturous in its beauty. Even the soreness deep inside her was magical. Wondrous proof that only hours before they'd been intimately joined. Their bodies moving together as one, their hearts laid open, everything that stood between them banished to the realm of memories and darkening dreams.

Well, almost everything.

Her head did ache a bit from the effort of trying to push Kendrew from her mind. Instead, she thought only of Alasdair and the life they'd enjoy together. He still felt as close as if he were in the next room, possibly even here at Nought, in her tower bedchamber with her.

She could almost see him looking at her still. His eyes smoldering as he reached for her, gripping her face in his hands and kissing her deeply, his tongue gliding into her mouth, twirling against hers, the earthy pleasure of their shared breath. And how his hard-muscled shoulders tensed beneath her hands, proving how fiercely he desired her.

She sighed and touched her ambers, wishing their magic could conjure him.

Tendrils of steam rose from her bath, reminding her of how the mist had pressed so closely about them as they'd thundered across Nought's rocky terrain.

The rain had returned, beating against the castle walls,

the night's cold, wet darkness all the more romantic now that she'd ridden with Alasdair across half of Nought in the storm's blustery embrace.

She'd always loved wild weather.

After the shelter of the Thunder Caves, her blood had quickened to share more of the rain- and windswept night with Alasdair.

Even now, she shivered with excitement.

The storm whisked her back into his arms, the memories of his wild passion making the lingering ache between her thighs tingle anew.

She closed her eyes, listening to the rain and refusing to be sad that she was again in her bedchamber, miles separating them.

Soon, he would come for her.

He'd promised.

Content in his word, she slid even deeper into the tub, letting the steaming water tease her chin. She enjoyed her baths. In truth, little was more delicious than soaking in the large, linen-lined tub, a well-doing wood fire on the hearth and a fine Nought wind serenading her.

Someone had thoughtfully lit the room's small coal brazier. Her little dog, Hercules, took advantage. He'd pulled one of her best embroidered cushions from her bed and dragged it before the brazier, treating himself to a luxurious and warm resting place.

But Hercules wasn't sleeping.

He'd stretched out on the cushion with his head resting on his paws, his ears pricked and his alert gaze on the bedchamber's closed door.

Hercules enjoyed guarding her privacy.

He wouldn't rest until she left the bathing tub and

slipped into her bed. Even then, he'd keep vigil, jumping up to growl if so much as a dust mote drifted too near to her.

Marjory glanced over at him, remembering how he'd almost played a favorite trick on Alasdair during one of his visits to Nought. Blessedly, she'd stopped Hercules just as he'd started to lift his little leg.

She shifted in the tub, sitting up a bit higher. "You're a wee blackguard at times, aren't you?"

One of Hercules's ears twitched, his mouth curving as if he were smiling in agreement.

"I'll give you a treat shortly." Marjory looked past him to where whoever had lit the brazier had also set her table with a late-night repast. Oatcakes, cheese, and butter along with wild fruit and honey winked at her, making her realize how long it'd been since she'd eaten all of two oatcakes at Hella's that afternoon.

Hercules followed her gaze, making an appreciative gurgling sound deep in his chest.

They could both do justice to such a feast.

She certainly was famished.

Yet she couldn't bring herself to end her bath.

She'd been drenched by the time Alasdair and his men had left her at the secret stair that led up to Nought's stone garden. Alasdair had argued, and lost, his intent to deliver her to the hall door. At her insistence, he and his men had ridden past the gatehouse's main stair to the stone garden's little-used entrance where chances were good no one would see her slip into the stronghold.

No one had.

Nor had Alasdair known she'd stood in a sheltered bower of the stone garden, peering over the wall to watch him and his men turn and ride away from Nought.

The rain increased then, the heavens opening as the storm raged around them, quickly blotting them from view. But she'd heard the thunder of their horses' hooves long after she'd caught her last glimpse of Alasdair's broad back disappearing into the blowing mist.

Not wanting to think about Alasdair hastening through the cold, wet night on his way back to Blackshore, she lifted the pitcher of rinse water, pouring its contents over her soapy scalp.

"Brrr..." She shivered and reached for the second rinsing jug, glad that the water in both had gone so cold. She welcomed the icy shock.

She'd never sleep if yearning for Alasdair kept rekindling the fires inside her, her awareness of the dull throbbing in intimate places making her burn to be in his arms again.

Across the room, Hercules barked once, and then again, sounding upset.

"Hush, sweet," Marjory called to him, pushing to her feet and reaching for her drying cloth.

It was then that a rush of cold air warned that she wasn't alone.

Someone had opened her door.

"Who's there?" She whipped about, whirling the drying cloth around her nakedness.

"It's only me." Isobel closed the door behind her and came into the room, a terrible look on her face. Hercules dashed over to her, running circles around her, yapping noisily.

Isobel didn't even glance at him.

She did come farther into the room. Her expression was even more unsettling now that she'd left the shadows of the door and the light of a wall torch fell across her, revealing her paleness, her state of disarray.

"Dear saints, Isobel. What is it?" Marjory stared at her friend, alarmed by the wariness in her eyes and how her unbound hair was tangled, still damp from her own bath.

She wore only her nightshift and she'd thrown one of Kendrew's plaids around her shoulders. Her feet were bare, her breath coming fast, as if she'd been hurrying.

She was clearly upset.

"Speak, please." Marjory felt her own pulse quickening. "What is it? Don't tell me you truly did hurt yourself falling from Ewan's horse?" She looked Isobel up and down, concerned. "You seemed fine when we spoke earlier, just after Alasdair brought me back."

"I am fine." Isobel raised a hand and shook her head. "You know, I could land headfirst in a leap from a horse and not hurt myself. It isn't that." Staying where she was, she looked around the room and then at the closed door as if she thought someone stood on the other side, listening through the wood.

When she turned back to Marjory, regret clouded her eyes. "Kendrew is speaking with several of his men. They're in the solar that opens off our bedchamber. And"—she reached to grip Marjory's arm—"the talk is of Alasdair."

"Alasdair?" Marjory blinked. Her heart clutched. Fear chilled her blood that something might've happened to him on his return journey. "Has he been injured? The storm—"

"Nae, nae, it's nothing the like." Isobel glanced over her shoulder at the door. "I didn't hear enough to know what was being said."

"If he's not dead, it can't be so bad." Heat was beginning to flood Marjory's face, her ears ringing so that her own voice seemed to come from a deep well. "Yet"—her palms were damping—"you wouldn't be here if it wasn't awful."

"I don't know that it is." Isobel glanced down at Hercules, reached to tug her hem from his teeth. That accomplished, she turned another worried look on Marjory. "But I think you should come with me to listen. There's a crack in the solar door. If we're quiet and press our ears to the wood, we should be able to hear what they're saying. I'm worried because Kendrew sounded very pleased." Isobel released Marjory's arm and pushed back her hair. "He never speaks of Alasdair in jovial tones. That's why I'm concerned."

"As am I!" Marjory threw aside the drying cloth and yanked on her night robe. She trembled, her fingers shaking so badly she could hardly tie the robe's belt. Of a sudden, it was chilly in the room, freezing nearly.

But the cold came from inside her.

It also felt ominously like the chill she'd experienced in the Thunder Caves.

Not wanting to make the connection, she bent to snatch up Hercules just as he made to nip Isobel's hem again. Her pulse racing, she placed him on the cushion before the brazier and gave him a warning look to stay there.

Hercules's sharp yipping was the last thing she needed if she and Isobel were to sneak down the corridor, into her brother's privy chamber, and listen at his solar door. If he caught them, there'd be hell to pay.

Hercules peered up at her, looking as if he'd relish the excitement.

The little dog loved nothing more than annoying Kendrew.

"You must stay here and be still. I will return soon." Marjory reached down to pet him and then hurried after Isobel into the night-darkened passage.

"I caught only bits." Isobel took her hand as they hastened through the gloom. "The door was closed and the wind howls louder on our side of the tower. But"—she hesitated, biting her lip before rushing on—"I think you should know before we get to the solar. I fear Hella was mistaken. Worse, I suspect Alasdair might've kept something very important from you when you were with him in the Thunder Cave."

Marjory froze. "What are you saying?"

"Come, let us hope I am wrong." Isobel tugged on Marjory's hand, hurrying her. "We need to get there before the men go down to the hall."

"Nae." Marjory dug in her heels. "Tell me what you know."

"I know nothing, dear heart." Isobel sounded as if she knew lots. Terrible things that knotted Marjory's stomach and made her knees quiver. "But..." She pulled on Marjory's arm again, urging her along the corridor. "From what I did hear, Alasdair must've agreed to marry the Mackinnon's daughter, Lady Coira."

"What?" Marjory's eyes flew wide, her heart nearly stopping. Icy shock raced through her veins. "That can't be so."

If it was, she couldn't bear it.

No, it wasn't possible.

She wouldn't believe it.

"I'm only guessing." Isobel shot a glance at her. "I could be wrong."

"You have to be." Marjory pressed a hand to her breast, hurrying. They were almost on the other side of the tower. Kendrew and Isobel's quarters loomed just ahead, the door ajar.

"Let's hope so. I know it would be a blow. I was stunned myself." Isobel stopped outside her bedchamber door, pushing gently and then wincing when the hinges creaked. "Shhh..." She ushered Marjory into the darkened room and over to the closed solar door. "Put your ear here." She spoke softly, touched a barely visible crack with the tip of her finger. "You will hear them."

Marjory didn't move. "Was Lady Coira mentioned by name?"

"Nae." Isobel shook her head. "The talk was of a 'marriage agreement that, once and for all, would keep Alasdair at Blackshore.' It sounded like an arranged union, already settled upon.

"Who else could they mean but Coira Mackinnon?" Isobel lowered her voice even more, clearly unhappy to be the bearer of such ill tidings. "We know her father has been after Alasdair to agree to the match."

"He'd have told me." Marjory was sure of it.

She also knew everything he *had* said to her.

She'd trusted him.

She still did.

But she couldn't resist pressing her ear to the crack in her brother's solar door. She wished at once that she hadn't. Kendrew's deep voice was unmistakable. She wasn't quite certain who was in the room with him. Several men, to be sure, just as Isobel had warned. Their words were indistinct, but their tone couldn't be mistaken.

They were mightily pleased about something.

And she did hear the words "marriage agreement" and talk of a "large settlement of coin and land." Most disturbing of all were the two names repeated again and again.

Alasdair and Blackshore.

Marjory's world turned dark, all the light and air rushing out of it, leaving her a shell. Distantly amazed she was still standing, that her legs hadn't given out on her, she pressed her forehead against the door's cold, uncaring wood and closed her eyes.

If what she heard was true, she wanted to die.

She couldn't live without Alasdair.

Not now, not after all that had transpired at the Thunder Caves.

She felt Isobel slip an arm around her waist, gently guiding her from the door and out of the room, back into the chill dimness of the corridor. Quietly, her friend closed the door behind them, already guiding Marjory back through the night, toward her own bedchamber.

"Now you see why I came for you." Marjory glanced at her as they rounded the first curve in the passage. Her pretty face wore a world of regret. "You had to know, my dear. I am so sorry."

Marjory couldn't speak.

Something had happened to her tongue. It'd vanished, perhaps chased away by the hot, burning thickness rising in her throat.

She blinked hard, refusing to dash at the stinging heat blurring her vision. She hated tears and wouldn't acknowledge them. She did keep walking, sheer will alone helping her put one foot in front of the other. She breathed in the same manner, though she'd also swear she *wasn't* breathing. She felt as if all the life had been sucked out of her. But deep inside her, a steely thread of hope wouldn't die. Clinging to that hope, she forced herself to think hard, searching for a reason to disbelieve.

"It doesn't make sense," she spoke at last, the words coming as they reached her bedchamber and Isobel hastened her inside. "He would've told me. I saw him only hours ago. We laid together in the Thunder Cave, on the bear- and wolfskins. It was beautiful, I told you—"

"My dear..." Isobel hugged her, the look on her face dashing Marjory's hope. "He knows you care for him, Norn. He didn't want to hurt you. We know he desires you." She released Marjory, stepped back. "He's always done so. If he is to wed Lady Coira, the arrangement will not have changed his feelings for you. I'm guessing his need for you overrode—"

"Pah!" Marjory's anger flared. "If this is true, how could he think I'd not find out? The Glen of Many Legends isn't so vast that—"

She broke off, brushed back her hair with both hands. Another thought came to her, sparking her suspicion. "How would Kendrew know this?"

Isobel shrugged, looking unhappy. "From what I gathered when Grim and I returned earlier, two wayfarers called at Nought while we were at Hella's." Leaving Marjory, she went to the table to pour them each a cup of night ale. "I didn't hear if they were passing pilgrims or just travelers, but"—she returned to Marjory, pressing one of the cups into her hand—"the men must've brought the word."

Marjory lifted the ale cup, taking a long, fortifying sip. "I see."

She truly did.

Passing wayfarers aye carried news through the Highlands.

They made the best couriers.

And as they usually held no ties to a particular clan, their word was accepted as truth.

Such men had no reason to lie.

"Did Kendrew say anything about the wayfarers' tidings?" Marjory was starting to hear a rushing noise in her ears again. "I know you'll have asked him."

She would've done.

Such men often brought the only entertainment into remote holdings such as Nought. Welcome guests, they were plied with food and ale in return for sharing tales and gossip. Their news a reason no laird ever turned them away.

"I did ask, yes." Isobel finished her ale, returned the cup to the table.

Marjory waited, the roaring between her ears almost deafening.

It worsened when Isobel went to stand before the closed window shutters, her entire stance revealing her reluctance to speak.

"Kendrew wouldn't speak of the men." She turned to face Marjory. "He said their news was so pleasing he wanted to savor it through his sleep. And"—she hesitated, the pause making Marjory wish she hadn't asked—"he said he wanted to tell you himself in the morning."

"So it does involve me." Marjory slowly shook her head, wishing she could undo all that had transpired that day—and the last two years since Alasdair had first crossed her path.

"I believe so." Isobel's words confirmed Marjory's worst dread. "And as we know Kendrew and his men

were speaking of Alasdair and a marriage agreement…"
She didn't finish, pressed the backs of her hands to her
eyes as if to stem tears of her own.

"Then I will be the one to break our pact." Marjory
reached down and scooped Hercules into her arms, needing his soft warm weight to comfort her. "There will be
no third wedding between the clans."

"You needn't marry Alasdair to fulfill our oath, Norn."
Isobel came over to her, stroked back her hair. "There are
other fine MacDonalds and even Camerons who would
make good and worthy husbands."

Marjory scarce heard her, for the buzzing in her ears
had reached a fever pitch. Her ambers were also blazing.
The stones burned her skin as if each one had been set
afire and was scorching her.

That pain, too, she hardly noticed.

Of course, they'd warn her that her heart was breaking.

Was there any greater tragedy?

She didn't think so.

And she didn't care if another MacDonald or Cameron would step in and take her hand. Such a union might
honor the vow she, Isobel, and Catriona had made on the
evening of the trial by combat two years before, but it
wouldn't assuage the ache in her heart.

A hollowing she'd suffer until she drew her last breath.

Only Alasdair could save her from such sorrow.

And that wasn't likely to happen because if she and
Isobel were guessing rightly, Alasdair would soon be wed
to Lady Coira Mackinnon.

Marjory stood straighter, lifting her chin as she pretended a vise wasn't clamped around her chest, crushing
the life from her, squeezing her heart.

"You must get back to your bedchamber." She took Isobel by the arm, leading her to the door. "If Kendrew doesn't go down to the hall with his men, he'll wonder where you are."

"I'll handle him." Isobel broke free, turning to face her just as Marjory maneuvered her into the passage. "I don't like leaving you—"

"I'll be fine," Marjory lied, forcing a smile. "A warrior forewarned is a warrior prepared."

"You're a woman, not a warrior."

"I'm feeling strengths I never knew I had." That wasn't true at all, but Marjory meant to make it so.

Isobel didn't look convinced. "The morrow will be difficult."

"That I know."

"Kendrew will make a grand flourish, announcing Alasdair's betrothal with relish. He'll—"

"He'll not get the better of me." Marjory wished she felt as confident as her words.

In truth, she dreaded facing her brother in the morning.

Worse than that, she hated the weakness that made her lean against the closed door and listen to her friend's footsteps disappearing down the corridor. Isobel was returning to a bed warm and beckoning, soon to be occupied by the man she loved. A husband and lover who eagerly awaited her.

Marjory would never know such a pleasure.

If she couldn't have Alasdair, she wanted no man.

Her heart was already shrinking. She felt ill, cold, and crushingly disappointed. She was also angry, her entire body so tense she feared she'd break if she pushed away from the door. She did fist her hands, pressing them hard to her chest as she forced herself to breathe.

To think.

It was possible she and Isobel misinterpreted what they'd heard.

Lady Coira's name hadn't been mentioned. They'd only caught talk of "a marriage agreement that would keep Alasdair from champing at Nought's door."

Perhaps one of Alasdair's men was marrying? A grand ceremony that would cost time and preparation and keep him occupied as clan chieftain?

Such an event would be something he probably wouldn't have mentioned to her at the Thunder Caves. Not as occupied as they were with their own passion.

A glimmer of hope flickered in Marjory's breast.

She swallowed hard. "Aye, that will be the way of it." She looked down at Hercules, who peered up at her, worryingly. "A clan matter requiring his attention."

Hercules leaned into her, pressing his head against her knee as if he knew that wasn't so and wished to comfort her. She reached down to pet him, her eyes stinging when he licked her fingers.

Hercules knew her so well.

She did need comforting.

On the morrow she'd be strong.

No matter what came at her, she would meet Kendrew's proclamation with a straight back and squared shoulders, a calm mien, or even a smile.

It was the only thing she could do if his tidings proved as grave as she feared...

That something had happened that would keep Alasdair so near to her, yet forever out of her reach.

Chapter Seventeen

❖

Early the next morning, Alasdair stood at one of the tall window arches in his painted solar and looked out on Loch Moidart. He took a deep breath of the chill, clean air, keenly aware that his days of standing at this particular window could well be numbered. Indeed, he was sure they were. And it split his heart to think of leaving Blackshore. He couldn't imagine living anywhere else.

The very notion was unthinkable.

Yet...

Life without Marjory would pain him more.

He clenched his jaw, ignoring the ache inside him, thinking only of her. He held a ribbon in his hand, a fine length of silk the same clear, dazzling blue of the sky. A deeper blue, the loch shone like polished glass, colored spears of light dancing across its surface. The storms of the night were gone, the morn glorious. He'd almost believe the gods were mocking him, taunting him with the blue of Marjory's eyes everywhere he turned his gaze.

Or letting him know they were aware he'd kept her ribbon after finding it in the birchwood. And like a wee laddie caught doing something he shouldn't have, his punishment wasn't a rap on the knuckles but a fresh-laundered blue day that could only remind him of her.

How sweetly she'd lain in his arms in her Thunder Cave. The bliss they'd shared and the promises he'd made her. Vows he had every intention of keeping.

He did love her.

So much that it hurt him inside.

Enough that he'd turn his back on everything he held most dear to have her.

He just needed to clear his head. To find the words to declare himself to his council, the clan who depended on him. Men, women, and children who would reel when he told them he was walking away. That chances were good he'd never again set foot in his beloved Glen of Many Legends.

He wound the ribbon through his fingers, clutching its silken softness against his palm. Only hours ago, he'd linked his hand with Marjory's, lifting her arm above her head as he'd loved her. She'd undone him, looking so abandoned and pleasured, the passion blazing in her eyes. Her joy, her trust, had made his heart soar. He wanted to see that exultation on her face always, every day of their lives.

He just wished their happiness wouldn't bring sorrow to others.

Leaning harder against the broad window ledge, he looked out across the loch, knowing he'd miss Blackshore fiercely. As if to tempt him into staying, his land was showing its best face. Not a thread of mist marred the day's brilliance. Nary a cloud graced the horizon, poised to soften the dazzling blue sky. Even the hills rose in star-tling clarity against the fine, bright dawn. A brisk wind rippled the loch and the air was clean and crisp.

It was a day he knew Marjory would love.

Blackshore at its finest, dressed to impress a lady.

And so different from the night before when he'd returned from Nought to find great curtains of rain sweeping in from the sea, bringing the sharp tang of salt, fish, and seaweed. Now, even the stone of the causeway sparkled as if a giant's hand had cast diamonds along its length, clear to the opposite shore.

Alasdair rubbed his thumb along his jaw, not taking his gaze off the view before him.

He knew better.

He wasn't alone in the painted solar.

If he turned to face the room, he'd see his great-uncle, Malcolm, sitting so straight-backed on his stool. An early riser, the graybeard had been in the solar when Alasdair arrived, already having claimed his favorite seat and bus-ily carving little wooden animals for the two small sons of one of the kitchen lasses.

And—Alasdair set his jaw—determining to ruin Alasdair's day.

Geordie was another reason he kept his back to the room.

He wasn't of a mood to come face to face with the old dog. Geordie was sprawled on his plaid before the hearth where a huge wood fire blazed. And his soured mood was apparent. The ungrateful beast missed the twists of dried beef Grim had given him in Nought's birchwood.

Alasdair refused to consider that Geordie might miss Grim.

Such a possibility was wholly unacceptable.

Outrageous, even.

He frowned, ignoring how both the dog and Malcolm were eyeing him suspiciously.

At least, they did when they thought he wasn't looking.

Alasdair turned his face to the morning wind, tightening his grip on Marjory's ribbon. At the moment, the bit of blue silk made him feel close to her. Until now, he'd never been a sentimental man. Leastways not about women. The last thing he needed was an aging warrior and an old dog prying into his business, guessing that Marjory had haunted him the entire journey home.

That he couldn't string the words together to tell his people of his plans because all he could think of was pulling Marjory back into his arms, tearing the clothes from her and then sinking deep into the tight, wet heat of her. Kissing her everywhere...

He frowned, fisting his hands around the blue ribbon.

She'd robbed him of his senses!

The air shifted beside him and Malcolm appeared at his elbow, proving that his infirmities didn't prevent him from moving with annoying stealth. "You will ruin your trophy if you keep crushing it."

"What trophy?" Alasdair whipped about, glaring at the ancient.

Malcolm only cocked a brow, looking irritatingly fit and hardy. "If I must tell you, then you disappoint me greatly."

"I found the ribbon in the wood." Alasdair couldn't keep the belligerence from his voice. "It means nothing," he lied, heat surging up his neck when Malcolm's expression showed he knew the ribbon meant everything.

Marjory's perfume even clung to the silk, the fresh wildflower scent fuddling his wits every time a whiff of it wafted near his nose.

Malcolm reached to pull the rumpled blue ribbon from Alasdair's fist. "A gift of such worth should be treated with care," he said, his tone erasing the years and making Alasdair feel like a brash, callow youth. "Most especially if it is all you are to have of her."

"You're babbling nonsense." Alasdair leaned against the wall and crossed his arms, feigning casualness.

Malcolm shook his head slowly. "You've been bitten hard, lad."

"All that's biting me is the chill of the wind."

"Aye, worse than I thought." Malcolm chuckled low.

Alasdair glared at him.

Malcolm only stroked his neatly trimmed beard and nodded. Then, with the smooth gait of a much younger man, he defied the battle wounds that plagued him and he sauntered over to Alasdair's table where he placed the ribbon on the gleaming oaken surface.

Not yet satisfied, he straightened the ribbon to its full length and then carefully smoothed out the wrinkles with his big, war-scarred hands.

Annoyance beat through Alasdair as he watched him.

"Have you naught better to do, Uncle?" Alasdair angled his head to the open windows, grateful to catch the ring of steel against steel coming from a courtyard around the tower's curve. The younger warriors were training there, starting their day with sword practice. "Ewan would appreciate your help instructing the lads at swordcraft."

Malcolm crossed the room as if Alasdair hadn't

spoken. Calmly, he reclaimed his seat on the stool. "A good warrior's training is more than how well he swings a blade."

This time Alasdair pretended not to hear.

He continued to lean against the wall, but turned his head, gazing pointedly at the loch. Experience had taught him that whenever Malcolm made such comments, and in that tone, a lecture was forthcoming.

With luck, ignoring his uncle would dissuade him.

Sage words were the last thing he needed.

Unfortunately, the graybeard was clearing his throat most demonstrably. And the instant Alasdair slid a glance his way, Malcolm pounced.

"Take these wooden toys…" Malcolm picked up a half-carved goose, examining it closely. "In a good clan, all hands pull together. It is fine when a laird's sons learn to be braw warriors. Yet"—he turned the goose in his hand, peering at it as if the toy held all the world's wisdom—"even lads born to a kitchen wench or a cottar's wife can, and should, hold their weight in battle.

"Truth is, such men, once grown, often make the deciding difference." He looked up then, his gaze piercing. "Remember how such folk supported Robert Bruce, our hero king, at the great battle of Bannockburn. They ran onto the field in the most desperate hour, shouting and wielding whatever weapons they had.

"Their bravery helped Bruce win the day." Malcolm looked back down at the little half-finished goose, one corner of his mouth hitching up in an annoyingly sage smile. "You should remember that," he added, reaching for his whittling knife. "Aye, you should."

"I dinnae see what the Bruce's triumph has to do with

me." Alasdair frowned at the toy in Malcolm's hands. "Even less a little wooden goose."

Malcolm ignored him, whittling away.

Geordie gave a huge, old-dog sigh and rolled onto his side, clearly tired of keeping a long, accusatory stare fixed on Alasdair.

It couldn't be easy to go so long without blinking, even for a dog well-practiced in such irksome habits.

Peace returned to the painted solar. A log popped on the hearth and the increased ringing of steel from the courtyard proved his lads were learning well.

Alasdair drew a long breath, welcoming the return of normalcy to his morning.

If he was left alone, he'd manage to think.

He began to relax, some of the tension easing from his shoulders.

"Rearing lads to feel special builds confidence in them." Malcolm's deep voice shattered the tranquility. "They know they're appreciated, valued as a strong member of the clan. They learn pride, to keep their chins aye raised and meet your eyes when you speak to them. In time, they may get cocky, talking back to you or walking with a swagger. Then the day comes when men must fight and they're often the first to reach for their weapons, ready to give their all for kith and kin. Such lads, and the men they become, should ne'er be forgotten.

"That's why I'm carving barn animals for Anice's boys." Malcolm set down the wooden goose, now finished and startlingly lifelike. "Such lads are the lifeblood of every clan. They should have a few toys when they're so young."

Alasdair just looked at him, feeling chastised even though he couldn't figure out why he should.

He did see to the well-doing of every man, woman, and child in the clan. Even now, his mind raced, making plans to ensure their weal when he was gone.

He was a good chieftain.

And Malcolm knew it.

"You're up to something." Alasdair was sure of it.

"You asked if I didn't have aught better to do." Malcolm reached for a new chunk of wood, turning it this way and that as if to decide what animal it wished to become. "I answered you, no more."

"Nae, you're leading into a lecture." Alasdair pushed away from the wall and strode over to Malcolm's stool, dropping to one knee to be on eye level with him. "I'd hear what it is. I know you'll tell me anyway."

Malcolm's lips twitched, but he caught himself quickly, assuming a swift air of innocence. "I'm simply carving toys, lad. You ken I like children."

Alasdair stood, ran a hand through his hair. He couldn't argue with Malcolm.

The graybeard did love children. He spent much of his time with the clan bairns, as Alasdair well knew. But there was one thing he didn't know.

Alasdair studied his great uncle, his gray head once more bent over the new piece of wood. "Why didn't you ever have sons of your own?"

Malcolm looked up at once. "I ne'er married now, did I?"

"Why didn't you?" Alasdair knew his mistake as soon as the question left his tongue.

"The same reason you'll no' be wedding, I'm thinking." Malcolm began carving the wood as he spoke. "I fell in love with the wrong lass. She was a MacKenzie, daughter to a cousin of Duncan MacKenzie, the Black Stag of Kintail. A more beautiful maid ne'er walked the hills, I say you. She had hair black as a raven's wing, eyes like sapphires. And she had spirit, a fiery temper, and so much passion a man could singe himself just looking at her." Malcolm paused, turning aside to knuckle his eyes. "Yet it was me she wanted, no other."

Alasdair bit his tongue, stunned to see a tear spill down Malcolm's cheek.

Then his eyes cleared and he fisted his hands so tightly on his thighs that his knuckles gleamed white. "She begged me to marry her," he said, his voice rough with emotion. "She insisted our love mattered more than the troubles between our clans. My grandfather told me she was right." A little smile touched Malcolm's lips, but it was sad, reminiscent. "He spoke of the old days when even in times of feuding, a man's worst transgression would be forgiven if he'd acted out of love for a lady."

"He suggested you offer for her?" Alasdair was surprised.

"Nothing the like." Malcolm laughed and slapped his knee. "He told me to ride to Eilean Creag and snatch her out from under the Black Stag's nose, is what he said."

"But you didn't."

"Nae, I didn't. My honor and loyalty to our clan stayed me. Even though she wished to be taken, I knew that stealing her away would fan fires of enmity that already blazed too bright."

"And now you regret it."

"More than anything else in my life." Malcolm closed his eyes, took a long, deep breath. "I'd give the rest of my days for one moment to go back and undo my thickheaded posturing. My refusal to risk everything I loved most for the one woman I loved even more."

Alasdair rubbed a hand across the back of his neck. "What happened to her? Do you know?"

"Och, aye." Malcolm's lips twisted. "As the fates willed it, a MacLeod snatched her away while she was out berry picking one fine summer day. The MacLeods, as you ken, are much more hostile to the MacKenzies of Kintail than we ever were. Yet"—Malcolm leaned forward, his gaze on Alasdair—"the great Black Stag eventually forgave the man, even welcoming him into his hall.

"It was a fruitful union, producing eight strapping sons and one bonnie daughter, last I heard.

"And"—Malcolm reached again for the new chunk of wood and his whittling knife—"the heather didn't vanish from the hills and the mist didn't slip away to hide just because she wed a man from a warring clan. Truth is I doubt her children, or Duncan MacKenzie, even cared how the pair came to be wed. They made a good match and raised a fine family, to the weal and benefit of both their clans."

"And those nine children should've been yours." Alasdair spoke what his great uncle left unsaid.

"They could've been, aye." Malcolm didn't look up from his whittling. "If I'd accepted that sometimes what's in a man's heart matters more than what's expected of him."

Alasdair frowned.

His head was beginning to ache with a vengeance.

Malcolm said nothing, his attention focused entirely on his wood carving.

It was a show, Alasdair knew.

So he went back to the window arch before Malcolm

could see how much his words moved him. Even so, the Highlands were different now. Much had changed since Malcolm's grandfather or even Malcolm might've stormed a stronghold and tossed their ladylove over their shoulder, riding off with her into the night. Such acts were barbaric.

Men were civilized now.

Alasdair rubbed the back of his neck, feeling anything but. He cursed beneath his breath, his gaze on the hills to the north. Not surprisingly, he couldn't see them clearly. As so often in the Highlands, the weather had changed, turning dark and blustery. The loch was now iron gray and long swaths of mist drifted in from the sea to curl across the water. Thick clouds had chased the blue from the sky, the day's gloom suiting his mood.

In such weather, any man could feel a tail growing, horns to mark his bold intent and cloven feet to brand his daring before the eyes of all men who kept their honor.

Soon, he'd break his word to the King.

Yet what was honor if it kept a man from claiming the woman he held most dear?

Alasdair flattened his hands against the cold stone of the window ledge. With the wind bringing the chill, the wet smell of rain, and the mist blurring the hills, it was easy to imagine a black-painted coracle slipping into the loch, gliding past Blackshore's walls. Knowing such a craft had been at Nought's Dreagan's Claw made it even easier to believe such intruders had something to do with Marjory.

Indeed, he was sure of it.

He knew trouble when it danced beneath his nose.

Truth was, he knew it from afar, too.

His entire body tensing, he cleared his throat, his gaze

on the loch and the whirling mist. "Malcolm," he spoke with deliberate calm. "Are the men still going on about a sea serpent in the loch?"

"Every night, aye."

"What do you think?"

"I know I've ne'er seen a swimming beastie here-abouts, or anywhere."

Alasdair rubbed his brow. He'd hoped Malcolm would give him a different answer. But he wasn't going to mention his suspicions. Not yet, anyway. He needed to think before alarming the clan. There were other, more serious matters weighing on him.

Such as...

He glanced at the table where Marjory's blue ribbon gleamed in the light of a candle. Its blue shimmered, reminding him of how the ribbon had delighted her at Castle Haven's Harvest Fair. How he'd purchased the ribbon for her and how much she'd loved wearing it in her hair. The way his heart had slammed against his ribs when he'd spotted the ribbon in the birchwood. How it now reminded him of her racing into the clearing to challenge him. Their ensuing journey across Nought and—his heart squeezed—everything that had then come to pass between them in the Thunder Caves.

Malcolm was right.

The ribbon was a grand prize.

The graybeard was right about a few other things as well, but Alasdair wouldn't swell his head by admitting anything the like.

He did push away from the window, briskly brushing his plaid into place. Then he strolled across the room to where his sword, Mist-Chaser, rested on a bench beside the door. If Malcolm noticed that he picked up the ribbon as he passed the table, so be it.

He also didn't care if he was observed raising the ribbon to his lips and then tying it around Mist-Chaser's hilt.

The deed done, he placed Mist-Chaser back on the bench and dusted his hands.

Across the solar, Malcolm was still on his stool, whittling industriously, his head bent low over what was beginning to look like a lamb.

But Alasdair didn't miss the glint in the old warrior's eyes. Malcolm had seen everything. And the brief nod he gave Alasdair was his approval.

Alasdair stepped in front of him and placed his hand on Malcolm's shoulder. "I wish you'd have gone after your MacKenzie lass."

"So do I, lad, so do I."

This time it was Alasdair who nodded gruffly. He also made a promise to himself to never be an old man sitting on a stool, regretting what he hadn't done.

His lady wasn't beyond reach.

She was even waiting for him to come for her.

And he'd be damned if he'd allow anyone to stop him from claiming her.

Later that morning, but on the other side of the Glen of Many Legends, Marjory walked briskly, her head high as she approached Nought's great hall. Hercules hurried beside her, his steps jaunty, as if he anticipated the mayhem about to erupt at the high table.

Hercules loved chaos.

Marjory preferred calm. So she'd spent much of the night preparing to accept Kendrew's news with grace.

She'd even thought of an enthusiastic response so that no one would guess how hurt she was by Alasdair's unexpected betrothal.

Only Isobel would know of her devastation.

That her world had been ripped apart, her heart torn, and her dreams shattered on the night the stars had shone their brightest for her.

How quickly their dazzle had faded.

Now there was nothing else for her to do but save what she could, her pride.

Unfortunately, as she neared the hall's arched entry, she caught the low rumble of male voices, including her brother's. She couldn't make out all his words, but she heard Alasdair's name. Her breath caught and her heart lurched. Images of their hours at the Thunder Caves whirled through her mind, as did everything she and Isobel suspected about Alasdair and Lady Coira Mackinnon. She forgot the rebuttal she'd been repeating so carefully in her mind.

She'd been up since before sunrise, composing it. She'd practiced so that her voice wouldn't waver, her tone unconvincing.

Now she couldn't remember a word.

Equally distressing, her ambers were on fire again. The stones hummed from within, each one vibrating against her skin as if they'd sprung to life.

They surely knew she was about to receive tidings that would end all her hopes of happiness.

Quickening her pace, ready to hear the worst and be done with it, she vowed to have the necklace delivered to Alasdair as soon as she could make arrangements for someone to carry it to Blackshore.

Now that her pact with Isobel and Catriona would not be fulfilled, she couldn't keep the ambers.

They belonged to Clan Donald.

Alasdair could give them to his bride as a wedding gift.

The thought made her feel sick and dizzy. It also sent heat rushing to her cheeks, so she stopped outside the hall door to take a deep, steadying breath. Then she lifted her chin, summoned her brightest smile, and sailed into the hall.

As soon as she was spotted, the men went silent, the sudden quiet almost louder than the din. Her heart began to pound as men parted to clear her path to the dais end of the hall.

It was then that she saw Kendrew.

He wore the smile she loved best on him. It was a crooked, boyish smile that, before Isobel, drew women to him in droves. He was looking right at her, his eyes alight with brotherly affection. He'd clearly been waiting for her and the pleasure on his face dashed her last hope that she and Isobel might've erred about Alasdair's nuptials.

Little else would put Kendrew in such a good mood.

So she did the only thing she could do and took her place at the high table.

"Everyone is in fine fettle this morn." She reached for a freshly baked bannock. She began buttering it with care, casting Kendrew a look from beneath her lashes. "You appear particularly pleased."

"So I am." He beamed. "I have grand tidings. Great news that will—"

"Let me tell her." Beside him, Isobel gripped his arm. She looked even unhappier than the night before in

Marjory's bedchamber. Her face was pale and she had dark circles under her eyes, her expression tense.

Marjory wished she could reassure her, but she couldn't reveal they'd met in the night. "There's no need for anyone to tell me. I already know."

"You cannae." Kendrew flashed a suspicious look at his wife. "No' unless—"

"Don't blame Isobel." Marjory glanced at Hercules, standing with his front paws on her knee. She gave him a tiny piece of buttered bannock. When she returned her attention to Kendrew, she spoke calmly. "You were speaking of Alasdair last night. Voices carry at such late hours. I heard you from the tower stair. That's how I know Alasdair is to—"

"Hah!" Kendrew snorted at the mention of his archfiend. "I dinnae care what he's up to, so long as he stays away from Nought. And your ears must be on backward. All I said about him was that I hope he chokes on a herring when he hears our news."

"Our news?" Marjory glanced at Isobel.

She looked as though all the blood had drained from her face. "I'm so sorry, Norn."

Marjory's chest tightened. She turned back to Kendrew. "What is this about?"

"Your betrothal, that's what." Kendrew beamed again, pride ringing in his words. "I've finally found a husband worthy of you. A Viking warlord of considerable note. By all counts, he's a handsome devil. Tall and blond, with looks to rival Thor. Word is he wears more arm rings than I do."

He grinned at her, as if expecting her to swoon.

Marjory feared she'd be ill.

"A true Viking, Norn. *A warlord*."

"I don't care if he's Thor and Odin in one." Marjory stared at him, the weight of his words crushing her as surely as if the ceiling had crashed on top of her. "How did you find him? There weren't any other Norse lords on your list."

"So there weren't." Kendrew took a long drink of ale. "But we're fortunate. Word spreads as quickly in Norway as in the Highlands. I didn't have to seek another suitor. He came to you. And he wants you badly enough to offer a hefty sack of silver as your bride price."

Hercules barked and darted beneath the table, no doubt planning to bite Kendrew's ankle.

"Hercules." Isobel scooped the little dog onto her lap, stroking him. "That's a good lad."

Marjory scarce noticed, her gaze on her brother. "You'd sell me for a bag of coin?"

"Sakes, Norn! You speak nonsense. I wouldn't sell you for all the world's gold." Kendrew leaned forward, gripping the table edge. "I will see you made a shining light of the north. Our old homeland, Norn, think of it. You'll be married to a man about to become a great noble. All Norway will know your name, respect you." He sat back, looking pleased. "The silver means naught. I'll save it as a birthing gift to your first child. It'll be our secret. Your husband need ne'er know. He's a warlord of untold fame." He looked round at the others lining the table, his chest swelling. "Men in the north sing ballads of him. He's a legend there and he wants you as his bride."

"Indeed." Marjory didn't know how she managed that one word.

"He holds vast lands in the Trondelag on Norway's rich western coast, directly on the Trondheimsfjord. Soon he will lord it over even more territory." Kendrew was enthusiastic, unaware that the floor had split open beneath his high table. That his sister was sliding into a deep, dark abyss, scrabbling desperately at the edge to keep from falling any farther.

"All the most powerful Norse lords hail from the Trondelag." He made it sound as if that truth sealed everything. "It is a fine match. You could do no better."

"That is not so and you know it." Isobel spoke up, her voice strained.

"I know she won't waste herself as a brine drinker's wife." Kendrew's tone hardened. "She'll be a fine lady—"

"She already is." Isobel met her husband's gaze, her own challenging.

Marjory stared at them both, hoping she didn't look as aghast as she felt. "Who is this man?" She had to know. "He surely has a name."

"And a fine one, it is." Kendrew's enthusiasm returned. "He is Ivar Ironstorm and he's already on his way to claim you."

Marjory's relief that he wasn't Rorik the Generous vanished upon hearing the man would soon arrive at Nought.

"How do you know this?" Her stomach clenched painfully. Yet there was still a chance Kendrew erred. That he'd read too much into the ramblings of wayfarers. So she took a moment to school her features and then asked the question that would determine her fate.

"I know you heard this from the travelers who stopped here yestere'en. Did they bring a missive with them? Something more substantial than gossip gathered on the road?"

"I take no stranger's word without proof." Kendrew's

answer sent her heart plummeting. "They brought a letter," he announced, retrieving a scrunched parchment from beneath his plaid.

He held up the proclamation and she saw the inked lines, the imprint of a seal in the broken glob of wax that had kept the scroll closed.

"Ivar Ironstorm's overlord wishes him wed so that he can settle greater lands and riches on him." Kendrew tucked the scroll beneath his plaid again. "In Norway as here, high-ranking nobles need heirs. And"—he patted the place where the parchment rested—"they are far-seeing enough to ken that a highborn daughter of a good Scottish house will make a worthy bride."

"Then I hope they find one for Lord Ironstorm." Marjory took another bite of her bannock, chewing delicately. "I appreciate your efforts to see me well wed, but I shall not be journeying to the Trondelag. I will not marry a Viking warlord."

"It's too late." Kendrew's expression was hard again. "I've agreed to the match."

"No one asked me." Marjory dabbed her lips with a linen napkin. "I'd remember if that were so."

Around them, the hall fell silent again. The men who were craning necks or crowding the aisles, pushing forward to hear what was going on at the high table, now froze. Each man looked on in stunned horror as if expecting a thunderbolt to slam down into the hall.

Marjory waited, too.

Her palms were slick and her knees trembled. Her stomach was a tight, painful knot and the place where her heart should be felt like a hollow, empty void. But she was pretty sure her face was all cold, hard refusal.

She hoped so, anyway.

"Next time"—she raised her ale cup, took a sip—"you might ask me first."

"What's this?" Kendrew's brows rose. "You're my sister. It's my duty and privilege to see you wed. I want only the best for you."

"That I know. I still wish to remain unwed." Marjory held his gaze, letting her own pierce him until he blinked first.

A test of wills she'd always won.

"I gave my word." He stood, turning to glance out over the hall, glaring at his men until they returned to their trestle benches. "I'll no' have you shame us by making a liar out of me."

He sat back down, his face closed. "You'll marry Ivar Ironstorm when he comes for you and you'll make him a good and willing bride."

"We shall see." Marjory sat straighter in her chair. Composure was her best weapon.

"Nae, you will see." Kendrew narrowed his eyes at her, a muscle jumping in his jaw. "If you think to refuse, I'll lock you in your bedchamber until Ironstorm's arrival."

"You wouldn't dare."

"Humph." Kendrew took a big bite of cold roast, chewing with relish. It was a sign Marjory knew and answer enough.

He would indeed ban her to her quarters if she defied him.

Except...

She wasn't about to let that happen.

Above all, she wasn't going to marry Ivar Ironstorm.

Her mind raced. Somewhere in the distance thunder rumbled and wind rushed past the hall's high, narrow windows. A few candles gutted as cold air swept the dais, bringing the smell of approaching rain. A movement near the hall's entry caught her eye, making her heart leap. In that moment, she hoped to see Alasdair striding in to challenge Kendrew and put an end to this madness.

But it was only Grim.

The big warrior didn't advance into the hall. He remained in the shadows where he leaned against the wall, his arms crossed and his face expressionless.

He didn't even look her way.

Marjory's heart sank, knowing no support would come from him. If she hoped to wriggle out of this mess, doing so would fall to her.

So she leveled her most direct gaze on her brother. "The Trondelag?" She let a bit of worry edge her voice, trying a different angle.

Beneath his misguided attempts to do right by her, he did love her.

That she knew.

So she'd appeal to his brotherly concern rather than his lairdly pride.

"So I said, aye." Kendrew eyed her suspiciously.

"You surely know the Trondelag is the most uninhabitable region of all Norway." She set down her eating knife and glanced around the high table, hoping for agreement.

But none of the men present would meet her eyes. Most kept their gazes on the food before them, busily eating or sipping their ale. One rubbed at a wrinkle on his sleeve. Another had drawn Hercules's attention and was feeding the little dog bits of cold roasted mutton. A glance across the hall showed that even Grim was gone, his disappearance proving how alone she was.

Only Isobel's face held sympathy.

"I've heard nothing good of the Trondelag." Isobel took her side. "It's known to be craggy and barren, a wasteland of ice where even the soles of your shoes freeze to the ground. The men there keep many wives because one wouldn't be enough to warm them in the long, endless winters."

"Hah!" Kendrew looked between his wife and Marjory. "So little do you both know of the Tronds and their vast and prosperous land. Trondelag is a favored place, much prized for its rich grazings and the fine crops of its well-doing farms. If a bit of snow falls in winter"—he tossed an annoyed look at Marjory—"since when is my sister one to complain of the cold?"

Marjory smiled. "Perhaps since I have no wish to marry a red-nosed, icy-fingered Trond."

"Nae, you'd rather wed a web-footed, brine-drinking MacDonald." Kendrew grabbed his ale cup, quaffing a long swig. "Ironstorm is a warlord, not an ice fisherman. Nor has he ever waved a sword in my face or slain good Mackintosh men just because they lifted a few scrawny cattle beasts in well-deserved retribution for Clan Donald's repeated harassment."

"I never said I wished to marry Alasdair." Marjory flicked a speck of lint off her sleeve.

"You dinnae have to." Kendrew's voice took on a hard edge. "A man only has to see you look at him to know. Ironstorm is far worthier for you."

"I've said no, so it scarce matters."

"Aye, it does. Ironstorm wants you for his wife and his lord is aged, already on his deathbed. It's the noble's dying wish to see his best warlord wed to you before he draws his last breath."

"A dying overlord?" Marjory and Isobel exchanged glances.

"Aye, and that's why Ironstorm is eager to fetch you and be away." Kendrew leaned forward, ignoring Hercules, who'd popped up beside his chair, growling. "His lord cannae wait much longer. Ironstorm hopes to wed you before his lord's burial."

Marjory's insides went cold. Her ambers caught fire, burning her so badly she lifted a hand and slipped her fingers between the heated stones and her skin.

Beneath the table, Isobel nudged her foot, showing she shared Marjory's suspicion.

Marjory tried to speak, but words wouldn't come.

Isobel spoke for her. "Who is Ironstorm's overlord? Do you know the man's name?"

"To be sure, I do." Kendrew didn't hesitate. "He is Rorik the Generous."

"Dear saints." Isobel's eyes rounded. "She'll be killed if these men take her."

Kendrew blinked, shook his head. "What kind of tall tale is this?"

"The truth." Marjory found her tongue. "I dreamed of this. These people mean to send me to Rorik the Generous's funerary pyre. They want me to take the place of his wife. I saw it clearly, remember all of it. That's why I know the names." She glanced at Isobel. "Ask your wife. She knows."

"I know the two of you love to scheme." Kendrew sat back and folded his arms. "It won't work this time. Ne'er have I heard greater foolery. I understand you're no' pleased, but you'll forget the MacDonald in time and—"

"I already have forgotten him." Marjory stood. "And

you can forget any plans to wed me to Ivar Ironstorm or any other Viking warlord."

Kendrew pushed back his chair, standing as well. "Now see here, lass—"

"I have seen. That's why I'm refusing." Marjory didn't wait to hear whatever he might say. The loud rushing was back in her ears and she wouldn't have heard him anyway.

So she simply left the hall, Hercules running after her.

She didn't know what her rebellion would get her into, but she knew what it would save her from.

That was enough.

Chapter Eighteen

✦

*E*scape.

The word sat like a carrion crow at the back of Marjory's neck, pecking at her until she lifted a hand and rubbed her nape. But the hot throbbing between her shoulder blades didn't go away. The pain only worsened, spreading through her until her temples pounded, her stomach knotted, and her chest tightened so fiercely she could hardly breathe.

It was gloaming and she stood in her favorite bower of Nought's stone garden. Isobel was at her side. And Hercules squirmed in a small wicker basket at her feet.

This was the most beautiful hour of the day at Nought.

Her beloved peaks soared all around her, a clean cold wind blew, mist was just beginning to curl through the stony vale beneath Nought's walls, and the deep tranquility of this special place almost broke her heart.

What she was about to do nearly crushed her spirit.

Fleeing wasn't in her nature.

Living was.

And now that she'd known such joy in Alasdair's arms, she was especially keen to enjoy a long and happy life. If the gods were kind, that would be at his side. In time, they'd surely find a new home they could both love. They'd enjoy their days, glory in their nights, and—a ray of hope warmed her—raise many strong, strapping sons and equally strong, vibrant daughters.

But to seize such happiness, she first had to run.

"You must go, my heart." Isobel touched her cheek, her dark eyes glistening.

Marjory gripped her friend's hand, squeezing tightly. "I will get word to you as soon as I can, letting you know I've reached Blackshore safely."

Isobel nodded, blinking rapidly. "I do not like this any more than you," she said, proving she understood how much it grieved Marjory to steal away. "Desperate measures are never good. I'll try to make Kendrew understand. He will someday, I promise you."

She didn't add that she hoped such a day wouldn't come too late, but Marjory heard the unspoken words as clearly as if Isobel had voiced them.

"He'll be livid." Marjory leaned down, slipping her fingers into Hercules's basket to calm him.

"He'll be more than that." Isobel looked unhappy. "He'll know exactly where you've gone and will set out after you. I daren't think what will happen."

"Blackshore is impregnable." Marjory hoped that was truly so. "Alasdair has told me there's a fresh-water well inside the stronghold and even if their stores were depleted, there are always fish in the loch. Kendrew would tire quickly of such a senseless siege."

"If Ironstorm brought his Vikings, their ships, Black-shore could be attacked." Isobel spoke what Marjory didn't want to consider.

"Alasdair has galleys. MacDonalds have a history of fighting Norsemen." Marjory bent to settle Hercules again when he began whining.

When she straightened, she glanced at a heavy cloth sack on a nearby stone bench. Prepared with care, the sack held more than oatcakes, cheese and cold slices of meat, and two flasks of wine. Also hidden in its depths were a rolled plaid to sleep in if necessary, swaths of black linen, jars of peat juice, and a small leather pouch filled with soot. Goods she'd use to make herself a night-walker once Isobel returned to the hall, leaving her alone in the stone garden.

"I should help you with the night-walker gear." Isobel followed her glance. "I've seen Kendrew and his men don the like often enough."

"So have I," Marjory reminded her. "And if you did assist me, someone would surely see your blackened hands when you go back inside. Kendrew would know what you'd done and come after me much faster than if you don't attract attention by entering the hall wearing smudges of soot and peat juice. Our father taught me how to night-walk at the same time he taught Kendrew. A wise man, he believed such a talent as slipping through the night unseen might someday benefit his daughter as well as his son. Truth is, all Mackintoshes know such secrets." Marjory went over to the sack, began pulling out the lengths of black linen.

She hoped Isobel would understand and leave.

She couldn't bear good-byes.

A sniff behind her proved Isobel knew their parting was nigh.

"I shall miss you so!" Her friend hugged her, holding her tightly.

"And I you." Marjory squeezed her back. "Now go, please." She glanced at the night sky, saw the moon was just rising over Nought's peaks. "I should be away already."

But when she looked back at Isobel, her friend was gone.

Marjory blinked, glancing about. Had Kendrew schooled his wife in night-walking? She wouldn't have been surprised. Then, from across the stone garden's stillness, she heard the low *thud* of the hall door closing.

Isobel was once again within the keep.

And she should be on her way.

But first she closed her eyes and took a long, deep breath, filling her lungs with the familiar scent of cold, damp stone and crisp night air.

Then she said a silent prayer to all the gods of her beloved home, asking them to bless every soul within Nought's bounds, most especially her brother.

She truly did love Kendrew.

But she loved Alasdair more. And so she removed her clothes, stashing them deep inside the cloth sack. Then she opened the first jar of peat juice and began smearing its blackness on her skin.

A short while later, as the gloaming turned to night, Nought's clean, cold winds picked up and the curling mists thickened. And in the stone garden, a shadow moved out of an empty bower to slip through the high garden gate and then down the steep stone steps to the rocky vale below. No one blinked at the shadow's passing and the night's deep tranquility was broken only by the soft whimpers of a tiny dog.

But the good men of Nought loved dogs.

And cherished as they were, the beasties had free rein of the grounds.

A wee dog's scuffling of an e'en were nothing unusual.

And so it was that Marjory and Hercules made their escape from Nought, slipping away into the darkness, their passage unnoticed.

Hours later, but on the opposite end of the Glen of Many Legends, at Blackshore Castle, someone else's appearance was anything but quiet. Horns blared from the castle walls, dogs barked, and a small party of mussed and mud-stained Lowlanders rode hell-bent across the stronghold's low stone causeway, racing for the castle gates.

Alasdair stood there, watching their approach with disbelief.

He recognized one of them as a man who'd not been to Blackshore since the trial by combat over two years before. He was a courtier who hadn't been welcome then and wasn't seen gladly now either.

Sir Walter Lindsay, the King's man.

Only as he reined in before Blackshore's steps and swung down from his costly leather-tooled saddle, he didn't look half as lofty or arrogant as he had so long ago when he'd come to declare the King's will.

He looked shaken to the core.

And—Alasdair now saw in the torchlight of his gatehouse—Sir Walter wasn't just mussed and muddied. He was also bloodstained.

"Sir Walter—I greet you!" Alasdair strode over to

him. "What brings you to Blackshore?" He eyed the red smears on the noble's cloak, the tears in his thickly embroidered tunic. "I see you've had a rough journey."

"A terrible one!" The man glanced at his companions and then back at Alasdair. "We came upon a group of wandering pilgrims who'd been set upon by brigands. Slaughtered to a man for a priceless relic they carried, or so one of them claimed before he died."

Alasdair frowned, ushering Sir Walter and his men inside the hall, leading them to the hearth fire so they could warm themselves. "It appears you were also in an affray? Is that why you've come here, to refresh yourselves before returning to court?"

"The court sent me here." Sir Walter's answer surprised Alasdair.

"Indeed?" He arched a brow, a suspicion rising. "Can it be that Kendrew Mackintosh summoned you?"

Ewan and Malcolm appeared at Alasdair's side, both men unsmiling. Others quickly joined them, none greeting the strangers kindly. Lowlanders weren't generally welcome at Blackshore. And those from the crown were regarded even more warily.

"I came here on the King's business, MacDonald." Sir Walter kept his gaze on Alasdair, ignoring the other men. He stood straighter, brushed at his sleeve, a bit of his old loftiness beginning to glimmer through. "Word came to us that you have been stirring trouble again. The accusation was made by someone much higher than Nought. A man whose concerns were taken seriously by the King and so I was to inform you—"

"Was?" Alasdair gripped Sir Walter's arm. "Are you no longer?"

"I think not." Sir Walter held his gaze, clearly displeased by his admission.

"Explain." Alasdair released him, stepping back and crossing his arms. "You have no' made much sense since pounding up to my door. Indeed"—he glanced around at his men standing in a tight circle around them—"I'm of a mind to show you that door if I dinnae care for your answer."

Sir Walter's mien changed at once, his arrogance fading. "I want no trouble here," he said, glancing at Alasdair's men, surely noting that they stood with hands on their sword hilts. "Truth is, we only require baths if we may have them. A bit of bandaging for our cuts, and beds for the night, and we'll be on our way at first light.

"And"—he swallowed, sounding pained—"I would apologize in the name of my King for inconveniences caused you in recent times."

Alasdair frowned. "Now you are speaking in riddles. You'd best explain yourself."

Sir Walter glanced at his companions. To a man, they slunk away, retreating on the pretense of holding their hands to the fire.

Alasdair lifted a brow. "Well?"

"My men and I pursued the brigands who'd massacred the pilgrims. When we caught them, there was a fight." He paused, clearly uncomfortable. "My men and I are expert sworders. To our surprise the ruffians fought with equal skill and finesse. After we finally prevailed, cutting them down, we discovered why they swung their swords so well.

"They were court men, disguised as common thieves. We knew their leader well. He serves one of the King's bastard sons, a young man whose aspirations exceed his station and who—"

"What are you saying?" Alasdair stepped closer to him, looming over the smaller man. "Dinnae tell me one of the King's own brood would set men upon pilgrims?"

Sir Walter shifted, swallowing again. "I fear it is worse than that, sir."

Alasdair just looked at him, waiting.

"One of the men took a while to die," Sir Walter explained. "Apparently his imminent end loosened his tongue, making him fear God more than the man he served. He told us they'd heard the pilgrims carried a precious saint's relic and when they found no such treasure on the men, they were angered and so slew them, innocents though they were.

"He also spoke of you, claiming his lord had often sent troops of broken men here, to your Glen of Many Legends, to cause havoc. His lord, the King's bastard, hoped to stir enough malcontent and woe here, always putting the blame on you and the other glen chiefs, so that the King would grow fed up with the lot of you and make good his threat to banish your clans from the glen."

"And then this man would step in and claim our lands as his own?" Alasdair felt his temper rising. "Tell me that isn't so."

Sir Walter just looked at him.

"Is there more?" Something told Alasdair there was.

Sir Walter nodded. "Isn't there a maid you favor? Can she be Lady Marjory? Kendrew Mackintosh's sister?"

"What of her?" Alasdair's vision hazed red. He grabbed Sir Walter by the arms, lifting him off the floor. "What has she to do with this?"

"Nothing, sir, nothing at all." Sir Walter wriggled in Alasdair's grip. "It is only"—he gasped, nearly dropped to his knees when Alasdair released him—"the brigand we questioned claimed payment was made to a Norseman so that he would offer for her hand. The plan was that such a union would outrage you and you'd fight her brother, giving the King's bastard enough reason to urge his father to banish you once and for all time."

"By all the saints!" Alasdair roared. He could feel his blood boiling, his face heating. He threw back his head and clenched his fists, everything around him blurring, his pulse pounding in his ears.

When he looked again at Sir Walter, he almost felt sorry for the man.

He'd blanched. And—Alasdair could scarce believe it—he appeared to be trembling.

Still, Alasdair bellowed again. "I have ne'er heard such perfidy!" He whirled about, pacing a few steps before he stopped and ran a hand through his hair. "Even Mackintosh wouldn't stoop so low. Is there more?" He strode back over to Sir Walter, disbelief and fury sluicing him.

Somewhere his men were arguing, he could hear their raised voices. And the castle dogs had gone wild, barking a storm, the din almost deafening.

Alasdair ignored the chaos, his gaze only on the Lowlander. "Well, is there?"

"If there is, I cannot say. The man died before we could question him further. I can promise"—Sir Walter drew a deep breath, again looking discomfited—"that I will report the entire matter to my King. He will be informed of your continued honor and loyalty. And he is sure to punish the young man responsible." He straightened then, seeming to regain his dignity now that he'd said all that he must. "I am close enough to the crown to give you my word that you and the other glen chiefs will never again be harassed. Like as not, you will also receive recompense for such troubles in the past."

"I do not care about recompense." Alasdair began pacing again. "I care about Marjory Mackintosh. She is to be my wife, see you?" He spoke loudly and clear, lifting his voice so that every man in the hall could hear him. "I meant to ride to Nought for her this very e'en and would've been on my way had you not appeared."

"I am sorry, sir." Sir Walter did sound regretful.

"Viking ships have been seen hereabout of late." Alasdair glanced at Ewan and Malcolm, at Angus and Farlan, so many of his other men, all gathered round.

Not a one of them looked shocked or outraged.

Far from it, they were grumbling among themselves about Norn, praising her and fretting about her safety, vowing to tear apart anyone who'd dare harm her.

Only Malcolm wasn't speaking.

The old man had turned aside, was dabbing at his eyes with his sleeve.

"Damnation," Alasdair snarled, his own eyes heating.

It appeared he wouldn't have to leave Blackshore at all.

Although, after all that had transpired, if something happened to Marjory, he doubted he could bear to stay on here without her.

He turned back to Sir Walter, his anger rising again. "If any harm comes to my lady, even your King will not be safe from my wrath."

The little man almost spluttered. "I am sure all will be well with her, sir. Word travels fast in these parts. Could be the King is already aware of the treachery and has taken due measures."

Alasdair scarce heard him.

There was another commotion at his door. Sir Walter's companions were huddled together staring round-eyed and aghast into the shadows of the hall's arched entry. And Alasdair's own men were laughing and shouting, running forward, whooping like fools.

Sir Walter also looked about, blanching as he raised an arm to point at the door. "Holy saints, protect us! It's a haint!"

"A ghost?" Alasdair couldn't stop a shiver, for one crazy moment wondering if Drangar had decided to visit his old stronghold.

But then the men surging the entry parted, making way for the *spirit* to enter the hall.

She was Norn.

Black-haired, dark-skinned, and swathed head to toe in sooty linen, but her sparkling blue eyes gave her away.

As did the smile she gave him as she came forward.

And perhaps the cheeky little dog who pranced along beside her, barking at Alasdair's hounds.

"Norn!" He ran across the hall, sweeping her up into his arms and crushing her against him. "Praise God, you're safe, my heart."

He set her on her feet and grabbed her face, holding her fast as he kissed her deeply, only vaguely noting the sudden cheering of his men. Their foot stomping and ale cup clanking, all the hoots and shouts of glee. Even Sir Walter and his companions were smiling, though none of them ventured too close to Marjory.

She did look a fright.

"Sweet lass, what have you done to yourself?" Alasdair dragged the back of his hand over his lips, noting that she tasted of peat. "And how did you get here? Surely you didn't walk."

"I flew." She smiled, glancing after Hercules who was now running circles about the hall, chasing Alasdair's beasts as if he already held sway here.

"Dinnae jest with me, sweet." Alasdair picked her up again, started for the stair tower that led to his quarters. "I ken something dire has happened or you wouldn't be here in such a state."

"I'm here as a night-walker." She shifted in his arms to look at him. "You'll know my clan uses such magic to move through the night unseen. It's a skill of all Mackintoshes, not just the men. And"—she lifted a hand to touch his face, that simple contact filling him with such happiness he thought his heart might burst—"using such a guise was the best way for me to escape Nought. I had to—"

"Dinnae tell me Kendrew threatened you." They'd reached his door and he kicked it open, not caring if he split the wood. "I'll tear him apart and—"

"He didn't hurt me, though..." She paused just long enough to make his blood boil. "In his attempts to be a good brother, he accepted a marriage offer for me that I had to avoid. And not just because of you. There were other reasons..." She slipped from his arms, began unwinding the lengths of black cloth she'd wrapped about herself. She told him everything as she did, finishing in the bath that several of his servants had brought to the room. They'd appeared unbidden, carrying in the tub and ewers of steaming water and bathing linens in a show of acceptance and loyalty that made Alasdair's heart split.

His people were welcoming her.

He would never let her out of his sight again.

"You're ne'er leaving here again, Norn." He told her so, just to make certain she understood. "I'll still speak with your brother. I'll take you to visit Nought whene'er you wish to visit. But you're mine now. We'll wed as soon as possible and then—" His voice broke. "You do still wish to marry me?"

He had to know.

He couldn't bear to lose her now, not after all they'd been through.

"Why do you think I'm here?" She smiled, the love in her eyes answer enough.

Alasdair crossed the room in swift strides and she stood and reached for him, naked and dripping. His heart slammed against his ribs and he lifted her from the bathing tub, pulling her into his arms.

"Sweet Norn!" He held her tightly, running his hands up and down her wet back and then gripping her arms as he lowered his head to kiss her fiercely.

"I thought I'd lost you!" He pulled back, looking at her, drinking her in as if he could never get enough of just having her near. "When Sir Walter mentioned a Viking lord receiving payment to offer for you, I thought the world ended. The black-painted ships that have been seen about—"

"They are surely on their way back to Norway now." She sounded so sure, her beautiful smile bright and confident. "I am safe here. I knew I would be—"

A loud horn blast cut her off, the sound repeated again and again. Then the pounding of running feet approaching, someone hammering on the door...

"Stay here." Alasdair grabbed a spare plaid off a chair and swirled it around her nakedness. Then he ran to the door, flinging it wide.

Ewan stood there, sword in hand.

"The Vikings," he blurted. "They're coming in the loch, full-manned and armed for war."

"Then we'll fight them on their terms—our best men and best galleys will make short work of them." Alasdair hoped it was so.

Ewan didn't look so confident.

And he avoided Marjory's gaze, even flushing when she hurried over to them, clutching the plaid around her.

"How many Viking ships?" She looked from Ewan to Alasdair. "I believe the MacDonald galleys are more."

"Aye, they are, my lady." Ewan answered before Alasdair could speak. "The Viking ships are two. The black-painted dragonships we've seen hereabouts for a while."

"If they are only a pair, we'll be done with them quickly." Alasdair wrapped his arm around Marjory, drawing her close, hoping to chase her worry.

Ewan's gloom wasn't helping her.

Alasdair frowned at him. "Be gone, lad. Make haste and pass on my orders to man the ships. I'll be in the hall right after you."

The lad didn't move.

"There is something else." He looked again at Marjory, pity in his eyes.

"Then out with it. Now!" Alasdair was getting angry.

"The Vikings aren't the only problem, Cousin." Ewan tightened his lips for a moment, inhaled sharply. "Kendrew is here as well."

"Kendrew?" Alasdair stared at the younger man.

Ewan nodded. "Aye, he is, and he's brought all his fighting men with him. They're no' coming to the keep. They're lining up on the cliffs, their purpose clear."

"Mother of God!" Alasdair shoved both hands through his hair, dread sluicing him.

"Dear saints, what is it?" Marjory gripped his arm, her eyes round. "What purpose?"

"I can't tell her." Ewan sounded miserable.

Alasdair scowled. "They'll be readying fire arrows, my sweet. We won't have much chance of fighting Ivar Ironstorm because your brother and his men will set our ships aflame as soon as we sail out."

Chapter Nineteen

❖

This can't be happening."

Marjory stood at the arched window of Alasdair's painted solar not caring if no one heard her. Hercules, still for once, and Alasdair's old dog, Geordie, sat beside her. They were listening to her, for sure. Both dogs, she knew, understood the dire portent of the scene unfolding outside the solar window.

Alasdair was running along the narrow shoreline beneath Blackshore's walls, cupping his hands to his mouth as he yelled orders to his men in the water or boarding the MacDonald galleys.

All the men were busy.

They were readying the ships to attack the two black-painted Viking dragonships beating back and forth just inside the loch's entrance.

Most terrifying of all were her brother's warriors.

Looking more savage than she'd seen them in a long while, they lined the cliffs along the loch, their broad shoulders draped in wolf- or bearskins. Mail glinted everywhere, as did the flash of steel.

And in an unwelcome memory of the trial by combat, most of the warriors had already unsheathed their axes and swords and were beating the weapons on their shields.

The knocking was terrible.

It echoed everywhere. Across the loch and hills and inside Blackshore's walls. The ghastly clanging even rang in her ears.

The war music was a precursor of slaughter.

It was a way to fire the blood of warriors, making them fearless, even bringing them to crave the fight.

But it wasn't the knocking that frightened her the most.

That honor belonged to the fire arrows. The archers she knew were expert enough to send them zinging right where they were aimed.

Alasdair would die this day.

And she would perish with him because even if her body survived, a little bit more of her soul shriveled each time she saw another archer step between the shield beaters.

"He's locked me in here." She pushed away from the window arch, started pacing, speaking to Hercules and Geordie who dutifully scrambled up to trail behind her. "Can you believe it?"

She stopped, planting her hands on her hips as she looked at the dogs.

"I ran away from Nought because my brother threatened to lock me in my bedchamber and now"—she blew out a breath, started pacing again—"after coming here, Alasdair has imprisoned me in his solar.

"He's running about without a sword!" She went back

to the window arch, leaning out as far as she could. Sadly, she wasn't mistaken.

Of all the men on the little shore and in the galleys, only Alasdair wore no weapons.

"He's lost his wits." She tried to call to him, but her voice was already hoarse from doing so.

Nor was he looking her way.

He kept glaring across the loch to where her brother—and Grim, the traitor—had joined the archers and shield beaters on the cliffs.

Then, just when she was sure she'd lose her mind as well, a loud splintering *crack* shook the walls.

Marjory cringed, placing her hands over her ears. She knew the sound from storytellers. It was the shattering of ship wood, vessels pierced by an iron ramming spear. Or"—she leaned even farther out the window, craning her neck to see—the sound of oars breaking off when another ship plowed through them at speed, the attack most times making quick work of the men aboard along with the broken oars.

"I can't stand it." She dropped to her knees, wrapping an arm around each dog, pulling them close. "Any moment, Kendrew will send the fire arrows and then..."

She couldn't finish the thought.

The yelling and noise of fighting was worsening, the sounds coming from everywhere, echoing loud in the little room. The shield knocking, especially, seemed louder. More like banging now, the crashing terrifying her.

Somewhere, amid the sound of thrashing and churning water, men screamed. Their shrill, ear-piercing yells left no doubt that they were dying.

Marjory shuddered, trying not to hear.

"Are you brave enough to go out on the shore with me, lass?" A deep voice startled her and she leaped to her feet, whirling around to see Alasdair's great-uncle, Malcolm, standing in the open doorway.

His face was grim, his eyes full of worry.

Marjory's heart broke. "Alasdair?" Again, she couldn't put her fear into words. "Is he?"

"He's fine, though I doubt his wits!" Malcolm frowned, shaking his head.

"We're losing, aren't we?" She hoped the old warrior would know she meant MacDonalds.

"No' yet, my lady." He nodded respectfully, his words and gesture giving her an unexpected rush of happiness.

And hope.

"But I fear we'll lose Alasdair if no one can talk sense into him." His words dashed her budding confidence. "That's why I'd like you to step out onto the shore with me. He's wanting to swim across the loch to confront your brother man to man. He'll never make it halfway. One of the fire archers will take him down as soon as he dives into the water."

"Dear saints!" Marjory's heart stopped. "That's why he isn't wearing his sword!"

She started running, bursting past Malcolm and then through the empty hall. The great doors stood open and she dashed outside, racing past the gatehouse and over a jumble of rock to the island's narrow shore.

Malcolm and Hercules and Geordie chased behind her. She could hear them coming, especially Hercules, who was barking louder than she'd ever heard him.

Panting, a sharp pain stabbing her chest, she pounded onto the shingled shore, not stopping until she reached the water's edge. Alasdair's weapons were there, braced against a rock. A blue silk ribbon was tied to the hilt of his sword, the sight, and its significance, making her heart clutch. The ribbon was hers and its ends trailed in a tide pool, floating dulled and lifeless on the water's gleaming surface. She prayed to all the gods that she wasn't seeing a portent. Panic constricting her chest, she looked up and down the narrow strand, searching for Alasdair.

Malcolm and the dogs arrived a moment later.

They were all too late.

Alasdair was already in the water, swimming furiously toward the opposite shore. He was well past the halfway point, beyond hearing them if they cried out to him. Any moment he'd reach the strand. And if Kendrew's fire archers didn't get him before he did, they'd surely hit him when he left the water and started climbing the cliff.

"O-o-oh, no!" Marjory fell to her knees in the surf, pressed her fisted hands to her cheeks.

Hercules and Geordie began to howl.

Malcolm simply stood staring out at the water, a thoughtful look on his once-handsome face.

"Come, lass, I think we should row over there." He held out his hand, helping her to her feet.

Not waiting for her reply, he tightened his grip on her hand and led her down the beach toward a small coracle. He pushed the little round boat into the water, holding it steady as she clambered aboard, Hercules and Geordie climbing in with her. Then he jumped over the side and reached for the oars, quickly maneuvering them onto the water but careful to stay close to the shore's edge.

He clearly meant to reach the other side by circling the loch.

It would take longer than rowing straight across, which was much too risky to do.

"Alasdair may be dead before we get there." Marjory tried to see him, but couldn't.

It was getting dark and the mist was thick now, swirling everywhere in great billowing sheets like a shroud.

She shivered and wrapped her arms around herself.

"Dear heavens, please let us get there in time." She couldn't bear it if they didn't.

Surely Kendrew would listen to her.

But then there was another terrible crashing of wood near the mouth of the loch, the ghastly noise filling the night, terrifying her.

She risked a glance in that direction, only able to make out galleys flashing to and fro. There were also two ships that appeared sealed together, men with swords running on the decks, fighting ferociously, their shouts and curses, and screams, terrible.

And then the heavens brightened, the night sky turning light as day.

Kendrew was unleashing his fire arrows.

The end was imminent.

"Mackintosh!"

Alasdair roared the bastard's name even as he pulled himself up and over the edge of the cliff. Panting, he bent double, bracing his hands on his knees as he struggled to catch his breath.

Never had he been in a sorrier state.

Shivering from the loch's icy water, he was also half naked, wearing only his wet and clinging shirt. He'd even kicked off his shoes.

And he carried no weapon.

He didn't need one.

He meant to rip Kendrew apart with his bare hands.

"Kendrew!" He straightened, cupping his hands around his mouth as he shouted for the miscreant. "Come here, you flat-footed he-goat! Fight me like a man, one on one, fists only and to the death!"

"Dinnae tempt me, you arse." Kendrew appeared out of the mist, striding forward with a cocky grin. "It's no' every day I have to admit I'm wrong. Goad me again and I'm done with you. I'll take my men and hie us out of here."

Alasdair blinked.

He shook his head, tilting it to the side and hitting his ear with his palm. Just in case he had water in his ears, clogging his hearing.

"We're getting the better o' them, did you see?" Kendrew thrust an arm out toward the loch and the ships and men fighting there.

He was also laughing, the sight terrible.

But then Alasdair followed his outstretched arm and saw that his foe spoke true.

The two black-painted Viking ships had foundered in the mouth of the loch. A welter of boulders on the ships' broken decks hinted at what had sunk them.

Alasdair's own galleys circled the shattered dragon-ships. And when he held a hand to his brow and squinted, he saw that his men were on the decks of the Viking vessels, using their swords to cut down any men who hadn't drowned when someone—Kendrew's men?—had rained down the boulders on the ships as they'd attempted to beat into the loch.

One or two other Viking ships had made it.

But those burned bright, flames like balefires swiftly consuming them.

Alasdair's galleys didn't bear a single scorch mark.

They flashed about, clean and untouched, more than proud.

And still Kendrew was laughing.

He stood with his legs spread apart and his arms crossed and the more Alasdair stared at him, the more he, too, felt like laughing.

To his shame, he felt something else, too.

A strange, damnable *kinship* that burned his fool eyes like hell.

"Damnation, who'd have believed this?" He strode over to his erstwhile foe, clapping him on the shoulder. "To what do I owe the honor?"

Kendrew didn't miss a beat, jerking his head toward a big, black-bearded man just stepping up to them.

He was Grim.

And he carried a spare bearskin, coming up to sling the fur about Alasdair's shoulders.

"A good e'en to you, Blackshore!" He stepped back, dusting his hands. "I took you on your word, see you? The things you said about black-painted dragonships and our Dreagan's Claw inlet. I went there myself"—he raised his voice above the shouting below—"creeping down the cliff and hiding out behind the rocks. Thon Ironstorm and his captains came ashore that night. I heard everything they said and—"

"Like the good captain that he is"—Kendrew boomed—"he made haste back to Nought and told me. We came here as fast as we could. Truth is"—he smiled almost sheepishly—"I would've brought my sister to you myself. But when I went to look for her, the fool lass had vanished."

He glanced about, his eyes twinkling. "She wouldn't be here, would she?"

"She is safe in my painted solar at Blackshore." Alasdair was relieved that she was. "She'll be pleased to see you when we're done here. I'll take you—"

"There is no need." Marjory ran up to them, throwing herself into Alasdair's arms. "I am here, as you can see. What I'd know is what *you're* doing here?"

She glanced at her brother, but he just threw back his head and gave a great shout of laughter.

"Later, Norn, at your man's high table." He winked at her and then punched his captain in the arm. "We have men's work to do yet," he boomed, already striding off into the mist.

Grim tossed them a look. Not quite a smile, but not unfriendly either. Then he turned on his heel to follow after Kendrew.

The mist closed around them quickly.

They were gone.

"What is happening here?" Marjory looked after them, frowning at the spot where they'd disappeared.

Alasdair followed her gaze, shaking his head.

"Nothing you won't hear all about in the hall this e'en." He reached for her, pulling her into his arms. "I'd sooner learn what *you* are doing here?"

He shot a dark look at Malcolm, who smiled back at him and then blew his nose.

Hercules and Geordie were also staring at him.

Geordie sported a look Marjory now recognized as his expecting-a-treat look. And Hercules —she blinked, hardly believing her eyes—was wearing an expression of pure hero worship. Eyes bright, tongue lolling, and his little tail wagging.

On the loch, the sounds of the fighting were winding down, replaced now by the roar of flames. The acrid stench of burning wood hung thick in the night air.

Marjory shivered.

Another flaming Viking ship flashed across her mind. She pushed the image away. Truth was, she'd brave a thousand burning ships, even the fires of hell, if they stood between her and Alasdair.

So she leaned harder into him, baring her heart. "I'm here because I love you."

She lifted up on her toes, curling her hand around his neck and then kissing him. "I also thought you might need saving from my brother."

"Indeed?" Alasdair cupped her face, giving her a kiss of his own, a long and deep one that sent warmth spilling clear to her toes.

"And what if he needed rescuing from me?" He straightened, winking at her.

"Then..." She glanced aside, down to the burning Viking ships on the loch. "It would seem we're all even, wouldn't you say?"

She didn't mention he'd once rescued her from a burning Viking ship.

There'd be time later to tell him of her dream.

For now...

She nestled closer to him, trying not to see that Malcolm was watching them, dabbing at his eyes.

She did see that wonders are always possible.

That magic is real.

And then Alasdair was turning her face up to his. "Will you be disappointed that we won't be leaving the glen, lass?" He kissed her, claiming her lips with such passion that it was clear he had no problems with his great-uncle and two dogs watching them. The bold smile he flashed her when he broke the kiss proved it.

"Well?" He wrapped his arms around her, pulling her closer. "You didn't answer me?"

"Ah, but I didn't, did I?" Tapping her chin, she pretended to consider. "I might regret not seeing more of the world, it is true."

He blinked, looking genuinely surprised. "Indeed?"

"It could be, yes. Unless..."

He started to smile again, seeing that she was teasing him.

"What is it, sweet?" He played along, his lips twitching. "Name your pleasure and it's granted. I dinnae want an unhappy wife."

"Then..." She slipped her arms around his neck, returning his smile. "I would like us to visit the Thunder Caves at least once a week."

"The Thunder Caves?" He frowned, looking puzzled.

Marjory laughed. "Oh, yes, we should go there often."

Then his eyes lit and he laughed, too.

"I understand, and we will visit them, I promise." He leaned down to nuzzle her neck, nipping the sensitive spot beneath her ear. "As often as you desire."

Epilogue

❖

THE GLEN OF MANY LEGENDS

At the Thunder Caves
Autumn 1398

*D*id you hear me?"

Marjory kept her voice low, not wanting anyone but Isobel and Catriona to hear her. The three women stood at the far end of the Thunder Cave, near a long table spread with all manner of festive victuals, wine ewers, and ale. In the center of the cave, the stone floor shone bright, the mounds of wolf- and bearskins that were usually piled there cleared away to make room for dancing.

After all, this was Marjory and Alasdair's wedding feast.

As if the heavens knew, the bands of moon- and star-light that always lit the cave shone with especial brightness this night, lending to the magic.

Unfortunately, Isobel and Catriona were spending too much time tipping back their heads to peer up at the naked couples cavorting about the ceiling.

Neither one of them had heard a word she'd said.

Marjory took them by the arms and led them deeper into the shadows at the rear of the cave.

"So-o-o!" She released them and stepped back, more than pleased with herself. "What did I just say?"

Isobel and Catriona exchanged glances, clearly unable to tell her.

"That it was good of Alasdair to give Clan Donald's special sword to Kendrew?" Catriona risked a guess, glancing to where Kendrew sat next to Alasdair.

Marjory and Isobel followed her gaze.

Looking as if they'd been close friends for life, both men were examining Honor, the sword that'd been pried from the hand of the last MacDonald clansman to die at the trial by combat. Aptly named, the blade was held in high respect by the clan, a gift of untold value.

"Nae, I didn't mean Honor." Marjory shook her head, turning back to her friends. "I agree, it was a meet gift, though. Alasdair wouldn't have parted with it if he hadn't truly made his peace with Kendrew. He felt it was fitting after Kendrew's timely arrival at Blackshore not so long ago, and I heartily agree."

"I know." Isobel beamed, aiming another quick look at the ceiling.

"No, it isn't the painted couples." Marjory felt her face heating.

"But you admit the Thunder Caves are a fine place to celebrate your wedding feast?" Isobel winked, not about to back down.

"Aye, that is true." Marjory flicked at her sleeve. "Still, I was thinking of something else. A matter of great importance to us all."

"Oh?" Catriona and Isobel spoke as one.

Marjory smiled back at them. "Indeed."

"Then what is it?" Catriona stepped closer, clearly curious.

Isobel cast another glance at her husband, her love for Kendrew so bright in her eyes. But then she, too, edged nearer, waiting.

Marjory pressed her hands together, tapped her chin with her fingertips. "You will not believe it! I have solved Gorm's riddle. The prophecy he gave to James just before the trial by combat. You'll remember what it was?" She dropped her voice, repeating the words:

" 'Peace will be had when innocents pay the price of blood and gold covers the glen.' "

Catriona and Isobel now gave her their rapt attention.

"You'll recall," Marjory went on, "everyone believed the men who'd perished in the battle were the innocents and the autumn turning of leaves was the gold covering the glen.

"But our peace has aye been fragile, the truce endangered many times.

"Until now." Marjory looked at her friends, waiting for them to guess.

When they didn't, she tsked at them, softening the scolding with a smile.

"The innocents," she began, "were the poor pilgrims who were slain by the men serving the King's blackguard bastard. Sir Walter and his men slew them and, last I heard, the King had dealt harshly with his son, imprisoning him for life, I believe. And"—she took a breath, lifting a hand to touch the ambers at her neck—"the *gold* covering the glen is our own enchanted necklace."

"Ahhh!" Catriona and Isobel again spoke as one. "The amber necklace has circled the glen, hasn't it?"

"Yes, it has." Marjory curled her fingers around the stones, feeling so privileged to wear them. "First they were Catriona's, leaving Blackshore to go to you, Isobel. And then after their time with you at Castle Haven, you passed them on to me at Nought. And now"—Marjory blinked, her eyes beginning to sting—"I have brought them back to Blackshore, where they belong."

"You are right!" Catriona was blinking, too, her smile a bit wobbly.

When she dashed at her cheek and coughed, both Marjory and Isobel pretended not to see.

Not that it should matter, for their eyes were just as misty.

"So we kept our pact in all ways, then?" Isobel discreetly dabbed her own cheek.

"I believe we have." Marjory would've said more, but Alasdair was coming toward her, the look on his face warning that he wished a moment alone with her.

"Ladies!" He drew up before them, resplendent in his MacDonald plaid and with Mist-Chaser, her gleaming amber pommel stone riding proudly at his side. "I'd have a word with my wife, if you dinnae mind?"

"O-o-oh, not at all." Catriona beamed, flitting away as quickly as the star- and moonbeams dancing throughout the cave.

Isobel gave Alasdair a long, piercing look and then, smiling mischievously, also took her leave.

Alasdair reached for Marjory's hand, lifting it to his lips and nipping her fingertips. "Have you decided, my lady?"

"Decided?" Marjory blinked, pretending not to know what he meant.

He stepped closer, looking down at her with heat in his eyes. "Then I'll tell you I'm favoring the couple then."

He slid a glance at the ceiling, toward a particularly well-made pair. The woman rode astride the man, her head tipped back as if in ecstasy, her long hair spilling free down her back. "What say you to them?"

Marjory leaned up on her toes, whispering her agreement in his ear.

And before she pulled away again, she let her hand glide ever so briefly over a certain most masculine part of her husband.

"Norn!" He inhaled sharply, his gaze darkening even more. "How will I ever wait until the festivities are over?"

"I can't imagine." Marjory didn't know how she'd wait either.

But she couldn't resist teasing him.

So she leaned close again, this time letting her breasts brush his side. "Perhaps we can slip away early?"

"Ah, lass!" Alasdair flashed a smile. "I always knew you were the woman for me."

Then he captured her hand, linking their fingers. Walking briskly, he led her away. Out of the Thunder Cave and into the night, the revelry continuing on behind them.

"Did you ever see a pair more in love?"

A soft, familiar voice startled Drangar as he hovered in the Thunder Cave, watching Alasdair and his lady depart.

Scarce trusting his ears, he spun about, his heart almost bursting to see his beloved Seona shimmering before him.

"Seona!" He reached for her and then lowered his arms when she flitted out of his grasp. "What are you doing here?" he voiced a simple question, not wanting to frighten her away.

To his delight, she shimmied nearer. "Perhaps I wished to attend Alasdair and Marjory's celebration? Unlike you, my husband, I have not forgotten what it is like to be young, passionate, and in love."

Drangar frowned. "You think I have?"

His wife sniffed, looking so lovely in her agitation. "You know much of the like. That is what I think."

"Seona..." He reached for her, his heart thundering again when she didn't vanish when he took her hands. He brought one to his lips, kissing her wispy knuckles. "You are as beautiful now as you were then. Can we no' let bygones be bygones, here on this neutral ground?"

"And when we return to Blackshore?" She lifted a brow, plainly determined to provoke him. "Shall I then remain on my rocks of doom near the castle while you sulk about your Warrior Stones on the cliffs?"

"I dinnae sulk, woman." He scowled at her. "I guard the coast, as I have aye done."

"And do you still chase Selkie maids?"

"I erred once, my heart."

"Say you." Seona turned her back on him. "Your erring had dire consequences."

"Think you I have not regretted that all my life? And"—he whisked himself around in front of her—"every bluidy day of my afterlife?"

She appeared to consider.

"I did not mean to leave you, you know." Her voice was soft, low. "I wanted to reclaim you for my own. That's why I perched on the tidal rocks. To show the seal people that you were mine and I wouldn't let another of their females have you. But then...

"The tide rushed in faster than I'd anticipated." She

paused, her gaze on the slanting swirls of moon- and star-light. "My skirts became tangled in the rocks. I couldn't get away. And then—"

"I never knew!" Drangar reached for her, pulling her close. "Sweet Seona, can you forgive me? Will you believe I ran down to the shore, tried so desperately to save you. But you were gone. And with you, my heart—"

"Your heart?" She looked up at him, her eyes misting. "Did I ever have it?"

"You have always had it." He cupped her face, smoothed back her glittering hair. "You still do. And you always shall, whether or not you claim it."

"Drangar..." For a moment, she shimmered brighter than the sun.

Encouraged, Drangar took her hand again, lacing their fingers. "Dare I take that as a yes?"

She smiled. "You may."

"Then shall we celebrate in style?" He nodded toward the center of the cave where couples whirled, smiling and laughing, love in their eyes.

"That would make me very happy." Her smile brightened as Drangar led her into the most lustrous of the twirling star- and moonbeams.

And they danced.

The festivities lasted well into the small hours, a grand time had by all. And although it's only clan lore, there are many who will swear that the Glen of Many Legends smiled that night.

Some say the glen is smiling still.

"The Devil" of the Highlands
knows no weakness—until
a flame-haired beauty
tempts him to abandon
his loyalties.

Please turn this page
for a preview of

Sins of a Highland Devil

The first book in the Highland
Warriors trilogy

The Legacy of the Glen

❦

Deep in the Scottish Highlands, three clans share the Glen of Many Legends. None of them do so gladly. Each clan believes they have sole claim to the fair and fertile vale. Their possessiveness is understandable, because the glen truly is a place like no other. Bards throughout the land will confirm that the Glen of Many Legends is just that: an enchanted place older than time and steeped with more tales and myth than most men can recall.

Kissed by sea and wind, the vale is long and narrow, its shores wild and serrated. Deeply wooded hills edge the glen's heart, while softly blowing mists cloak the lofty peaks that crowd together at its end. Oddly shaped stones dot the lush grass, but the strangeness of the ancient rocks is countered by the heather and whin that bloom so profusely from every patch of black, peaty earth.

No one would deny the glen's beauty.

Yet to some, the Glen of Many Legends is a place of ill fame to be avoided at all costs, especially by the dark of the moon. Strange things have been known to happen there, and wise men tread cautiously when they must pass that way.

But the MacDonalds, Camerons, and Mackintoshes who dwell there appreciate the glen's virtues above frightening tales that may or may not have credence. Good Highlanders all, the clans know that any storyteller of skill is adept at embroidering his yarns.

Highlanders are also a proud and stubborn people. And they're known for their fierce attachment to the land. These traits blaze hotly in the veins of the three clans of the Glen of Many Legends. Over time, their endless struggles to vanquish each other have drenched the glen with blood and sorrow.

Peace in the glen is fragile and rare.

Most times it doesn't exist at all. Yet somehow the clans tolerate each other, however grudgingly.

Now the precarious balance of order is about to be thrown into dispute by the death of a single woman.

A MacDonald by birth, and hereditary heiress to the MacDonalds of the Glen of Many Legends, she was a twice-widowed woman who chose to live out her days in the serenity and solitude of a nunnery.

Sadly, she neglected to set down her last wishes in a will. This oversight would not be so dire if not for the disturbing truths that her first husband had been a Cameron and her second, a Mackintosh.

On her passing, each clan lays claim to the dead woman.

Or, it can be more aptly said, they insist on being her rightful heirs.

Soon land-greed and coveting will once again turn the

glen's sweet grass into a sea of running red and many good men will lose their lives. But even when the last clansman sinks to his knees, his sword sullied and the end near, the real battle is only just beginning.

When it is done, the Glen of Many Legends will be forever changed.

As will the hearts of those who dwell there.

Chapter One

❖

BLACKSHORE CASTLE

THE GLEN OF MANY LEGENDS

AUTUMN 1396

A battle to the death?"

Alasdair MacDonald's deep voice rose to the smoke-blackened rafters of his great hall. Across that crowded space, his sister, Lady Catriona, stood frozen on the threshold. Alasdair's harsh tone held her there, but she did lift a hand to the amber necklace at her throat. A clan heirloom believed to protect and aid MacDonalds, the precious stones warmed beneath her fingers. She fancied they also hummed, though it was difficult to tell with her brother's roar shaking the walls. Other kinsmen were also shouting, but it was Alasdair's fury that echoed in her ears.

His ranting hit her like a physical blow.

Her brother was a man whose clear blue eyes always held a spark of humor. And his laughter, so rich and catching, could brighten the darkest winter night, warming the hearts and spirits of everyone around him.

Just now he paced in the middle of his hall, his handsome face twisted in rage. His shoulder-length auburn hair—always his pride—was untidy, looking wildly mussed, as if he'd repeatedly thrust angry fingers through the finely burnished mane.

"Sakes! This is no gesture of goodwill." His voice hardened, thrumming with barely restrained aggression. "Whole clans cut down. Good men murdered—and for naught, as I and my folk see it!"

Everywhere, MacDonalds grumbled and scowled.

Some shook fists in the air, others rattled swords. At least two spat on the rush-strewn floor, and a few had such fire in their eyes it was almost a wonder that the air didn't catch flame.

Only one man stood unaffected.

A stranger. Catriona saw him now because one of her cousins moved and torchlight caught and shone on the man's heavily bejeweled sword belt.

She stared at the newcomer, not caring if her jaw slipped. She did step deeper into the hall's arched entry, though her knees shook badly. She also forgot to shut the heavy oaken door she'd just opened wide. Cold, damp wind blew past her, whipping her hair and gutting candles on a nearby table. A few wall torches hissed and spat, spewing ashes at her, but she hardly noticed.

What was a bit of soot on her skirts when the quiet peace of Blackshore had turned to chaos?

When Alasdair spoke of war?

As chief to their clan, he wasn't a man to use such words lightly. And even if he were, the flush on his face and the fierce set of his jaw revealed that something dire had happened. The stranger—a Lowland noble by his finery—didn't bode well either.

Men of his ilk never came to Blackshore.

The man's haughty stance showed that he wasn't pleased to be here now. And unlike her brother, he'd turned and was looking right at her. His gaze flicked over her, and then he lifted one brow, almost imperceptibly.

His opinion of her was palpable.

The insolence in that slightly arched brow, a galling affront.

Annoyance stopped the knocking of her knees, and she could feel her blood heating, the hot color sweeping up her neck to scald her cheeks.

The man looked amused.

Catriona was sure she'd seen his lips twitch.

Bristling, she pulled off her mud-splattered cloak and tossed it on a trestle bench. She took some satisfaction in seeing the visitor's eyes widen and then narrow critically when he saw that the lower half of her gown was as wet and soiled as her mantle. She had, after all, just run across the narrow stone causeway that connected her clan's isle-girt castle with the loch shore.

She'd raced to beat the tide. But even hurrying as she had, the swift-moving current was faster. She'd been forced to hitch up her skirts and splash through the swirling water, reaching the castle gates just before the causeway slipped beneath the rising sea loch.

It was a mad dash that always exhilarated her. As she did every day, she'd burst into the hall, laughing and with her hair in a wild tangle from the wind. Now she might look a fright, but her elation was gone.

"What's happened?" She hurried forward to clutch

Alasdair's arm, dread churning in her belly. "What's this about clans being cut down? A battle—"

"Not a true battle." Alasdair shot a glance at the Lowlander. "A trial by combat—"

"I see no difference." She raised her chin, not wanting the stranger to see her worry. It was clear he'd brought this madness. That showed in the curl of his lip, a half-sneer that revealed his disdain for Highlanders.

Alasdair noticed, too. She hadn't missed the muscle jerking in his jaw.

She tightened her grip on him. "If men are to die, what matters the name you cast on their blood?"

Behind her, someone closed the hall door. And somewhere in the smoke-hazed shadows, one of her kinsmen snarled a particularly vile curse. Catriona released her brother's arm and reached again for her amber necklace. She twirled its length around her fingers, clutching the polished gems as if they might answer her. Her own special talisman, the ambers often comforted her.

Now they didn't.

Worse, everyone was staring at her. The Lowlander eyed her as if she were the devil's own spawn. He surely saw her fiery-red hair as the brand of a witch. Almost wishing she was—just so she could fire-blast him—she straightened her back and let her eyes blaze. MacDonald pride beat through her, giving her strength and courage.

She turned to Alasdair. "You needn't tell me this has to do with the Camerons or the Mackintoshes. I can smell their taint in the air."

"My sister, Lady Catriona." He addressed the Lowlander, not her. "She sometimes forgets herself."

"I but speak the truth. As for my appearance, I was

enjoying the day's brisk wind—a walk in our hills." She flicked her skirts, righting them. "Had I known we had guests"—she met the man's hooded gaze—"I would have returned before the tide ran."

It was the only explanation he'd get from her.

"Lady." The stranger inclined his head, his dark eyes unblinking. "I greet you."

She refrained from asking who greeted her. His rich garments and jewels had already marked him as a fat-pursed, well-positioned noble. Not that such loftiness counted here, deep in the Highlands, where a man's deeds and honor mattered so much more than glitter and gold.

As if he read her mind and knew she was about to say so, her brother cleared his throat. "This, Catriona"—he indicated the Lowlander—"is Sir Walter Lindsay, the King's man. He's brought tidings from court. A writ from the King, expressing his royal will."

Catriona bent a chilly look upon the man. The churning in her stomach became a tight, hard knot.

Somehow she managed to dip in a semblance of a curtsy. "Good sir, welcome to Blackshore Castle." She couldn't bring herself to say my lord. "We've never before greeted such a noble guest to our glen."

Sir Walter's brow lifted. He said nothing, but a slight flaring of his nostrils showed he knew she wished she weren't forced to greet him now.

"It is because of the glen that he's here." Alasdair's words made her heart go still. "The King wishes that—"

"What does our glen have to do with the King?" She didn't want to know.

"The crown is greatly interested in this glen, my lady." Sir Walter rested his hand lightly on the sword at his hip.

"Your King would see peace in these hills. He is weary of the endless provocations between your clan and the other two who share this land. I am here to inform you that"—his gaze went to Alasdair—"he orders a trial of combat to ensure his will is met."

"Highland men keep their own peace," someone called from near the hearth.

Other voices rose in agreement, and Catriona's heart leapt. Surely the men of the clan would send Sir Walter on his way, King's courier or not. But Alasdair only strode to the high table and snatched up a rolled parchment, its red wax seals dangling and broken. When he turned back to the hall, his face was darker than ever, the writ clenched in a tight, white-knuckled grip.

"There are many here, Sir Walter, who would say this"—he raised his hand, shaking the scroll—"has too much blood on it to be worth any peace. We of this glen have our own ways of handling trouble. Even so, you'll no' see a single MacDonald refuse the King's challenge." Slapping the scroll back onto the table, he dusted his hands, demonstrably. "No' under the terms set before us."

The kinsman standing closest to Catriona, a young lad built like a steer and with hair as flame-bright as her own, spat onto the floor rushes. "Threatening to banish us from the glen be no terms!"

"They are the King's terms." Sir Walter's voice was impervious. "Be assured the Camerons and the Mackintoshes will receive the same warning."

Catriona heard the terrible words through a buzzing in her ears. Her head was beginning to pound, but she wouldn't show weakness by pressing her hands to her temples. She did flash a glance at her brother. Like every other MacDonald in the hall, he looked ready to whip out his sword and run the King's man through.

If she weren't a woman, she'd pull her own steel.

As it was, she suppressed a shudder and chose her words with care. "I missed the reading of your tidings, Sir Walter." His name tasted like ash on her tongue. "Perhaps you will repeat them for me?

"And"—she tilted her chin—"his reasons for placing us under his vaunted regard?"

"With pleasure, my lady." Sir Walter took her hand, lowering his head over her knuckles in an air kiss that jellied her knees in an icy, unpleasant way. "The King's will is that a trial of combat—a fight to the death—should be held in the glen. King Robert proposes within a fortnight."

He looked into her eyes. "Thirty champions from each of the three clans of the glen must face each other. They shall fight stripped of all but their plaids and armed with swords, dirks, axes. A bow with three arrows per man shall be allowed, and a shield. But no quarter may be given.

"Spectators will attend, and specially dispatched royal guards will assure that no man leaves the field." His gaze narrowed on her, his mien hardening. "At the trial's end, the clan with the most champions standing will be the one who wins your glen."

Catriona went hot and cold. "The Glen of Many Legends already is ours, the MacDonalds'. Robert Bruce granted it to my great-great-grandfather in tribute to our support at Bannockburn. Our men should not have to spill blood for what they fought and won with such honor."

"She speaks the truth, by God!" Alasdair banged his fist on a table. "Would your King see the good King Robert's charter undone?"

"King Robert Stewart would see an end to the strife in his realm." Sir Walter's voice was clipped. "The unrest and lawlessness in these parts—"

"Lawlessness?" Alasdair's face darkened. "What do you, a Lowlander, know of—"

"Do you deny the murders of three Mackintoshes this past summer?" Sir Walter examined his fingernails, flicked a speck of lint from his sleeve. "Innocent men killed in cold blood not far from these very walls?"

"They were stealing our cattle!" The redheaded youth next to Catriona stepped forward. "They chose to stand and face us when we caught them. It was a fair fight, no' murder."

Sir Walter's face remained cold. "Clan Mackintosh made a formal complaint to the court. Their chief informed us they were taking cattle to replace revenue tolls they lost because you menaced and threatened wayfarers trying to use the mountain pass above their stronghold."

"Aye, and what if we did?" Catriona began to shake with fury. "Every time our drovers attempt to use that pass to drive our beasts to the cattle trysts, the Mackintoshes block the way, barring passage to us. Even"—she drew a hot breath—"when we offered them double their toll."

"They cost us revenue!" The shout came from the back of the hall. A clansman riled by such absurdity. "They've been blocking that pass to us for years. We tired of it."

"The Mackintoshes are troublemakers." Catriona could scarce speak for anger. "Clan Cameron is worse."

A shiver ripped through her on the name, her heart pumping furiously as the insolent face of the dread clan's chief flashed across her mind. Worse than the devil, James Cameron ridiculed her every time their paths crossed.

There were few men she reviled more. Though just now she'd almost prefer his bold gaze and taunts to Sir Walter's superior stare.

Eyes narrowed, she fixed him with her own frostiest air. "Camerons cannot breathe without spewing insults." She tossed back her hair, knew her face was coloring. "They are an ancient line of Satan-spawned—"

"Ahhh..." Sir Walter spread his hands. "With so many transgressors afoot, you surely see why the King's intervention is necessary?"

"Necessary a pig's eye!" someone yelled near the hearth fire.

Catriona agreed.

Though, with Sir Walter harping on the past summer's squabble with the Mackintoshes, she could imagine that an overblown account of the incident might have reached the King's royal ear.

"Are the Mackintoshes behind this?" She could believe it. The cloven-footed trumpet-blasters wasted no opportunity to shout their claim to the glen. "Did they send another complaint to court? Asking for the crown's interference?"

Sir Walter's mouth jerked, proving they had. "They did send a petition in recent days, yes."

Catriona flushed. "I knew it!"

"They weren't alone. Clan Cameron also sent an appeal, if you'd hear the whole of it." Sir Walter's tone was smooth. The glint in his eye showed that he enjoyed her distress. "Indeed"—he actually smiled—"it surprised us that we did not hear from your brother, considering."

"Considering what?" Catriona's belly clenched again.

Sir Walter's smile vanished. "Perhaps you should ask your brother."

Catriona turned to Alasdair, but when he fisted his hands and his mouth flattened into a hard, tight line, her heart dropped.

Whatever it was that she didn't yet know was grim.

"Lady Edina has passed." Alasdair spoke at last. "She did not leave a testament. Nor, according to the abbess at St. Bride's"—he drew a deep breath—"did she ever make her wishes known to anyone."

Catriona swallowed. Guilt swept her.

She hadn't thought of the old woman in years. She'd been little more than a babe in swaddling when Lady Edina went, by choice, into a Hebridean nunnery. At the time—or so clan elders claimed—she'd desired a life of serenity and solitude behind cloistered walls.

But Edina MacDonald was hereditary heiress to the Glen of Many Legends.

She was also twice widowed. Her first husband— Catriona's heart seized with the horror of it—had been a Cameron and her second, a Mackintosh.

And now Lady Edina was dead.

Catriona wheeled to face Sir Walter. "This is the true meaning of your visit. Now that Lady Edina is gone, and without a will, the King means to take our lands."

Again, shouts and curses rose in the hall as MacDonalds everywhere agreed. Men stamped feet and pounded the trestles with their fists. The castle dogs joined in, their barks and howls deafening.

Even Geordie, a half-lamed beast so ancient he rarely barked at all, lent his protest from his tattered plaid bed beside the hearth fire.

Sir Walter stood unmoved. "These lands are the King's, by any right, as even you must know. Be glad he wishes only to bring you peace," he said, his weasel-smooth voice somehow cutting through the din. "When he received petitions from both the Camerons and the Mackintoshes claiming their due as Lady Edina's heirs, he knew strong measures would be needed to settle this glen. He wishes to see these hills held by the clan most worthy."

Alasdair made a sound that could only be called a growl. His face turned purple.

Catriona's ambers blazed against her neck, the stones' pulsing heat warning her of danger. She took a deep breath, drawing herself up until the disturbing prickles receded and her necklace cooled.

"How did the Camerons and Mackintoshes know of Lady Edina's death?" She looked at the Lowlander. "Why weren't we informed, as well?"

"You know better than me how swiftly—or errone-ously—word travels in these parts." Sir Walter shrugged. "Perhaps a missive meant for you went astray? Either way—"

"You mean to see good men slaughtered." Catriona felt bile rise in her throat. "Men who—"

"Men who fight, yes, until only one remains stand-ing." Sir Walter set his hand on his sword again, his fin-gers curling around the hilt. "If they do not"—his voice chilled—"you must face the consequences. Banishment from this glen to parts even wilder. Resettlement, if you will, in places where the crown can make use of men with ready sword arms and women adept at breeding."

The words spoken, he folded his arms. "The choice is yours."

Across the hall, Geordie barked hoarsely.

Out of the corner of her eye, Catriona thought she saw

the dog struggling to rise. She wasn't sure, because the hall was spinning, going black and white before her eyes. Around her, her kinsmen shouted and cursed, the noise hurting her ears. Even more alarming, something whirled and burned inside her. It was a horrible, swelling heat that filled her chest until she couldn't breathe.

Slowly, she felt down and along the folds of her skirts, seeking the lady dirk hidden there. But she caught herself in time, clasping her hands tightly before her just before her fingers closed on the blade.

Ramming a dagger into the King's man would bring even more grief to her clan.

But she was tempted.

Fighting the urge, she looked from the Lowlander to Alasdair and back again. "I believe, Sir Walter, that my brother has given you our choice. MacDonalds won't be driven from their land. These hills were our own before ever a Stewart called himself a king. If our men must take up arms to avoid the Stewart wrongfully banishing us from a glen we've held for centuries, so be it."

A curt nod was Sir Walter's reply.

Returning it, Catriona dipped another curtsy and then showed him her back. She needed all her dignity, but she kept her spine straight as she strode to one of the hall's tall, arch-topped windows. Once there, she stared out at the sea loch, not surprised to see its smooth gray surface pitted with a light, drizzly rain. Dark clouds crouched low on the hills, and thin tendrils of mist slid down the braes, sure portents that even more rain was coming.

The Glen of Many Legends was crying.

But she would not.

She wouldn't break even if the Lowland King and his

minions ripped the heart right out of her. Highlanders were the proudest, most stoic of men. And MacDonalds were the best of Highlanders.

So she stepped closer to the window, welcoming the cold, damp air on her cheeks. Countless MacDonald women before her had stood at this same window embrasure. In a fortnight's passing, her brother and cousins would ensure that they would continue to do so in years to come. It was just unthinkable that they were being forced to do so with their lives.

Incomprehensible and—she knew deep inside—quite possibly more than she could bear.

When Geordie bumped her hand, leaning into her and whimpering, she knew she had to try. But even as she dug her fingers into the old dog's shaggy coat, the sea loch and the hills blurred before her. She blinked hard, unable to bring her world back into focus. The stinging heat pricking her eyes only worsened, though she did keep her tears from falling.

On the day of the battle she'd do the same. She'd stand tall and look on with pride, doing her name honor.

Somehow she'd endure.

Whatever it cost her.

Nearly a fortnight later, James Cameron stood atop the battlements of Castle Haven and glared down at the worst folly to ever darken the Glen of Many Legends. Wherever he looked, Lowlanders bustled about the fine vale beneath the castle's proud walls. A different sort than the lofty souls gorging themselves on good Cameron beef in his great hall, these scrambling intruders were workmen. Minions brought along to do the nobles' bidding, whose busy hands erected viewing platforms while their hurrying feet flattened the sweetest grass in the glen.

Already, they'd caused scars.

Deep pits had been gouged into the fertile earth. Ugly black gashes surely meant to hold cook fires. Or—James's throat filled with bile—the bodies of the slain.

On the hills, naked swaths showed where tall Scots pines had been carelessly felled to provide wood. Jagged bits of the living, weeping trees littered the ground.

"Christ God!" James blew out a hot breath, the destruction searing him with an anger so heated he wondered his fury didn't blister the air.

He went taut, his every muscle stiff with rage.

Beside him, his cousin Colin wrapped his hands around his sword belt. "They haven't wasted a breath of time," he vowed, eyeing the stout barricades already marking the battling ground where so many men would die.

A circular enclosure better suited to contain cattle than proud and fearless men.

James narrowed his gaze on the pen, unable to think of it as aught else. "Only witless peacocks wouldn't know that such barricading isn't necessary."

Colin flashed a look at him, one brow raised in scorn. "Perhaps they do not know that Highland men never run from a fight?"

"They shall learn our measure soon enough." James rolled his shoulders, keen to fight now. "Though"—he threw a glance at the men working on the nearest viewing platform—"I might be tempted to flee their hammering!"

Half serious, he resisted the urge to clamp his hands to his ears. But he couldn't keep an outraged snarl from rumbling in his throat. The din was infernal. Any moment his head would burst from the noise. Each echoing bang was an ungodly smear on the quiet of the glen, most especially here, in this most beauteous stretch of the Glen of Many Legends.

Equally damning, the MacDonald wench once again stood at the edge of the chaos. On seeing her, he felt an even hotter flare of irritation. He stepped closer to the walling, hoping he erred. Unfortunately, he hadn't. She was truly there, hands on her hips and looking haughty as she glared at the Lowland workmen.

Joining him at the wall, Colin gave a low whistle. "She's Catriona MacDonald, the chief's sister. Word is she's the wildest of that heathenish lot."

"I know who she is." James glared at his cousin, not liking the speculative gleam in his eye. "And she is wild— so prickly some say she sleeps in a bed of nettles."

Colin laughed. "She's bonnie all the same."

"So is the deep blue sea until you sink in its depths and drown." James scowled at the lass.

Pure trouble, she'd clearly come to show her wrath. As she'd done every day since the Lowlanders began setting up their gaudy tents and seating. If Colin hadn't noticed her before now, James had. He always noticed her, rot his soul. And just now, she was especially hard to miss with the sun picking out the bright copper strands in her hair and her back so straight she might have swallowed a steel rod. And if he didn't want to lose his temper in front of workmen who—he knew—were only following orders, he would've marched down to the field days ago and chased her away.

He'd done so once, running her off Cameron land years ago, when he'd been too young and hotheaded to know better than thrusting his hand into a wasp nest.

She'd stung him badly that day. And the memory still haunted him. At times, sneaking into his dreams and twisting his recollections so that, instead of sprinting away from him, she'd be on her back beneath him, opening her arms in welcome, tempting him to fall upon her and indulge in the basest, most lascivious sins.

Furious that she stirred him even now, he tore his gaze from her and frowned at the long rows of colorful awnings, the triumphal pennons snapping in the wind. The festive display shot seething anger through his veins. Truth be told, if one of the King's worthies appeared on the battlements, he wouldn't be able to restrain himself.

Apparently feeling the same, Colin stepped back a few paces and whipped out his sword, thrusting it high. "Forget the MacDonald wench and her jackal blood. We could"—he made a flourish with the blade—"have done with yon mummery in the old way! Cut down the Lowland bastards and toss them into a loch. We then block every entry into the glen, keep silent, and no one need know they even reached us."

He grinned wickedly, sliced a ringing arc in the cold afternoon air.

James strode forward and grabbed Colin's wrist, stopping his foolery. "The old way ne'er included murdering innocents. The workmen"—he jerked a glance at them— "are naught but lackeys. Their blood on our hands would forever stain our honor. Sir Walter's blood, much as I'd love to spill it, would bring a King's army into the glen. No matter what we did, they'd come. Even if every clan in the Highlands rose with us against them, their number alone would defeat us.

"And"—he released Colin's arm, nodding grimly when

his cousin sheathed the blade—"King Robert would then do more than scatter us. He'd put us to the horn, outlawing us so that we'd lose no' just our land but our very name. A fire-and-sword edict passed quicker than you can blink. That, he would do!"

Colin scowled, flushing red. "Damnation!"

"Aye," James agreed, his own face flaming. "We are damned whate'er. So we do what is left to us. We keep our pride and honor and prove what hard fighters we are. With God's good grace, we shall be victorious."

Colin's chin came up, his eyes glinting. "Perhaps He will bless us now." He flashed a wicked grin and strode for the door arch. "I'm off to the hall to see if God in His greatness might cause Sir Walter to choke on a fish bone. I shall pray on the way."

James's lips twitched. On another day, he would have thrown back his head and laughed. As it was, he watched Colin hasten into the stair tower without another word. Only when his young cousin's footsteps faded did he glance at the heavens and mutter a prayer of his own.

Then he whipped around to toss another glower at Lady Catriona, even though she couldn't see him.

He snorted when he saw her.

She'd edged even closer to one of the viewing platforms, her glare pinned on the workmen. James shuddered just looking at her. He almost felt sorry for the men flamed by her scorching stare. Deepest blue yet piercing as the sun, her eyes could burn holes in a man if he didn't take care.

James knew it well, much to his annoyance.

Fortunately, their paths didn't cross often, but each time they'd had the displeasure, he'd regretted it for days.

Just now, with the wind blowing her skirts and her hair

whipping about her face, he almost felt an odd kinship with her. There was something about the challenging tilt of her chin and the blaze in her eyes that—for one crazy, mad moment—made her not a MacDonald but every Highland woman who'd ever walked the hills.

Almost, he was proud of her.

But almost was just that—something that hovered just short of being.

He let his gaze sweep over her one last time, glad that it was so. Catriona MacDonald was the last woman he wished to admire.

Blotting her from his mind, he strode to another part of the battlements, choosing a corner where the sight of her wouldn't spoil his view. Then he braced himself and stared past the fighting ground to the hills beyond, deep blue and silent against the sky. Directly across from him, a sparkling rock-strewn cataract plunged down a narrow gorge cut deep into one of the hills. It was the same vista he enjoyed from his bedchamber window. The sight—as always—took his breath and made his heart squeeze. This day, the falls' beauty also quenched any last shred of sympathy he might have felt for the MacDonald she-wolf.

In Cameron hands since distant times, the glen was his birthright and his joy. Cloud shadows drifted across its length, the gentle play of light and dark bleeding his soul. His eyes misted at the well-loved scene, his throat thickening. He'd always believed his children would one day love the glen with equal fierceness. That they'd carry on tradition, bound to the land and appreciating their heritage, teaching their own offspring to do the same.

Now...

He wrenched his gaze from the glen, fury whipping

through him like a flame to tinder. He should've known better than to come up here. But Colin had wanted to see the workmen's progress. And, truth be told, brisk winds always blew across the ramparts and he'd relished a few moments in the cold, clean air before courtesy demanded he join Sir Walter and his ravenous friends in the hall.

The man's lofty airs and barely veiled insults were more than any man should have to tolerate within his own walls. And watching Lindsay and his henchmen eat their way through Castle Haven's larders—with neither the MacDonalds nor the Mackintoshes helping with the costs—was as galling as it was enlightening.

No matter how the trial of combat ended, the other two clans of the glen would never change their colors.

Most especially the MacDonalds.

The she-wolf's presence on the field vouched for their obstinacy. Just as her flay-a-man stares proved they had a touch of the devil in them.

It was a taint that might serve them well when they soon found themselves in hell.

James's pulse quickened imagining them there.

It was a fine thought.

A well-met fate that sent a surge of satisfaction shooting through him. He could see them landing on Hades' hottest hob or in a deep, icy pit where they could languish for eons, pondering their treacheries.

They deserved no better.

Pity was so many Camerons would be joining them.

THE DISH

Where authors give you the inside scoop

From the desk of Kendra Leigh Castle

Dear Reader,

"Everybody's changing and I don't feel the same." That's a lyric from Keane, one of my favorite bands, and it could easily be applied to Bay Harper. She's the heroine of the fourth book in my Dark Dynasties series, IMMORTAL CRAVING, and she's grappling with the kind of changes that would send even the most well-adjusted people into a tailspin.

Bay is a character near and dear to my heart. In a series where just about everyone grows fangs, fur, or wings, she's incredibly human. And though I myself haven't had to deal with my best friend becoming a vampire, I found it very easy to relate to her struggle with the upheaval around her. I'm a Navy wife—it's a job that involves regularly scheduled chaos. Every few years, I pack up kids, pets, and boxes of stuff that seem to reproduce when I'm not looking. Then I move to a different part of the country and start again. It can be exciting, or infuriating, or just completely overwhelming...sometimes all three at the same time. In IMMORTAL CRAVING, Bay's going through all of those feelings. The difference is that in her case, she's not the one moving. It's everything around her that refuses to stay still. With her best friend now a vampire queen and her town being overrun with vampires and werewolves, Bay is clinging to what shreds of normalcy she can.

We all need things to hang on to when times get tough. For me, I rely on my family, my constant companions on this crazy journey. Bay takes solace in her cozy nest of a house, her big slobbery dog (I also have a pair of those, and I can attest that sometimes a dog hug makes everything better), and her job. Still, no matter how hard you fight it, nothing ever stays the same. And when lion-shifter Tasmin Singh shows up on Bay's doorstep—well, floor—she's finally forced to decide which things in her life she really needs to be happy, and which she can let go of.

Change happens to everyone eventually, whether you're a Navy wife or have lived in the same town all your life. I hope you'll enjoy watching Bay and Tasmin discover, as I have, that even when your entire world seems to have been upended, the people by your side can make all the difference in the end.

Happy Reading!

Kendra Leigh Castle

♥　　♥　　　　♥　♥　　♥　　♥

From the desk of Anne Barton

Dear Reader,

Don't you just adore makeovers?

I do. Give me a dreary, pathetic "before" with the promise of a shiny, polished "after," and I'm hooked. The obsession began with Cinderella, when a wave of her fairy godmother's wand changed her rags into a sparkling ball gown. (With elbow-length gloves!) If only it were that easy.

Reality TV (which I also happen to love) serves up a huge variety of makeover shows. When I'm flipping through the channels, I can't resist them—room makeovers, wardrobe makeovers, relationship makeovers, and more. Even as I'm clucking my tongue and shaking my head at the "before" pictures, I'm envisioning the potential that's underneath, seeing what could be. Of course, every makeover show ends the same way—in a big (often tear-filled) reveal. The drama builds to the moment when we finally get to witness the person or thing transformed. And it feels sort of magical.

In WHEN SHE WAS WICKED, Anabelle gets a little makeover of her own. When we first meet her, she's a penniless seamstress with ill-fitting spectacles and a dowdy cap. She resists change (like a lot of us do) but eventually finds the courage to ditch the cap and trade in her plain dresses for shimmering gowns. But her hot new look is only half the story. Her *real* transformation is on the inside—and that's the one that ultimately wins Owen over.

Makeovers inspire us, and I think that's why we're

drawn to them. We may not have fairy godmothers, but we have hope...and reality TV. We all want to believe we can change—and not just on the outside.

Happy Reading!

Anne Barton

♥ ♥ ♥ ♥ ♥ ♥ ♥ ♥ ♥ ♥ ♥ ♥ ♥ ♥ ♥

From the desk of Sue-Ellen Welfonder

Dear Reader,

Do you ever wonder where characters go after their story is told? If the book is a Scottish medieval romance, can you see them slipping away into the mist? Perhaps walking across the hills and disappearing into the gloaming?

SEDUCTION OF A HIGHLAND WARRIOR ends my Highland Warriors trilogy, and I'm betting readers will know where Alasdair MacDonald and Marjory Mackintosh enjoy spending time these days, now that their happy ending is behind them. Their favorite "hideout" is extra-special, as I'm sure readers will agree when Alasdair and Marjory take them there.

Scotland brims with special places.

Is there anywhere more romantic? Anyone familiar with my work knows how I'd answer that question. Nothing fires my blood faster than deep, empty glens, misty hills, and high, rolling moors purple with heather.

Toss in a chill, damp wind carrying a hint of peat smoke, a silent loch, and a spill of ancient stone, and my heart swells. Add a touch of plaid, a skirl of pipes, and my soul soars.

My passion for Scotland has always been there.

So has my belief in Highland magic.

I always weave such whimsy into my books, and my Highland Warriors trilogy abounds with Celtic myth and lore. Readers will find an enchanted amber necklace, a magical white stag and other fabled beasties, and even a ghostie or two. There are mystical standing stones and enough Norse legend to lend shivers on cold, dark nights. My characters live in a world of such wonders. The Glen of Many Legends, the sacred glen shared by the three clans in these stories, is a magical place.

But at the heart of each book, it's always love that holds the greatest power.

Alasdair fought against his love for Marjory. If, at the beginning, you asked him what matters most, he'd answer kith and kin, and Blackshore, his beloved corner of the glen. He's a proud chieftain and a fierce warrior. He knows that giving his heart to Marjory will destroy his world, even causing the banishment of his people. As clan leader, the weal of others must come first. Yet for Marjory, he risks everything.

A strong heroine, Marjory is sure of her heart, refusing to abandon her love for Alasdair even in her darkest, most dire hours. She also desires the best for the glen. But as a passionate woman, she battles to claim the one man she can't live without.

As Marjory and Alasdair enjoyed the special place noted above, a bit of Highland magic entered my own world. In the story, Marjory has a much-loved blue ribbon.

The day I finished copy edits, I received a lovely, hand-made quilt from a friend. On opening the gift, the first thing I saw was a beautiful blue ribbon.

I smiled, my heart warming.

I'm sure the ribbon was a wink from Marjory and Alasdair.

Highland Blessings!

Sue-Ellen Welfonder

www.welfonder.com